Impossible Things

Impossible Things

Kate Johnson

Published 2014 by Choc Lit Limited
Penrose House, Crawley Drive, Camberley, Surrey GU15 2AB, UK
www.choc-lit.com

A CIP catalogue record for this book is available
from the British Library

ISBN 978-1-78189-059-2

Printed and bound by CPI Group (UK) Ltd, Croydon, CR0 4YY

I would like to dedicate this book to whatever I'd been eating the night before I had that really weird dream about the devil, because he positively insisted I wrote a book about him.

Acknowledgements

Thanks must go to:

Natalie James, who explained to me not only how to break someone's arm in the most painful manner, but also how to fix it. I do hope it's knowledge I won't need again.

Christina Courtenay, who gave me the recipe for pepparkakor and even sent the pomerans to go in it.

Jan Jones, who gave me 'crocogator'. Well, not literally. I'd never get it in the bathtub.

My brilliant cover designer, who not only has exquisite taste in vampires but somehow knew exactly what the perfect cover for this book would look like before I did.

My wonderful editor, who not only made this book much better but let me keep 'splendiferousness' in it.

Everyone else at Choc Lit, who thought this book was a good idea even when it was still called The One About The Warlord, The Blind Slave, And The Dog Called Brutus.

Everyone in the Romantic Novelists' Association, as ever. You guys keep me sane. That is, as sane as I am.

Chapter One

She lay motionless on the bed, a skeleton in a red silk dress with a tangle of matted dreadlocks obscuring her bony face. Kael couldn't quite believe that anything so thin could still be alive.

'Do you know why you're here?' he asked for the third time.

For the third time she answered, 'To please you, my lord.'

He couldn't think of anything less pleasing. She was utterly terrified of him and wasn't even trying to hide it. Hadn't once lifted her gaze from the floor or the richly embroidered bedspread. She'd stumbled into the room on her crippled leg and declined his offer of a seat, simply collapsing onto the bed like a bag of bones. Even the barest of touches had her flinching away from him in horror.

Kael had never taken an unwilling woman in his life, was famous for it in fact. Or perhaps infamous was a better word. The skin of the last man on his crew to have attempted raping a woman was still stretched across the prow of his ship.

Krull the Warlord. He didn't mind having a reputation as a pirate, a thief, a killer and a right evil bastard, but he was damned if he was going to be that most cowardly of things, a rapist.

He tried being friendly. 'My name is Kael. To Samara I'm Krull the Warlord, but my name is Kaelnar. My friends call me Kael. What do your friends call you?'

She shook her head. Probably didn't have any friends. Samara had called her 'the little witch' and 'the little cripple'. The second one was self-explanatory, given the malformed shin of her right leg. But it was the first that intrigued him.

'Why does Samara call you a witch?' he asked.

The slave was silent for a long moment, then she held out her left hand, palm up, and said in a voice that was like a death rattle, 'I'm good with herbs, my lord.'

'You heal people?'

She nodded. The fluttering in Kael's chest that had started when he first saw her grew stronger.

'And do you just heal with herbs, or can you do it by touch?'

She frowned, wrinkling skin that was already stretched tight over her skull.

'Can you sense an injury by touching a person?' he said, trying to remember how Karnos had described it to him. 'Can you feel what's wrong with someone and make it right, fix a problem inside them, without opening them up?'

Her frown turned to puzzlement. 'No, my lord. I don't ... no.'

He sighed. Well, that was to be expected if she had no crystals. Out here in the New Lands so few people had even heard of the Chosen that he wasn't surprised she didn't understand about the crystals. No wonder Samara thought she was a witch, with the Healer's mark on her palm.

But the mark on her right arm ... that wasn't the mark of a witch. That was the mark of a Warrior. And women weren't Warriors. He'd never heard of a female Warrior, outside of fairytales.

'Choose any of them, my lord,' Samara had said languidly, gesturing to the dead-eyed girls draped around her throne like decorations, 'to warm your bed. As many as you like.'

And Kael had ignored them all and pointed to the girl by the fire, the girl with the inky black marks on her skin. 'Her. Send her to me.' And Samara had been unable to disguise her astonishment.

He strode over to the bed and lifted her arm. She went rigid, and he could feel the tremors under her skin.

'I'm not going to hurt you,' he repeated for the millionth time since she'd been thrown into the room.

2

She nodded stiffly. She clearly didn't believe him.

'I just want to see this mark. On your arm. How long have you had it?'

She licked her dry, peeling lips, eyes still on the bedspread. 'I don't know. Five winters?'

He tried to work out how old that would have made her, but it was impossible. He couldn't guess whether she was fifteen or thirty. 'And the other? On your palm?'

'Seven?'

'How did you get them?' he asked, because it wasn't unknown for deluded twits to tattoo themselves in hopes of being mistaken for Chosen.

'They're tattoos,' she whispered. 'I was foolish.'

He sighed and dropped her arm. 'Right. Why did you get them?'

'I was foolish,' she replied, fingers nervously pleating the red silk.

You're not the only one. How had he thought this wretched creature might be one of the Chosen? Probably she was some runaway who thought tattoos were cool and had got herself kidnapped into slavery. A terrible story, but not his problem. He couldn't go around saving every slave in the New Lands. He'd fought slavers before, but on his own terms, with his own army, and most crucially, with the sanction of the Emperor. He wasn't about to start a war over here, all because of some skinny wretch who'd tattooed herself.

He ran his hand through his hair, annoyed with himself and even more annoyed with her, which was irrational since it wasn't her fault she was a skeletal wreck of a human being.

Maybe he could make things a bit better for her, though. Salve his conscience a tiny bit.

'What happened to your leg?' he asked. He could see her malformed shin bone where the red silk of the dress had ridden up. Instead of a smooth, straight line, the bone stuck out, as if it had been snapped in two and simply left like that for the skin to heal back over. A compound fracture, which he'd seen before, but never just left like this.

Her face twisted in what looked like shame. 'I was clumsy.'

'Didn't anyone help you? Didn't you try to help yourself?'

She shook her head. 'No. I was foolish.'

And his patience snapped, because 'foolish' probably wasn't even her word, it was Samara's, and she was so broken she couldn't even think for herself. 'Will you stop saying that? And will you swiving look at me when I'm talking to you?'

So saying, he grabbed her chin and tipped her face up so she was forced to look at him. Her lids fluttered in surprise and fear, her breath quickened and her eyes darted about in confusion. They flickered in the direction of his face, but she didn't seem to see him.

She didn't seem to see anything.

Kael stared, but her gaze never rested anywhere. Her eyes remained unfocused. They were a clear, pale blue, with no signs of blindness, and yet—

And yet. She was blind.

'Merciful gods,' Kael breathed.

'I'm sorry,' she whispered, which irritated him, because she shouldn't be apologising about it. He let go of her hair and stepped back, watched her calm herself, fingers smoothing the crumpled silk of her dress. Her lids dropped again, as if to hide her useless eyes. Kael waved his fingers at her, even stuck his tongue out at her, but she paid him no attention.

His gaze dropped to her crippled leg again. A blind girl could trip and fall so easily. Become an object of ridicule. No one would help her set her broken leg, and he doubted she'd have the strength, let alone the guts, to try it herself.

Slaves were valuable. Mistreating them was like buying a horse just so you could flog it to death. There was no point.

Why had Samara let this happen? She didn't seem stupid. Maybe she was mad.

'Were you really clumsy?' he said, and she nodded. Kael sighed, knelt on the bed and took her arm in his. The patterns looked so real. Half to himself, he said, 'But why would a blind girl tattoo herself?'

'I wasn't always blind,' she rasped.

He looked up at her eyes again. There was no sign of injury to them. 'How did it happen?'

'I—' she flinched again. 'I was foolish.'

Kael regarded her face for a long time. He wondered how many times he'd have to ask her before she stopped parroting the same answer. If she ever would. If the flickers of guilt and shame he'd seen earlier had just been the shallow emotions of a misbehaving animal expecting a reprimand.

Her face was pale, cheekbones protruding hard under those useless eyes. Her lips were cracked, her hair in matted locks hanging to her bony shoulders. He wondered if she'd always been like this. If before the blinding and the beatings and the starvation she'd once been a normal person. If she'd ever been free.

And suddenly he was angry. At whoever had broken this girl into a brainless animal, but also at the girl for allowing it. Didn't she fight? Didn't she rebel? Had she never attempted to keep her own dignity, her own mind? Maybe she didn't deserve to be treated like a human being. Maybe she'd never been one.

He ran his hand over her uninjured leg, and she flinched. Her body said no. But when he again asked, 'Why did you come here?' she still replied without hesitating, 'I came to please you.'

'Well, you ain't pleasing me much sitting there quivering.' Not even sure if he meant it, he continued, 'If you wanted to please me you'd take your clothes off and open your legs.'

A long heartbeat, then she rose to her feet and pulled the dress over her head. Kael stared, amazed and repulsed at the same time. She was quite hideously thin, every one of her ribs standing out in sharp relief, her breasts almost non-existent, her hipbones protruding like knives.

But she lay down on the bed, her legs apart, and waited.

What would happen if he sent her back untouched? Would Samara *check*?

Kael ran his tongue over his teeth and regarded her. Hell, he'd been with uglier women.

Giving her one last chance, he said, 'Are you willing, girl?'

She nodded frantically. 'Yes, my lord. I'll—I'll do anything.'

Maybe she'd get a reward for it. Food, clothing, somewhere warm to sleep. He might actually be doing her a favour.

Kaelnar Vapensigsson, you can be a real evil bastard.

'Will you, indeed,' he said softly, and let his jerkin fall to the floor. His shirt followed as he toed off his boots, and he watched her tremble as she listened to the rustle of clothing. She could say no at any time. He'd given her the opportunity to say no.

Naked, he slid into bed beside her. 'Don't be afraid,' he said, touching her shoulder. 'I won't hurt you.'

She nodded rigidly, and Kael stroked her face. Her body was stiff. She was terrified.

'Is it your first time?' he asked gently. She quivered in response. 'Are you frightened of what's to come?'

She gave a bare nod, and Kael cupped the small swell of her breast. 'Relax,' he told her. 'It will be better if you relax.'

He kissed her neck – at least she'd washed before she came – and stroked her skin, trying to calm her. If he gave her this, some warmth and pleasure, even if it was only for one night, he might be able to leave Samara's compound without tarnishing his soul any more.

Murmuring soothingly, he slipped his hand between her legs, and she suddenly jackknifed against him, shoving with her scrawny arms, jerking her knee up and very nearly spearing his vitals with it. The rigid, supine slave beneath him flashed into a spitting wildcat, made strong with anger, propelling him off her bony body and onto the floor, where he landed hard and lay for a moment, stunned.

On the bed, she'd frozen too. Kael shoved himself to his feet and glared at her, not caring whether she could see him or not.

'*Now* you change your mind?' he growled, and she cowered, scrambling back and falling off the far side of the bed. 'You said you were willing, girl!'

She hauled herself to her feet, shaking so violently he thought she might break another bone. Kael rounded the bed and grasped her by the arms, shaking her.

'What is wrong with you?' he shouted. 'Why couldn't you say no when I asked you? Why can't you say anything you haven't been told to? Are you simple, girl? Are you mad? Or are you just a bloody prick tease?'

Her teeth were chattering. He nearly expected her to faint.

'Oh for gods' sakes,' he spat, shoving her away from him and throwing the silk dress after her. 'Get out of my sight.'

She stumbled, clutching the dress to herself, and began to feel her way around the bed. Kael, all patience lost, roared, 'Get out!' and she fled, tripping and crashing into things, scurrying through the door with the dress still grasped in her hands.

Kael kicked the door shut after she'd gone and glowered at it, furious. At Samara, at the girl, and now at himself.

Wrenching the door open, he strode across the hall and into the common room where his men were getting drunk with Samara's pleasure slaves. Naked and angry, he grabbed the two nearest girls and hauled them into his room.

* * *

Out from the darkness of sleep a huge red cat loomed.

The wall was covered with fangs and claws, beaks, crowns. Fearsome animals, and yet they didn't frighten her. Flames burned low in the huge fireplace. The bed was soft and warm.

Something tickled her cheek, but when she turned her face to rub at it, her gaze fell on the man sleeping beside her. A handsome man, a strong man. A man who opened his eyes and smiled at her.

She smiled back, and then he reached for his sword and plunged it into her belly.

She woke up screaming.

Chapter Two

Kaelnar Vapensigsson rubbed his hands together in a vain attempt to get some heat into them. He was used to hard, mean winters, but they were winters at home, clean and crisp and cruelly beautiful; they were *his* winters, not these unfathomable New Land winters with their heavy falls of hail and dirty, scraggy snow.

'Do we have to go back to see her?' he asked. 'Can't we just get on the boat and go home?'

Verak snorted. 'You want to leave a woman like Samara mad at you?'

'I don't intend on ever coming back here.' He gazed around at the desolate beach, the sort of beach where ships came to die. No one had ever frolicked on this beach, built a jaunty sandcastle or shrieked with delight at the coldness of the water. This was a beach where the hard things you tripped over might be the bleached ribs of a long-wrecked ship, or of its long-dead crew.

It was a hideous place, but it was still a better place to camp than Samara's compound. The guest rooms might have looked luxurious, but ever since he'd woken up there the morning after the blind girl, he'd had the uneasy feeling that all the silks and sweet herbs were like spices disguising rotten meat.

He'd muttered something about needing to supervise repairs and set up camp by the shore.

'Still, international relations ...'

'I don't give a rat's fart about international relations,' Kael snapped. 'I'm Krull the Swiving Warlord.'

'Is that how you're announcing yourself now?'

Kael glared at the hull of his ship as it swayed with the tide.

If it hadn't been for this hideous weather they wouldn't have been blown into that stupid reef and he could have checked Samara's exports at the port, like he'd planned. But no, he'd been stuck here three weeks and beholden to a sadistic hag who treated her slaves as disposable commodities.

An image of the blind girl from his first night at Samara's came into his mind, stabbing guilt into him, and he dismissed it. Not his problem.

'And she'll want presents,' he grumped. 'We can't pay her for loaning us slaves, but she'll want presents.'

'We have plenty of brandy and silks on board,' Verak said. 'We can spare some.'

Kael nodded. 'And crystals,' he said, the blind girl haunting him again. 'We've always got loads of crystals.'

The great hall of Samara's estate had a throne on a dais. Kael wondered if she'd be waiting there for his farewell as she had on his arrival nearly three weeks ago, dressed in silks and satins, surrounded by dull-eyed slaves in a horrible parody of a court scene.

Kael, who'd attended more royal courts than he could remember, snorted. His own court consisted of a chair and a desk and a queue of people complaining about crop harvests. If he wore silk and satin he'd be laughed out of the place.

The horde marched behind him. Today they really were a horde, armoured and fearsome, and he'd instructed Johann, the signifer, to don his full bearskin cape as he carried the standard. Behind him, the horde's banner snapped in the freezing wind.

He stopped dead in the doorway, the horde coming to a complete stop behind him. The clang of every fist on every breastplate was deafening, and judging by the uneasy reaction of Samara's fat, bullying guards, it had the impact he wanted.

But the throne was empty. The room was dark and cold,

the huge fireplace spilling ashes. One of the toadying, greasy men Samara called her courtiers came scurrying towards him. 'What's the hold-up?' Kael demanded.

'Um. Her ladyship is ill.'

'I'm sorry to hear that,' Kael lied. 'I need to see whoever's in charge.'

The man twisted his gloved hands. Samara liked to surround herself with richly-dressed men, apparently under the illusion she was some sort of queen. Kael was fairly sure they were simply another sort of slave – just ones who didn't realise it. They were there to warm her bed and fan her ego.

This one looked entirely at sea. It was clear that without Samara to order everyone around, no one knew what to do. Gods, did no one in this place have a shred of initiative?

'Apologies, gentlemen, but—'

'Do not apologise to me,' Kael snarled, towering over the little man, who cowered gratifyingly. 'I am Krull the Warlord, and you will do as I say.'

The courtier nodded rapidly, and Kael thought he saw some sort of relief in the man's eyes.

Briefly, he wondered what would happen to these people without Samara. They truly didn't seem able to function by themselves.

'My men need food, and we need provisions for the ship. Lady Samara has promised to help us with this.'

She hadn't, but the courtier didn't know that.

'We will of course pay for the supplies we take,' he said, confident that with Samara out of commission, no gifts would be required. 'Now get out of my way, little man.'

The courtier did just that, and Kael thought he saw a hint of a smile on Verak's face as they strode back into the courtyard. Outside, the air was brutally cold, but it was better than the chilling emptiness of the hall.

'You,' he pointed at a random slave. 'Show my men where

your food stores are kept and assist them with whatever they need. Understood?'

The slave nodded, looking terrified, and Kael signalled to his quartermaster to follow. The men wheeled after him, boots stamping on the snowy courtyard.

'What do you suppose she's ill with?' Verak asked as the courtyard emptied.

Kael shrugged. 'Maybe she's been attacked by her own conscience.'

'Didn't think she had one,' Verak replied. 'I mean, what if it's something contagious?'

'Karnos can handle it.' His Healer could handle most things.

'Still, I'd rather not spend a three-week voyage cooped up with plague-ridden sailors.'

'It's not the plague, or this place'd be full of corpsified slaves.'

'Corpsified?'

'It's a word,' Kael said defensively.

'Krull the Warlord: scourge of the seas, terror of the Empire and maker-up of words.'

'And don't you forget it.'

Verak grinned at him, and Kael grinned back, but it was a grin that withered as he watched a burly guard carrying a frail body out of a side door.

'That's not a plague victim,' he said to Verak, even as he started forward. 'You there,' he accosted the guard, 'what did this slave die of?'

It was a slave, undoubtedly so. Matted hair, inadequate clothing, stick-thin limbs.

Limbs with tattoo-like markings on them.

Oh, *hell*.

'It's not dead,' said the guard, and Kael resisted the urge to hit him for the 'it'. 'Not yet, anyway.'

'What's wrong with her?'

The guard shrugged. 'Displeased her ladyship.'

Kael frowned. Beside him, Verak made a noise of disgust.

'You mean, she's going to be executed?'

'Nah, just chucked back inna cell until it's dead.'

Kael stared hard at the emaciated arm bearing the impossible tattoo.

'You mean,' he said slowly, 'she's to be starved to death?'

The guard shrugged. The movement made the slave's head loll.

He wasn't entirely sure how his sword ended up in his hand, the tip against the guard's throat. Verak said, 'Kael,' warningly but he wasn't listening.

'This is what's going to happen,' he said to the guard, whose attention was riveted on Kael's crystal-studded double-handed war sword. 'You're going to give that girl to my friend here, and then you're going to go back to Samara and report that she's already dead and disposed of. Aren't you?'

The guard nodded, terrified.

'Now,' Kael said, and the man nearly threw the slave at Verak before rushing back inside.

'She weighs nothing,' Verak said, appalled, cradling the unresponsive creature in his arms.

Kael pushed back the tangle of her hair and swore. On her left cheek was a crusted, oozing mess of a wound, blistered and burnt.

'Karnos could heal that,' Verak began, and Kael shook his head.

'Karnos isn't here.' The Healer had remained with the crew who were dismantling the camp by the shore and preparing the ship for departure. Kael had only brought enough men to intimidate Samara. 'She has marks on her hand – she said they were tattoos, but ...'

'You think she's a Healer?' Verak said doubtfully.

Kael looked at the dreadful creature. 'I don't know what to think,' he said truthfully. He held out his arms, and Verak handed her over carefully, as if she might break. 'Go find the men and bring me a chest of crystals. I'll be in the guest quarters.'

Verak nodded and ran off, and Kael strode to the low building where Samara had housed him and his men the night of their arrival. The doors weren't locked, but neither were there any signs of recent occupation. He shoved open the door to the room he'd used before, laid the girl on the bed and glanced at the fireplace. Gods be praised, someone had laid a fire there. He lit it and covered the girl with a blanket for good measure.

Then he sat beside her and took her left hand, her Healer's hand.

And swore.

This also bore the blistered, crusted skin of a burn. Unlike the one on her face, which was a few weeks old, this one was fresh, angry and red and probably too much for her to bear.

'Can you hear me?' he asked, shaking her gently. Nothing. 'I order you to pay attention to me!'

That caused a flutter of her eyelashes. Her lips moved, and she made that death rattle noise again.

'I'll swiving murder that bitch,' he cursed. 'I'll cut her to pieces. Starve you to death! I hope she does have the plague.'

'For all our sakes I hope she doesn't,' said Verak, entering the room with the chest of crystals. 'And try not to kill her, the Emperor won't be pleased.'

'You think I care about the Emperor?' Kael said, positioning the chest next to the girl and plunging her hand in.

She gave a startled yelp and tried to pull it out again, but Kael held her there, his fingers wrapped tight around her twig-like wrist.

'Leave it. Just for a few moments.' Just until we can tell whether you're a Healer or not. If you're not …

He glanced up at Verak, his face tense and worried, and saw his own thoughts mirrored there. If she wasn't a Healer, they'd have to take her to Karnos and he really didn't think she'd survive the journey. His own field-medic skills weren't enough to save someone as weak as this.

'Kael, her face,' Verak murmured, and he peered at the crusted mess which was, incrementally, becoming less crusted and less messy.

'Water,' he said, his heart thumping. 'And a cloth. Soap.'

Verak nodded and moved away, and Kael waited impatiently until he returned, watching the ugly wound on the girl's face heal itself.

She's a Healer, he thought deliriously. She's Chosen. She's Chosen and I nearly left her here to starve to death. Oh gods, the Emperor really isn't going to be pleased if he hears this.

Carefully, gently, he soaked away the crusts of dried blood and fluids from her face. She flinched weakly, but didn't stop him. The skin underneath was raw and red, and he thought she might always have a scar there, but then he cleaned a big lump of dirt away and his heart nearly stopped when he saw what was beneath it.

'Verak,' he said. 'Her *face*.'

'Has to be a hoax.'

'She's a Healer, Kael, we've seen that.'

The fire crackled as he tossed another log on. The sky was getting dark, so he'd told the men to bunk up for the night and they'd leave in the morning. He couldn't move the girl now; she was far too weak.

He glanced over at her, lying apparently asleep in the big bed, her body barely making a rise under the heaps of blankets. Her hand was almost totally healed, and her face bore the marks of an old wound. They'd given her sips of water and tiny bits of food, heated water in a tub and soaked away the dirt ingrained in her skin. There wasn't much for her hair but to shear it all off, which Verak did, cutting away the worst mats and burning them.

She was crawling with lice, her body covered in infected bites and sores which the crystals gradually healed. What they couldn't heal, however, were the old scars, the marks of beatings and whippings, cuts and burns that had hardened into ugly lumps of scar tissue under her skin. He'd paid these no mind before, so focused on her Marks and her blindness that he hadn't even looked much at the rest of her. When he looked closely he saw scars around her wrists and ankles that could only have come from manacles. There was even the faint suggestion of a collar that had once bitten into her skin too, although he'd seen no such collar on any of Samara's slaves.

She was as clean and healthy as they could make her now, and maybe by the time Karnos had treated her and they'd got her back to Ilanium, she might resemble something approaching a human being. If, perhaps, they fed her sticks of lard. Kael had never seen anyone so thin in his life. It made a mockery of the Ilani fears that fashionable women were a bit too skinny.

'She can't be a Warrior. It's impossible.'

'It's never happened before,' Verak corrected. 'That we know of.'

'A female Warrior? You don't think something like that might have made the history books?'

Verak shrugged. 'Maybe not the history books, but what about all those fearsome warrior women of myth and legend?'

'They're *myths*,' Kael emphasised, 'and *legends*.'

'Just because—'

'Look, stop playing Devil's advocate, will you? I know you don't believe it.'

Verak was silent a moment, staring down into his wine.

'You can't believe it,' Kael said. He glanced over at the girl again and wondered vaguely if her body was strong enough to withstand the weight of the blankets on it. 'And even if such a thing were actually possible, then what about the third mark?'

Verak shook his head helplessly.

'It wasn't there before. I'd have remembered it if it was. It could be a tattoo,' Kael suggested half-heartedly.

'A blind slave getting a tattoo in a frozen mining compound in the middle of nowhere. That's more likely than a third mark, is it?' Verak glanced at the mark on his own forearm. 'Mine turned up overnight.'

'Mine too. Both of 'em separate.'

Kael looked back at the girl. Now that the crusted blood and dirt on her face had been washed away, now that the crystals had healed the worst of the injury to her face, the inky black patterns twining around her left eye were clearly visible. The mark of a Seer.

The Healer's mark on her palm was once more whole. And on her right forearm twined an unmistakable Warrior mark.

She bore three marks of the Chosen. Three.

'Come on, Mr Devil's Advocate, explain that one to me.'

'I don't know,' Verak said. 'I just … Look, a female Warrior I can just about get my head around, but Thrice-Marked, that's …'

'Just as impossible,' Kael finished. He drained his wine and reached for more. 'A Seer and a Healer, then. That's possible. That's got precedent. Probably.'

'It's plausible,' Verak said. 'On a child of the Citizenry. A child whose parents both came from long lines of the Chosen. How many Twice-Marked have there ever been who weren't Children of Two Marks at the least?'

There was a short pause. Verak winced.

'Well, me for one,' Kael said as drily as he could. His mother had been from a very old family, but much to the regret of her family she'd remained unmarked and chosen to marry a warlord from a frozen wasteland, a Citizen only by the skin of his teeth and the grace of a family who'd thrown up a few Warriors many generations ago.

'But you've got lines of Chosen stretching back on both sides as far as the Book records. Have you ever heard of a Twice-Marked being born to a plebeian?'

'No.' Kael stared glumly at the fire. He was never going to be able to explain this to the council. He'd need a Truthteller to verify her marks, and he wasn't sure they even had one at the Academy any more.

A man like himself, who came from two long bloodlines of the Chosen, whose father was already a renowned Warrior, had no need to have his Warrior mark checked. There was no reason why he'd cheat, and he was quite aware of the penalties.

She could demonstrate her Healing talent quite easily, he supposed. And once she'd regained some strength he could perhaps test her for Warrior abilities. But how in the seven hells he was supposed to check whether she was really a Seer or not, he had no idea.

She couldn't be Thrice-Marked. She couldn't be a Warrior. Those were two impossible things about her. But the third ...

The thought that anybody with her gifts was living as a slave was just inconceivable. She could only be Twice-Marked if at least one of her parents came from a very old Chosen family. It simply wasn't possible otherwise.

And no Chosen would ever allow their child to become a slave.

The children of the Chosen were cosseted, adored – and very carefully recorded in the Book of Names. It was impossible to simply disappear.

He pinched the bridge of his nose. Well, it was very hard, he'd put it that way. There were always loopholes, always exceptions. The gods knew he'd found a few in his time.

Clearly some weird things were going on with this girl. Some almost impossible things.

He was going to have a hell of a time explaining this to the council.

She couldn't ever remember comfort like this.

She was warm, which in itself was almost a forgotten sensation. And she was clean, which wasn't a state she'd been able to achieve for a horribly long time.

But the strangest thing, the most alien sensation, was the lack of pain.

She concentrated. Her belly was still empty, but the clawing pain of a hunger so intense it felt as if her body were trying to eat itself, had faded. Her face didn't feel as if it were on fire any more, her eyeball boiling with agony, her flesh crawling with fire. Her hand was so painless she had to check it was still there.

The everyday bruises, sores, bites and lashes hurt so little she barely noticed them.

She realised she must, therefore, be dead.

Which was why it came as something of a shock to hear a deep, dark voice asking, 'Are you awake?'

She froze, not sure how to answer.

'You are. I can tell you are. Do you want something to drink? You're still quite dehydrated.'

She licked lips that were dry but no longer blistered, and nodded.

A hand touched the back of her neck, and she barely had time to register the surprise of strong fingers against her bare scalp before a cup was pressed to her lips.

'Just little sips now. Your body can't handle much more.'

She drank as directed, trying to take small sips but too frightened he'd take it away from her.

It was him, undoubtedly. The stranger who'd strode into the great hall and, out of all the female slaves, chosen her to warm his bed for the night.

The warlord she'd been ordered to please. The big man, smelling of sweat and blood and sage, who'd spoken to her gently, almost as if he didn't want to hurt her. She wasn't fooled. They all wanted to hurt her.

The man she'd so insulted, so offended, she thought he was going to kill her there and then.

'How are you feeling?' he asked now.

A terrible question to answer. Would it please him more if she were hurt? If she told the truth – that she felt a lot better – would he hurt her? If she said she felt terrible, would he punish her for lying?

'Your colour's improved,' he said, taking the cup away and pulling her into a sitting position. 'Have something to eat.'

This was dangerous. This was frightening. He was pretending to be kind to her, but why?

A bowl of something savoury was held under her nose and she felt her mouth fill with saliva. Forcing herself to be sensible, she inhaled and concentrated on separating the scents. Vegetables, herbs … She breathed in again, but the herbs were just seasonings. Nothing to harm her.

Probably, it was information he wanted. That's what Ladyship had implied that first night. 'See if he talks in his sleep,' she'd said with a laugh.

Maybe Ladyship would be forgiving this time …

The soup was delicious, the taste almost too rich to stand. When he took the bowl away she wanted to stop him, to bring it back, to eat and eat. But she did nothing. She wasn't greedy. She was grateful. She must remember to be grateful, or Ladyship would be upset again.

'I know you're hungry,' he said. 'I know you're so far beyond hungry it's a miracle you're still alive. Clearly the gods have plans for you. But I can't let you eat too much, not just yet. A little more each time until you can manage a whole meal. We've got to do this gradually.'

She nodded. She'd nod at anything he said if it made him happy.

'But by the time we get to Ilanium you'll be a lot healthier. We've got weeks on this journey for you to get stronger, and plenty to eat. Especially if you like fish.'

She nodded again. She truly had no idea if she liked fish or not.

Then she caught up with herself. 'Journey, my lord?' she said, her voice cracked and weak.

'Yes. We're going to Ilanium.'

He paused, clearly expecting a reaction to this. 'Yes, my lord?'

'Do you even have any idea where that is?'

Ilanium. It snagged vaguely in her memory, like something from a long-forgotten story. Bracing herself, she admitted, 'I'm sorry, my lord.'

'No. Right. So. Born here, were you?'

She shook her head. 'I don't know.'

'No. Right then, look. You're clearly a lot better than you were last night. Do you think you can move? You'll just have to go as far as one of the wagons. I can carry you if you need me to.'

'Wagons?' She licked her lips again. Of course, she wouldn't be travelling with Ladyship. Ladyship would have her own carriage, or possibly a litter. But ... 'I need to see her.'

'Who? You have family here?' he asked sharply.

'Ladyship.'

He barked out a laugh. 'You want to see Samara before we go? Are you really a glutton for punishment, girl?'

'She's been unwell. I need to make sure she's well enough to travel.'

'Well enough—? She's not going anywhere. And she thinks you're dead. No. You just come quietly out to the wagons, we'll pull one right up to the door so no one sees you, and—'

'Not going anywhere?'

She cringed automatically. She'd interrupted him.

'No. I'm not taking her to Ilanium! Ha, unless I can actually pin this smuggling thing on her. If I saw that woman in chains I think I might actually dance a jig of happiness. And I do not dance.'

If she could see she'd have stared at him in bemusement. He was taking her away? 'But Ladyship needs me.'

'Needs you.' He said it flatly, heavily, like a slab falling flat on the ground. Like the wall that had crumbled last year and taken out three men and a woman instantly, flattening them so utterly she could only tell who was missing by counting up the survivors.

'Samara does not need you,' said the warlord. 'Any more than she needs a practice target, or a punchbag, or perhaps a butterfly she can pull the wings off. Samara has whored you out, burned you, imprisoned you and tried to starve you to death. Samara does not need you.'

'She's ill. I have … some skill with herbs …'

'You have much more than that.' He was close now, sitting on the bed near her. 'You have no idea of the skills you have. Look, your hand, your face – you did that. You healed that.'

He touched her palm, stroked her cheek. She willed herself not to flinch.

'I can't leave her.' Ladyship would be so, so angry if she left. 'Bad things happen when you leave.'

'I'll bet they do. Bad things like being shot in the back with an arrow.'

He didn't seem to understand. 'It's not safe out there,' she whispered.

'It's not swiving safe in here!' he yelled, and backed off. 'Seven hells, girl. Are you telling me you actually want to stay?'

She nodded.

'Right. And is this like you "wanted" to please me that first night?'

She did cringe this time. She nodded.

He let out a string of sounds she didn't entirely understand, but she recognised by the tone they were profanities.

'You'd rather stay here with this woman than—? She'll throw you back in that cell, you know that? Probably burn you again, and this time there'll be no crystals to heal you. She doesn't *need* you. She wants you to *die*, slowly and horribly.'

'Ladyship will give me what I deserve,' she whispered.

He swore again. 'What you deserve is a slap in the face. Look – what *is* your name?'

She opened her mouth, and no sound came out.

… what is …

A memory stirred, deep and forgotten

… name …

'Are you going to answer? Do you even know?'

… my name …

His voice came from very close to her face, and very far away all at the same time.

'Do you *have* a name?'

… my name …

'Can you even hear me? Oh, I give up. Samara can bloody well have you.'

'My name,' she mumbled.

'Are you even listening? I said you can go back to that filthy cell and *rot* for all I care—'

'My name,' she said slowly.

He paused in his ranting. 'Yes?'

She lifted her head and said clearly to the warlord, 'My name is Ishtaer.'

Chapter Three

The little slave looked up, and if he hadn't known she was blind he'd swear she was looking right at him.

'My name is Ishtaer,' she said clearly.

For a long second Kael stared, the wind knocked out of him. 'Ishtaer,' he repeated automatically.

'My name,' she said again, slower this time, 'is Ishtaer.' It was as if she was trying to persuade herself of it.

'That's a very pretty name,' Kael said weakly, and shook himself. 'That's a Draxan name. Are you from Draxos?'

Again, that expression on her face, as if she didn't understand the question.

'I'm from,' she began, and paused. But this time her face cleared to frustration. 'I don't know,' she said. 'I don't remember.'

'You're not from here?'

She frowned, and Kael thought he recognised the expression from his own days at the Academy, when he'd struggled so hard to recall the names of the great families of Ilanium or the correct form of address for a senator's wife.

A Draxan name. One of their old goddesses, he thought. Perhaps she'd been kidnapped, or … perhaps lost in the riots there. Four years ago now? Five, maybe. They simply hadn't been able to account for everyone.

'All right, Ishtaer. How about this. How old are you?'

She brightened a bit at the use of her name. No, brightened wasn't the right word. She seemed to become more solid, more real. More alive.

'I think …' she trailed off, and he saw her fingers tapping against her palm as if she was counting. 'I think … twenty?'

She still cowered as she said it, as if she expected this to be the wrong answer. Kael let it slide. 'Twenty it is.' Which would make her maybe sixteen at the time of the riots. No Chosen would have gone missing without someone creating a stink, the type of news he or Verak would certainly have been privy to, which meant she'd have to have been unmarked at the time. She thought she'd been marked for seven years, but then she also thought her marks were tattoos and that her beloved Ladyship was her benefactor. Samara had really done a number on her.

Sixteen was a little old to have come into her first mark, but not unheard of. It was possible she'd been from an old family who hadn't produced a Chosen in generations, forgotten outside the pages of the Book of Names, or perhaps that she was just too old to be expected to manifest a mark. Or maybe both.

It shouldn't be hard to track an Ishtaer on the lists of the missing after those riots. The thought cheered him. He might even be able to reunite her with her family. Although what the hell he'd tell them about where he found her he had no idea.

'Right then, twenty-year-old Ishtaer who may or may not be from Draxos, I'll ask you again. Do you want to come with me?'

She was still a moment, then said, 'Away from here?'

'Yes.'

'Away from Ladyship?'

He ground his teeth. 'Yes.'

A longer pause, then Ishtaer whispered, 'She'll kill me.'

He said nothing, waiting for her answer. Waiting, it seemed, forever.

When she spoke her voice was almost inaudible, and her whole body shook as if the words had to be forced from her, pushed past some impossible barrier.

'I want to leave. I want to get away from this place. I want—'

Then she ran out of things to say, and her body slumped as if she couldn't continue the effort of speaking any more. It seemed to Kael as if it had taken all her energy to say those words, to even think them. What had Samara done to this girl to break down even the thoughts inside her own head?

'Right.' He felt more relieved than he'd expected. 'Good, then. We'll leave as soon as things are packed up. Smuggle you out. Shouldn't be hard, she already thinks you're dead.'

She shook her head. 'She'll want to see me. A body.'

'Well then. Close your eyes and play dead.'

Another shake. 'She won't …' Then she seemed to pull herself together, and her head came up. 'I know a concoction. Herbal. It makes you look dead. Unconscious. Slows the heart right down. No breathing. She wouldn't be able to tell …'

Kael frowned. 'Is that necessary?'

Ishtaer flinched. 'She doesn't like to lose,' she said quietly.

It was eerie, how still and limp she became after drinking her carefully mixed potion. Kael and Verak had watched her mix it, and the older man had stopped Kael from interfering about five times when he simply couldn't believe she knew what she was doing.

'You can't even see what you're putting in there!' he exploded.

'No, my lord.' She added a pinch of some herbs that looked identical to at least three other kinds set out before her.

'So how do you know—'

'I assume she's familiar with the texture,' Verak said, in the same voice he used to quell arguments between his children. 'And the smell, perhaps, Ishtaer?'

She nodded, concentrating on what she was doing. If nothing else, Kael really couldn't doubt that she was a Healer now. The frightened wretch who'd cowered from him and begged to stay had vanished, leaving behind a calm and competent woman, measuring out herbs as if she did it every day.

Only the Chosen had such calm confidence in their work, and that usually came after years of training.

Soon after she swallowed the potion her head began to loll, and the pulse Kael was monitoring in her wrist decelerated until it was barely a flutter every few minutes. Her eyes stayed open, glassy and unfocused and unnerving as hell.

'She's too clean,' he said to Verak. 'Samara will never believe we just found her like this.'

'And too warm,' Verak said. 'I'll get some snow.'

'And dirt,' Kael called after him. 'Her face is all healed up.'

They made her as dirty and cold as they dared, then Kael wrapped her in his cloak and took a deep breath and picked her up. Her body weighed nothing, a fragile bundle of sticks wrapped in thin skin.

'Gods, I hope she isn't actually dead,' he said as they carried her out of the guest quarters and across the frozen courtyard. 'Can you imagine telling the council about her? "We found potentially the highest-ranked Chosen the world has ever seen, and then we let her poison herself." They'd love that.'

Dread curdled in his gut as the very real possibility occurred to him that all this could have been a form of suicide. His steps faltered. Had Samara brainwashed her that badly?

'Hush,' Verak said. 'She'll be fine. You saw the way she handled those herbs. She knew what she was doing.'

'Yes, that's what worries me.' Right then. There was nothing for it now. If she'd killed herself no Healer in the world could bring her back.

Samara lounged on her throne in the great hall, looking wan and pale. Kael almost felt sorry for her, then he remembered that she'd branded Ishtaer's face and palm and left her to starve in a freezing cell. He wondered if the Emperor would mind if he cut the head off one of the Empire's most important oil suppliers.

'My lord,' she said, but whatever she was about to follow it up with, Kael cut her off.

'My lady,' he said, bowing his head. 'I would not have disturbed you except to ask where your burial ground is.'

Samara's forehead creased. 'Burial ground?'

He indicated the limp body in his arms. 'The slave who so pleased me on my first night appears to be dead. I would bury her according to the traditions of my people.'

Samara beckoned him closer, and when he held out Ishtaer's body her nose wrinkled.

'The little cripple,' she said. 'Pity, it was occasionally useful. Still, that's what it deserves for such insolence.'

'Insolence, my lady?'

She motioned to one of the slaves by the fire and said to Kael, 'It was so pleased with itself after one night with you, my lord, that it evidently got ideas above its station. Drew something on its face. One of its witch marks. They're all lies, of course. That's why I burned it off immediately. The little cripple had no magic.'

'Indeed, my lady?' Kael said, his mind racing. So Ishtaer's Seer's mark had appeared the night he first met her? Interesting.

'That's why I bought it, you see. For the witch marks. I understand among your people they denote magical ability?'

Kael kept his face expressionless. Everyone in the Empire knew what the marks meant, but the Chosen kept the details of their gifts shrouded in mystery. Better not to let the general populace know that their 'magical abilities' were dependent on a handful of crystals.

'Yes, my lady,' he said.

'But they were lies. Tattoos or some such. You needn't bury it according to your customs, my lord. I doubt it's one of your people. We can just throw it in the furnace.'

'As you say, my lady,' Kael said, holding onto his temper. 'But our traditions demand that every body is treated with respect. Even,' he added, 'those of our enemies.'

Samara looked surprised at this, but shrugged tiredly and said, 'As you wish. But before you do, my lord, let me just check it's really dead, and not just trying to fool us.'

She turned to a nearby slave, and Kael's heart leapt in his throat as he saw what the man held. A brand fresh from the fire, the stylised S shape burning bright yellow and white.

Samara took the brand carefully and looked at Ishtaer with disgust. 'Well?' she said to the slave. 'I don't want to touch it.'

Kael willed himself not to panic as the slave pulled back a fold of the cloak covering Ishtaer's body and pulled out her hand. Her right hand, not the one Samara had already maimed. Not the one resting healed and perfect inside the cloak.

'Is that necessary, my lady? I am quite good at knowing when a body is dead,' he said.

'I don't trust this one,' Samara said, and thrust the brand against Ishtaer's naked wrist.

He didn't hide his expression this time. The smell of burning flesh was disgusting. Verak caught his eye, and it was a good job Samara was focused on the torture she was inflicting on Ishtaer's corpse, because Verak looked like he wanted to kill her.

The look of excitement on Samara's face was almost sexual.

'I think that proves it,' Kael said, a little sharper than he intended, and Samara looked up, disappointed. 'We must treat her with *respect*.'

Samara looked genuinely baffled, but she carelessly handed the brand back to the slave, forcing him to take it by the hot end.

'Bury it where you like,' she said, 'just not anywhere it's going to get in my way.'

'Of course, my lady. I wouldn't want to disturb you,' Kael said, and left before he accidentally killed her.

Ishtaer awoke to the sway and creak of a ship and every one of her muscles tensed in immediate, helpless panic. Or at least they tried to. Her body felt sluggish, heavy, the way it had felt in that cell after days of eating snow and licking the moss from the walls.

The ship …

She couldn't remember why the thought frightened her so much. She didn't remember a ship of any kind. Didn't remember anything before Ladyship. But the smell of the sea and the rocking of the bunk on which she lay, and the creak of the ship's timbers, the calls of the crew to one another, all brought back a deep, paralysing terror.

Bad things happened on ships.

When the door opened she tried to still herself, to feign sleep, but the erratic rise and fall of her chest gave her away. A man spoke, but she couldn't make out his words, her blood was pounding in her ears, her own breath rattling and scraping so loudly it deafened her.

'Please,' she gasped. 'Please don't …'

A hand held her head still. Something was pressed to her lips. Unable to fight, her weak and treacherous body letting her down again, she thrashed uselessly, sobbing with blind panic.

The next time she woke the lethargy was gone from her limbs. She was still on the ship. Still in the bunk.

A hand held hers.

'Now, no theatrics this time,' said a deep voice, the warlord's voice. 'No one's going to hurt you, Ishtaer.'

Ishtaer. My name is Ishtaer.

She yanked her hand back, but he held firm. Her heart hammered so fast and hard she thought it would break right out of her chest. She felt like a rabbit, inches from the jaws of a mad dog, panicked and utterly helpless.

'You gave poor Karnos a black eye,' said the warlord, 'which I have to say was actually quite impressive given the level of sedation you were under. Perhaps I ought to take that Warrior mark more seriously.'

She cowered, waiting for the inevitable punishment.

Instead, the warlord sighed. 'I said I'm not going to hurt you,' he told her. 'Only cowards pick on the weak, and you, little Ishtaer, are about as weak as they get. Now. Can you promise me you're not going to try and fight me?'

Her breath jerked in and out in shallow pants.

'Ah, so that's it,' he murmured after a long pause. 'That little episode in the guest quarters. You think I'm going to take advantage of you? Look —' he sighed again, his thumb idly rubbing the back of her hand. 'That wasn't my finest hour. I'm sorry. I thought – well, I don't know what I thought. That Samara might punish you for not giving me what I wanted. Which, ironically, isn't what I wanted.'

He paused.

'I mean – look, we both know why she sent you to me. You did say you were willing. But having seen more of Samara's handiwork I can tell that's not exactly true. You wanted to please her, didn't you? Not me.'

Ishtaer licked her lips. She nodded.

'She told you to give me what I wanted.'

Ishtaer nodded again.

'And did you want to do that? Did you want me?'

She couldn't answer. He'd be so angry.

'I won't get angry,' he said, and that was so like what she'd been thinking that she was startled into honesty.

'No,' she said. 'I didn't want it. I'm sorry, I— I didn't know what to …'

His hand squeezed hers, unexpectedly comforting. 'It's all right,' he said. 'My ego will recover. And listen, just for the record, I don't take unwilling women. Never have, never will, don't tolerate it among my men. If your eyes worked properly I'd take you to see what decorates the prow of my ship, but I don't suppose there's any sense in scaring you. Suffice it to say that not one man on this ship will touch you unless you ask him to. I promise you that. They're all far too frightened of me to even think about it.'

Ishtaer didn't know what to say to that. She just nodded, jerkily.

'Now. Since we've established no one's going to be swiving anyone they don't want to, and no one's going to be beating anyone else up,' he added pointedly, releasing her hand, 'let's get on with things. Might I ask you to try moving your right leg?'

She frowned, unsure what he meant by that. Her right leg was the bad one, had been for … actually, she couldn't remember how long. Ugly and twisted, it made walking awkward, and if someone kicked her there – which they did, regularly – the pain brought her to her knees.

She shifted under the covers – and gasped.

The warlord let out a low laugh.

'Have a look at it,' he said. 'That is – I mean, have a feel at it.'

Ishtaer shoved back the covers and ran her hands over her leg, suddenly cautious, a little afraid to believe what she thought she'd just felt. Her crippled leg, moving free and easy beneath the blanket.

Hesitantly, she touched her shin, then ran her fingers down the length of the bone.

It was smooth and straight.

She ran her hand back up, astonished. The bone remained straight. The surface of her leg unmarred by the painful lump of bone that had protruded, aching and awkward, for as long as she could remember.

'But—but—'

The warlord laughed again, a rich sound of amusement. 'Karnos reset it,' he said. 'He's my Healer. Lots of experience with broken bones, although admittedly he usually gets to them a lot sooner. How long ago did this happen?'

Ishtaer couldn't stop touching her newly healed limb. 'Three winters,' she replied, and then blinked, surprised at her own answer.

She remembered. She just didn't know that she remembered.

'You've been walking around on a compound fracture for three years?' He let out a low whistle. 'Was this before or after you were blinded?'

She couldn't stop herself flinching. The touch of her own hands suddenly repelled her. Shaking her head rapidly, she managed, 'Same time.'

The warlord said nothing for a moment, then he said, 'That must have been some accident.'

Ishtaer said nothing.

The warlord cleared his throat. 'Listen,' he said, 'Karnos wants to talk to you about the injury. He's been with you, by the way, most of the time since we boarded the ship. He says you'll probably always have a scar, and it'll take some time to build the muscle back up, but there's no significant nerve damage or ... actually, I lost track after that. He wondered if you healed any muscle damage, or if there was an infection?'

She shook her head again, the nightmarish memory of

those awful days pressing in on her. All the things that had been lost in the fog of her memory, all the small things that were benign and unfrightening, but what crept into her mind like an evil demon whenever she let her guard down was this.

'I don't remember,' she said, her voice small.

'Right. Fine. Never mind.' He paused again, and let out a sigh. 'Look ... the other thing is ...'

Ishtaer rearranged the covers over herself and waited.

'You still can't see me, can you?'

She shook her head apologetically. 'No, my lord.'

'Karnos looked at your eyes. Can't find anything wrong with 'em. No injury, and nothing in your head that could cause it. That is, the skin around one eye was a little burned after Samara's charming attentions – oh, the burn on your arm is much better, by the way, and he's been making headway on some of the other stuff – but it's all fine now.'

Ishtaer felt at her arm. What burn did he mean? There was still the scar of an old brand there, nothing fresh, the S every slave had. Ladyship's mark of ownership. She'd always had it. Hadn't she?

'There's a little bit of scarring on your face,' the warlord went on, 'but you ought to be able to see.'

Ishtaer blinked, but her vision remained as blank as it had been for the last three years.

'What caused it?' the warlord asked bluntly.

She willed herself not to think about that night. 'I hit my head,' she muttered.

'But there's no head injury.'

She shook her head. 'I'm sorry, my lord.'

He blew out another sigh. 'Yeah. Me too. How the hell am I going to present a blind Tyro to the council?'

Ishtaer didn't understand that, so she kept silent.

'Maybe someone in Ilanium can figure it out. Delicate surgery isn't exactly Karnos's forte.' She heard the furniture creak as he stood up. 'Are you hungry? Stupid question. Bet you're always hungry.'

She gave a meek nod.

'Stay there. I'll get you something to eat.'

And with that, the warlord departed the room like a servant.

Chapter Four

Within a few days Ishtaer was on her feet again. The ship's carpenter fashioned her a crutch and then a cane to keep the weight off her leg, but even Karnos was impressed at how fast it healed.

'Malnourished wretch like her, didn't think her body'd have the strength,' he said to Kael.

'She is a Healer herself,' Kael replied. 'And don't call her a wretch.'

Karnos raised his eyebrows but only grunted in reply. The old Healer was grizzled and surly, but Kael could count at least five times in his life when he'd have died were it not for Karnos.

Verak fashioned a little leather pouch to hang around Ishtaer's neck, filled with a variety of crystals. None of them were entirely sure what sort of crystals a Seer might use, but then again, nobody really knew what it was that Seers did. They gave her the most commonly used crystals for Healers and Warriors, and watched her carefully.

After a week she had no need for her cane and walked carefully around the deck with Kael or Verak. To begin with, Kael alerted her to every obstacle, but when he forgot to remind her of a hatch lid he realised she stepped over it anyway.

'How did you know that was there?' he asked.

She looked surprised. 'I remembered it from last time.'

'Just that one, or all of them? Every coil of rope, every step, every single obstacle?'

She frowned, but nodded. Kael took her arm – she only flinched a little now – and led her around the deck again, saying nothing about anything in their path.

She avoided every obstacle, even ducking under the boom as it swung over their heads. Kael, who'd been about to shield her head with his arm, stared at her.

'How did you know that was there? It wasn't before!'

'I heard it. I felt the air move.'

'But we're on deck in the middle of the ocean. There's a lot of air moving around.'

Ishtaer just shrugged. 'I don't know, my lord. I just knew it was there.'

Kael caught Verak's eye, and the other man motioned to the mark on Ishtaer's face. Kael shook his head. Could her Seer's powers really be helping her to find her way around?

She certainly knew where everything was in his cabin. He'd decided to keep her there, out of the way of his curious crew, partly for her own protection and partly for theirs. He'd assured her no man on the ship would touch her, but he wasn't stupid enough to rule out arse-pinching or catcalls, and he honestly didn't think Ishtaer was strong enough to handle it. Three weeks was a long time to be confined to the same small space with no women, and he wasn't about to throw temptation right into their way.

Added to which, he still wasn't entirely sure she might not suffer some sort of panic attack at deserting her beloved Ladyship and attempt to throw herself overboard. He, Verak and Karnos kept an eye on her all throughout the day, and he kept her locked in his cabin at night.

It panicked her to be locked in with him, but then as far as Kael could tell, pretty much everything panicked Ishtaer. While she'd been unconscious, first due to her own eerie drugs and then from the concoction Karnos gave her to keep her under while her leg was fixed, Kael had slept in the same bunk as Ishtaer. It was a large enough bed, and she took up less room than one of the ship's cats.

But when she woke up and found herself sharing the space with him she'd gone rigid and started trembling so violently he thought her bones would shatter.

'Don't worry, lass, you're really not my type,' he said, but she didn't even seem to hear him. He'd been unable to snatch more than a few minutes' sleep the rest of the night.

His shadowed eyes made most of the crew snigger. 'Up all night, were you, cap'n?' 'Demanding lady, is she, sir?'

He ignored them, but the scarlet flush on Ishtaer's cheeks just made them laugh harder.

'Treat her with respect, or I'll have you keelhauled,' Kael said flatly, and the laughter abruptly stopped.

He brought in a hammock for her, but kept it quiet. He figured if the crew thought Ishtaer was his woman they'd be less likely to hassle her. Although he had to wonder if they thought he'd lost his mind. Although she gained in strength every day, she was still a painfully skinny creature, constantly trembling in fear and flinching from the most fleeting of touches.

Kael thought that even if she could see, she'd never meet his eye.

But he made a point of physical contact with her. She couldn't expect to survive at the Academy if she was so frightened of being touched. Hell, if she took the route of privilege and decadence most Chosen did, she'd have to get used to a bevy of body servants washing and dressing her and … er, doing whatever it was those people did.

So he took her arm and walked around the decks with her, gave her a wooden practice sword and taught her a few basic moves and steeled himself to teach her unarmed combat so she could at least defend herself next time a bully like Samara tried to take advantage of her.

And all the time he wondered. Who was she? Where had

she come from? How had she ended up as a slave? And why was she just so frightened of absolutely everything?

'... to the Academy, which is in Ilanium. And Ilanium is the capital of ...? Ilania, that's right,' the warlord said as if Ishtaer had answered him herself.

He speaks to me like a child, she thought, and was astonished at such a rebellious thought.

'Now Ilania is the country, but its empire is known as the Ilani Empire. Encompasses most of the mainland, including countries such as Draxos. You remember me talking about Draxos?'

'I remember,' she said obediently, although the memory was fuzzy and indistinct, clouded with the fear and pain and confusion of that day.

'Draxos is quite a hot country, to the south and east of Ilania. A lot of people there have dark hair like yours. Although,' he faltered, 'they're not usually as pale as you. But then you're probably just pale from lack of sunshine. Get back to Draxos and you'll be brown as a nut in no time.'

Ishtaer was nonplussed. She genuinely had no idea what she looked like. Even when she could see she had no recollection of ever looking in a mirror.

'My hair is dark?' she asked. One hand, the hand that wasn't tucked into his arm, moved up to touch her hair. Someone had hacked it all off, taken away the painful mats that tugged at her scalp and were home to more crawling creatures than she could get rid of. Not that she recalled trying much. There had been a time when it had bothered her, but for some reason, after a while with Ladyship it just seemed ... unimportant.

Now it covered her clean, unbitten scalp in a layer no more than an inch long. She wondered if it made her look ugly. Then she wondered where that thought had come from.

'Yes, your hair is dark. Rather like mine. Not quite black, but getting there. And your eyes are blue, did you know that?'

She shook her head.

'Quite a nice pale blue, actually,' he said, and from his voice and his breath on her face she could tell he was peering at her. 'Not terribly Draxan,' he added, straightening away from her. 'Was your mother Draxan?'

'I don't know,' Ishtaer said.

'Did your father have blue eyes?'

'I don't *know*.'

'What do you know about them?'

'Nothing,' she answered automatically, and then shook her head and tried, really tried, to remember.

She must have had parents. Everybody had parents, even slaves. Someone had given birth to her and nursed her, and ... then what? Someone had inspected the cleanliness of her hands, had beat her with a cane for misbehaving, had dabbed stinging ointment on scrapes and bruises. But that someone wasn't family.

'I don't ... think I knew them,' she said slowly.

'An orphan?' asked the warlord.

Orphan. The word slotted into place in her head, like a key opening a door. 'Yes, an orphan. In the ... the place, where they put people who have nowhere else. The ... the ...'

'Orphanage?'

'No,' she said, frustrated with herself. The stern voice telling her to turn her hands over, enquiring whether her fingernails were clean ... the smell of tripe and disinfectant ... the high, barred windows ... the tubs of water and the wringers and the red, raw knuckles ...

'They send people there to work. People who have nothing. And children. The ones without families. We did the work. The laundry and mending and picking and cleaning. We worked—' she broke off, unable to find the words.

'A workhouse,' said the warlord beside her. He sounded shocked.

'Workhouse,' Ishtaer repeated in relief, and that word opened up another door, another memory. The inside of the workhouse, the huge central hall where meals were taken at long tables, everything smelling of tripe and cabbage. The laundry, endless, steaming and scalding, the ache in her fingers that she could still feel now. The hard bed, scratchy blanket, the pervading chill from the stone floors. Always a small child crying somewhere. Always a bell ringing, for some task or some punishment. Always a line of penitents standing in the hall, watching the others eat, waiting to be caned for the day's misdemeanours.

'I remember,' she breathed, bathing herself in the memory, the cold and the boredom and the smell, all of it. *That was me. I existed before all this. I have memories.*

'I wasn't always a slave,' she said.

'She's from the Saranos,' Kael said, and watched the table go silent. For a long moment the only sound was the creak of the ship's timbers and the patter of rain against glass. Kael was glad he wasn't out on deck tonight.

'She told you that?' Verak said eventually.

'She grew up in a workhouse,' Kael said, emptying his wine and reaching for more. The table, hanging from a pair of brackets on the ceiling, swayed as he set the flagon back down.

'But they were all shut down,' Karnos began.

'After the war they were,' Verak said. 'More than five years ago they'd still have been operating. Seven hells, Kael. She lived in one of those places?'

Quite a large proportion of his crew had been there in the

Saranos Islands five years ago. Kael had personally walked into one of the cathedrals of misery where the Saraneans put their poor and hopeless, had seen the defeated faces of men drowned in debt, unmarried mothers, orphaned children. He hadn't been much older than Ishtaer was now. He'd thought it was the worst place he'd ever been.

That was, of course, before he'd seen Samara's compound.

'Does she remember the war?' Karnos rumbled.

'No idea. She got as far as the workhouse then had to go and lie down.'

'She eaten today?' Verak asked.

'Yes, *Papa*, she's eaten properly,' Kael said. Verak rolled his eyes. 'In accordance with Healer's orders.'

'Don't recall as I gave any order about how she should be fed,' Karnos said, watching them with amusement.

'No, you don't need to, because laddo here knows all about hunger, don't you?'

Kael pointed at his second with a chicken leg and said, 'Aye, more than you do, so shut it. Does a man good to know what it's like to be hungry. I've half a mind to strand the crew on an island somewhere and pick 'em up a week later, then we'll see how they complain about hard bread and rotten meat.'

Verak held up his hands. 'Spare me the tale, I've heard it often enough.'

Kael wrenched some more meat off the bone with his teeth, good humour gone. He'd hated his father at the time for sending him out into the wilderness like that, unarmed and unprepared, a boy of eleven with nothing but sheer bloodymindedness on his side. He could still hear the old man's voice telling him that if he was so sure he was going to be a great fighter he could learn to take care of himself.

Kael had done better than that. He'd learned how to catch

small animals and fish, how to construct a shelter and make a fire from almost nothing, and one day when his feet were frozen and his belly cramping with hunger, he'd fought a she-wolf over a dead rabbit, and won.

Of course, later he discovered the wolf's pups, and still couldn't work out whether he was proud of himself for showing them mercy, or whether he'd been a coward not to slay them. Two had died anyway, and the third bit him hard enough to leave a scar before wandering off, never to be seen again.

When Kael returned home, it was with the Warrior's mark on his arm.

'If you two are done bickering,' Karnos broke into the memory, 'perhaps we should try to work out why a girl from the Saranos, from the Empire, ended up as a slave.'

'Maybe that's what the workhouses did with an excess of inmates,' Verak said darkly.

'She must have left before the war,' Kael said, trying to put it together in his head. 'The Islands were a lawless place back then. Remember all those smugglers we caught?'

'I remember,' Karnos said. 'Those smugglers paid for my cottage out at Offerhöjden.'

Kael grinned. 'What a piece of legislation the Privateer Act was.'

'Maybe she was kidnapped,' Verak said. 'There were still slavers operating out of the Saranos.'

'Maybe,' Kael said. 'I still can't work out how she ended up in a workhouse in the first place. With those marks she has to be from the Citizenry. Even if she was orphaned she shouldn't have ended up there.'

'Was she? Orphaned?' Verak added, and Kael nodded.

'She remembers that. Says she doesn't know anything about her family. Remembers the workhouse. And that's it. I'll try again tomorrow.'

Karnos picked up his glass and said, 'By the time we get her to the Academy she might even have a last name.'

She didn't have a last name, despite Kael's increasingly inventive questioning. By the time the ship rounded the Excelsis Cliffs he'd ascertained that she'd worked in a kitchen of some kind and that she'd been called Agnes there because 'I won't have filthy foreign names in my kitchen,' but when he asked who exactly she'd been quoting Ishtaer got that frustrated look on her face and said she didn't know.

He tried to explain about Ilani naming structures to her, but could tell about five words in that she found it utterly baffling. He couldn't entirely blame her. His own name in High Ilani went on for so long he needed to start saying it five minutes before he introduced himself.

'Look, you're from the Saranos, so we'll call you Ishtaer ex Saraneus,' he said. 'The names are in High Ilani so the words are a little different. *Ex* just means *from*. It's for Chosen and Citizens who aren't from Ilania. Okay?'

She nodded in the way he was beginning to recognise as meaning she didn't understand at all but was prepared to pretend she did so he wouldn't get angry with her. This in itself made him angry, since after nearly a month she still couldn't comprehend that he wasn't going to hurt her.

'You'll be called Tyro while you're at the Academy,' he said, 'because that's the High Ilani word for student. Don't worry, everyone there speaks Common Ilani. You won't be expected to learn another language, except for a few terms. When you pass out of the Academy, you won't be called Tyro any more, but your new title will be added to your name. Mine are Militis Viscus, because those are the marks I have. So, when you qualify as a Healer they'll call you Ishtaer ex Saraneus Medicus, all right?'

The same uncertain nod.

'Then there are victory titles. They're usually awarded by the Emperor for a victory or great service. I've a couple,' he added casually.

He wondered if she ever would. Then it occurred to him that in some way she'd already accomplished a victory of a kind: simply staying alive for so long in Samara's compound. Retaining a shred of humanity. Surviving.

Hmm.

Kael opened his mouth to explain about the order of precedence for the Twice-Marked, but then shut it again. There was absolutely no point confusing her further when he didn't even know if her other marks were genuine.

'You'll be fine,' he told her, which was a huge lie and he knew it.

The breeze was fresh off the Great Ocean as Ilanium came into view, the sun just beginning to set, and as ever Kael stood in awe of the sight for a few seconds.

'I wish you could see this, Ishtaer,' he said, not even looking to see if she stood beside him at the rail. She nearly always did. 'The city's built on one huge rock in the bay at the mouth of the river, and it's backed by the white cliffs of the bay. When the sun hits them you've no need for a light anywhere in the city, so they say. And there's the Turris Imperio, the Tower, rising up above the city with the Emperor's palace at the top, closer to the gods than any other mortal. See how it spirals up with roads and—' he caught himself. 'That is, I mean you ought to see it. Feat of engineering. The whole tower is bigger than some cities, but it's just the centrepiece of Ilanium. The city's built in a circle around it, avenues like the spokes of a wheel. They say the gods must have designed Ilanium, the view from high above must be so pleasing.'

He trailed off, aware he was prattling. Beside him, Ishtaer murmured, 'It sounds very impressive, my lord.'

'Yeah. Well.' He cleared his throat. 'I mean it's not bad.

For the Empire. Bit showy, if you ask me. I prefer my cities a bit more organic. I like castles with battlements on them.'

She nodded politely. Kael ran his hand through his hair and turned to study her. In less than an hour he'd be presenting her to the council. What would they think? Would they be appalled at the blind, cowering skeleton he brought them?

Her hair was beginning to grow out, which meant that it looked like she'd lost a fight with a set of hedge clippers. He made a mental note to attempt to even it up a bit. Her face had lost its gaunt look, and although she was still very thin she wasn't as painfully, cadaverously emaciated as she had been when he found her. To his surprise she stood quite tall, at least she did when she wasn't cowering.

The scar on her face had lessened considerably, but Karnos fully admitted he wasn't one for fine work, and she might always have a mark there. It marred the otherwise beautiful lines of her Seer's mark, the delicate tracery around her eye that wasn't quite leaves or feathers but something ethereal and lovely.

He'd been able to heal the fresh burn on her wrist completely, no such luck with the scar on her arm where she'd been branded, like a cow, whenever it was that Samara had acquired her. But at least that was something she could keep covered up, if she chose. And since it had received immediate attention, her own nascent healing skills had taken care of the brand on her palm. The Healer's mark there was whole and clean, manifesting itself as something almost like writing on her skin.

And that Warrior mark on her arm. Bold, thick lines curving and chasing each other over her whole forearm, marks like exotic blades conducting a battle of their own.

He still didn't know what he was going to say to the council about that.

It was dark by the time they moored up. The structure of the city, surrounded wholly by water, meant that the docks circled the whole of Ilanium; but even so there was never quite enough room, especially for large ships such as his.

This didn't, however, cause much of a problem for Kael.

He glanced at the jack he'd personally run up as they sailed in, and grinned. Toeing off his boots, he ran barefoot up to the bow and leapt onto the bowsprit, stepping nimbly out over the waves and steadying himself with one hand on the forestay. The wind flew through his hair, his cloak streamed behind him and the mighty sword he wore at his hip gleamed in the dying light of the day.

He glanced back at the foresail, emblazoned with his red and black banner, and when he turned back to the harbour his grin was fierce.

Below him on the bow stretched that tattered piece of human skin.

'Tell the Empire Krull the Warlord has returned,' he howled to the wind, and behind him the crew cheered, blades raised to catch the light.

Ships fled before him like mice from a cat.

The *Grey Ghost* slid into dock with insolent ease and Kael leapt down onto the ground, landing in a crouch.

'Sir Verak, my boots if you please!' he yelled, and a few seconds later they came thudding down beside him. 'And the girl,' he added.

The few passers-by who hadn't been able to get off the dock in time froze, horrified, as if they expected her to be thrown over the side too. But by the time Kael had got his boots back on she was walking down the gangplank on Verak's arm, looking remarkably composed for someone who had just sailed into the largest city in the Empire on the most notorious pirate ship in the world. Behind them strode half a dozen men, dressed in dark cloaks bearing the insignia of Krull the Warlord, every one of them very visibly armed.

'I love a show of strength,' Kael said.

'Want me to come with you?' Verak asked as he handed over custody of Ishtaer.

Kael shook his head. 'No. You take care of the ship. It's too late for a meeting now. I'll send for you tomorrow if I need you.'

Verak saluted him and Kael acknowledged it with a nod.

'My lady,' he said to Ishtaer, taking her hand and placing it in the crook of his arm. 'Don't worry about stepping over things or around people,' he added as he strolled off the dock and onto the first solid ground he'd seen for weeks. 'They generally get the hell out of my way.'

He led her on foot through the city, the streets gently rising as they neared the centre. As darkness fell, wheeled conveyances were allowed onto the streets, but Kael never stepped out of the way of a single one. He watched with amusement as one poor man nearly drove into a wall to avoid him.

He frowned in thought as they approached the Academy, which had the effect of making a couple of small children cry.

The Academy, occupying more horizontal space in the city than any other institution, stood concealed behind high walls and permanently manned gates. Kael strolled up to the main door and used the hilt of his sword to pound on it.

A voice from behind it said, 'It's the middle of the night!'

One of Kael's men sniggered.

'Lad, I don't think that's what you're meant to say, is it?' Kael said. 'Especially since it's barely past twilight.'

'Admittance ends at twilight,' said the voice. 'It might as well be the middle of the night. You're too late, you'll have to find somewhere else to stay tonight, and Sir Flavius will be—'

'Shut up, lad,' Kael said amiably, and slid his sword back into its sheath. It made a silken sound, which caused the voice on the other side of the door to go silent.

'No. Here's what's going to happen. You're going to ask me my name, and then you're going to open that hatch and check I am who I say I am, and then you're going. To swiving well. Let. Me. In. Understand?'

'Er … yes, sir. What is your name, sir?'

Kael took a deep breath. 'Lord Kaelnar Vapensigsson ex Krullus Militis Viscus Saraneus Drax.'

There was a pause while the voice on the other side of the door processed this.

'You might know me better as Krull the Warlord,' he added, and the hatch shot open.

He smiled at the young man revealed there. It wasn't a nice smile.

The door was dragged back in a hurry and Kael strolled right in without looking at the boy. Ishtaer kept pace with him, her gaze appearing as though fixed straight ahead. She wore a long cloak with the hood pulled up, but the light from the Academy's torches clearly showed the mark on her face. She looked unexpectedly regal in the firelight.

'Will, er, you all be coming in, sir—my lord?' asked the boy, dancing around the squad as they marched into the outer courtyard.

'No. My men will be returning to the ship,' Kael said without turning to look at them. His men knew when they were getting an order from him. 'Just me and the lady will be coming in.'

'Er, yes, my lord. And can I take the lady's name?' the boy asked, reaching tentatively for a clipboard.

'Tyro Ishtaer ex Saraneus Medicus Militis Aspicio prior Inservio.'

He wasn't sure what made him add that last part. She

might not be happy with him when she found out what it meant.

The boy scribbled it down, eyes wider with every cognomen Kael uttered. When he mentally translated the victory name his head jerked up and he stared at Ishtaer, who thankfully couldn't see his naked shock.

'Tell the council I want to see them tomorrow. And find a room for us.'

'My lord, I'm sorry, but they're only single rooms. Single beds, I mean.'

'Lad, I'm Krull the Warlord. I want a room with a double bed. And my own water pump. You're going to find one for me. Understand?'

'Er … yes, my lord. Er … wait here, please.'

The boy ran off, and Kael noticed with mild interest how he had an awkward gait, one he'd only seen before on men with one leg.

'Back to the ship,' he told his men, and they saluted him, fist over heart, before turning and wheeling back out onto the street. Damn, even after weeks at sea they marched in formation.

'Makes a warlord proud,' he said. 'Right then, Ishtaer. Here we are. When that damn fool boy comes back we'll get some rest, have some supper and wash the sea off us, then you'll be perfectly presentable to see the council tomorrow.'

She nodded silently.

'Don't mind sharing a bed with me, do you?' he probed. 'Just for one night. Wouldn't want to leave you all alone in a strange place.'

'I—' she began, but couldn't seem to go any further.

'I won't do anything you don't want me to,' he added with only a hint of mocking.

'Yes, my lord,' she stammered.

'Ah, come on Ishtaer, you're bad for my ego. Can't I tempt you a little bit?'

'No, my lord, sorry, my lord,' she gasped, as if simply refusing him was the hardest thing she could do. He supposed slaves weren't used to having much choice.

'Well, your loss,' he said as the boy came running back to them.

'My lord, I've found you a room.'

'Good lad,' Kael said, striding on into the inner courtyard. 'Somehow I knew you would.'

She didn't know why he insisted on keeping her with him. Did he think she was going to run away? She might be terrified of this big, dangerous man, but for the first time she could remember she was clean, healthy and not hungry, and it was all thanks to him.

If only Ladyship had offered her those basic comforts, Ishtaer might have stayed.

She was so shocked at that thought that she hardly noticed the warlord pumping water into a bucket and taking his clothes off. It was only when he touched her arm and she turned, startled, that her body came up against his and she realised he was naked.

'I've clean clothes for you, once you've had a wash,' he said. Ishtaer nodded automatically. 'You might need to get undressed first,' he added when she just stood there.

'I—'

He sighed. 'Said I wasn't going to touch you, Ishtaer, unless you wanted me to. Do you want me to?'

She shook her head rapidly.

'Sure? It's an experience most women would pay for.'

I know. I've been paying for it for years.

That thought shocked her too.

'Come on, get your clothes off. I ain't sharing a nice clean bed with you all covered in the sea. Funny how you notice it all the more on dry land, eh?'

She nodded stiffly and began to undress. He'd seen her naked before, of course, and had hardly been inflamed with passion. And she knew he'd taken off his clothes in her presence, quite often actually. She could hear the rustle of cloth, smell the scent of his skin. He seemed to do it on purpose, to needle her.

He probably wasn't used to women turning him down.

She washed herself quickly and put on the nightshirt the warlord handed to her, just as someone knocked at the door.

'Your supper, my lord, and … um …'

'Lady,' the warlord said absently.

'Er … yes.'

The door shut, and the warlord said, 'Well, you'll be a lady when you graduate. Assuming those marks of yours aren't faked.'

It was a loaded statement. 'No, my lord.'

'And for the love of the gods stop calling me "my lord". My name is Kael. We've shared a cabin for weeks, girl. You can at least call me by my first name.'

'Yes, my … Kael.'

He laughed softly at that, and told her to eat.

She'd learned to eat carefully, slowly, her stomach still unused to such huge amounts of food. A few pieces of meat and one bread roll and she was stuffed.

'You'll soon get used to eating more,' the warlord – Kael – said.

Ishtaer nodded politely. She didn't think she ever would.

He told her to get into bed and she did, lying stiff and trembling as he climbed in beside her. But all he did was settle beneath the covers, not even trying to touch her. She heard his puff of air as he blew out the candle, and silence settled over the room.

'Ishtaer?' he said after a few minutes.

'Yes, m—Kael?'

'Stop bloody trembling. I can't get to sleep.'

'I—I'll try.'

'Are you cold?'

'No.'

'Pity. I could have warmed you up.'

She edged a little further away from him.

'Sure you don't want me to touch you?' he asked idly.

'Yes,' she gasped.

'Your loss. Well, night, then,' he said, and she heard nothing from him until the morning, when he shook her awake, told her to get dressed and follow him.

She'd expected to go straight into a meeting with this council he'd talked about, but instead he took her across a courtyard and into a large, busy room filled with heavenly scents.

People went oddly silent as Kael approached, but he ignored them all and handed Ishtaer a tray on which he placed various items of food, then guided her to a table.

All around them, Ishtaer was conscious of the whispers.

'... *fifteen hundred in Draxos.*'

'*I heard he killed fifteen thousand.*'

'*I meant personally, numbhead.*'

Beside her on the bench, Kael calmly ate his breakfast, with no sign of having heard them.

'*So did I. He just slaughtered that many.*'

'*No one could kill fifteen thousand men all by himself.*'

'*Lord Krull could …*'

'Coffee, Ishtaer? It's better than the stuff we had on the ship.'

Ishtaer nodded mechanically.

'... *you know he's Twice-Marked?*'

'*Yeah, but no one knows what his second mark is.*'

'They say his Militis mark covers, like, his whole arm and half his chest! But no one's ever seen ...'

'Enjoying your breakfast?'

'It's delicious,' Ishtaer said with heartfelt sincerity. It was porridge, but not the tasteless stuff they'd had on board the ship. This porridge had cream and honey and fruits and spices in it. This porridge was like food for gods.

'... oh my gods, that's Lord Krull!'

'So I see. You know,' he dropped his tone and spoke close in her ear, 'if you'd let me touch you in bed, I could put that look on your face.'

Her whole body tightened at his nearness, even before he spoke.

Kael made a sound of disgust. 'But that'll never happen, will it?' he said. 'You'll get that expression from porridge, but not from me.'

'... on the seas, and his father was a great warlord ...'

'Krull the Warlord!'

'... pirate ...'

'Shh, don't look, that's Krull the Warlord!'

Eventually, as her bowl emptied and Kael finished his several plates of food, he shoved back his chair and stood up. 'Come on, then,' he said, and once again everyone went silent as they passed.

'Gone a bit quiet in there,' Kael remarked as they emerged into the cool morning.

'They all knew you,' Ishtaer ventured.

'Nah, they knew of me. I love having a reputation,' the great warlord remarked as they crossed the cobbles. 'Always gets girls into bed. Well, except you.'

Ishtaer had, technically, been in his bed, but she didn't really want to remind him of it.

'Although maybe you haven't heard about me. I'm Krull the Warlord, you know.'

'I've heard, my lord,' she said evenly. All those whispers …

'Really? Did I tell you how I slaughtered – how many were they saying in there? Fifteen thousand, in Draxos?'

'Barehanded,' she agreed, feeling slightly sick.

'And the pirate booty. Got a castle full of gold in Krulland. No? I kill pirates, you know,' he added jauntily. 'They're afraid of me.'

'Everyone's afraid of you, my lord,' Ishtaer said.

'Including you,' he sighed. 'Okay, fine. Whatever. Try not to look so terrified when we meet the council, will you?'

She nodded, but she had the distinct feeling that he knew as well as she that it was a lie.

Chapter Five

The chamber he took her to was up a wide flight of stone stairs and along a passageway open to the courtyard below. Whenever they passed someone, conversation would stop, footsteps slow, and once she even thought she heard the shuffle and scrape of a curtsey. Kael ignored it all.

The day was cold, the air crisp, but Ishtaer wore a woollen dress and cloak that covered her head and hands. The day was cold, but she was not.

Kael opened a door that creaked heavily and led her to a wooden chair in a room where tapestries muffled echoes and a large fire crackled.

'Now then, Krull,' said a man's voice. An older man, his voice used to command. 'What have you brought us?'

'Will this take long?' asked a woman, not unkindly. 'We're run off our feet in the clinic. I swear every second person in the city has flu.'

'You won't be long here, Julia,' said a second man, his voice thin with age, but sure of itself.

'It will take as long as it needs to,' said a third man, his voice calm, friendly, and just a little bit too smooth to be trustworthy.

Kael ignored them all. 'Coffee, Ishtaer?'

She shook her head automatically, then added, 'No, thank you, my lord.'

She heard the glug of liquid and clink of crockery as he poured his own, and the woman's impatient sigh. Finally, he settled beside her in another chair, and said, 'You'd best introduce yourselves. Sir Scipius I know, but I'm afraid it's been a while since I visited the clinic, ma'am.'

'Julia Quintia,' said the woman.

'Madam Julia, the senior Healer here at the Academy, is that correct?' Kael said. Ishtaer assumed the woman nodded as there was no rebuttal to this. 'If she believes your mark to be genuine, she'll be in charge of your training.'

Ishtaer nodded. Her eyes were downcast, as usual. She'd been told for too long how annoying it was to have them flickering about all over the place. Best that her lids hid them.

'I am Sir Flavius Fulvius Viator, child,' said the smooth-toned man. 'I run the Academy.'

'And also takes charge of all the dull stuff every Chosen needs to know, whether or not it actually relates to his or her field,' said the elderly man in a quiet tone. 'I really can't see how High Ilani is even relevant any more, except as a way of excluding those who don't know it. To which end, I might as well call myself simply Killen.'

'I am Sir Scipius Durian Militis,' said the man who'd spoken first, 'and I've no idea what I'm doing here. Why am I verifying the marks of a woman, Krull?'

There was a pause, during which she heard Kael swallow and set down his cup. 'The same reason Madam Julia is here,' he said.

Another pause. 'She has a Healer's mark also?' Madam Julia said. She made a noise of annoyance. 'You know there's no way to test if her Seer's mark is real.'

'No. But just as you can test if she's a real Healer, Sir Scipius can test,' here he took Ishtaer's wrist and pushed up her sleeve, 'if she's a real Warrior.'

Someone sucked in a breath. Someone laughed softly.

'Is this a joke, my lord?' asked Madam Julia.

'If it is, then it's on me as well,' Kael replied smoothly. 'And you know I'm not fond of being laughed at. I found her with these three marks. I've seen her heal herself so I've no reason to distrust that mark, and she's shown a little aptitude with a sword, although in her present sorry state it's rather hard to tell what she might be good at. You've no idea how to stand up for yourself, have you, Ishtaer?'

'And I don't suppose you've had any handy visions that have come true, have you, child?' asked Killen.

Ishtaer shook her head.

'But,' said Sir Scipius, 'a woman. A woman Warrior?'

'Just because it's never happened before doesn't mean it can't happen in the future,' said Sir Flavius.

'Yes, but that would make her Thrice-Marked,' said Madam Julia tensely. 'It's impossible.'

'Merely implausible,' said Killen.

'Who are you?' asked Sir Flavius. 'Who are your people? Are you related to Lord Krull?'

'Gods, I hope not,' Kael said, and against all her expectations, that hurt Ishtaer. 'Sirs, Madam, may I present Tyro Ishtaer ex Saraneus Medicus Militis Aspicio prior Inservio.'

'Yes, but,' began Sir Scipius, and then he went silent.

'Inservio?' asked Madam Julia sharply.

Kael let out a long breath.

'Will you not speak, Ishtaer?' asked Killen softly. The rest started squabbling.

'My lord,' she whispered sideways.

'Mmm?' Kael said.

'I don't understand. Inservio?'

A pause. 'Never mind,' he said. 'You'll get a new name soon. Once you've graduated the Academy. And maybe we'll find out who your people are. Then you can be named for them.'

'You don't *know*—' Madam Julia yelped.

'Perhaps you'd better start at the beginning,' said Sir Flavius crisply.

A pause, and the rattle of Kael's coffee cup. Then he said, 'As you say,' and proceeded to give a potted history of Ishtaer as he knew her.

A very potted history. He managed to glaze over their entire time at Samara's compound with, 'I noticed she bore the marks of the Chosen and brought her back to my ship,' and utterly failed to mention how she'd nearly gelded him and he'd left her to die in a cell.

He told the committee what he did know of her life before she became a slave, and as he spoke it became clearer to Ishtaer too. 'She was raised as an orphan in a workhouse on the Saranos,' he said. 'She doesn't know who her parents were. She worked in domestic service before escaping to sea, where she was sold as a slave.'

No, that's not right. She'd never been sold. She'd been ... captured, that was more the word. From the terror and pain and anger of the ship to the chaos on deck, the crash of timber and the smash of swords, men screaming and dying and the deck running red with blood, and the devil raising his sword and roaring at her—

'Ishtaer?'

The old man's voice. Startled, she shook herself.

'Are you all right?' That was Kael.

Rapidly, she nodded. Footsteps sounded, and the swish of cloth, and someone smelling of medicinal herbs was in front of her. Madam Julia. Her fingers were cool against Ishtaer's wrist.

'She's terrified, my lord. What have you been doing to her?'

'Me? I've been saving her life, that's what I've been doing. Should have seen her when I found her. Starved, crippled—'

'Crippled?'

'Yes, she – look, you tell her, Ishtaer. You've hardly said a word all morning.'

You hardly gave me opportunity. 'I broke my leg,' she said, and then frowned and corrected herself. 'My leg was broken.'

'Not usually enough to cripple someone,' Madam Julia said. 'Especially not a Healer. Had your mark manifested by then?'

Ishtaer nodded. 'But she had no crystals,' Kael put in for her, 'and had never heard of the Chosen, anyway.'

'Hmm. So it was never set? I suppose that would cause problems,' Madam Julia mused. 'May I see?'

Ishtaer nodded, and the Healer pushed up the skirts of her dress to the knee. She chattered with Ishtaer about the injury and about how Karnos had set it. 'That old misery,' Julia called him.

'A misery who's saved my life a handful of times,' Kael told her.

'Hmm. We might work on that scar, Ishtaer, but the bone has healed quite nicely. What have you healed since you got your crystals?'

Ishtaer showed the woman the palm of her hand. 'I was burned here.'

'And there's not a mark on it. Very good. What burned you?'

She hesitated. 'Tell her,' said Killen's voice.

'A a brand,' she stammered.

A short silence, then Scipius said, 'Like a cattle brand?'

'Exactly like a cattle brand,' said Kael. 'Lady Samara is not a pleasant woman. I imagine I'll have an interesting conversation with the Emperor about her later.'

'I see,' Madam Julia said, although it was quite clear she didn't. 'And have you any knowledge of herbs?'

Ishtaer forced herself to be still. *Don't try to impress them. Don't pretend to be better than you are.* 'Some,' she said.

'Some? Ishtaer – look, will you look at me, please? How I'm supposed to carry on a conversation with the top of your head, I've no idea.'

Ishtaer breathed in.

'Ah,' said Kael. 'Yes, that's the other thing.'

'She can't,' said Killen.

Madam Julia's hand went under Ishtaer's chin and forced it up. Ishtaer opened her eyes fully; there was no point hiding now.

Scipius swore. Ishtaer felt the breeze of the Healer's hand waving back and forth. 'You're blind,' Madam Julia said sharply.

'No,' Ishtaer said, surprising herself. 'I just can't see.'

'Isn't that what blindness is, girl?' Sir Flavius asked.

'There's nothing wrong with her eyes,' Kael explained as Madam Julia poked at her eyelids. 'Karnos has examined them over and over. No injury, no cataract, she wasn't born this way. We were rather hoping someone here might be able to shed light on it.'

Madam Julia sounded thoughtful. 'It's not my field,' she said. 'I'm sure I can find someone who specialises. It will make it harder to teach you, Ishtaer,' she added, as if Ishtaer had done it on purpose.

'And impossible for me,' said Sir Scipius. 'Even if that mark is real.'

'It is,' said Killen, but Sir Scipius came striding over to take her arm in his hands. She felt his breath on her skin as he peered close, and fought revulsion.

Kael muttered something under his breath, then said aloud, 'We're wasting time here. Your sword, sir.'

Sir Scipius dropped her arm. 'You can't mean —'

'A demonstration, yes. And if she's hurt, well then. What better way to demonstrate her healing abilities?'

Killen laughed softly. After a moment, she heard the silken glide of a sword being withdrawn from its scabbard, and then the hilt of it was pressed into her right hand.

It was a serviceable weapon, she decided, not fancy with crystals and carvings, like Lord Krull's. This one was shorter than the practice swords she'd used on the ship, it had leather binding the handle and no cross guard, but it was light and felt secure in her hand.

She unfastened her cloak and laid it over her chair.

'You've given her a gladius against your longsword?' Sir Flavius said doubtfully. 'Is that fair?'

'No,' the warlord said, and swung at Ishtaer.

Her arm flew up across her body and the short sword pushed him back, steel sliding against steel. He whirled the longsword in an arc above his head and came at her again, from the left this time, the sword slicing upwards. Ishtaer chopped down and was rewarded with the clash of steel on steel again.

'But—' Sir Scipius murmured.

Krull's sword slid up along hers, up and to the right, and she pushed back in the same direction until he'd swung away, and this time he chopped down at her.

Use the momentum, she thought, and drove the point of his sword to the ground. Then she lifted her weapon and jabbed sharply forward, the blade an extension of her arm.

Someone sucked in a sharp breath, and she remembered too late that this was a real sword, not a practice wooden dummy, and that Kael hadn't dressed in padded practice armour as he had on the ship. She faltered, halted her thrust, and the warlord let out a short, harsh laugh as he swept the flat of his sword against her arm, slicing through her sleeve and the skin of her inner arm.

The gladius clattered to the ground and Ishtaer clutched at her arm, feeling hot blood seep through.

For a moment no one moved, no one spoke, and then Kael said, 'Now would be a prime time to demonstrate your healing abilities, lass.'

Madam Julia *tsked* and pushed Ishtaer to her seat. 'A small cut would suffice.'

'That is a small cut.' Kael sounded disinterested.

'I meant a little slice of the finger! Not a – oh dear, that's bleeding quite a lot, Ishtaer. Do you know how to slow the blood?'

She nodded, covering the wound and willing the flow of blood to cease. That was what Karnos had told her on the ship. 'You just have to tell it what to do, kid. That's the only way I can describe it.'

'And knit the blood vessels back together … yes, that's it. Layer by layer, that's the way to treat a cut like this. Start with the most important bits and then the most badly damaged, and after that simply work your way out.'

'How did you know where his sword was?' Sir Scipius asked her. 'If you can't see … Is this some Seer's trick?'

'No,' said Killen's voice. He sounded amused.

'I don't think so,' Ishtaer said. 'It's just … I listened, and I felt for the air currents and I … I worked it out. Where the sword was going to go. Using the momentum.'

'We had a couple of practice fights on the ship,' Kael said. 'Yes, but …'

'If she could see, she'd be better,' Kael conceded. 'But do you think she could do that if she wasn't a Warrior?'

Madam Julia held the edges of the wound together while Ishtaer concentrated on fusing the skin closed.

'Do you know how to dull pain?' she asked, and Ishtaer shook her head.

'I—the crystals fade it a bit,' she said. 'But I don't know if it would work on someone else.'

'No. That's a technique you can learn. And which I'll teach you.' She paused. 'It's going to be difficult, Ishtaer, if you can't see anything. But I'm willing to try if you are.'

She was firm, but she was kind. She was offering to teach Ishtaer.

People have been kind before. And it's been a lie.

She thought about the sword Kael had knocked from her hand. About the instinctive way she'd moved with it. *This whole place could be crawling with armed men who are bigger and faster than I am.*

But they don't seem to mind me fighting back.

'I will try,' she said, and Madam Julia made a satisfied noise.

'You'll need to clean that wound,' she said. 'Come with me down to the clinic and we'll sort it out properly for you. These boys can squabble over whether you're a Warrior or a Seer, but I'm satisfied you're a Healer. Come on, then.'

Ishtaer followed.

Chapter Six

The sun was as high in the sky as it was going to get at this time of year. Kael emerged from the council session with knots in his shoulders and grabbed a passing student at random to run down to the ship with his message. The kid, a Bard by his clothing, ran off like a frightened rabbit.

Kael made his way to the Militis training grounds, discerned which group were the most skilled and informed one of them that he'd be a gold aureus richer if he could beat Kael in a fair fight.

Of course, Kael didn't fight fair if he could help it, but the lad didn't realise this until it was too late. Kael kept his aureus, but in deference to the fact that the lad had fought him for ten minutes and nearly cost him his sword at one point, he gave the boy ten denari.

'What's your name, lad?' he asked.

'Tyro Marcus Glorius Livius Militis, my lord,' said the boy, who was tall and blond and had an arrogant cast to his features. And no wonder: a name like Glorius Livius said that both his parents were Chosen. The kid had been born Child of Two Marks at the least. Even if his Mark had never manifested, he'd still have been raised like a prince.

Kael was beginning to regret giving him the denari. His defining memory of the Glorius family was that they were richer than Kael would ever be.

'I know you're a Tyro, kid. That's why you're here. Work on your footwork.'

He picked up his sword and turned to leave. Behind him, the Glorius kid muttered, 'Work on your footwork,' in the sort of tone that had Kael wondering if he'd get away with turning back and stabbing the boy.

No. Probably not.

A lad from Kael's horde was waiting by the training ground, a large chest on wheels by his side. Kael motioned to him to follow to the changing rooms, and the boy opened the box to reveal the gleaming black piles of Kael's dress armour, heaped like giant malevolent beetles.

'Are the rest of them here?' Kael asked as he stepped into the fine black chain mail that went under the plate armour. The stuff wouldn't stop a rubber arrow, but unless things had radically changed at the Tower, he didn't expect he'd need it for actual bodily defence. Dress armour was all about putting on a show.

'They'll meet you outside, sir,' said the boy. He was maybe twelve or thirteen, the nephew of one of his men. Kael didn't need to ask if he could fight – he could probably best half the lads in the training ring. He didn't take helpless children along in his horde.

'Did you get me a horse?'

'Yes, sir, a black destrier. He's used to armour, too. Sir Verak has a chestnut who bucked and reared when we tried to dress him.'

Kael smiled. 'He'll love that.'

'We've just caparisoned him for now, sir, although Sir Verak says we can try for the armour if you really want.'

'No, the caparison is fine.' Let Verak ride a horse wearing skirts. The spectacle was the thing.

The boy – Kael thought his name might be Lars, but wasn't about to embarrass either of them by getting it wrong – began to fasten the ornate plate armour over the top of the mail on his legs. Kael's dress armour was made from steel containing an ore that turned it to a matte black, and he'd had replicas of his marks carved and enamelled in red over his arm and chest. At every join, the plate was studded with red and black crystals that flashed in the light. Unlike some Warriors, he had decided against bearing his sigil on his breastplate, which made the black and red all the more stark.

'How's the ship?'

'Shipshape, sir. Almost nothing to do to it.' Lars buckled plate armour to his legs. 'Steward wants to know when you want to leave next, and where to, and he'll get it provisioned.'

'Soon as possible. We'll sail on the tide tonight if we can. We're already cutting it fine, this time of year.' Kael rolled his shoulders and pulled on his mail shirt. It was made from the same black steel as the plate armour and seemed to suck the light from the day.

He shook his head when offered the coif, however. He wasn't actually going into battle – and what was the point of dressing like Krull the Warlord if no one could see his face?

Over the mail shirt went the enamelled breastplate, buckled to the backplate at the shoulders and sides. Kael took a deep breath to test the fit, and nodded. He hated being trussed up like this, truth be told. A man couldn't fight half so well when he was wearing half a ton of steel.

Lars tied on the vambraces, then laced the shoulder plates to the breastplate. Kael knew all this stuff had special fancy names, but he'd be buggered if he was going to sit around learning them all like a first-year Tyro.

'Will you want the gauntlets, sir? Or just gloves?'

'Gauntlets,' Kael said. He'd take them off as soon as he'd made his entrance. 'Carry my helm, would you?'

The boy nodded and scrambled into his surcoat. Every man of the horde who marched with them on these occasions wore the same coat: black on the left, red on the right, with the crest of Krulland emblazoned across the chest in bright silks.

Kael marched from the changing rooms across the training ground and was gratified to note that this time, everyone stopped to look. Even Glorius's boy, although his handsome face was schooled into a sneer.

Waiting at the gates to the Academy, causing a hell of a disturbance to traffic, was a century of his men, each of them armoured and coated and helmed, the relentless darkness of their dress armour like a black hole in the noon light. They saluted, fists to breastplates, with a deafening clang.

Kael saluted right back and swung himself up into the saddle of the huge black destrier Lars held ready for him. Behind him to the right, Verak stilled his horse, with Karnos flanking to his left. Ahead of them, Johann the signifer stood with Kael's mighty banner.

'Stand you ready?' Kael roared, and a hundred men roared back, 'Aye!'

'Show off,' muttered Verak, and Kael hid a smile.

'We ride,' he called, and the men saluted again, marching after the three horses in perfect time.

Just as he'd told Ishtaer, people generally got the hell out of his way, and that was never truer than when he was putting on a show. After a few hundred yards the crowds had formed an avenue, watching in awe.

'What's it like being the most feared man in the Empire?' Verak asked, riding up beside him. On the other side, Karnos did the same. His men knew about pageantry just as well as he did.

'Oh, you know,' Kael said offhandedly. 'The money's good but the hours aren't great.'

'And the uniform is frankly appalling,' Karnos grumbled.

Verak laughed. His arms were a golden cockerel on a maroon field, plain and uncluttered with the detritus of family legacies and victory cantons. Karnos, on the other hand, came from a line sparsely populated with undistinguished Chosen, and had inherited arms bearing an ass and a beaver. Worse, the purple and yellow diagonal stripes of the background were described in heraldry as 'bendy sinister purpure and gules'. Kael had laughed so hard when he first heard the description of the sinister bendy ass and beaver that he'd nearly choked.

'Put me in Krullish livery then,' the grizzly Healer had said, but Kael refused. Partly because the man was Chosen and had the right to bear his own arms, and partly because it was so damn funny seeing his face when he had to wear the stuff.

'How's our girl settling in?' Verak asked as the horde passed under the Queen's Gate and began down the Processional Way, flanked by bas reliefs and walls made of jewelled and enamelled bricks so bright and vibrant Kael's armour seemed dull in comparison.

Kael shrugged, which was a noisy business when he wore so much armour. 'Hard to say. She's still a frightened little mouse, but she seems to forget some of that when she gets to healing. Madam Julia has accepted her at any rate.'

'Julia Quintia?' Karnos rumbled. 'She's running the place now, is she? No surprise. Intelligent woman.'

'Sensible too,' Kael added, because in his experience the two didn't always go together.

'What did Scipius say?' Verak asked.

Kael sighed. 'Doesn't believe she's really a Warrior. I showed them she could fight—'

'What? No she can't!'

'Yes, she can, a damn sight better than any other half-starved slave I've ever seen,' Kael said bluntly.

'Especially considering she can't see,' Karnos added.

'Right,' said Kael. They passed under the Warrior's Gate, the second of many along the Processional Way. Kael supposed they'd been built in antiquity as additional defences for the Tower. Despite the crowded streets of the city pressing right up against the Tower, the Processional Way was still the only entrance to it. He didn't know precisely why some of them were named for the Chosen. Probably there was some legend about it. Probably that had been explained in the same class as the silly names for armour.

'What will you tell the Emperor about her?' Verak asked, and Kael glanced at him in surprise.

'Why should he need to know?'

Both men stared at him in silence.

'Look, until we're really sure she is Thrice-Marked then what's the point in getting him excited?'

'He's the Emperor,' Verak said. 'He'll find out sooner or later.'

'And then you'll be in the shit for not telling him,' Karnos added.

Kael made a face and stared out at the overly decorated walls of the Way.

'And don't sulk,' Verak said.

Kael rolled his eyes.

The Tower was so huge that the Empire liked to pretend it went right up to the sky to touch the gods themselves. Kael thought this was a load of bull, but he had to admit the place was impressive. Roadways spiralled around it, right up to the top, which made him baulk the first time he was summoned there. But inside were several huge elevators, operated by pulleys and teams of horses, enough to carry the cartloads of goods the inhabitants of the Tower required every day.

The horde approached the King's Gate, where men in the Emperor's livery saluted them and waved them into the outer courtyard, where the two spiralling roadways began to chase each other around the Tower. The place was heaving with people and horses and goods, but they all went markedly quiet as Krull the Warlord rode through.

A steward hurried forward to tell them the Emperor awaited in the Mirrored Court.

'Hear that, lads? The Emperor awaits me. Didn't think he awaited anyone.'

The steward smiled nervously and beckoned them on. Kael rode forward, Verak and Karnos flanking him, the men remaining where they were. It never failed to impress when his men obeyed silent orders, and yet Kael couldn't figure out why. Did people think they were all psychic? Didn't they realise he told them what to do in advance?

'Oh, I hate this bastard thing,' Karnos muttered as they approached the nearest elevator.

'Not as much as your horse will,' Verak replied.

They rode in, the gate was shut and they waited as instructions were given to the relevant team. 'Take us to the exit below the Mirrored Court,' Kael said, and while the steward looked puzzled he agreed. He fastened the two sets of gates and the three men swung down from their horses, in Verak's case not a moment too soon. Kael stopped laughing when the creature tried to bash his friend's skull in, and left his own calm, battle-trained horse to Karnos while he helped Verak steady the terrified chestnut.

The Mirrored Court was less than a third of the way up the Tower, but Kael was still beginning to regret bringing the horses with him. By the time they arrived, the cage stank of urine, and by the steward's mortified expression Kael suspected not all of it had come from the horse. He flipped the man a gold aureus and led the horses out to the bright sunshine of the roadway, where the chestnut calmed almost instantly.

The roadway was bordered by a wall of about waist height, but that was the only barrier between the horse trough they led the animals to and a few hundred feet of nothingness. Kael gazed out over the city huddled on its rock, the eight major roadways spreading out from the Tower like the spokes of an immense wheel, and past it to the glittering harbour and the sprawl of buildings on the shore. Beyond them, fading into the mist, rolled fields and forests and, somewhere in the distance, mountains.

And far, far beyond that, over the sea, lay Krulland.

A horse's snort brought him back to the Tower. 'Remind me who thought riding horses was a good idea?' Kael said, watching Verak soothe the chestnut. 'I've seen cornered mice with more sense.'

'If we were all three inches high, I'm sure we'd ride mice,' Karnos said.

A boy waiting nearby with a cart sniggered. Kael shot him a look that had him hiding behind his master.

'Next time I'll ride in on a bull,' he said.

'Oh, aye, famously calm are bulls,' Verak said, splashing water on his slightly yellowed boots.

'Impressive though,' Kael said thoughtfully. 'Get a Bard to sing to one, maybe we could train it to be ridden.'

The other two stared at him.

'What? Bet you no one else has ever ridden a bull into the Mirrored Court.'

'Yeah, and there's a reason for that!'

Kael winked and swung back into his saddle. 'Aye. That reason being, no one else is Krull the Warlord!'

Karnos snorted. Verak rolled his eyes. But both men mounted up and followed him up the roadway, around a full turn of the spiral, falling automatically into formation. By the time they reached the outer courtyard of the Mirrored Court, Verak's horse had recovered from the elevator, and Kael doubted that any rumours of a less-than-impressive exit from the contraption would go very far. It was amazing what being a big guy on an armoured horse did to frighten people.

They rode past the elevator banks and towards the portcullis that shielded entrances to every level of the Tower.

'Krull the Warlord,' Kael yelled, not bothering to slow his horse. 'His Imperial Majesty awaits me.'

The portcullis was lifted and the three of them rode on.

'We getting off any time soon?' Karnos wanted to know.

'Nope.'

'Just checking.'

Inside the Tower the floors and walls were inlaid with an even higher level of enamelled and bejewelled insanity than the Processional Way. They rode down a corridor lined with gilt and jewels and courtiers in rich clothing who stared in astonishment at the three warhorses bearing down on them at a steady pace. People began to look nervously at the huge doors to the Mirrored Court, standing closed with only a couple of footmen and a major domo to guard them. From behind the doors came a babble of voices, some shouting, some laughing, some singing along to lute music.

'Open the doors,' Kael said lazily, and the two bewigged footmen glanced at each other.

Kael drew his sword, and before the silken sound had even died away, the doors were open and the major domo was gliding forward ahead of them.

'Lord Kaelnar Vapensigsson ex Krullus Militis Viscus Saraneus Drax,' he bellowed, and Kael silently prayed Verak's horse wouldn't have another meltdown. 'Sir Verak Torsis Militis Saraneus Drax. Sir Karnos Atrius Medicus Saraneus.'

His voice echoed around the suddenly silent room. Kael walked his horse forward, Verak and Karnos following in formation. The only sounds in the room were the horse's hooves and the slide and clank of armour.

Kael kept his gaze on the figure seated on the throne dead ahead. The Mirrored Court lived up to its name, however, and the myriad mirrors reflected the astonished, amused, and in some cases terrified reactions of the courtiers filling the room. Every one of them was dressed in fabrics that cost more than the average worker's yearly wage and adorned with jewels and gold and intricate hairstyles. Kael knew that the hair on the heads of a lot of these women had initially grown on the heads of much poorer girls.

He was all for putting on a show, but that was just ridiculous.

The Emperor liked to hold court in this room because, aside from its blinding splendour, it rose in a series of steps to a throne higher than most men's shoulders. This meant that anyone petitioning the Emperor was forced to look up and be reminded of his own smallness.

Which was why Kael had decided to ride in on a huge warhorse.

The Emperor was a man of middling height and slightly past-middling years. He wore a neat goatee, which was the same textured grey as his close-cropped hair, and he tended towards austerely cut clothes in dark-coloured, expensive fabrics. His Empress was a handsome, intelligent and hard-working woman, who had unfortunately failed to give him children. While Kael knew this to be a great source of personal sorrow for the couple, he also knew that the Emperor's three sisters had given him several nieces and nephews who were all being carefully educated and watched to see who would be the best successor.

His eyes tracked Kael's progress across the great expanse of floor with no small amount of amusement.

'Imperial Majesty,' Kael said, reining in his horse and saluting in a way he rarely had cause to. Right fist to breastplate and then raised ahead of him, in the direction of the Emperor.

Kael might speak to the man as an equal in private, but he wasn't about to disrespect him in front of the entire court by failing this show of fealty.

'Lord Krull,' the Emperor replied. 'Sirs. Please, I am sure you would be more comfortable on foot.'

Nice try. 'With respect, Your Grace, we have been travelling for a long while. To remain seated is more comfortable.'

'Atop a horse?'

'Were we to sit on the ground we might cause offence, Your Holiness.'

The Emperor actually laughed at that.

'There are chairs in my salon,' he said. 'Would that suffice?'

'Your Imperial Splendiferousness is too kind,' Kael said, but he didn't move to get down from his horse until the Emperor had risen and footmen had opened the doors to his private salon. Then he swung down, followed incrementally later by Verak and Karnos, and marched off after the Emperor, mounting the mirrored steps and ignoring the surprised murmur from the Mirrored Court. Not many people got a private audience with the Emperor.

The door shut behind them, and suddenly the only sound was that of a fire crackling cheerfully in the massive fireplace. The salon was a large room, but it was a manageable sort of large. There were carpets on the floor and the chairs looked comfortable.

They weren't alone – various aides and servants stood around, but Kael knew they could be dismissed if necessary.

The Emperor gave Kael a look. 'Splendiferousness?'

'Too much?' Kael said.

He shook his head, as if Kael was a naughty child.

'See our horses are cared for,' Kael told a man in livery. 'And find somewhere comfortable for my men to rest.'

'Is this my palace, or yours?' the Emperor complained as he took a seat. Kael followed, and then Verak and Karnos did the same.

'I believe it belongs to the Empire, sir,' Kael said smoothly.

The Emperor rolled his eyes and made an economical gesture to the servant to do as he was told. 'You always did like to make an entrance,' he said to Kael.

'I can't disappoint my fans.'

The Emperor snorted, but made another subtle gesture,

and a servant began pouring wine. 'What news from the New Lands?'

Kael unbuckled his gauntlets and tossed them on the floor, where they clattered noisily. The day was cold, and up here the air rarely got warm, but he could have done without a full suit of armour.

'We found no trace of Venerin in any ship, container, or warehouse,' he said, and watched the Emperor deflate. 'The effects of it, yes, all over; and plenty of people offering to sell it to us. But whoever supplies them is pretty damn cunning, sir. Every supplier only knows one link back in the chain, and often not as far as that. We followed one man who collected his supplies from a dead drop. We stationed men there for weeks, but nothing happened.'

'We thought it must be a different location each time,' Verak put in.

'Finally we managed to get someone to speak to us,' Kael said, and the Emperor was too polite to ask if this was because Kael had used force. Which he had. 'He said he picks up the stuff from a new location every time, never knows where or when until two weeks before, when the information is passed in another dead drop. The trail just goes all over the place, sir, often going completely dead.'

The Emperor drummed his fingers on the arm of his chair. 'And what about the exports?'

'Not a word, sir. Nobody knew anything about sending it abroad. We checked every damn ship coming in and out of port, but there wasn't a trace of it. False holds, concealed barrels, barrels with fake bases ... we found lots of other stuff, but no Venerin.'

'"Other stuff?"' asked the Emperor delicately.

'I believe I am still covered by the Privateer Act, sir, while on Imperial business?'

He damn well hoped so, or he'd have to cough up for all

the illegally exported silk, tobacco and weapons he'd sold on in the New Lands.

'Happily,' the Emperor's tone suggested anything but, 'you are. Except for illegal drugs.'

'Wouldn't touch 'em, sir. I've seen what they can do.' He hesitated. 'Sir, one plantation owner ... seemed to have a very free supply of Venerin.'

Verak shifted in his chair. Karnos shot him a warning look. 'Indeed?'

'But no traces of it going in or out,' Kael said. 'We checked every wagon, every barge.'

The Emperor sat upright. 'You think he's manufacturing his own supply?'

'Her, sir. She calls herself the Lady Samara.'

Instantly a flunky appeared with a piece of paper, which he handed to the Emperor. 'Ah ... yes. Looks like you spent several weeks in her region. Exporter of oil.'

'Very rich exporter of oil,' Kael corrected, wondering where the hell the man got his information from. 'The Empire can't afford to get on her bad side.'

'Hmm.' He gestured to another flunky, who brought forth more paper. 'And did you notice any crops of ... ah, no, our Healers say it's made from mundane herbs ...'

'But can't figure out how it's treated to create such an effect,' Karnos rumbled. 'Sir, they use it in the East. I still think we should be looking there.'

'The aphrodisiacs coming out of the East might be related to Venerin, but they're not as devastating,' the Emperor said, shaking his head.

'We found some Venerin in Samara's kitchens,' Verak volunteered.

'And did you question her staff?'

'Slaves, sir. Not staff,' Kael said darkly, remembering the frightened huddle of skinny wretches. 'Not one of them could have given you a straight answer. That was the problem all over, sir. Slavery is still rife in the New Lands and there's nothing to regulate it. You can't follow a money trail because nearly everything's generated by slave labour. There are no laws governing how slaves are kept, so they can be beaten and starved into submission …'

'… which means they won't answer any questions put to them,' the Emperor finished for him. He sighed again and gestured for more papers to be brought over. 'I see. With respect, Lord Krull, if you can't frighten the information out of them I don't see who can. I'll put this to my Council and see what conclusions they can draw.'

Kael knew a dismissal when he heard one. But Verak was giving him a very pointed glance, and he sighed and cleared his throat. 'There was one more thing,' he said.

The Emperor looked up from his papers and said, 'Oh?' in a manner that suggested he knew what Kael was going to say before he said it.

'At Samara's compound we – I – found a slave with the marks of the Chosen.'

The Emperor said nothing, just waited for Kael to continue.

'Not just one mark, either, sir. She has the mark of a Healer, and that of a Seer …'

This time Kael said nothing and waited for the Emperor to show his hand.

'A fortunate young woman, to be Twice-Marked,' said the ruler of the Empire.

Gods damn him. Kael glanced at Verak, who nodded. 'She also has the mark of a Warrior,' he said finally.

For a long while the Emperor didn't respond. Then, very quietly, he said, 'I see.'

Did he? What did he see?

'I can't speak for the veracity of her Seer mark, sir, but I've seen her heal herself, and …'

'And?' Finally the Emperor looked at him. 'And? You are Krull the Warlord, the most famous soldier and pirate in the Empire and beyond. Possibly the most famous Militis we have ever had. You can't tie your shoe without the gossips spreading the news all over the city. I heard about this girl the second she stepped off your ship.'

'Nonetheless, I considered it a courtesy to tell you in person,' Kael said, fighting the feeling that he was a boy being told off by his father.

'Indeed.' The Emperor glanced back down at his papers. 'The consensus at court is that it's some kind of joke.'

'In that case, then it's not a very funny one,' Kael said. He took a breath and said, 'Her Militis mark is real.'

'Your professional opinion?'

Kael nodded.

'I see,' said the Emperor again. He appeared to think for a while, then said, 'What does Scipius make of her?'

Kael made a face. 'He's not happy about it – but that's more because she's blind than because she's a girl.'

The look on the Emperor's face was priceless. Kael thought this must be the first time he'd surprised the man.

'Blind?'

'Nothing anyone seems able to do about it. Madam Julia says there's nothing wrong with her eyes or her brain or … oh I don't know, all that stuff Healers rabbit on about. But the fact is she can't see.'

'A blind female Thrice-Marked Militis,' said the Emperor slowly, pausing between each word.

'Who is also a Medicus and Aspicio,' Kael added helpfully.

The Emperor stared into the distance.

'The gods do have a sense of humour,' he said eventually.

'My sentiments exactly.'

Chapter Seven

She didn't see night fall, of course, but heard matches being struck, the hiss of something she dimly recalled might have been gas. Somewhere, a bell tolled. Fires had been lit around the room, and from their smell she guessed they were coal, not wood.

'It's late,' Madam Julia said eventually. She'd given Ishtaer a sandwich for lunch, and now told her to get some dinner. 'You do know your way to the dining hall?'

She hesitated. She'd known this morning, but since then she'd been shepherded from one room to another, offices and meeting rooms and classrooms and now the sick bay, all of them up stairs and around corners and across courtyards.

'I'll talk to Sir Flavius in the morning and see if we can get someone to show you around. We have maps for new students, but I don't suppose they'll be much use to you if you can't see.'

'Yes, ma'am.'

'I'll show you around,' a voice said. A new voice, not one of the other Medicus students or one of the patients. A young man, his accent slightly different to the cultured students or poor city-dwellers. He sounded vaguely familiar, but she'd met so many people in the last twenty-four hours, she couldn't place him. 'I've got loads of free time.'

'Mr Fillian,' said the Healer, a slight trace of exasperation in her voice. 'You do get around.'

'Astonishingly, yes,' the young man replied.

'Do you have no classes to attend?'

'Too dark,' he replied cheerfully. 'And anyway, for some reason I'm not Sir Scipius's favourite pupil.'

'He says you're like a bad ass,' Julia said crisply.

'Always turning up,' agreed the young man. 'You're Ishtaer. I saw you last night. You came in with Lord Krull.'

A slight lull in the noise of the ward around them followed Krull's name, as Ishtaer was learning it usually did.

'Yes, I did.'

'I'm sorry, that should be Lady Ishtaer—'

'No,' she interrupted. 'It's Tyro.' Then, shyly, 'I'm told it should be Tyro Ishtaer.'

'Well, you're both Tyros, so just get on with it.' Madam Julia sounded exasperated again, but then this seemed to be her usual state of being. 'Eirenn, take her to the dining hall, would you? She's hardly eaten all day. And see if she's been assigned a room yet. And get her something suitable to wear.'

'Yes, ma'am,' Eirenn said, making a noise that sounded to Ishtaer like a heel click. 'Ishtaer?'

There was a pause, and then he took her hand and rested it in the crook of his arm, just as Kael had done on the ship. He led her out of the ward, walking confidently but with a slightly unusual gait.

'This is very kind of you,' Ishtaer said as he took her down the corridor she thought led to the outside.

'Not a problem. I'm the Academy's gopher anyway.'

Ishtaer tried to work this one out. Her face must have showed her confusion, however, because Eirenn Fillian laughed and said, 'Gopher this, gopher that. I'm the runner. Ironic, really.'

She gave up on trying to work that one out.

'Why did Madam Julia call you a bad ass?'

He laughed again. It seemed to come very easily to him. 'Lots of reasons, but an ass is a small coin. You know, if you flip a coin and the wrong side always comes up … it's a bad ass.' When she was silent, he added, 'Sort of a pun. Never mind. If you're not too hungry, I reckon we should go to Admin first and see about your room. It's useless trying to get anything out of them after dinner.'

Ishtaer nodded, and he turned a corner in what she thought was the opposite direction from the one she'd come in by.

'So, you're from the Saranos? What's it like there?'

I have no idea. Vague memories jumbled together in her mind, some half forgotten, some possibly invented. Kael had kept suggesting things to her, and now she wasn't sure if she'd just agreed to the things that sounded realistic, instead of actually remembering them.

'Different,' she said. 'I—they don't really have Chosen there.'

'Yeah? I thought they were part of the Empire now.'

She shrugged. 'Maybe. I don't know.'

'You grow up there?'

Ishtaer nodded. She bit her lip. Then she said, 'I don't really want to talk about it.'

'Fair enough,' Eirenn said easily. 'Generally when people ask about where I'm from it's so they can make fun of it.'

'You're not from the Empire?'

'Oh, yeah, but out in the arse end of nowhere. When my mark manifested the major concern was how the hell they were going to get me all the way to Ilanium. That is, not the major concern, but not far off.'

'What was the major concern?' Ishtaer asked politely, because he seemed to have left that one hanging there.

Eirenn laughed. 'Right. I'm used to people knowing. And if you can't see ...' she felt the slight breeze of him waving his hand in front of her face, and said nothing. 'So. Drumroll, if you please.'

Ishtaer didn't know what he meant by that, so she just said, 'There's something wrong with your leg. The ... the right one, I think.'

Eirenn was silent a moment. 'How the frilly heck did you know that? Did Madam Julia tell you?'

'Why would she tell me? I could tell by the way you walk. The sound of it, and now I'm beside you I can feel that you slightly favour one leg over the other.'

'I'm impressed. And yes, it is the right leg. Want to take a guess at what's wrong with it?'

She thought for a moment and listened to a few more footsteps. He walked as if he couldn't bend his foot or ankle, but she didn't think he wore a cast or splints, and could sense no injury anywhere. It was possible he had some wasting disease, or had suffered from one as a child, and his leg had needed to be splinted for strength or to keep it straight, but that didn't feel quite right to her either.

'It's a wooden leg?' she guessed eventually.

Eirenn laughed, the sound one she'd later categorise as admiring. 'I'm twice impressed. It is indeed. You don't get many around here. I guess it's more common out in the Saranos? I mean, if they don't have Chosen there aren't Healers, right?'

'Right.' She chewed her lip again. 'What happened?'

'Rock fall. I lived up in the mountains, you see. Farming. Mostly goats and sheep. The land is practically vertical around there. All it takes is one footfall in the wrong place and half a hill shears off and slides down. Just one goat hoof on the wrong pebble. It was like a river,' he added, almost wistfully. 'A river of stones. Beautiful, really. That is, until it landed on me. Then it was less beautiful, and more intensely painful. And like I said, no Healers, so it just got chopped off and I was considered lucky.'

'Lucky?'

'Could've killed me. Or the wound could have been infected, or … Well, anyway. When my Militis mark appeared a few years later no one really knew what to do with me. Think they were ashamed to send a one-legged boy off to the Academy.'

'But the Academy accepted you?'

'Oh, sure. I can fight, you see, I'm good with a sword, although my footwork's not up to scratch. And I'm ace with a bow and arrow. Strong, too. They said the gods must just have a sense of humour.'

'They said that about me, too,' Ishtaer said, and he briefly squeezed the hand she had tucked into his arm.

Eirenn took her to an office smelling of paper and coffee where he charmed a rather brusque woman into assigning Ishtaer, 'a good room. Not one above the training yard where she'll get no sleep, not one where the water pump is leaky, one with a good bed. Ah, you're a star, Augusta.'

Next he took her to a large laundry, where he held up various garments against her until he had a collection he deemed suitable. When a tired-sounding woman asked him what he was doing, he said, 'I'm outfitting Lord Krull's protégée. You have heard he has a protégée? Well now, who wants to get on his bad side?' And the woman left them alone.

'Whose clothes are these?' Ishtaer asked as he bundled them into a basket and led her away.

'The Academy's. You're lucky, both Warriors and Healers get through a lot of dirty clothes, so there's a constant supply to change into. I've no doubt you'll want to go shopping for your own soon, but this'll do you for now. Don't worry, it's all standard stuff, I won't make you look weird.'

I have hair an inch long and a tattoo on my face, Ishtaer thought, *I can't see where I'm going and I weigh as much as a small bag of feathers. I'm pretty sure I already look weird.*

He led her back to the main courtyard and then through a set of doors to a smaller quadrangle.

'There are a couple of sets of accommodation around the place, but they all have the same layout. Three atriums leading off a central courtyard. Each atrium has a lounge, study area and eight bedrooms on the ground floor, and then upstairs there are twelve more on each storey. You've got a second floor room,' he explained as he led her through the atrium, 'which means more stairs to climb but fewer people thundering past your door at all hours.'

He told her about the central fountain which rose from a square pool open to the sky, and took her past it to a passageway leading back further. 'There's a lounge there to your left, and a study room to your right, but if the girls' accommodation is anything like the boys', they're just hangout clubs for the popular kids. Best avoided until you've found your feet.'

Eirenn led her up two flights of stairs and along a corridor, allowing her to count the doors until they reached the right one. He put a key in her hand and guided it to the lock.

'Housekeeping will have a key to the room,' he said, 'but no one else. If you want you can bolt it from the inside, okay?'

He let her go into the room and explore it by herself, silently, carefully, moving about in her own private darkness. There was a rug to muffle her footsteps. A bed touching her shins. It was already made up with blankets and pillows. Beside it was a small locker, and at the foot a chest for clothing. There were also shelves and hooks on the walls. A small fireplace was already laid, with extra coal beside it, and hooks to heat the warming pan and kettle she found on the washstand, beside a large ewer and jug.

'There's a water pump at the end of the hall,' Eirenn said. 'I'll show you.'

Ishtaer nodded, dumbstruck. There was one bed in here. She had the only key.

Was this really her room?

'I know,' Eirenn said softly behind her. 'I couldn't believe it either when I first came here. I'd never had my own room. Never even had my own bed.'

'And it's so … it's so …'

'A palace compared to the dark little cottage I came from. Dunno what houses are like in the Saranos, but only rich people live like this where I come from.'

Flashes of memory hit Ishtaer like slaps. Lady Samara's huge bed, hung with silks and velvets; the tiny, covetable cubby where her personal servants slept; the bare floors and dirty straw for the rest of the slaves; the freezing cell …

… and more memories, tumbling over each other, jumbled and incoherent. A small dark room with two clean, comfortable beds; the frills of a silk comforter; rows of iron bedsteads and a small child weeping; the cold pantry floor; a hammock, a ship's bunk, a ship's bunk—

'Ishtaer?'

Eirenn's voice brought her back to herself with a gasp.

'Are you all right?'

She nodded, her hands pressed to her stomach, and took a deep breath.

'Sure, it's a bit overwhelming at first.'

She nodded again, gratefully.

'Come on, let's go and get some food. You must be starving.'

You have no idea, Ishtaer thought, but she washed her hands and face with water from the pump and followed Eirenn back down to the atrium. She heard a couple of girls giggling, and her heart sank. She knew that giggle. It wasn't a kind giggle.

'Eirenn Fillian,' one of them said, 'don't tell me you've got a girlfriend!'

'You know you're not supposed to be in here,' said the other.

'Just helping a friend out,' Eirenn said. 'Have you met Ishtaer ex Saraneus Medicus Militis Aspicio?'

He left off the last two words, Ishtaer noticed. The two she didn't understand.

There was a short silence, then the first girl said, 'Don't be stupid, Eirenn. She can't be Thrice-Marked.'

'Well, she can and she is, and she's also got perfectly good hearing,' Eirenn said, 'so you can address your remarks to her.'

A longer silence this time.

'No? Right then. See you around, girls,' Eirenn said, and took Ishtaer's arm to lead her away.

'... has to be fake,' one of the girls whispered as they left the atrium.

'Ignore 'em,' Eirenn said.

'I'll try,' said Ishtaer, who'd been ignoring worse for longer than he could imagine.

He took her back to the dining hall where she'd had breakfast with Kael all those hours ago and helped her navigate the loud, busy room, select a tray of food ('Is that all? No wonder you're so thin.') and find somewhere to sit that wasn't terribly crowded.

Eirenn proved to be an immensely likeable companion, with a friendly, lilting voice and casual manner of dropping hints and explanations before she quite realised she needed them. He was also a natural raconteur, managing to make everything – from his humiliations on the training field to his days herding his family's goats – into entertaining stories.

'So it's me and this mad nanny goat, right, and she's squaring off against me, head down, like she's ready to charge. And I never thought about how big a nanny goat's horns were before, but my gods, they could do you some damage if they hit you somewhere sensitive, you know what I mean? Although actually, you're a girl so you probably don't. Anyway, imagine it. Goat-head height. And she has these glowing red eyes, she's proper mad. And there am I, backed up against these rocks, and all I've got to eat all day is this packet of sandwiches which are in my trouser pocket, and she's about to charge, and I'm seriously thinking about whether I'd be more upset if she squashed the sandwiches or—ah, bollocks.'

Ishtaer found herself giggling. She didn't think she'd ever giggled in her life.

'Ishtaer, in advance, I'm really sorry.'

'Advance? You've already said it!'

'No – what? Oh, no,' he said distractedly. 'I mean I'm sorry for the waste of a Militis mark coming towards us.'

'What was that, goat boy?' said a rather cold voice, and Ishtaer felt her smile slip away.

'I said, "Oh look, there's Marcus coming towards us,"' Eirenn said, his voice losing a little of its warmth.

'No, you didn't.'

'Ah, so it's psychic you are, then, is it? Only I notice, unlike my friend here, you don't have the mark of a Seer.'

'Your friend,' sneered Marcus. 'I wouldn't believe you had one, but I hear on the grapevine there's a blind slave around the place. Hard to believe there'd be anyone more pathetic than you here, Fillian.'

'I know, it's what I told myself right up until I arrived,' Eirenn said, and there was a pause while Marcus digested this. Hopefully he was too stupid to understand it.

'What did you say?' Marcus demanded.

Oh, hell. Ishtaer braced herself.

'I said there are much more pathetic creatures around here, Marcus. Amazing, isn't it? And sad, so sad, that even those Chosen by the gods to receive such an amazing gift still feel the need to piss it away bullying those less fortunate than themselves—'

'Even the gods make mistakes,' Marcus growled.

'—and then insult the gods themselves by calling them fallible—'

'If my father heard of this,' Marcus threatened.

'—before invoking the names of their illustrious but unfortunately burdened fathers in order to justify their bullying behaviour.' Eirenn sighed dolefully.

Marcus's voice got closer. 'Don't think you can get away with insulting me like that—'

'Why, Marcus!' Eirenn feigned surprise. 'Whoever said I was talking about you?'

Marcus drew in a breath to retort to that, but Ishtaer never got to hear what he had to say. While she'd been listening to the exchange the room had got subtly quieter, but now the sound level dropped to a whisper.

The same whisper she'd heard that morning.

'My Lord Krull,' said Marcus, his voice a whole lot more respectful than it had been five seconds ago.

'Glorius,' Kael said, sounding bored. 'I see you've met my protégée.'

The whisper abruptly turned to deafening silence.

'Your—' Marcus swallowed audibly. 'The goat boy is your protégée?'

'Ah, if only I could be so fortunate,' Eirenn said. 'I believe his lordship is talking about my new friend Ishtaer here.'

The silence strained.

'Tyro Ishtaer ex Saraneus Medicus Militis Aspicio prior Inservio,' Kael corrected. 'Yes. I've agreed to sponsor her.'

For a long moment no one said anything. Ishtaer couldn't even hear anyone breathing. Then Eirenn cleared his throat and said, 'Very generous of you, my lord. I don't recall as you've ever sponsored a Tyro before.'

'No, I haven't,' Kael said softly.

'And we've never had a slave here before,' said Marcus, his voice dripping disdain. 'My lord, are you sure she's not faking it?'

'Who would fake slavery?' Eirenn said.

'I could cut you open here and now, Glorius, and let her heal you, if you want proof,' Kael said.

A short silence while everyone thought about this, then Marcus said, 'The Militis mark, my lord. It can't be real.'

'Are you calling Lord Krull a liar, Marcus?' Eirenn said.

'No … but … but she's a woman.'

'Well observed. I see your expensive education wasn't wasted.'

'I'm not training with a woman!'

'Then don't train,' Kael said crisply. 'The gods have chosen Ishtaer as a Warrior, and she shall be trained as one. And afforded the respect due to my protégée. I expect regular reports on her progress,' he added menacingly.

'I'll try not to let you down,' Ishtaer whispered.

'I'm sure you won't. You,' he added. 'Can you read and write?'

'Yes, my lord,' Eirenn said.

'Good. Write to me. I want to know how she's doing.'

'Yes, my lord.'

'Ish—for gods' sakes, don't you people have conversations of your own to listen to?' Kael snapped, and abruptly, people found things to talk about. 'Ishtaer, come with me.'

He took her hand and led her from the dining hall, trailing speculation behind him like a cloak. Outside, he took her around a corner, and Ishtaer heard another fountain splashing.

'Were those kids bothering you?'

She shook her head automatically.

'If Marcus Glorius is anything like his father he'll be a little shit, so keep your eye on him. Or – you know. Watch out for him. I mean—'

'I know what you mean,' she said quietly.

'I've just told the whole dining hall that you're mine, so no doubt by breakfast the whole city will know. It'll have reached the edge of the Empire by suppertime. That boy – Eirenn? You've made friends fast.'

'He was showing me around. He seems nice.'

'Hmm. Reserve judgement. Just because he's like you – I mean, he's an outsider too,' he covered fast, 'doesn't mean he's automatically on your side. And listen, when I asked him to report to me I don't want you to think I'm spying on you. I just want to know how you're doing, all right?'

She nodded.

'I have to leave soon. On the tide, if you don't need me here. Winter storms will be setting in around Krulland, and every day I delay makes it more likely we'll be caught in one. Could've done without that delay at Samara's place.'

Ishtaer flinched.

'Not that – look, I'm glad we were there and found you. And brought you here. She can't hurt you any more, you know that? You're safe here.'

Ishtaer nodded jerkily. A man like Krull the Warlord would never understand what safety meant. He'd never been threatened or helpless in his life.

He notched a finger under her chin and lifted her face to his. 'Do you want me to stay?'

She shook her head. 'I'm fine here. I'll be fine.' *In this strange place full of people who think I'm a freak and have history and customs I can never hope to understand.* 'I've been helping in the sick bay. I can do useful things here.'

'Good. That's good. And don't let twatfaces like Marcus Glorius bring you down. The gods chose you to be a Warrior, same as him.'

'Not quite the same,' she said.

'No, not quite. He's never had to fight for anything.'

She frowned at that, but he dropped his hand and stepped back. 'I've set up an account for you with the bursar, for clothes and books – or whatever – and weapons and things. When you buy something, tell the shop to charge it to my account here, all right? I can't see anyone refusing. If they do, get your friend to write it down and I'll give 'em what-for next time I'm in town. The bursar will give you petty cash too, if you want it. Spend what you like, I've way more gold than any man needs. Buy nice clothes, go for ices. There used to be a place on Seventh Street that sold fantastic ices when I was a student here.'

'You were a student here?' Ishtaer said, surprised. She couldn't imagine him needing to learn anything from anyone.

'All Chosen are students here at some point. We all have to learn.' He was silent a moment, then said, 'Are you sure you'll be all right?'

Ishtaer nodded.

'I'll be back in the spring. If you need anything, get your friend to write to me. Or hire a Viator if it's urgent.'

Ishtaer wasn't sure what a Viator was, but she nodded anyway.

'Remember the gods chose you for this. They wouldn't give you more than you could handle.'

'But they gave me so much,' she whispered.

'You're strong.' When her eyebrows shot up, Kael laughed. 'The girl who kneed an infamous warlord in the nuts is strong, believe me. You just need to remember that. You're more powerful than you know, Ishtaer. And don't be ashamed of your background. It's better to come from nothing than to do nothing.'

Says a man who came from something, Ishtaer thought, but kept that to herself.

'And remember it's all a show,' he said. 'The popular kids, the rich kids, the scholarship kids ... they're all pretending. Your friend Eirenn in there, he knows it.' He put a finger under her chin. 'Chin up. Shoulders back. Eyes right ahead. Behave like a lady, Ishtaer, and no one will ever think you're anything else.'

He took her by the shoulders and brushed a kiss over her forehead, as if she were a child. Ishtaer was too astonished by that to know how to react.

'Take care, then,' he said, and walked away. Ishtaer touched her fingertips to her forehead and listened to him leave.

Chapter Eight

The sea was calm, black and glittering where the *Grey Ghost*'s lanterns shone. Kael leaned against the rail, staring back at Ilanium – or at any rate, where Ilanium had been before the darkness swallowed it.

'If I didn't know you better, I'd say you were brooding,' Verak said behind him.

'I'm not brooding,' Kael said automatically. 'I don't brood.'

'Yes, you are, and you do. All the time.'

He sighed. 'Yeah.'

Verak leaned against the rail beside him, and Kael turned to put his back to the Empire. His friend waited silently.

'Did we do the right thing?'

'In what?' said Verak. 'Rescuing her? Bringing her here?'

'She doesn't know this world, she doesn't know how to … how to act, how to talk to people, how to do anything of her own volition.'

'Then she'll learn, Kael. She's a smart girl.'

'Is she?'

'She learned how to defend herself against you with a sword. Not many people could do that.'

'Aye, but she's also learned to blindly follow orders or she'll be beaten and starved. How's she supposed to cope with being Thrice-Marked? I don't even know what she'll be called.'

'Ishtaer, I should imagine.'

'Funny. I mean she's not a madam or a lady … what's next after that?'

'Queen. Empress.'

'I imagine Her Imperial Highness will have something to

say about that.' Kael groaned. 'Verak, how's she going to get on at court?'

Verak raised his palms. 'I don't know. But is standing here fretting about it going to help?'

Kael pinched his nose and glowered at the deck. 'No,' he said, 'but it makes me feel better.'

Ishtaer was woken by the bell.

Eirenn had explained it to her last night, that the Academy's day was timed by a series of bells. Bells to wake you up and tell you breakfast would be served in half an hour, bells to signal the beginning and end of the morning's lessons, bells to tell you when lunchtime was over and bells to announce the dinner hour.

'I'll meet you out here,' he said, leaving her in the atrium of her dormitory, 'after the first bell, and show you around.' Eirenn was supposed to spend most of his time in Sir Scipius's training arena, but it seemed to be pretty widely acknowledged that he'd never really achieve the skills he needed to graduate, so no one really minded him skiving off.

She rolled her shoulders and sat up. The room wasn't cold, thanks to the fire which had been burning cheerfully when she returned from dinner last night, but the stones beneath her were chilly.

She wasn't brave enough for the bed. Not yet.

She washed with soap and cold water, dressed in the clothes Eirenn had found for her yesterday, and made her way downstairs. Halfway there she heard footsteps coming towards her and paused as she listened acutely.

The footsteps didn't go around her. They stopped in front of her.

'You're the blind girl,' said a young woman.

'Yes.'

'They said you're gonna train as a Warrior?'

'Yes,' Ishtaer said again.

'Well, how can you?' said the other girl, her voice accusatory. 'That's for men only. Does Sir Scipius know about this?'

'Of course he does,' Ishtaer said.

'Well—' the girl began again, and then seemed to run out of things to say. 'There's never been a woman Warrior before.'

'I *know*.' If one more person told her that she'd scream.

'So how—'

'Hortensia?' said another girl. 'Are you coming?'

'Yeah, just forgot my scarf. Have you met the blind girl?'

The newcomer paused, then said quietly, 'You dined with your family yesterday, didn't you? She was at supper last night. With Lord Krull.'

The silence stretched.

'I'm his protégée,' Ishtaer supplied helpfully.

'Protégée,' Hortensia said.

The other girl whispered something frantically. Ishtaer didn't have to try hard to make out the supposed replay: Lord Krull had stormed in and insulted Marcus Glorius, then proclaimed to everyone that Ishtaer was his protégée before sweeping her outside where Livia's friend Attalus's brother saw them kissing.

'What?' Hortensia gasped, apparently under the impression that 'blind' meant 'unable to hear'. 'He's sleeping with her? With the blind girl?'

Ishtaer opened her mouth to correct the assumption, then abruptly remembered Kael's crew. *'Up all night, were you, cap'n?' 'Demanding lady is she, sir?'*

None of them had so much as tried to touch her. Because they thought she was his.

'But she's so ... so ...'

Ishtaer waited politely.

'Oh my gods, what do you think he's *like*?'

'He has very gentle hands,' Ishtaer said, and the two girls went instantly silent. 'Now if you'll excuse me, I'm meeting a friend for breakfast.'

She walked down the corridor, and as she turned the corner, Ishtaer was smiling.

'The whole class went utterly silent. We were training indoors, it being a filthy day – and you know Sir Scipius would usually rather we were out in it, but the rain was so heavy we couldn't hear what he said, so he sent us into the gymnasium. And it's full, maybe twenty or thirty students, even the youngest of them pretty proficient on the bars and the weights and no one pressing less than two hundred—'

'Two hundred what?' interrupted Mags the housekeeper, flipping a large quantity of dough over on itself.

'Pounds,' Verak explained. 'About a sack and a half of flour.'

'Why are they pressing flour?' asked Mags's son Durran.

'They're not. A bench press is … y'see, it's a thing they use in gyms there,' Kael said, and added, 'because they don't do proper work, like us.'

'What's a gym?' Durran asked. Mags rolled her eyes.

'A gymnasium. It's where they exercise. Anyway,' he said quickly, turning his attention back to the letter. 'So Ishtaer's just walked into the gym, which is full of bigger, stronger lads who've all been training there a while, and – look, this Eirenn puts it better. *You know how it was when you walked in there the first time, not knowing anyone, the new kid, and even if you're strong and you've been working hard, these are lads who've been learning how to kill people for months, maybe even years. And it's a good job she can't see the looks on their faces, especially Marcus Gloria'*—here Kael allowed himself a chuckle—*'who looks like he's swallowed a toad. Anyway, the silence is bad enough, everyone stopping what* they're doing, all the machines going silent, all conversations stopping, and if Sir Scipius hadn't been there I reckon they'd have turned on her like a wolf pack on a lamb.'

'Why would they turn on her?' Durran asked.

'Because people are afraid of things that are different,' his mother told him, thumping the dough. 'Especially stupid people, and bullies.'

'The two are often the same thing,' Verak said idly, bouncing his youngest daughter on his lap.

Kael reached out and grabbed a piece of dough, for which his housekeeper smacked his hand as if he were a child. Kael grinned and ate the dough anyway.

'*But he was there,*' he continued reading, '*and he told everyone, calm as you like, "This is Ishtaer ex Saraneus, lads, and Lord Krull and I have verified her Warrior's mark, so she'll be training with us. Anyone has a problem with that, you can take it up with me. And Lord Krull."*'

'I still don't know how you've managed to persuade the whole Empire you're some kind of bogeyman,' Mags said. 'You've got flour on your nose.'

Kael ignored that. '*So the class goes on training, except for Gloria and his cronies, and they walk over and he says, "A woman can never fight as well as a man, sir,"* and—'

'And she smashes his face in? I would,' said Mags, beating the dough to prove it.

'Aye, well, they don't breed 'em so tough in the Empire,' Kael said. 'Likely Gloria's never seen a woman stand up for herself.'

'Gloria's a girl's name,' said Durran scornfully.

'Indeed it is, which is why I shall endeavour to call the proud Marcus Glorius Livius that on every occasion.'

'Marcia Gloria Livia,' giggled the child.

'I am definitely going to call him that from now on,' Verak said.

'So Scipius doesn't say anything, just hands Ishtaer a sword, a real one, not one of the wooden practice ones like Gloria has, and bloody Gloria smirks, like he knows he can beat her anyway, and attacks her without waiting for a signal, and she just … it was amazing, my lord, just amazing, she defended herself as if she could see everything coming, every blow, every thrust, every feint, and then she got him with this amazing stop-cut to the wrist, and he drops the sword, like his whole hand's gone numb, and there's blood dripping on the ground.

'And he's proper mad now, 'cos not only has he been bested by a girl, but one with no training, and she's blind, and oh gods, I wish I could re-live that moment any time I wanted, my lord, because it's the most wonderful thing I've ever seen. Actually, I take that back; the most wonderful thing was when she lay down her sword and said very calmly, "I can heal that for you if you like." I thought I would die. It was perfect.'

'I like her already,' Mags said. 'When can we meet her?'

Kael folded the letter to finish reading later. 'Next time Eirenn sends a letter.'

'Can she come visit?' Durran wanted to know.

Kael looked at the child, all shaggy brown hair and huge eyes, and at the warm, bright kitchen full of people peeling vegetables and kneading dough, out of the window to the courtyard where a couple of lads were chasing after errant chickens, laughing breathlessly, and said, 'We don't have visitors, Durran. Not now, not ever.'

Chapter Nine

Kael pulled the last of the fishing boats above the waterline and stood back, surveying the harbour. The water was calm now, snowflakes dissolving gently in it, but when the big storms of winter hit they'd turn anything still floating into matchsticks.

'Reckon you'll get out again this side of the Dark?' he asked Valter Fiskaren, who shrugged.

'Hard to say. Short trips, yes, but what can you get so close to shore?'

It was the same conversation every winter. Out of respect for the older man, Kael never reminded him of this. By now he probably knew as much about fishing as Valter did.

'Line fishing from the harbour wall?' Kael said. The boats already had a thin dusting of snow on them.

Valter raised his palms. 'Couldn't feed my cat on what you catch there.'

'Have we got enough preserved to see us through?'

'Sure, but who can eat that much salted fish? After a few weeks of pickled herring, a day out on the boat in the middle of a squall starts to look really good.'

Kael clapped him on the shoulder. 'Not good enough. I'll go out hunting and get us some meat. And there's always the carp pond for feast days.'

Valter grunted. He didn't think much of freshwater fish.

'Have I let you starve yet?'

'No. You're a good lad,' said Valter, just as he had since Kael was eleven.

'Right. Look, if it gets bad you move everyone up to the castle, all right?'

'I'm not afraid of the Dark,' Valter scoffed, but Kael saw the fear behind his eyes.

'Aye, I know that, but I'm having no one trapped in collapsed buildings. Bring the animals too,' he added, remembering the year half their pigs had been wiped out by a bad storm.

'Aye, lad. I will,' said Valter, and Kael moved off, following the donkey carts up the path to the castle.

'Castle' was a bit of an overstatement. Skjultfjell had been built in the lee of the headland and roofed with turf, a longhouse hidden from the eyes of invaders. Over the years his ancestors had built around it, creating a series of courtyards, linking one building to another and even hacking into the rock to create more hidden rooms. Even now, in safer days, there were few buildings visible from the sea. Skjultfjell looked like part of a fishing village.

He took the narrow Lower Gate and climbed the steep path to the first courtyard, passing the donkey stables and loping up the steps past the goods hoist. Stellan Timmerman was poking at the wood with a frown.

'Problem?' Kael asked, watching the baskets being hauled up.

'No, not yet, but can you see here where it's starting to rot? Needs fixing before the next storm or it won't be able to hold a full load.'

'Do we have the timber?' Stellan nodded. Kael glanced at the sky, which was a dark yellowish shade and promised a lot more snow. 'Then get it done. This'll get worse before it gets better.'

Skjultfjell was composed mostly of steps and uneven ground. Ishtaer would have a nightmare here, Kael thought, taking the next flight two at a time and swerving to avoid two men carrying a pig carcass between them. Oh good, that meant bacon was on the menu.

When he entered the kitchen he found Mags scowling at her cloak, which was soaked with a big dirty patch at the back.

'Dare I ask?' Kael said, draping his cloak over the fireguard.

'Flagstones are starting to get slippery out there. We're going to need to salt them.'

Kael wondered if they had enough grids to put over the stones. He'd told old Smed the smith to make some last year, enough for pathways across the courtyard, but some had rusted before the end of the winter. 'Do we have enough? I don't want to waste it if we've meat to preserve.'

Mags batted at the stain, which didn't do much to shift it. 'We always have enough. You always buy too much. More came in today.' She nodded at a basket on the table. 'Some mail for you, too.'

He picked up the packet of letters. Mail took forever to arrive at Skjultfjell, mostly because he had it routed through a complex system of agents and offices. Most of it was to do with property and employees, some was news, and one was a letter from Eirenn Fillian.

The letters came regularly, arriving most weeks on the sled from Utgangen with their supplies, and he read them out in the kitchen or the hall like the latest chapter of a story.

Chapter One: In which Ishtaer gets three ribs broken by Marcus Glorius during a session of quarterstaff training but never complains and heals them herself.

Chapter Two: In which the other students badger Ishtaer for information about 'Skullfell' and Eirenn makes up a load of rubbish about it, for which he hopes his lordship will forgive him, but it all makes him out to be extra fearsome, ruling with an iron fist, and incidentally mentions his fantastic prowess as a lover.

For his own sanity, Kael chose not to share that last part with Mags and the kids.

Chapter Three: In which Ishtaer heals a young woman who's been hit by a cart, and not only mends her life-threatening wounds but, on discovering the woman is a seamstress, spends her whole night healing every injury to her hands, which earns her the quiet admiration of Madam Julia.

Chapter Four: In which Ishtaer attempts to ride a horse without help, and ends up breaking her ribs again ...

Mags recognised the handwriting and asked, 'What's your little project getting up to now?'

'Who knows? She may even have found the courage to speak to strangers.'

Mags tutted, giving up on her muddy cloak and washing her hands with lavender soap. 'Be nice. From what you say she's spent years being kicked around by this Samara woman. You probably wouldn't have any courage left after that.'

Kael shot her an incredulous look as he pulled the letter open. 'I'd have shot Samara in the head years ago.'

'Why didn't you? I mean, when you were there? If she treats people so badly—'

'Look, it's not my problem, okay? I'm not going to war with one of the richest and most important oil producers the Empire has over a few slaves.'

'No heart, you.'

'Shut up or I'll lock you in the donkey shed.'

Mags snorted. 'I'd like to see you try.'

He grinned at her and started reading.

'Out loud?' Mags said pointedly.

He rolled his eyes. 'Some technical stuff about training – she still can't fire a bow, or at least she can but the only reasonably safe place to stand when she does it is directly behind her.'

'Not surprised if she can't see.'

'No. Not great with horses either. He says he leads her around on one like a little girl.'

'I think this Eirenn has a little crush on your blind girl,' Mags said as her sons bounded into the room.

'Then this Eirenn must be blind too. You should see her, Mags. Like a scarecrow. A skeleton scarecrow.'

'I want a skelton scarecrow!' Durran said, taking off his parka and throwing it on the floor.

'Pick that up,' said Mags.

'No, *I* want a skelton scarecrow!' Garik yelled.

'Pick it up,' Kael said as the younger boy copied his brother and flung his coat on the floor. 'Or I'll lock you in the donkey shed.'

'And it's skeleton,' Mags said. 'Three syllables.'

'What's a syllable?' asked Durran, dropping his scarf on top of his coat. 'Is it like arms? Do skeltons have three arms?'

Mags rolled her eyes at Kael. She picked up her cloak and filled a tub with water and washing soap.

'Pick up your stuff,' Kael said. 'And stop interrupting.'

'But—'

'Donkey shed,' he said severely, and Garik looked nervous.

'I like donkeys,' Durran informed Kael.

'Good, then you can spend the afternoon mucking them out. Now quiet, I'm reading.'

The two boys stood silently next to the heaps of their outdoor clothing. Garik fidgeted. 'But the Huntsmen will get us!' he blurted.

'Huntsmen?'

'From the Wild Hunt! We heard the dogs! It's the Dark!'

Kael exchanged a look with Mags. The Wild Hunt was a myth told to children, but he knew a lot of adults believed it too. During the darkest week of the year, grown men he knew to be quite sensible would swear they heard the hounds of hell barking in the sky, the thunder of hooves, the horns of the spectral huntsmen. Kael was never quite sure how they differentiated these sounds from the perfectly normal dogs and horses he kept around the place. As for the horn, it sounded exactly like the wind howling, just like it did all year.

'It's a little early for the Dark,' he said.

'No, it's coming early! That's what Agda Bondesdottir said!'

'Agda Bondesdottir is a halfwit,' Mags said. 'The Dark comes the same time every year.' Durran looked sceptical, but Garik's eyes were still huge.

Kael said gently, 'When the Dark comes we'll light the candles and sing the songs—'

'And can we have pepparkakor?' Durran said, all fear forgotten at the idea of gingerbread.

'Yes, but only if you help to make it.'

The boys nodded eagerly, and Kael shook out Eirenn's letter theatrically. 'Now. Evil huntsmen banished, can I continue reading, please?'

Garik nodded solemnly.

Kael turned back to the letter. 'Right. She can't fire a bow or ride a horse, but she's coming along well with sword and staff. *To begin with Sir Scipius had her sparring against me since I'm the worst in the class, but this week he's had her fighting some of the other boys. Mostly the younger ones, but it's a step up. He's also trying to get her to do unarmed combat, but she's much more hesitant with that. She'll beat the sh—*' Kael glanced at the two boys, who were listening with interest, '*the life out of a punchbag, but when it comes to people she doesn't seem to know how to fight back.*'

He read the next part, and frowned.

'What?' Mags said, pausing in her washing.

'He says, *I know she used to be a slave, my lord, but I thought it was the way we had slaves here. Valuable property to be protected. But I wonder if it's not like that in the New Lands. I wonder if she was beaten there, and told not to fight back. When she forgets herself, she's as brave as anything, but if someone shouts at her she cowers. I don't think she even realises she's doing it. She still walks with her head down, and I don't think it's to hide her eyes from anybody.*'

She's got the body language of a person who's been made to feel like they're nothing. I know, because that's what I was like before I pulled myself together and started fighting back.

'And it doesn't help that Marcus Gloria has taken a personal dislike to her. He seems to be offended by the very idea of her. Shoves into her all the time when she walks by, and then laughs at her as if it's her fault. Always hits her a little bit too hard in the training ring. The other week we had a melee and he just went for her. I think he broke something again, but she wouldn't tell me and whatever it was she healed it herself. Again. I mean, I know he's a bully, and a loser, and that he trades on his father's name, I know it as well as you do, but Ishtaer doesn't, and she won't be told. She seems to think he's in the right.'

'Ooh, what I'd do to that Gloria boy if I was in Ilanium!' Mags said, thumping her wet cloak harder than was strictly necessary.

'It's not him you need to do it to,' Verak said. Kael hadn't even heard him come in. He caught Kael's eye and said, 'It's her. No amount of words or even beatings will make him stop picking on her until she learns to fight back.'

'Isn't that what she's supposed to be doing?' Mags said 'Honestly, Kael, you could train her better.'

'No,' he said distantly, still looking at the letter. 'I mean, I could, but Verak's right. She has to want to fight back. She has to believe she's worth it.'

There was a pause. 'So,' said Mags, who had never in her life doubted her own self-worth for so much as a minute, 'how do you make her believe that?'

Kael glanced at Verak, who shrugged.

'I honestly have no idea.'

Out from the darkness of sleep a huge red cat loomed.

Fangs and claws and beaks and crowns, and yet she was

unafraid. Burning bright, the gleam of fire upon metal. A bed of clouds and heat, and a man sleeping beside her. A handsome man, a strong man. A man who opened his eyes and smiled at her.

She smiled back, and then he reached for his sword and plunged it into her belly.

Ishtaer woke up screaming.

Darkness stared back at her, the same darkness she'd seen every morning and night for five years. Beneath her was hard stone; by her feet, the dying warmth of a fire.

Someone pounded on wood. 'Oi! Keep it down!'

She sat up, shivering despite the warmth of the room. Her own room at the Academy. Ishtaer forced her tight muscles to relax. 'S-sorry.'

'You got someone in there?'

A second voice said spitefully, 'You know we're not allowed men in here.' That was Hortensia.

'There's no one here.' But even so, she felt for her sword, just in case that handsome man lay in hiding. 'I had a bad dream.'

The same bad dream she'd had the night her Seer's mark appeared.

A shiver that had nothing to do with the temperature shocked through her.

Chapter Ten

The road to Utgangen was as icy as every other one in Krulland, but Kael's ponies had been bred in the harshest of conditions and didn't even seem to notice. Wrapped in heavy furs, face covered everywhere but his eyes, he steered the troika on through the blizzard. Once a week someone had to go into town, to collect whatever Skjultfjell couldn't supply itself with and to check for news.

In the middle of the Dark, few people were willing to make the journey. Kael figured if he was going to force anyone to do it, it ought to be himself. Besides which, the number of men he knew who could drive a troika wasn't high. Controlling three horses who ran abreast at two different paces using four reins had taken Kael years to learn, and he'd got the Chosen advantage to help him.

The lights of the small trading town finally shone through the gloom, and even the hardy ponies seemed to pick up their pace.

'Nice warm stable for you tonight, my friends,' Kael told them, 'and the biggest bucket of mash you ever saw.'

Nice warm bed for me too, he thought, and the biggest bucket of beer you ever saw. And should there be some amenable female company, I wouldn't exactly say no.

He steered the sleigh to the posting inn and handed it over to the cargomen. Inside the inn, the heat and noise hit him like a wall. The warm, bitter scent of hops brewing flowed across the low-ceilinged room, which was always a good sign that there'd be fresh beer available.

'Aye aye, you're a brave man to be out in the Dark!' called the landlord.

'I don't fear the Wild Hunt,' Kael said, smiling, and moved forward.

'Then you're either brave, or stupid,' said the man, and poured him a beer without being asked.

Kael took the beer, a packet of letters and a room key, and handed over Mags's list of supplies.

'Running low on sugar,' the man said, scanning the list, 'but we should be able to do the rest.'

Kael said he'd pick it up in the morning and retired to a table by the fire to read his mail. It wasn't hard to get a good table, even when people didn't know who he was: a man who'd braved the Dark, alone, was a man lesser men feared.

There was a letter from Eirenn, dated only three days before. Kael frowned and glanced around, eyes scanning the clientele. Most of them had the look of locals who'd scurried in for a quick pint before the darkest part of night, but there were two or three people he guessed had come in during the few hours of daylight and were staying the night. A man with the look of a fur trader. A nervous-looking lad clutching a kitbag. And a woman, drinking alone by the bar.

He smiled to himself and read the next chapter in the life of Ishtaer ex Saraneus: In which she'd attended the Midwinter Festival with Eirenn and all the city's Chosen, at the Templum Ilanium in the Emperor's Tower. Afterwards, the Emperor had sent for Ishtaer, who had stammered and choked her way through an excruciating conversation, and then gone on to drink a heroic amount of grappa in a local taverna, the bill for which would be added to Kael's account. When Marcus Glorius had stumbled into the taverna, drunk and surrounded by over-privileged posh boys, he'd tried to grope Ishtaer, and received a knee to the groin for his troubles. Ishtaer was now dreading the retribution of Lord Glorius, which Eirenn doubted would be coming since he didn't expect Marcus had the stones to admit to his father he'd been brought down by a girl, and a low-born slave at that.

Kael sat back, thinking. A low-born girl. Clearly, Eirenn

was projecting his own issues onto Ishtaer, who he obviously saw as an ally, but Kael just couldn't equate a Thrice-Marked Chosen with someone who'd been born to nothing. There had to be something more to her story.

He finished his drink and sauntered over to the woman drinking alone. She wore a cloak with the hood pulled up despite the warmth of the room. Pale blonde hair was just visible in wisps. She was nursing a small, gently steaming cup of fragrantly spiced wine.

'How's the glugg?' he asked, and she looked up at him from the depths of her hood.

'It's good.'

'A better drink than you'll get in Ilanium.'

She leaned back as he took the spare seat at her table. 'You've visited the Empire?'

'On occasion. Not the season for it now, though. Any man sailing a ship up the coast in this weather is a lunatic.'

'They think the same of you for braving the Dark,' she pointed out.

'Men fear the Dark,' Kael said, signalling the landlord and pointing to the empty wine jug, 'because of mythical huntsmen. I fear the sea because I've seen winter storms smash ships into splinters.'

'A sensible man.'

'I've been called many things, but sensible isn't one of them.' The glugg arrived and he poured himself some. She was right, it was good. 'I'll hold my hand up to being reckless, violent, bloody-minded and rude, but please don't call me sensible. You'll ruin my reputation.'

She smiled around her wine cup.

'I'll also admit to a certain level of perception. Lady Aspicio.'

She paused for the tiniest fraction of a second. 'You must have me confused with someone else.'

'Maybe. It could be a birthmark you're hiding, or a bruise,

or maybe you're just ugly. But I seem to recall a young man with hair like yours by the name of Celsus. Your brother?'

She put down her cup. Then she pushed back her hood. Her hair was indeed silvery blonde, and her face bore the delicate tracery of a Seer. It was, he decided, not quite as pretty as the mark Ishtaer had.

Kael pulled up his sleeve to show her the mark on his arm. 'Kaelnar Vapensigsson Militis ... all the rest of it.'

Her expression was pretty knowing. 'Lord Krull, in the Empire.'

'But we're not in the Empire, are we?'

'In that case, I'm Celsa Luccia Aquilinia Aspicio.'

'Aspicio *Viator*,' Kael corrected. No one else could have covered the distance she had in such a time. The Viatori were a shady lot; half messenger, half spy, and probably a whole lot else too.

She shrugged. As far as he knew, a Viator mark was on the foot, and he wasn't expecting her to pull up her skirts and take off her boots.

Well, not yet, anyway.

Kael smiled. 'In that case, Aquilinia, let me pour you another drink while you tell me all about your next commission.'

'I don't have another commission,' she said, her eyes deep and steady on his.

'Even better.'

'And you've never had any Seer training? Child, that is shocking. In my day there was always a representative of each of the Gifts here to train new Tyros. For many years, I was that representative.'

'But now you've retired?'

'Something like that.'

The elderly gentleman had been sitting in the courtyard outside the atrium when Ishtaer came down to wait for

Eirenn before they went to a training session together. She remembered Master Killen from her first day at the Academy, and when he'd hailed her across the courtyard and told her she was the first Seer he'd seen at the Academy for years, she'd found herself chatting to him about the only vision she'd ever had.

'What I find interesting,' he said now, 'is that you saw it at all. I have heard it said that the blind are blind even in their sleep, and that even those with perfect vision rarely see colour in their dreams. But you saw everything in vivid shades.'

Ishtaer nodded. 'The cat was definitely red. But it wasn't a real cat, it was … I don't know, a picture of one. And there was another creature, with a beak and wings. But it wasn't a bird.'

'Many mythical creatures have wings,' Killen suggested. 'It could have any one of several meanings. The cat itself symbolises mystery, but can also be an omen of treachery and deceit. The colour red, in a dream, generally augers good news.'

'But you said it may not have been a dream,' Ishtaer said uncertainly. 'More of a vision.'

'Indeed, I believe it to be so. Of course red is also the colour of the Warrior,' Killen added. 'You are a mystery, child.'

'So I've been told,' she said with feeling.

'Been told what?' Eirenn sounded out of breath as he loped into the courtyard.

'That I'm a mystery. Barely a day goes by that someone doesn't tell me how impossible I am.'

'Sir Flavius just called me impossible too,' Eirenn said, flopping down on the bench beside her. 'Just because I forgot to deliver a message that came in for him last night. That's why I'm late, sorry.'

'It's all right, I've been talking with Master Killen here. I'm so sorry, sir, this is my friend Eirenn Fillian.'

Eirenn coughed gently. 'Er, Ish? Who're you talking to?'

'Master Killen. The gentleman here,' she gestured with her arm, but found only empty space. 'Oh, where did he go?' She listened for footsteps, but heard only the wind in the trees and far-off conversations.

Eirenn was silent a disconcertingly long while. Then he said, 'Elderly gentleman, grey hair and a long beard, walked with a cane?'

'He had a cane, yes. Do you know him?'

'Lord Killen Derrus Aspicio Veradis,' Eirenn said slowly.

'Oh! I didn't know he was a lord. I was calling him sir,' Ishtaer said, her cheeks heating.

'A more accurate thing to be calling him would be "late",' Eirenn said. 'Lord Killen died four, five years ago. We haven't had a Seer here since.'

Ishtaer laughed at his joke, but when he didn't join in, the laughter faded.

'He was also a Truthteller. He used to verify the Marks of every new Tyro,' Eirenn said. 'We all met him. We all went to his funeral. I can show you his memorial if you like.'

'But that's impossible,' Ishtaer said.

'Not if you're a Seer it's not,' Eirenn said, and touched her arm. 'Congratulations, Tyro Aspicio, you just met your first ghost.'

The messages came on the sled from Utgangen.

Kael shut the door to his office and sat down, feet on the desk, to read. Eirenn's letter had arrived, containing, as he'd asked, the names of every Chosen of Draxan and Saranean origin who had been alive around twenty years ago. And the name of every Chosen who had disappeared, ever.

But it was Aquilinia's news he wanted to read first, fresh

from her visit to the Saranos Islands. He didn't know how she'd got there in the winter seas, or what methods she'd used to get her information, but what she told him made for interesting reading.

People remember the girl with the tattoos who worked at the Manor House on Gurundi. The cook there remembers her as called Agnes, but concedes this probably wasn't her real name as lower servants tend to get given the same names over and over. She was thrown out five years ago for getting herself tattooed again. There's a price on her head since a man was found bleeding to death in the street, saying he'd been attacked by a woman with a tattoo on her arm, who was freakishly strong and possibly a witch.

Kael smiled at that. Looked like Ishtaer had form.

Agnes came from the Gurundi Workhouse, as did most of the cheap labour in the Saranos at the time. The former matron there was persuaded to remember the birth of a child called Ishtaer, which she considered a filthy foreign name. The mother came in out of a terrible storm, never gave her name, and died shortly after Ishtaer was born, living long enough only to name the child and give her a crystal necklace. The matron remembers because the woman had a heathen witch mark on her foot. Also, I suspect, because she tried to steal the necklace and found that she couldn't. She remembers Ishtaer wearing it every day of her life, which is unusual in a place where most people don't even have shoes. I enclose the record of the child's birth.

The record had a rusty looking stain on it. Kael suspected it was blood.

Ishtaer reckoned she was around twenty, which fit the date Aquilinia had uncovered. The woman with the witch mark on her foot was almost certainly a Viator, which narrowed his search in some ways and made it impossible in others. While her name would have been recorded in the Book of the

Chosen, if she was a Viator on a mission the details of it may never have been written down. Shady lot, the Viatori.

He pulled Eirenn's list of Draxan Chosen towards him, looking for Viator women of the appropriate age. What he found first was a man whose name called out to him from over a decade. Sir Rellan Mallus ex Draxus Medicus. Kael's hand went to his knee and he rubbed it without even thinking.

Rellan, who'd had the pale eyes and dark skin peculiar to some Draxans, a quiet manner and a way of healing axe wounds that was nothing short of miraculous.

Rellan, who'd lost his wife and child all those years ago and never stopped searching for them.

Rellan, whose wife was a Viator.

His hands nearly tore Eirenn's letter in his haste to check the names of the missing Chosen. There she was, twenty years ago, Madam Saria Secunda Viator. Mission unknown. Never returned. No body found.

He sat back in his chair, remembering it. How Rellan didn't know where his wife was going, or even that she was pregnant until a hastily written note had arrived, and he'd pleaded with her to return before the winter seas got too rough. And she never had returned. And Rellan had spent the rest of his life searching for his wife and a child he'd never seen born.

The coincidences were too much. It couldn't be anyone else.

Kael picked up his pen and wrote down the names, crossed them out and reordered them in the Ilani fashion for addressing a woman of the Citizenry. Then he stared at it, for a long time.

Mallia Saria Ishtaer ex Saraneus Medicus Militis Aspicio.

'That's one hell of a big name to live up to,' he said.

* * *

116

Winter became spring, and with only a week to go, Eirenn asked Ishtaer if she'd got her dress for the Imperial Ball.

'The what?'

'The Ball. Capital B. Sir Flavius should have ...' he trailed off. 'No, you don't go to his classes, do you?'

'I haven't time.' She turned to the basin beside her and washed her hands. Her patient was a young man who said he'd tripped and hit his head, but the gash on his cheek felt to her like it had been caused by something sharp propelled at force. A ring, for instance, on a hand balled into a fist. 'Mornings with Sir Scipius—'

'—getting the merry hell beaten out of you by Marcus Gloria. Really, Ish, you've got to stop just defending yourself and go on the attack.'

Since it took every ounce of courage she had to defend herself, Ishtaer ignored this. 'Then it's classes with Madam Julia and all afternoon here.'

'You don't have to spend all afternoon here. Your other classmates don't.'

'No, they do mornings instead. I have twice the amount of classes to fit into half the time.' She felt for the roll of gauze and cut a length, folded it over and pressed it to the cut on the young man's face. 'Hold this.'

He complied. 'Will it scar?'

'Do you want it to?'

He looked surprised to be asked.

'I can erase all trace of the cut,' Ishtaer said as she cut the tape to hold the gauze in place, 'but sometimes scars are a useful reminder. Every time you look in the mirror you'll remember why she hit you.'

He flinched. 'My own stupid fault,' he mumbled, and then added sharply, 'I tripped and hit myself.'

Eirenn chuckled. 'Sure you did,' he said. 'Solitaire ring, was it? Did you give it to her, or was she someone else's wife?'

The young man jerked as if to hit Eirenn, but Ishtaer's hand on his shoulder kept him in place. Madam Julia often called on her to restrain unruly patients, or to hold down those she didn't have time to anaesthetise before a painful procedure. It had taken an embarrassingly long time for Ishtaer to realise that most Healers didn't have this kind of strength.

'Leave it,' the patient muttered, subsiding. 'I ought to be reminded.'

Ishtaer gave him some ointment and instructions to come back if there was any sign of infection, then took the items she'd been using to the row of large stone sinks, served by their own pump and a fire for heating water. She set about sterilising the equipment.

'You didn't answer,' Eirenn said. 'About the dress. You do know you need a new one?'

'Won't the one I wore at Midwinter do?' asked Ishtaer, who'd been bullied into buying more clothes than she possibly needed by the terrifyingly grand assistants at one of the city's premier tailors.

'Of course not,' Eirenn said, as if it was obvious. 'It's blue.'

'They told me blue was the colour for Healers.'

'And so it is, but not at the Ball. Not until you're qualified. It's all very ... symbolic.'

She put the scalpel and needle to one side and began scrubbing her hands. 'So what must I wear?'

'White is traditional for Tyros. Fine for girls but looks bloody stupid on men. An incentive to graduate as soon as we can, I suppose. If you ask me, you should get his Lordship to pay for something terribly expensive.'

'Why?'

'Just humour me, all right? I've had to wear the same damn thing every year since I stopped growing, and the Scholarship Fund won't shell out for anything new. You've got a sponsor with stupid amounts of money. Spend it!'

Ishtaer paused in scrubbing her nails. Eirenn had alluded once or twice to being a scholarship boy, but it had taken a while for him to admit that the gophering he did for the Academy was actually paid employment, and that half his clothes were second-hand, donated by the Academy.

'All right,' she said. 'I'll see if I can get some time off this evening.'

She didn't leave the shelter of the Academy often. Over the months she'd become familiar enough with its layout, the steps and uneven cobbles and walls and doors, to make her own way around. Within the sick bay she rarely put a foot wrong, although it often unnerved her patients that she did everything by touch and not sight.

But outside on the crowded streets of Ilanium, she found it nearly impossible to get around without help. She couldn't hear or feel where she was going, and the people and animals around her moved so fast she knew she'd be under a horse's hooves in minutes without someone to guide her.

'There was a circus here at the weekend,' Eirenn said. 'One of Lord Gloria's nobby friends had a private menagerie in his garden. Shame it didn't eat some of the guests. The wagons caused bloody havoc overnight. Half of them were still here in the morning, and you know there aren't allowed to be any wheeled conveyances during daylight hours? The Emperor sent out his guards to remove them. It was chaos this time yesterday.'

He took her to the Sartorum Ilanium, where she'd purchased the clothes she wore every day and the few finer items they'd recommended for days like Midwinter.

'A dress for the Ball?' said the horrified assistant. 'It's next week!'

'I know that,' Ishtaer began.

'We're run off our feet! Most of the Chosen ladies place their orders before Midwinter!'

'So that's a no, then?' Eirenn said, and the assistant utterly missed his sarcasm.

'It most certainly is!'

'Even for Lord Krull's protégée?'

The woman paused, and Ishtaer could feel her sudden agony. But even Krull's name didn't work its usual magic. 'I'm really sorry,' she said pleadingly. 'But there's nothing we can do.'

It was the same story in the next four boutiques they tried. In the fifth, Ishtaer was too dispirited to even ask, but Eirenn managed to catch someone's eye and enquire.

'For the Ball?' The girl whistled. 'Not a snowball's chance in – wait a minute. I know you.'

For a second nobody spoke. Then Eirenn nudged Ishtaer. 'She's talking to you.'

Ishtaer frowned. She didn't know anybody apart from Eirenn.

'You mended my hand.' Ishtaer's own hand was taken by the assistant's. Her fingers were long, the tips hardened, the nails cut right down to the quick. And the bones had been recently healed. Nearly all of them.

'The cart accident,' Ishtaer said. 'At Midwinter.'

'I would have *died* without you,' said the dressmaker's assistant earnestly.

'Really it was Madam Julia who did most of the work,' Ishtaer said.

'But you were the one who healed my hand. Without this,' the girl flexed her fingers, 'I'd be—' Her voice suddenly dropped to a whisper. 'I'd be out on the streets. I'm not a Citizen, I don't have any rights or a family who can protect me. Girls who can't work don't get paid. You have no idea what you saved me from.'

Ishtaer pulled back her hand abruptly, pretty sure she had.

'My name's Malika,' the girl said. 'Look – if you can come

back after we've closed, I'll see what I can do. I might be able to make you something, so long as it's not complicated and doesn't need a lot of embellishment.'

'The simpler the better,' Eirenn said. 'Malika, you're a lifesaver.'

'No, Lady Ishtaer is,' said Malika fervently.

'It's Tyro,' Ishtaer began, but Eirenn was already pulling her away and thanking the girl as he did.

'Let her call you a Lady,' he said. 'You won't be a Tyro forever.'

'Are you sure about that? You said yourself I need to learn how to attack, and as for being a Seer, so far all I've had is one vision that makes no sense and one ghost, who, thanks to the fact that I can't see even after the Emperor sent his personal physician to me, might just have been a normal person playing a joke on me.'

'But you took a seamstress's shattered hand and gave her back her livelihood,' said Eirenn, drawing her down the small street back towards the main avenue. 'That says Healer to me. I've seen how Madam Julia relies on you. She doesn't do that with just any first year student, you know.'

Ishtaer wasn't sure what to say to that. Madam Julia asked for her help, yes, but surely no more than anyone else. Ishtaer worked hard, that was all. Some of the other students seemed appallingly entitled, didn't like getting their hands dirty or working long hours. Ishtaer had been doing that for as long as she could remember, and nobody had given her three hot meals and a warm bed for her trouble.

Not that she'd actually got around to sleeping in the bed yet, but the offer was there.

The thought was cut short by a sudden whine that had her head snapping to the left.

'If you ask me,' Eirenn began, and Ishtaer held up a hand for silence. 'What?'

This time she put her hand over his mouth and cocked her head to the side, listening hard. Eirenn had commented that she seemed to have better hearing than anyone else, which Ishtaer didn't think was strictly true. She just relied on it a lot more than anyone else.

And what she heard now was the whine of someone in pain. It might have been an animal, but she'd heard people make the same noise. People who were degraded to the status of animal. People who thought of themselves as less than human.

People like she'd once been.

'It's coming from that alley,' Eirenn murmured very softly. She nodded. She could hear voices now too, laughing and jeering. And the thud of something blunt hitting living flesh. Both were sounds she heard every day in the training ring.

'Are you armed?' she asked softly.

'A knife,' Eirenn replied, 'but listen. There's at least three or four of them.'

She thought there might be more, all of them youths, none of them familiar. 'They're not Chosen,' she said. 'We'd know them.'

'You really want to go into a blind alley and fight an unknown number of men armed with the gods only know what?'

'You want to walk away and leave whoever that is to be beaten to death?'

Eirenn sucked in a breath. Then he took her hand and pressed the hilt of a small dagger into it. 'You take the knife,' he said. 'And try not to hit me.'

They walked together to the alley, and Eirenn said loudly, 'Well, well. It's a parlous state of affairs in this city when one small dog is such a threat that it takes five of you to subdue it. With rocks.'

A dog. Not that it mattered whether it was a dog or a

human or a horse. There were five of them against one, and Ishtaer had seen those odds before, had *been* those odds before.

An unfamiliar feeling built inside her, spiky and hot. She thought it might be anger.

'Piss off,' said one of the lads. He was probably a few years younger than Ishtaer, judging by his voice. There was another thud and whine as he threw another rock at the dog.

The anger pulled in on itself, drawing her in with it.

'Now, that's no way to talk to a lady,' said Eirenn. 'Especially when she *is* a lady.'

At this, the jeers stopped for a moment and she heard the rustle of clothing and feet as they all turned to look at her.

Her head went up. Her left hand curled into a fist, her right tightening its grip on Eirenn's knife.

'A Seer, in fact,' Eirenn went on conversationally, 'and she's just had the most fascinating vision of the near future. Would you like to hear it?'

'We ain't scared of a Seer,' said the boy who'd spoken before.

'Ah, but you would be if you knew what she saw. It's really exciting. Basically it involves the two of us beating the shit out of the five of you, and then walking away with this dog you've been tormenting for no good reason. Is that about the size of it, Ishtaer?'

'It's how I see things going,' said Ishtaer, amazed at the steadiness of her own voice.

'Wait a minute, Ishtaer?' said one of the other boys.

'Yes. Ishtaer ex Saraneus Medicus Militis Aspicio. You might have heard of her. She's very good friends with Krull the Warlord.'

'Yeah, right,' said the first boy, but the second whispered something. 'You don't get women Warriors,' came the scornful reply, but it sounded less certain.

Months of training every day pushed Ishtaer's body into an automatic fighting stance, body reduced to a smaller target, hands ready, knees loose.

'Would you like to test that theory?' she asked.

Chapter Eleven

'She did what?' Verak said.

Kael looked at Eirenn's letter again. 'Beat up five lads twice her size and adopted a wolf.'

'Yes, I thought that's what you said.' Verak took the letter and read it for himself. 'He says it looks like a wolf cub, not that it is one.'

'Does it make any difference? The rumours will have it as a wolf. It's a nice bit of mythology.'

The two men stared out over the rail of the *Grey Ghost* as it slid away from the headland. From here, Skjultfjell was completely invisible, hidden by the rocks and cliff face. A week's journey to the south was Ilanium, and the Imperial Ball, which Kael would usually avoid like something that came with festering boils but which he was suddenly eager to attend.

Besides, he had a plan for Ishtaer when he arrived. Beating up youths to save a puppy was one thing, but Eirenn's reports weren't getting any more optimistic about her ability to defend herself.

He could only remember one occasion when she'd fought back with any determination.

He might as well recreate it.

'How does it look?' Ishtaer asked, standing diffidently by the fountain. Eirenn had been silent for nearly a whole minute, ever since she walked in, and she was afraid she looked ridiculous. 'Malika said something simple would be fine, but I don't know ... If the fashion is for something really complicated then will I just look wrong? I don't know what fancy people wear. Eirenn, say something!'

'You look,' Eirenn began, then cleared his throat and started again. 'You look stunning.'

'In a good way?' she asked doubtfully. Malika had also given her hair a trim, and she had no idea how it might look.

'In a very good way. I shall have to send flowers to Malika for creating something that suits you so well. Or maybe ask her to marry me. You look wonderful.'

He took her hand and kissed the back of it. Ishtaer flinched and pulled it back. At her side, the dog growled.

He was only half grown, leggy and skinny, but he was already a large animal, his head at mid-thigh level. Since she'd brought him back to the Academy, washed his matted fur and fed him raw meat from the kitchens, he'd barely left her side. Madam Julia had forbidden him from the sick bay, although when he'd licked her hand and made a whining puppy noise, she'd allowed him to stay in her office while Ishtaer worked.

'He's like the guard dogs my father used to keep,' she'd said, her voice softer than it had ever been since Ishtaer met her. 'He'll be a big fellow one day.'

Big fellow or not, he now sat at Ishtaer's side, wearing a lead made from rope braided with the same red, blue and silver ribbons that edged Ishtaer's white dress. She'd looped it around her wrist, like a bracelet. Apart from the leather pouch of crystals around her neck, it was the only accessory she wore.

'Are you sure I'll be allowed to take him to the Ball?' she asked. She was still amazed she'd been allowed to keep him in her room, but Eirenn pointed out that a lot of sons and daughters of the Citizenry kept their own horses, hunting dogs and birds of prey within the Academy's walls.

'Oh, sure. Few years back there was a fad for women to wear wigs with birdcages in them, and actual birds. Of course, they were always escaping, flying all around the place. It was chaotic. Nobody stopped it though. So long as he behaves himself ...'

'He will,' said Ishtaer firmly. The dog licked her hand. 'I can't leave him in my room, he cries all the time.' She ruffled the soft fur between his ears. Despite her healing the injuries the boys had inflicted on him, the dog was still thin, still wary, and had latched onto Ishtaer as some kind of saviour. As a result, he'd also become fiercely protective of her. Even Marcus Glorius had backed off when faced with seventy pounds of growling canine.

'How's Gloria doing?' Eirenn asked as they set off towards the Academy's exit, along with a growing stream of excited students heading towards the Turris Imperio and its huge ballroom.

'I told him he'd be fine unless he threatened me,' Ishtaer said. 'The dog was out of sight while we were training. If he hadn't tried to trip me on my way out, the dog would never have snapped his lead like that to pounce on him.'

Eirenn laughed. 'Did Madam Julia heal his black eye?'

'No. She said he ought to keep it as a reminder, and that if he went running to his daddy to complain then she'd be forced to tell him how Marcus had attacked a girl, unprovoked.'

'I love Madam Julia,' Eirenn said. He scratched the dog's ears. 'But you know what? You can't keep calling this feller "dog". If you're going to keep him—'

'I am.'

'—then he needs a name.'

She frowned, pausing to let someone else ahead of her through the gate. Since the incident with Marcus, people had been giving her and the dog a wide berth. 'I don't know how to name a dog,' she said.

'Right then, let's see. You could call him something like Fluffy—'

'No.'

'Or … Grey Ghost …'

'Kael's ship?'

'Lord Krull to the rest of us,' Eirenn reminded her. 'He might like it if you name your dog after his ship.'

'Yes,' said Ishtaer, who suspected he'd like it too much, 'he probably would.' Her stomach fluttered at the thought of meeting the warlord again, even if she knew she wasn't the frightened wretch he'd left behind. All right, so she still couldn't bear to be touched and hadn't got up the courage to sleep in her own bed, but she was stronger, healthier, and even though she'd had Eirenn's help and the boys had mostly run away the moment they'd been threatened, she found herself carrying her head a little higher after word got around that she'd beaten up five men all by herself.

'He needs a strong name. After all, he broke that fence post clean in two when he went after Marcus. What's High Ilani for *strong*? Or *big*? Or … something like that.'

Eirenn thought for a while, then said, 'How about Brutus? It means heavy, immovable.'

'Brutus,' Ishtaer said, and the dog licked her fingers. 'He likes that. Well, then. Brutus it is.'

For a second Kael paused at the top of the stairs and looked down into the blinding confusion of the Imperial Ball.

Ishtaer, he thought as he descended the grand staircase, was probably lucky she didn't have to look at it.

The fashion amongst wealthy women seemed to be for skirts about a mile wide in every shade that could be conjured by the human imagination, and even some that couldn't. Bodices were low, spilling acres of cleavage where it had no right being. This season's wigs were huge, and also brightly coloured. And also worn by men. The modish look seemed to be for highly embellished coats with wide skirts that echoed the women's outfits, emphasising narrow waists and shoulders. Men and women wore make-up, and not in a way that could be called subtle.

They looked, Kael thought, quite demented.

Moving amongst these mad peacocks were the Chosen, generally more soberly dressed, each of them wearing a coloured sash. The majority were red or blue for Warriors and Healers, with a few purple Viatori dotted here and there, and the duller shades of the Bards and other lesser Chosen. Some of the Warriors had their sleeves embroidered with the patterns of their marks, and he saw at least one Healer with an embroidered glove.

Kael adjusted his own red and black sashes and idly scanned the crowd for anyone else with two of the damn things. His eye drifted over the clumps of Tyros fiddling self-consciously with their all-white outfits and picked out Lady Aquilinia in her purple and silver sashes. A faint smile curved his lips in remembrance. Aquilinia raised her brows at him but made no move to approach. They understood each other. She no more wanted a relationship than he did. It was incredibly refreshing after the endless advances made on him by fortune-hunting young – and often not-so-young – women. He wondered if he should invite Aquilinia back to his rooms later.

But then a slight commotion behind him made him turn back towards the stairs, where he saw two Tyros dressed in white. And a wolf.

Kael blinked, but they were still there when he opened his eyes again. Eirenn Fillian, his faithful correspondent, and a tall, slim woman in a draped silk dress that made her look like a goddess and displayed the bold, chasing lines of the Militis mark on her arm. She had dark hair cut unfashionably but attractively short, which meant that there was nothing to distract from either her lovely bone structure or the Aspicio mark around her eye. Wrapped around her left wrist was the leash of the wolf – a swiving wolf, by all the gods!—and her palm was turned outwards, revealing the Medicus mark there.

Kael stared.

She had high cheekbones and long dark lashes and her eyes blazed a curious pale blue that seemed at odds with her warm skin tone. Her breasts were small and high, her bare arms slender and strong with the sort of muscle few fashionable women ever had.

'Dear gods in heaven,' said Verak, who Kael hadn't even noticed standing beside him. 'That's Ishtaer?'

Kael could just about manage a nod.

All around him, people nudged and murmured, but Ishtaer appeared to ignore them. She took the arm of her friend, her head high and her blind eyes aimed straight ahead, and descended the staircase like a queen.

'Are you sure that's not a wolf?' Verak asked.

Kael shook his head, a little too rapidly. He cleared his throat. 'No. Can't be. Must be a big dog.'

'Looks like a wolf to me.'

'Why would she have a wolf? Must be a dog.' It had the same pale blue eyes as its owner and a shaggy winter coat in shades of grey and brown. It had a skinny, defensive look about it, exactly like Ishtaer when he'd first met her.

Eirenn murmured something to Ishtaer, and the odd trio made their way over to Kael, brushing past the society women with their ridiculous clothes and wigs and thick warpaint.

'My lord,' she said, with a very slight incline of her head. That was how most of the Chosen bowed. Someone had been tutoring her.

'Ishtaer,' he said. He stared at her some more, uncomfortably aware that while she didn't know he was doing it, both Eirenn and Verak did, and that he should stop. But he couldn't. 'You look ...' She looked a lot of things: strong, healthy, exotic, attractive. All the things she'd never looked before.

'You look different,' he said eventually, and she gave a tiny flicker of a smile that looked, of all things, disappointed. 'Nice pet,' he added quickly.

'His name is Brutus,' she said.

'Going to need to do a bit of filling out to live up to that name,' Verak said.

'He's only young. Less than a year, I think.'

There was a short silence, during which Kael attempted to unglue his gaze from someone who should have been a skinny, pathetic wretch but who was instead a rather lovely young woman. He failed, miserably.

But at least he wasn't the only one staring. Eirenn gazed at her with what Kael could only call adoration, and she drew curious and admiring glances from plenty of passing men. In this frantic sea of overdressed, overcorseted popinjays, she stood like a statue.

'It's a good turnout this year,' Eirenn said. 'I didn't think you usually came, my lord.'

Kael cleared his throat and tore his gaze from Ishtaer. 'No. Well. Long way.' He cleared his throat again. 'Thought I'd better come and see my protégée.'

When no one said anything, Verak said, 'We've been getting your letters, Eirenn. Great to see how Ishtaer is getting on.'

'She's doing really well,' said Eirenn. He was of a height with Ishtaer, dark haired and pale skinned. She seemed entirely comfortable leaning on his arm.

I wonder if they're lovers?

Kael physically shook himself at that. There was no way in this world or the next that Ishtaer was anyone's lover.

He'd seen her reaction back in the New Lands when he tried to seduce her. If his barest touch had repulsed her that much, he doubted any other man had got between those no-doubt muscular and firm thighs …

Stop thinking about her thighs! He gave himself a mental slap and forced his lustful thoughts to the back of his brain, saving them for later. At least he wouldn't have to do much acting if he wanted his plan to work.

'Well,' he said. 'I've got people to talk to. Oh look, the Emperor. I'll see you at the Presentation, Ishtaer,' and he walked off before she affected him any more.

Behind him, Verak laughed.

Eirenn accompanied her to her first Presentation, where each Tyro Militis was presented to each fully qualified Militis in attendance. There were a lot of them, each with hands to be shaken, and it was a tedious business. Ishtaer smiled politely as each and every man there, young and old, exclaimed how they never thought they'd see a woman Warrior. Some were curious, some were downright rude. Ishtaer simply tightened her hand on the woven rope connecting her to Brutus, and they quickly shut up.

When she reached Kael, he held her hand a fraction too long, and murmured, 'You look really good, Ishtaer.'

Her smile suddenly felt very hard to maintain.

After the Militis Tyros were presented, those who had been judged proficient enough to graduate were called forward and draped with a red silk sash. Sir Scipius and various other notable Warriors made speeches, although she noticed Kael wasn't among them. Everyone applauded. Brutus barked. Eirenn whispered in her ear that Lord Glorius looked livid that Marcus hadn't been selected for passing out. Marcus himself stomped out of the room, his tread as familiar to Ishtaer as her own.

They followed the newly graduated Warriors back into the main ballroom, where they were announced and applauded again, and then the man with the loud, ringing voice who'd announced the Militis Presentation called forward the Healers.

'Try not to yawn,' Eirenn advised, and Ishtaer retraced her steps. She'd been nervous about this evening, but now she had no idea why. Mostly, like the other official occasions she'd been obliged to attend, it was just mind-numbingly boring.

She followed the other Medicus students along the line of Healers, shaking hands with a fairly equal number of men and women, a surprising number of whom said things like, 'So you're the Ishtaer Julia's been telling us about!'

It took Ishtaer a while to work out why she was annoyed by that. Eventually she realised how damn patronising it sounded.

The only one who didn't patronise her or make some comment about her blindness was Sir Karnos, the old Healer who'd fixed her leg on Kael's ship. He gripped her hand and said gruffly, 'You're looking very well, Ishtaer.'

'I feel well,' she replied stupidly, and he laughed a little before letting her go.

She followed the rest of the group back to their side of the room and listened to the names being called out.

'Hirtia Daria Medicus.' Oh yes, Ishtaer had worked with her on an exploded appendix. 'Spurius Nautius Medicus.' Nice lad, good with children, ashamed of his illegitimacy. 'Meara Ciara ex Parvulus Medicus,' who occasionally talked with Eirenn about the small province they both came from. 'Rufia Quintia Medicus,' a girl she didn't really know. And on. And on.

Brutus lay down beside her, and she couldn't blame him. Eirenn's words whirled monotonously around her head. *Try not to yawn. Try not to yawn. Yawn. Yawn.*

'Mallia Saria Ishtaer ex Saraneus Medicus Militis Aspicio prior Inservio.'

She blinked. That had almost sounded like ...

The girl next to her nudged Ishtaer. 'You deaf as well as blind?' she hissed. 'Get up there!'

'But—'

'I do believe she is unfamiliar with the use of her full name. Ishtaer, come forward,' said Madam Julia, and Ishtaer did, dread sweeping over her. This was impossible. A mistake. She'd been here only a few months, there were people in the group who'd been there years, someone was doing this as a joke, maybe Marcus, his grandfather was in the room after all—

Someone draped a sash over her shoulder and settled it at the opposite hip. Something heavy weighed it down, a small pin with a design she couldn't quite trace with her fingers.

'Curtia Mercula Medicus ...'

Beside her, Brutus licked her hand.

The boy had watched her go with an expression of fierce longing on his face. Mags had been absolutely right: Eirenn had a crush on Ishtaer. A big crush. Not that Kael could throw stones. He'd been bowled over by her too.

'So it actually is a wolf.'

Eirenn glanced at him. 'It's not a wolf.'

'Lad, I know wolves.'

'Why would there be a wolf in the middle of an island city?' The boy sighed. 'It's probably a runaway from the circus. She got a bit ... upset about those boys pelting it with stones.'

'Upset?'

Eirenn paused, and appeared to be choosing his words carefully. 'She's never said what happened to her before she came here. But the way she reacts ... the look on her face when she found that dog ... I've never seen her so angry.'

Because she was once that dog. He could see the same thought in Eirenn's eyes. 'I've heard rumours of her fighting off a dozen large, big lads, all by herself, unarmed.'

'More like five,' Eirenn conceded, 'and she had a knife. And me. But yeah. Apart from that it's almost exactly as I told you. Might have invented a fire-breathing dragon or two.'

'On your side, or theirs?'

'Ah well, depends who you listen to.'

Kael smiled. It was impossible not to like Eirenn.

'How is her fighting coming along?'

Eirenn shrugged awkwardly. 'Technically she's quite competent, but she lacks ... I don't know ...'

'Courage?'

'Maybe. It's like she's going through the motions 'cos she's been told to, not actually fighting because she wants to, or because she's trying to defend herself. And gods' shield she should actually attack anyone. Until she went after that dog I thought she was physically incapable of it.'

Kael frowned, but before he thought of a reply the Emperor's braid-encrusted major domo bellowed the announcement of the newly graduated Medicus Chosen, and Kael clapped dutifully, wondering how far down the list the Seers would be, because he wasn't staying any longer than he had to. Even Krull the Swiving Warlord wouldn't leave before his protégée had been through her presentations.

Then he saw Eirenn's jaw drop, heard the murmured astonishment ripple through the room, and looked up for the second time to see Ishtaer standing at the top of the stairs, with her wolf, looking shell-shocked.

She was wearing a blue sash.

Eirenn started applauding, but Kael could only stare. She'd graduated? She was a fully qualified Healer? After less than four months? He'd heard of such things, but only occasionally, and usually with someone who'd been teaching themselves long before they came to the Academy. Kael himself had passed out of the Academy at sixteen, which was pretty damn young, but he'd been there over four years by that point.

Dammit. He couldn't be jealous of Ishtaer.

He clapped a bit, feeling as stunned as Ishtaer looked. Her dog began barking at all the noise, and her cheeks flushed bright red. She scampered away as soon as they let her, tripping down the stairs and landing in an undignified heap on the ground.

People started laughing.

Kael strode over, grabbed her by the arm and hauled her to her feet. Brutus growled.

'What,' he asked the assembled company icily, 'is so funny?'

The laughter stopped.

'You okay?' he asked Ishtaer, who nodded, her face even redder, and tugged her dog closer. 'Well then. Congratulations.'

'Congratulations? I just made a fool of myself in front of all the Chosen in the city.'

Yes, she had. And if Lord Krull's protégée did something embarrassing, it embarrassed Lord Krull too. He stamped down his anger and said, 'I meant about graduating. That's a phenomenal achievement.'

She shrugged awkwardly, and Kael realised he was still holding her arm. He let go, and she shook herself as if trying to rid her skin of the memory of him. That made him even more annoyed.

He looked down at her, standing as if she was trying to make herself smaller, fiddling with the caduceus pin on her sash, and he looked at the curve of her lip as she worried it between her teeth.

If Eirenn had fallen down those stairs he'd have made a joke about it. If Kael had done it he'd – well, he'd never have done it, but if he *had*, he'd have glared at everyone until they shut up.

Ishtaer looked like she wanted to crawl in on herself. He had never seen anyone who was so ill-at-ease with her own body before. *You're a Warrior,* he wanted to say to her. *Damn well act like one.*

Instead he took Brutus's lead from her hand and held it out to Eirenn. The boy had followed in his wake the second he'd moved towards Ishtaer.

'Take this,' he said. 'Ishtaer and I are going to dance.'

If anything, she looked even more mortified. 'I don't know how to dance,' she whispered.

'If you can move your feet, you can dance,' he told her. 'Just hold on to me.'

He fairly dragged her to the dance floor, angry with her for a lot of things he couldn't quite work out. For being a coward, certainly. For graduating so ridiculously early. Yes, all right, he was jealous. Probably everyone in the room was. And yes, he was angry because he was so attracted to her, which was hellishly shallow of him and he knew it. He was angry with himself for being angry with her, which in turn just made him angrier.

So angry, in fact, that the plan he'd been close to dismissing suddenly seemed a lot more feasible.

He pulled her close against his body and moved in time to the music. Ishtaer was rigid in his arms, her fingers tight in his hand and on his shoulder. She was lean, not skinny but strong. She should have felt good against him. She felt terrified.

'It's very unusual to graduate so early,' he told her.

She nodded. 'Madam Julia says she's never approved someone so soon.'

'Did she say why she made the exception for you?'

Her fingers flexed, and for a moment she said nothing. Then, 'The girl who made my dress. Malika. She was hit by a cart at Midwinter and suffered massive internal damage. Madam Julia and I healed her. But she'd also broken several bones in one hand. Madam Julia told me to splint them because we were too busy to heal something that would heal itself, but Malika told me if she couldn't work for several months then she'd starve. So I stayed up all night to heal her.'

Kael digested this. Eirenn hadn't told him she'd gone against Madam Julia's wishes. Maybe her cowardice was just in the training ring.

'You could have gone into crystal-debt,' he said, tightening his fingers on hers. He'd heard of it happening with young, hot-headed Chosen, high on the super strength and power their crystals lent them. They'd push too far, further than their bodies could take, but the crystals wouldn't relent. Eventually the Chosen collapsed from exhaustion. The mildest cases took weeks to recover from. Many went into comas. Many never came out of them.

'That's what Madam Julia told me. She was angry at the time, but I was all right. She was also pleased with a couple of medicines I created.' She faltered a bit, then added in a determined tone, 'I've always been good with herbs.'

She'd said that before, Kael thought, but he couldn't remember where or when.

'So I've seen. We should celebrate, Ishtaer. Don't you think?'

'I—I suppose so.'

'Suppose?' Anger rose back up again. 'You've just graduated as a Healer! You might still have to work on your Warrior and Seer qualifications, but you're a Citizen now, in your own right. World's your oyster. You can do what you want. Time to celebrate.'

'How?'

He had his hand on her back, cupping her shoulder blade the way he'd been taught all those years ago in Sir Flavius's damned etiquette classes. His finger stretched to the bare skin exposed by the back of her gown, and stroked her.

'Oh, I'm sure we can think of something,' he whispered in her ear.

Ishtaer stumbled.

'You're looking very beautiful tonight, Ishtaer. Have I told you that? Not many women could cope with hair as short as yours, but it highlights your pretty face.'

His hand left her back and stroked her cheek, her jaw. Lingered on the fullness of her mouth.

Ishtaer went even more rigid.

'And this dress. Your seamstress should be complimented. It clings in all the right places.' His hand slipped over her neck, her shoulder, the curve of her breast. 'To all your curves. Last time I met you, you didn't even have curves.'

She'd stopped moving entirely now, standing there before him completely still. Had he thought she looked like a statue before? She was barely even breathing now. The skin around her mouth had gone white.

Come on. React.

Kael pressed the whole of his body against hers. She was trembling. His hand slid down over her waist, her hip, cupped her firm backside and pulled her against his groin.

'You and me, Ishtaer. We could just skip out of here, find an empty room somewhere. Emperor's got lots of rooms. Lots of big, soft beds. Let me peel this admittedly fetching frock off you and celebrate the best way I know how.'

Her hand on his shoulder was like a vice. Kael lowered his head and murmured in her ear.

'Hot. Sweaty. Naked. You and me.'

She shuddered. Maybe, Kael thought, she was actually

considering it. Well, this was just a plan that couldn't backfire!

'Let me be your first, Ishtaer. I'd make it good for you. Very, very good.'

'No,' she whispered.

'No? Oh, I would. Believe me, sweetheart, with me it's always good.'

'I will never be with you,' Ishtaer said.

He drew back a little, looked at her face. She was completely white. Her eyes blazed blue fire.

'Why not?' he asked, and suddenly her hand wasn't in his any more, but on his face, finger and thumb pressed hard against his left brow and cheekbone. He stared in astonishment at the same place on her face, where her delicate Seer's mark feathered around her eye, and then—

—something lashed against my back, agonising, slamming into broken, bleeding skin, and I was trapped in that basement kitchen, Cook beating me with a belt, screaming about filthy foreign tattoos—

—I huddled in the cold and the dark, and a boy tussled with me, trying to get under my skirt, and I lashed out with strength I didn't know I had, and grabbed his knife and then his blood was spraying over my face—

—I only want to see, the captain said, so I gave him my crystal necklace but he wouldn't give it back, making me leap for it, and then the first mate grabbed me and tore my shirt and they saw the bindings on my breasts and shouted she's a girl, *and the bindings were torn away and I was exposed to their grabbing hands, and my breeches ripped off, and they held me down, and the captain laughed and grabbed at me and shoved himself inside me—*

—the rope cut into my wrists as I tried to get free, but they were relentless, one after the other, every man on board, the captain more than anyone else, over and over until I bled and

sobbed and they pushed me into fighting back, laughing and congratulating themselves on how clever they'd been to tie down and rape a fifteen-year-old girl—

—the rain lashed down on me as the pirates attacked, and I flew across the deck after the captain as he was thrown overboard with my necklace, my mother's necklace in his pocket, and the pirate king laughed like a god as he whirled in a storm of slaughter until the deck ran red with blood, never stopping me as I leapt into the cold dark sea—

—the cruel hands of the slavers, leg irons biting into my skin, and the kind eyes of the Eastern woman who taught me to heal myself with herbs, the lizard gaze of the slave buyer, the phrase I'll always regret—

—I'm good with herbs—

—the brand on my arm, branded like cattle, 'you belong to me now', the cold flags of the floor as Samara pushed me down, little witch, you're a liar, you can't do magic—

—the clawing pain in my belly, the hands grabbing me, always the guards, the courtiers, bringing the little witch down a peg or two, the crack of bone, the last time I fought back, the smash of my skull against the floor—

—darkness—

—the hands, the cold, the filthy invading bodies, the laughter, the hunger, the pain, the red silk dress, the devil promising he'd make it good for me—

'Stop, please make it stop!'

His own voice, begging, terrified. Ishtaer's hand falling from his face. Her chest heaving with anger as she stepped back and he crumpled to the floor, gasping for air, his whole body alive with pain.

Kael stared up at Ishtaer, standing there like an avenging angel, eyes hot with pain and fury, her wolf snarling at her side, surrounded by the Chosen and the Citizenry and several hundred of the Empire's most influential people.

'Ask me again why I could never be with you,' she said, and Kael couldn't speak.

Ishtaer turned and walked away, and Kael sprawled on the floor, broken.

Chapter Twelve

'That,' said Eirenn, 'was bloody brilliant.'

Ishtaer couldn't stand still. She'd strode out onto the roadway, high above the city, and gulped in huge lungfuls of cold night air, pacing up and down the slope. Fury pulsed in her veins, anger making her hot and cold, trembling, barely able to speak.

That he'd done that, that he'd said it, that he'd provoked her—

That she'd *shown* him. Oh, nicely done, Ishtaer. Now everyone will know, and there goes any respect anyone might have been thinking about having for you—

'It was nicely done,' said a cool female voice behind her, and she spun around. 'I know you've been having visions and you've seen a ghost, but I've never seen memories projected quite like that before.'

'Who the hell are you?' Ishtaer snapped, hating the quiver in her voice.

Eirenn cleared his throat. 'Lady Celsa Luccia Aquilinia Aspicio Viator.'

A Seer and a Viator? Ishtaer winced.

'Can't be anyone else,' Eirenn added.

'Indeed.' Lady Aquilinia sounded amused. 'Eirenn, I believe? Go and find my handmaiden and tell her to bring the silver sash. Her name is Atella. Go.'

Eirenn hesitated, then she heard him walk away, fast. Lady Aquilinia had the sort of voice that gave orders, not suggestions.

'I'm sorry, my lady, I didn't mean to be rude. I can't see, that's the thing.'

'Oh, but you can. You can see things other people can't see, you can see what is to come, you can even make others see. Don't worry, you didn't show anyone else those memories. The rest of the crowd in there simply saw you shove Krull the Warlord to the floor and walk away. It was magnificent.'

'It was humiliating.'

'He needed to be humiliated.'

'I didn't know I could do it.' She still wasn't sure how she had. She'd just been angry and wanted to show him how wrong he was, and … then it happened.

'It's often the way.'

Ishtaer hesitated. 'Did you see … what I showed him?'

'Some of it. I didn't want to pry. But a projection like that … it fairly shouted to me. I was keeping half an eye out for you anyway. Your Presentation this evening would have been only to me.'

'There are no other Seers here?'

'There aren't many of us in the first place,' said Lady Aquilinia. 'A lot prefer seclusion, especially if they're readers, like me. Have you ever picked up someone else's thoughts?'

Ishtaer hesitated. 'The odd intention, but usually when it was obvious. Not thoughts, no.'

'Lucky you. It can get very noisy. Your particular Gift seems to be for visions. What do you think the red cat means?'

'Lord Killen said—'

'No. Not Killen. He was a clever man and an exceptional Seer, but I want to know what you think it means.'

Ishtaer sighed. 'I don't know. Maybe it's a vision of my future. Maybe I'll see a huge red cat one day, and then a man will stab me. To be honest, it wouldn't be the strangest thing that's ever happened to me.'

'No. I don't expect it would. Not all visions are straightforward, Ishtaer. Some deal with metaphor and allegory, and some simply show you what's going to happen.

I wish I could have been more specific with my vision about Lord Krull, but you get what you're given.'

'Vision?'

'All I know is that his child will die to save him. Which child, and when, and how, I've no idea. You can imagine he wasn't pleased when I told him.' Before Ishtaer could say anything else, footsteps sounded and Lady Aquilinia said, 'Ah, Atella, thank you. Now go and tell that man in all the braid that I've had my Presentation with Ishtaer and that I'd like to announce her graduation as a Seer.'

For the second time, Ishtaer thought she must have misheard. Or imagined it. Two in one day? This was ridiculous.

'I must be dreaming,' she said as Lady Aquilinia placed the sash over her shoulder and adjusted the way it lay.

'Trust me, you're not. Now then, my lady, if you're ready?'

He was still getting strange looks three days later as he left the Turris Imperio with a sack of gold weighing down his horse's back. The general story had got around, and in the usual way had been inflated from an argument and a shove to an all-out brawl and several broken limbs, most of them his.

What hadn't got out, he was vastly relieved to discover, was any hint of what Ishtaer had shown him.

How could he have been so stupid? Of course she'd been frightened of what he was going to do to her back in that guest room on Samara's plantation. Why in the name of all that was holy had he thought it was because she was innocent?

He cringed as he rode through the streets, recalling pretty much everything he'd said and done with her, just like he had every spare minute since the Ball. Had he known ... But even if he had, would he have realised the extent of her abuse?

It was one thing to know she'd been raped and another to experience it, to feel the fear and helplessness and revulsion. Good gods in heaven, how did she function so normally? Kael continually had to resist the urge to curl into a ball and weep.

The horse took him back to the domus he'd moved into directly after the Ball. There was no way he could face the possibility of meeting Ishtaer at the Academy. He had no idea what he could say to her. Where to even start.

With an apology, you bastard, his conscience sneered.

Kael rubbed at his forehead, feeling a headache pulse into life. Yeah. An apology would be a good place to begin.

Ishtaer was used to conversations going quiet as she approached, but since the Ball things had been getting extreme. According to Eirenn, the rumour now was that she'd punched Lord Krull in the face and then let her dog savage him, which possibly accounted for why everyone was giving her and Brutus such a wide berth.

'But everyone at the Academy was there at the Ball,' she said. 'How can they have not seen it?'

'The thing is, until he started screaming and fell on the ground, there wasn't anything much to see,' Eirenn said. 'People just fill in the gaps, I guess. You could set the record straight and tell everyone what actually happened …?'

But Ishtaer shook her head firmly. She wasn't about to spill any more hideous secrets, not even to Eirenn.

Madam Julia called her in to talk about prospects, explaining to Ishtaer that although she'd be expected to continue with her Militis training, as a fully qualified Healer the possibilities for her future were many and varied.

'You could become a private physician,' she said, 'which admittedly does pay very well. You could set up a clinic and specialise in injuries, or women's problems, or caring for children, or anything. Or you could join an existing clinic. You could go anywhere in the world – I suppose, really, you don't have to finish your training with Sir Scipius. You might attach yourself to the Imperial Army, or a private military force – like Sir Karnos has with your Lord Krull.'

'He's not *my* Lord Krull,' Ishtaer said automatically.

'Well, not after the Ball he isn't, at any rate.' Madam Julia paused. 'Or you could stay here, with me. The pay isn't spectacular, but you get free room and board, and we can work shifts around your training.'

'I'd like that,' Ishtaer said, and Madam Julia squeezed her hand before changing the subject to a boil that needed lancing.

She left the sickbay that afternoon to find Eirenn sitting under a big tree in the main courtyard, teaching Brutus tricks. 'He'll sit and lie down, and he's pretty good at bringing back a stick if you throw it. But his number one talent is growling menacingly at anyone who says anything remotely unpleasant to me. He's ace at that.'

'Glad to hear it.' Ishtaer scratched Brutus's head and he leaned against her, large and solid and comforting.

'Listen,' Eirenn said, and there was something in his voice that made her pay attention. 'A letter came to the gate for you this morning.'

'A letter? But – I don't know anyone,' Ishtaer said. 'Except for you and Kael and he's, that is, I don't expect he'll be writing to me. Besides, I can't read.'

'No, which is why this one came with a note attached asking me to read it to you.' He hesitated. 'It's from Krull.'

Ishtaer sat down hard on the bench beside Eirenn, feeling hot and cold sweat prickle over her. 'I don't want to hear it.'

'And yet I think you will.'

'You've already read it?'

'Uh.' She felt him shift uncomfortably, 'I – er, yes. Well, he said I could!'

Ishtaer ran her hand through her short hair and rocked her head back against the tree. What could Kael possibly have to say to her? He was probably so disgusted by what she'd shown him that he'd never come near her again. This was probably a note to say he was withdrawing his sponsorship of her, and that she'd have to get by on what the Academy paid her to work in the sickbay.

She sighed. 'All right, then. Tell me.'

Paper crackled as he shook out the letter. He cleared his throat. And then he said, *'I'm sorry.'*

Ishtaer blinked.

'I made some assumptions about you and your past that were thoughtless and unfair. I only wanted to provoke a response in you that would get you fighting for yourself, which you unarguably did, just not in the way I expected. I'm sorry that those things ever happened to you, and I'm sorry I provoked you into showing them to me. I can't imagine how painful they are to recall. That is – I can, because I lived through them all, condensed into a few minutes, and I think they'll give me nightmares for the rest of my life. I'm sorry for the way I treated you. You deserved better. To be honest, I'm amazed you have the strength to carry on as normally as you do. So, I'm sorry. I really am.'

Eirenn fell silent, and Ishtaer realised she'd been holding her breath. She let it out in a rush.

'Well,' she said, and ran out after that.

'I know. I didn't think he was capable of apologising like that. Must've been something awful you showed him,' Eirenn said.

'Must have,' Ishtaer said briskly. 'Right. Come on, Brutus, time to get you fed.'

Brutus bounded up, but Eirenn said, 'Wait, there's more.'

'I'm not sure I can take more.'

'It's not more apologies. It's – look, just listen.'

Reluctantly, she settled back down again.

'I don't know how far this will go to make things up to you, but I've been trying to find out who you are and where you came from. I've asked Eirenn to do some research for me and sent a Viator to the Saranos, and what I've found simply can't be a bunch of coincidences.'

Ishtaer sat in the spring sunshine, her dog at her feet, and listened to Eirenn tell her the story of a woman on a secret mission, a child born in a storm and a father who never stopped searching.

'If only you still had the crystal necklace your mother gave you, we'd know without doubt, but I guess I know where that ended up. Maybe one day we could hire an Aqualis to search for it. But I remember your father; he treated me a few times. Thanks to him I still have the use of my right knee. He had warm olive skin and pale blue eyes, and dark hair that took the sun. And he was tall, taller than me. He was quiet, he was kind, he was clever. And he never stopped searching for you or your mother. He never gave up. Right up until his death he kept looking for you. Your father loved you even when he'd never met you.'

Her hand clenched in the thick fur at the back of Brutus's neck. Her eyes prickled.

'He died seven years ago. I think he'd have been proud of you. I'm sure his brother will be. I didn't know whether I should contact him on your behalf or not, but I decided not. I'll let you decide. His name is Citizen Garados Mallus, and he is a well-respected and successful merchant in Liman, on the Draxan coast. I believe he's married with a child around your age. His mother died a number of years ago, but she was named Ishtaer. You're named for your grandmother.

'With respect to your mother's family, you can find out all you want about them, but I'm not sure you'll ever want to go near them. Your mother was the second daughter of Citizen

Aculio Sarius, a family with a long history of being Chosen and an even longer history of being cold-hearted bastards. They used to trade in slaves and vociferously opposed the abolition of slavery. I think Sarius is dead now, and good riddance. The whole family cut your mother dead when she married your father. They're friends with the Gloriuses and their like. I wouldn't recommend you have anything to do with them, but it's up to you.

'*The Emperor has contracted me to sort out the mess in Palavio, so I'll be back in town when I'm done, but don't worry, I won't bother you. And I won't tell anyone what I saw. You have a family now, kid. And you have status, higher than nearly every other female in the Empire. You're a Citizen now. You can own property and vote and you don't even have to get married to do it. Well done, and good luck. Kael.*'

Eirenn folded the letter back up, and Ishtaer stared at the blackness behind her eyes. She didn't realise there were tears on her face until Brutus licked them off.

She cleared her throat and said, 'What mess in Palavio?'

Eirenn sounded surprised. 'Uh, tribal skirmishes, I think. Been going on a while. They're the riverlands out east.'

'Oh.'

'You want to talk about anything in that letter?'

'No.' *I have a family.*

'You want to get something to eat?'

'No.' *Will they like me? Will they accept me?*

'You want me to leave you alone so you can think about this?'

'Yes, please.' *Will I like them?*

'All right.' He got up to leave.

'And, Eirenn?'

'Yes?'

'Thanks.'

*   *   *

150

Palavio was a gods-forsaken swamp delta that no one in their right mind would ever want to live in. Unfortunately for Kael, the residents weren't in their right minds and constantly squabbled over who owned which bit of bog. Like Krulland, it was an Ilani protectorate. Unlike Krulland, it had no less than seventeen people claiming to be the rightful prince. All of them had armed forces, ranging from armies to militia to a few blokes waving pitch forks. All of them were at each others' teeth.

Kael stamped his feet. They squelched.

'You know,' he said, 'there are people in the Empire who reckon being a warlord is all romance and excitement.'

'The same people who've never heard of trench foot,' Karnos said.

'Or bog gators who can have your hand off before you've even seen them,' Verak added.

Kael gazed at the mud-coloured shrubs, mud-coloured sky and mud-coloured water that passed for scenery in Palavio. 'Why the hell would anyone want to be prince of this place?'

By dint of bribery, they'd added some local soldiers to the horde. This meant they were less likely to find their camp sinking into the mud, but Kael was never quite sure he could trust these small rivermen not to lead them to a patch of quicksand and let them drown. Or whatever the hell you did in quicksand.

'I swiving hate this place,' he muttered.

'You said that about the New Lands,' Verak reminded him, and Kael's arms wrapped around his body in an involuntary reaction. He shuddered.

Verak and Karnos exchanged glances.

'You sure you're all right?'

'Fine.'

Verak touched his shoulder, and Kael flinched away.

'Yeah, you look fine.'

'I don't want to talk about it.'

Karnos said, 'That girl in the tavern at that last place we stopped. She was all over you. Why didn't you take her up on her offer?'

—the hands, the filthy invading bodies, the laughter, the hunger, the pain, the red silk dress, the devil promising he'd make it good for me—

'Not my type,' Kael muttered through clenched teeth.

'Not your type,' Karnos spluttered. 'She was gorgeous!'

'Anything with a pulse is usually your type,' Verak added.

'Not this time, all right? Gods.' Kael turned and strode back to his tent.

'What did Ishtaer do to you?' Verak called after him.

Kael willed himself not to shudder. He failed.

'Nothing that wasn't done to her,' he said.

'Then there's the symbol for a Seer,' Sir Flavius said. 'Many like to choose an eye or a variation thereof. Lady Celsa Luccia Aquilinia has an eye peeking out from behind a veil, combining the symbols of a Viator and Aspicio—'

'Sir Flavius,' Ishtaer interrupted, and paused to marvel at herself for doing so. 'What do Viators do?'

'Viatori,' he corrected. 'The correct plural is Viatori.'

'In High Ilani,' Ishtaer said, 'but what about Common? I'm a Medicus, but everyone says Healer, and an Aspicio, but everyone says Seer, but with the Viatori …?'

Sir Flavius cleared his throat. 'Might I ask your interest?'

Annoyance rose up in her. 'I've spent all morning learning the correct way to describe a coat of arms I can't even see, and learning the history of the Book of Names, and every time I say someone's full name I get things in the wrong order—'

'If you're descended from a Chosen, his or her family name comes after yours if you're male and before if you're female. It's very simple.'

'Right, so if I'm learning all this stuff, why not something as simple as what the Viatori do?'

Sir Flavius was silent for a moment. Ishtaer wondered if she'd gone too far, but found herself curiously unafraid. She still had no idea what she'd really done to Kael at the Imperial Ball, but it felt to her as if she'd passed on some of her fear, her helplessness, the hideous heavy sensation of worthlessness. She felt lighter. Stronger. Much less afraid.

'The most literal translation is *messenger*,' Sir Flavius said eventually, and Ishtaer recalled Kael telling her to hire a Viator if she needed to contact him urgently. 'Every Viator has a different skill set, much like every Seer having different powers, or every Healer having a different speciality. But most possess an ability to move extremely fast. We're occasionally known as Runners. But stealth and silence play a big part. We're good at hiding in the shadows, and listening. We can retain a huge amount of information. During the Third Battle of the Saranos, one Viator went behind enemy lines, memorised troop information about every single unit and relayed it not just to the general but all his colonels, majors and captains, word for word. The Saraneans were convinced the gods were against them as our victory was so complete.'

Ishtaer digested this. Was that what her mother had been doing in the Saranos? But ... no. The war hadn't even fully broken out until after Ishtaer had left the islands, a full fifteen years later. Eirenn had told her how the islanders had cut themselves off from the Empire, had rejected Imperial rule and eventually started blockading ports and sinking ships.

Kael had been one of the Warriors fighting on behalf of the Empire. If only he'd come a day earlier, or found her ship, or ...

She shook herself. Dwelling in the past would do nobody any good.

'I remember your mother,' Sir Flavius said quietly. 'That's

why you're asking, isn't it? She was a Viator, and a very good one. When Saria Secunda was sent on a mission, you got the results you wanted, and fast.'

'Except her last one,' Ishtaer said.

'Yes. Intelligence-gathering. Deep undercover.' He paused again. 'Believe me when I say nobody knew she was expecting you. Not even your father. It's my belief she kept it quiet so she could continue her mission. The intelligence we received was extremely useful ...'

'Worth losing her for?' Ishtaer asked, her voice trembling a bit.

Sir Flavius merely said, 'She knew the risks.'

Ishtaer got up and walked out before she did something she'd regret.

Theoretically, she outranked the vast majority of Chosen, who in turn outranked any other member of the Citizenry, who in their own turn outranked the vast number of freeborn and plebeian residents of the Empire. Theoretically. But she still didn't expect that attacking Sir Flavius for letting her mother die was a particularly good idea.

Brutus headbutted her hip as she walked. Was it simply the confidence of having a large, potentially lethal dog by her side that had changed things? Or had that exchange with Kael actually done something to her?

She heard Marcus Glorius approach, and tensed, but he just walked on by.

Sleep didn't come easily to Ishtaer that night, her head full of what-ifs and if-onlys. The parents she never knew tried to take nebulous form in her mind. A dark-haired woman, pale and lovely, her features indistinct, fading into blackness no matter how fast Ishtaer ran to keep up with her. Snatches of a children's song floated through her mind ... *run run run, as fast as you can, you can't catch me, I'm the invisible man ...* and a wobbly, distorted image of a young girl with dark hair and skin and startling, unnerving blue eyes. The same eyes that looked out from her father's face, strained and unhappy, calling, 'Ishtaer, Ishtaer!'

She sat up abruptly on the cold floor, the images vanishing into blackness. Brutus grumbled as she stretched past him for the beaker of water on the nightstand, and drank. They weren't dreams, weren't visions, just miserable imaginings from an orphan child.

'When I was a child,' she told Brutus, 'every kid in the workhouse would imagine who their real parents were. Everyone knew we were the unwanted kids of convicts and whores and runaways, but it never stopped us wishing, believing secretly, that our real parents were lords and ladies, that we'd been stolen away and that our real parents were searching for us.'

Brutus licked her face. He didn't seem to care a fig who his real parents were.

'And I always knew it was a fantasy. I never thought they would be searching for me, or I figured that if they were they would be as potless as everyone else I knew.'

Brutus thumped his tail.

'Not that it does me, and I use this term in its fullest sense, the blindest bit of good.'

She lay back down, determined not to think about it, yet sure she *would* every time her new name was mentioned. Mallia Saria Ishtaer ex Saraneus Medicus Militis Aspicio prior Inservio. *Former slave.* That name told her whole life, if anyone cared to listen to the end.

She closed her eyes, and this time when the visions returned, she knew they weren't just dreams.

Kael looked up at the high walls of the stockade and nodded grimly. He was fighting a disparate bunch of people who leapt out of nowhere, attacked either Kael or each other or both, and then disappeared again. After a disastrous few days, he'd gathered together his brightest men and the least insane of the local leaders, and hashed out a plan.

The insurgents needed food, weapons and recruits. They could only do that if the local populace was on their side. To this end, Kael had developed a policy of being open and honest with the locals: he rode into town – or more often, given these damn marshes, rowed into town – and paid over the odds for whatever he needed. He'd offered employment to the populace, protection from their enemies, and plentiful food for those who were running out, which was most of them.

In two months, he'd got maybe half of them on side. The Emperor's bigwigs were doing their diplomatic thing with the locals, working out who was going to run the place when they'd all stopped fighting each other, but Kael was concentrating mostly on keeping the peace.

The stockade contained the fighters he and his men had rounded up. He'd planted a few of his own lads in there to identify the ringleaders and see what, if anything, they wanted. In Kael's experience quite a few of them were just fighting because they liked fighting.

He swiped the sweat from his brow and pushed back into his own tent, where Verak was marking things off on a map. 'Reckon the Carvelli are the next ones we should target,' he said.

Kael looked the map over. Carvelli territory occupied a significant fork of the river delta. They were a nomadic tribe, their camp consisting of a small flotilla of ragged boats and tents pitched on whatever solid ground they could find. 'Agreed. We get past that, we've got access to a huge chunk of the country.'

'And we can control who escapes out to sea.'

Kael glanced out through the tent flap at the sun, which

was sinking in the sky but not taking much of the heat with it. He longed for the cool, fresh air of Krulland. 'Midnight raid sound good to you?'

'Whatever happened to "open and honest"?'

'We can be open and honest once we've captured the bastards who want to turn us into gator feed.'

'Fair point.' Verak slid his sword into its scabbard. 'Midnight raid it is, then.'

Their boats moved almost soundlessly through the dark, swampy water. Kael was an excellent sailor, but this murky bayou was alien territory to him. They had no lamps to light the way and give away their position. In the dark, everything looked like a threat. Skeletal tree roots surged out of the thick water, moonlight glinting on rocks and logs that might well be insurgents or gators. The air was thick with heat and insects, and Kael was glad he'd left his heavy mail back at camp. Getting a mosquito stuck under that didn't bear thinking about.

'Swiving hate this place,' he muttered, taking a two-handed grip on his sword.

'I'm going to start counting the number of times you say that,' Verak muttered back.

Kael opened his mouth to tell Verak he'd be running out of fingers and toes pretty soon, when the oar in front of him slithered loosely down into the water. *What the hell?* He reached for the oarsman, who flopped limply off his bench, a small dart in his neck.

Kael had his bow in his hand before he'd even formulated the words to tell Verak they were under attack. He was on his feet, scanning the indistinct shore.

'They've seen us,' he said, and Verak started hissing orders as Kael strained to see movement among the trees. He slid a fire-blackened arrow from the quiver on his back.

There! The tiniest flash of moonlight on the metal tip of a dart, dead ahead. Kael raised his bow.

He never fired a shot. Something hit the back of his neck, and the black swampy water rose up to swallow him.

Chapter Thirteen

Ishtaer woke, gasping, and was on her feet before she knew what she was doing. Her hands moved automatically, dressing in her training gear, rolling a spare tunic, breeches and dress into a ball and pressing them into a satchel. Despite the incipient warmth of the season, boots went onto her feet and a cloak around her shoulders. The satchel went over one shoulder, across her body. Her medical bag went on the other shoulder. Brutus's lead slipped around her wrist.

She was halfway out the door when it occurred to her to stop and check with herself that she wasn't going mad.

But she'd seen Kael in the swamp, seen him fall into the dark water where monsters lurked, seen him hauled out not by his men but by strangers painted green and brown. She'd seen them haul his unconscious body along the rough ground, drag him cheering into a raggedy camp of tents and boats lashed together, hoist him up by his bound wrists to a tree hanging over the mangrove swamp where his blood dripped down to beasts with huge, snapping jaws. She'd seen them laugh and throw stones at him, whip him, drain him of strength and blood and life.

She'd seen them sort through a pile of bodies, carve a message into the torso of one of them, then dump it in a boat and watch it drift away downriver.

And she'd heard a voice, an insistent voice as deep inside her as her own heartbeat, urging her to go after him.

He will die without you. He will die.

'I don't know what to do,' she whispered to her midnight bedroom.

I will show you, said the voice, and Ishtaer saw herself doing it.

She closed her door and went to wake Eirenn.

'Just so I'm clear,' Eirenn said as the sleek mail ship slid into port at Terafin, the last stable town before the badlands of Palavio began. 'We hire a small boat, row downriver to the Carvelli camp, shoot, stab or otherwise disable anyone who gets in our way, cut down Krull from this tree above the swamp monsters, and then continue on our merry way through enemy territory until we reach Krull's camp?'

'That's the plan,' Ishtaer said, drawing the hood of her cloak closer around her face.

'Just checking.'

He handed Ishtaer ashore and went to see about hiring a row boat. When he returned, she handed him a heavy sack.

'What's this?' He peered inside. 'Chain mail? Ishtaer, the air is like soup, we'll dehydrate in seconds. Not to mention what'll happen if we go overboard wearing forty pounds of metal. You might be curious what the bottom of a swamp is like, but I'd rather not know.'

'They fire poison darts,' Ishtaer said. 'You leave any bit of skin exposed and you'll end up the same as Kael. If you're lucky.'

'Chain mail it is,' Eirenn said.

Something buzzed near his head. Kael figured this was an improvement over what snapped by his feet. He knew there was a proper name for it, but all he could think of was dragon. A dragon who swum and grinned its jagged teeth at him and opened its mouth about thirty feet wide, snapping shut, taunting him.

A snake slithered over Kael's hand, and he'd have flinched if his fingers had been capable of movement. The creature twined around his arm and slid its head out into the soupy air, curling back to hiss at him. It had red and yellow stripes and a glob of green poison hanging off the edge of its forked tongue.

The snake opened its mouth wide enough to engulf Kael's whole head. 'My dragon friend isss going to eat you,' it hissed at him. 'Toesss then feetsss then legsss. Piggy by piggy.'

He was just lucid enough to think he might be hallucinating.

Ishtaer didn't need to see the swamplands to know how creepy they were. She'd seen it all in her vision anyway. The huge eerie trees with their roots half out of water, the strands of hanging moss, the ripple and glide of a huge beast under the water. The air was foetid and thick with insects that batted constantly against the boat, her face and her gloves. She thought one or two might have got under the mail shirt she wore. She itched abominably.

But Ishtaer was good at ignoring discomfort.

'You need to keep going,' she murmured to Eirenn, reaching down to pet Brutus. She'd rubbed salve into his coat to try and stop the worst of the insect attacks, but he still gave a miserable whine. 'Past the camp, until you get to Kael.'

'Uh, won't the banks be watched?' Eirenn asked. 'Guarded?'

'Not after I'm done on shore, they won't.'

'Those, er, lizard things. Croco … gators?'

'What's a crocogator?'

'Something with really big jaws attracted to blood.'

'Then I won't shed any.'

Calm descended on her.

Eirenn slid the boat to the bank, and Ishtaer leapt out. Brutus made to come after her, but she pushed him back. 'No, boy. Stay.' As much as a large dog might be handy for intimidating people, she needed not to have anyone to worry about.

'Are you sure you know what you're doing?' Eirenn asked.

She nodded, unsheathing the longsword from her right hip and the gladius from her left. 'I've seen it all. I know where to go and who will be waiting there and what I have to do. Go. I'll see you at the tree.'

'What tree?' Eirenn hissed as she began to run, cursing the heaviness and noise of the chain mail.

'You'll see it.'

And she ran.

The first part would be easy. *Run until you reach the path, turn right, there are three guards on the way.*

Her hand moved of its own accord, taking out the first man with the hilt of her longsword. He made no sound as he fell.

The second man heard her coming, but she whirled the sword and his blood spattered her face.

The third man got in a blow that glanced off her arm. Her gladius went through his belly.

Take out the first hut you come to. She paused very quickly to strike a match and touch it to a small clay pot drawn carefully from her pocket, then threw it at the hut before running as fast as she could past it.

The *whumph* of the fire could be heard all over the settlement. Ishtaer felt the sudden heat against her back, and continued running.

They'll run to the fire. Kill anyone who stops you.

At first she darted through the crowd, but at the first shout she brought her swords up and ... danced.

The longsword had the greater reach but the gladius had more power to stab. Her right arm whirled in a graceful arc, she stepped and ducked and crouched and thrust the gladius back, scything the longsword above her head. Rolling back to her feet she twirled both swords and stabbed one forward, one back.

The fire heated her right side.

Kael is suspended from a tree at the end of a floating dock. Destroy it as you go.

Ishtaer ran, planting her foot on a fallen man, a dog, a horse, flying through the air, over people's heads, hacking at any hand that tried to stop her. She leapt onto the dock, shoving her swords back in their sheaths. She raced along the slimy wood and threw an unlit clay pot behind her.

Eirenn will be waiting. He will fire two shots.

'Now!' she screamed, and leapt off the end of the jetty.

Kael's body fell heavily into her arms as Eirenn's first arrow severed the rope holding him. Ishtaer's foot landed on something which bobbed in the water. Jaws snapped at her.

She raced over the huge lizards, dancing from one to the next as she had with the tribesmen. Kael's body was heavy, a dead weight in her arms, making her ungainly. Her muscles burned.

Behind her, heat blossomed as Eirenn's second arrow hit the dock. This one was on fire, and the clay pot exploded.

She could almost see the flames.

'Come on!' Eirenn yelled, and she made one last push, her boot landing on wood. The small boat rocked alarmingly as she collapsed in a heap with Kael's body under her, covering it as best she could.

'Go, go,' she gasped, and Eirenn put his Militis muscles to good use, whirling the boat away from the burning Carvelli as fast as he could.

The snake had stopped talking to him, but since the village had exploded into flames and spewed forth Ishtaer, swords whirling, armour gleaming, Kael figured he was still hallucinating.

In his hallucination Ishtaer tore him from his bonds, threw him into a boat, and rowed away faster than the wind. She also tore away his clothes while her wolf watched, his tail thumping.

Darkness descended for a while, hot and thick, and next time he opened his eyes his body screamed with pain. His arms had been torn from their sockets, his foot was ripped to shreds, his flesh on fire and crawling from his body.

'He's coming round,' said a half familiar voice. Kael tried to focus on a figure with pale skin and dark eyes. He wore full mail and appeared to be rowing a boat. He also had an identical twin beside him doing exactly the same.

Both of them said, 'You need to put him back under again, Ish.'

'I can't,' said a voice right by his ear. He tried to turn and see but strong, delicate hands kept him from moving. 'It's all I can do to keep him breathing. The venom's in his blood. Let me concentrate.'

His blood, which had been pumping as sluggishly as the river, suddenly roared with pain. Kael screamed, and clutched willingly at the blackness as it reached out to him again.

When he woke again the pain in his body had been downgraded to merely agonising, and he could just about focus through the pre-dawn gloom on Eirenn, calmly rowing, apparently without an identical twin.

'Do us a favour, and don't scream this time,' he said. 'I've hardly any arrows left if anyone else comes after us.'

Kael blinked. He lay back in a small boat, making its way at a leisurely pace through brown water, flanked by slimy trees dripping moss, and attended by swarms of insects. He didn't seem to be wearing much, but then he hadn't since he fell out of the boat.

'Oh, and also keep your hands inside the boat. There's a crocogator been following us the last half hour or so.'

'Croco …?' Kael croaked.

'I don't know what it is, and I'm not about to find out.'

Eirenn pulled on the oars. At his feet lay Ishtaer's wolf, looking thoroughly miserable.

'Swiving hate this place,' Kael groaned.

'You and me both. Now shush, Ishtaer needs to concentrate.'

'Ishtaer?'

'Sure. You might remember her. Pretty girl, Seer's mark on her face, knocked you on your arse last time you saw her. Just saved your life and is continuing to patch you up even as we speak.'

Belatedly, Kael noticed that he was being propped up by a woman, whose hands rested on his chest. Not large hands, but long-fingered, calloused and capable-looking. Her fingers shifted delicately against his skin, but she said nothing.

'How did ... What happened?'

Eirenn grinned at him. 'You'd never believe me if I told you.'

Kael drifted off to sleep again, waking once or twice more as the heavy night turned into a scorching morning. The brackish river gave way to stronger, clearer water, and despite being visibly exhausted, Eirenn continued to row. The banks widened, the trees grew taller and greener, and Kael thought it was beginning to look familiar.

The wolf began to bark, which was interesting since Kael didn't think wolves could bark. Almost too tired to move, he turned his head and saw a man on the bank, pointing an arrow at them.

'How many more arrows've you got?' he asked Eirenn raggedly.

'Four, but I'm not going to shoot him.' The boy started steering the boat towards the shore.

'What? But he's aiming at us ...'

'But not actually firing, eejit. I reckon ... yep, see that insignia? He's one of yours. Thought we ought to be coming up on your camp soon. Hey,' Eirenn yelled to the archer. 'Can you give us a hand? A stretcher or maybe two.'

The man peered at the boat, and as they got closer Kael realised he was familiar. He returned the archer's salute somewhat shakily, then realised what Eirenn had just said.

'Two stretchers?'

Eirenn looked grim. 'Not a word out of Ishtaer for a few hours.' He hauled on the oars. 'She'd better just be asleep.'

Alarmed, Kael felt for her pulse. He hadn't registered whether or not she was breathing behind him.

Her blood thudded dully in her veins. He forced himself to turn, to kneel before her. Her face was white, her lips tinged blue. Her hands fell limply to her sides, her head lolling.

'Shit,' Eirenn said. 'I warned her. I bloody warned her. Is it crystal-debt?'

Kael nodded. He was so tired he could barely speak and there wasn't an inch of him that didn't hurt. He picked up Ishtaer's hand and pressed it over his heart.

'I'm sorry,' he said.

Chapter Fourteen

She was back in the cell, lined with ice and drifts of snow, her belly cramping with hunger, too weak to move. Soon the guards would come, poke at her with their boots or their spears, check if she was dead yet, and leave. She was meant to die here, a slow race between freezing and starving to death.

The warmth began in her heart, spreading out through her body. She was made of lead, of ice, immovable and cold. Blood too cold to move couldn't push through her veins, and yet, and yet ...

Heat fluttered through her. Arms held her. Warmth cocooned her. Ishtaer struggled feebly.

'Shh, love. I'm helping you. You're in crystal-debt. I'm helping you.'

The Warlord's voice. Kael. He smelled of blood and sweat and old wounds, but under that he smelled of Kael, and his skin was warm against her face.

She stirred, and he held her against his body, murmuring to her if she were a sick child, stroking her back, cradling her head on his shoulder. Pain thrummed through him.

'You're hurt,' she croaked.

'Nothing that won't heal. Go back to sleep. You need rest.'

She wasn't afraid of him. A man held her close in his bed and she wasn't afraid.

He took nothing from her. He asked for nothing but for her to rest. He gave nothing but warmth and comfort.

Ishtaer fell into sleep, and dreamed of nothing.

The sun was falling in the sky and the air began to cool to a manageable temperature. Kael still needed to shade his eyes from the light.

Once, when he was a boy, he'd fallen through some thin ice and nearly drowned trying to break his way back out. The heavy, numb sense of defeat that had weighed him down, right before the final punch that broke the ice, was exactly how he felt now.

He stumbled only once on his way through the camp. If anyone noticed, they pretended not to. The number of men sitting around outside their tents, drinking and cooking and talking, seemed a lot smaller than he was used to.

'Those bastards and their darts,' Verak had groaned when Kael mentioned this yesterday. 'Half the horde overboard, a damned feast for those scaly lizards in the water.'

Kael shuddered at the very thought of said lizards. Alligator, crocodile, dragon – he didn't know what they were and didn't want to. His foot still throbbed. He'd been lucky to be recognised by the enemy and pulled out of the water.

Well, lucky was a relative term.

He found Eirenn sitting at a cookfire, stirring a pot and telling tales.

'... and I thought she was completely mad, right? I mean, all right, she's a Seer, but her powers are mostly untested and I've absolutely no idea whether this vision she's had is just a dream or not, but you know, what can I do? Can't let her go off on her own with her dog.'

'Dog?' said one of the men at the fire. He was about twice Eirenn's size, bearded and scarred and battle-hardy. In this, he was typical of most of Kael's horde. He made Eirenn look like a little boy. 'That swiving thing's a wolf if ever I saw one.'

'But what would a wolf be doing in the middle of a city?' asked Eirenn with wide-eyed innocence. The men laughed. 'So anyway. She waits until we're actually in the boat, on that filthy pestilence of a river, before she tells me the plan. Calm as you like. "You just row past the settlement and find where they've got His Lordship, and when you see me fire two arrows."'

'Just fire them? At anything?'

'Oh no. One at the rope above yer man's head, and mind it goes clean through because she hasn't the time to cut him down, and the other she wants me to set alight and fire at what she's going to throw at the deck.'

'What did she throw?'

'Devil fire,' Kael said, emerging from the gloom and enjoying the startled looks on their faces. Eirenn just rolled his eyes. 'At a guess,' he added. 'The whole camp burned. You don't get that from just ordinary fire arrows. Where the hell did she get it?'

'Oh, you can buy anything at the docks,' Eirenn said, stirring his pot, 'especially if you're Thrice-Marked, accompanied by a wolf and have recently knocked Krull the Warlord on his arse.'

The assembled men went very still.

'I'm glad to see she's learning,' Kael said, and his men relaxed. He limped towards the nearest empty seat, which had all the comfort of a log. Mostly because it was a log.

'How's she doing?' Eirenn asked, his voice entirely different.

'Resting. Another day and she'll be out of the woods.'

Eirenn's gaze flew to him. 'But – she was in debt. It takes weeks, doesn't it?'

'Not this time.' Kael met the younger man's gaze and held it. Eirenn opened his mouth, then shook his head and looked back at his stew.

'Lads,' Kael said, 'bugger off, would you?'

The half-dozen or so men glanced at each other, then got up and went without a word.

'You've got them trained like dogs,' Eirenn said.

'I take that as a compliment. What're you cooking?'

'It's a stew of these shellfish things and some pork and—'

'Is it ready?'

Eirenn glanced down at him, and Kael stopped trying to hide his fatigue. He slid to the ground and leaned back against the log, wondering if he'd ever been this tired.

'Here,' Eirenn pressed a clay bowl into his hand and set down a piece of wood with some bread on it. 'I'm exhausted myself, and I didn't get strung up to be eaten by crocogators.'

Kael tore off a hunk of bread as Eirenn sat down beside him with his own bowl. 'That's not what they're really called, is it?'

'No clue,' the boy said cheerfully. 'Didn't feel like sticking around to ask. How's the foot?'

'It hurts,' Kael said, 'exactly as much as you'd imagine a foot which has been chewed by a crocogator would hurt.'

Eirenn made a face.

'She got most of the skin to grow back, though. Impressive, I thought. Never seen that before. Then again, I've never seen a flayed foot before—'

'Eirenn, shut up.'

'Shutting up now.'

They ate in silence for a while, and when Eirenn finished his bowl he refilled Kael's without asking.

'What's your name, kid?' Kael asked when Eirenn sat back down again.

Eirenn gave him a sidelong glance that questioned whether Ishtaer had indeed got all the snake venom out of Kael's body.

'I'm asking you, Eirenn Fillian, to give me your name.'

Clearly wondering what the hell Kael was getting at, the boy said, 'Eirenn Fillian Militis.'

'Tyro—'

'Tyro Eirenn Fillian Militis.'

'Ex – where're you from?'

'Glengower. Tyro Eirenn Fillian ex Glengower Militis.' Eirenn paused. 'Am I in trouble?'

'No. Do you know my name? All of it?'

Eirenn cleared his throat. 'Lord Kaelnar Vapensigsson ex Krullus Militis Viscus Saraneus Drax.'

'Right. The name tells you something, lad. Yours tells me you ain't left the Academy yet, that you come from the arse end of nowhere, that your parents were nobodies—'

'Thanks,' Eirenn said.

'—but you're still Chosen. And mine? Bit by bit.'

'Lord means you're Twice-Marked. Or twice-graduated, I mean,' he amended before Kael could correct him. 'Vapensigsson is your father's name, I think. He wasn't Chosen, or that name would be in the Book of Names. Neither was your mother since you don't have her name.'

'Very good. Next?'

'Right, ex Krullus is fairly obvious, and Militis, and … well, to be honest I've never been sure what the Viscus bit means. The last two I know, they're victory titles. You led battles in the Saranos and Draxos.'

'Spot on. See what I mean about it telling you a lot? Except for the Viscus bit.' Kael set down his bowl and carefully, painfully, pulled off his shirt. Eirenn's face carefully gave nothing away, which was clever of him since Kael knew he was still covered with nasty red insect bites, many of which had swollen to blisters, and with the marks of a whip Ishtaer hadn't fully healed.

He ignored them. 'Here,' he said, gesturing to the bold black lines covering his left arm and chest. 'How far up does your mark go?'

Eirenn motioned to his upper arm.

'You probably see a lot of these marks. Ever seen one cover the chest?'

Eirenn shook his head.

'That's because it's not just Militis. Took endless hours of examinations and conversations with Truthtellers and book after book of history, but they eventually found what it means. Viscus, also sometimes called Animus.'

He saw Eirenn working it out. 'Something to do with life? Life force?'

'Exactly that.' Kael pulled his shirt back on, just in case those little bastards came back for another nibble. It hurt, everything hurt, his shoulders a bit worse than the rest of him. He'd been strung up by his wrists for several days. According to Verak, both his shoulders had been dislocated, painful enough without the snake venom and the crocogator bites and the dehydration and the insects ... No wonder Ishtaer had put herself into crystal-debt. She'd pretty much brought him back from the dead.

'They told me what it could do, but I've never used it before. Never had to. Never met anyone foolish enough to put themselves into debt. But that's what it does, lad. Restores life force to a Chosen who's pushed too far. Not useful on a daily basis, but the sole reason Ishtaer isn't spending the rest of her life in an invalid bed.'

Eirenn swallowed. 'Was it that bad?'

Kael took in a deep breath and let it out. 'It was worse.'

She was cold, and she was tired. But Ishtaer had been those things before, and survived. She lay in a bed that was about as comfortable as a bed in a military camp was ever going to get, swaddled in blankets, her dog snuggled up by her side. Someone held her hand. She thought it was probably Kael.

He was talking quietly to someone, and the more she concentrated the more she could make out their conversation.

'... burn the swiving lot of them as far as I'm concerned.'

'That'll foster goodwill.' Verak's voice, dry and warm.

'They hung me up to be eaten by crocoga – to be eaten alive. I don't give a rat's arse for goodwill.'

'We're supposed to be gaining the trust of the populace.'

'Fuck the populace.'

A pause, then Verak said quietly, 'Is this because of Karnos?'

Karnos, the Healer? Ishtaer listened hard.

'Find me one of their bodies,' Kael said, and she was astonished to hear – no. It couldn't be. There weren't ... tears in his voice?

'We are not doing the same.'

'Find me one of their bodies and carve a swiving ransom demand on it, see how they like it. Nobody does that to my men.'

'Kael—'

'Burn them. Feed them to the gators. I don't care. Get the bastard lot of them out of my sight. And pack up camp. We're leaving tomorrow. If there's anyone else between here and Terafin who wants to fight they can swiving well fight.'

'We're down on men—'

'But high on captives. Give 'em a sword or a noose. Their choice. And get the ringleader of the Carvelli. Whoever's highest up. Bring me his head. I want it for a banner.'

Verak let out a harsh breath, but he didn't argue. He just left, the tent flap swishing shut behind him.

'And you,' Kael said, squeezing her hand, emotion high in his voice, 'don't you pretend you didn't hear that.'

Ishtaer turned her head towards him, which was an effort. 'How many were left alive?'

'Not many. You burned a lot. River hemmed them in on two sides. Some of them came north—'

'I know. They kept shooting at us.'

'Good job your friend Eirenn is a good archer. Verak says there were dozens of half eaten corpses on the riverbank, all with Academy arrows sticking out of them.'

'They had those little darts. By the time they realised they wouldn't work on us, Eirenn had usually shot back. One of them got you, though. I should have brought some mail for you.'

Kael sighed. 'None of us wore it after the first day, not with all those bastard insect bites. I don't know what's worse, being eaten alive one itchy red bump at a time, or being eaten alive by whatever crocogator manages to jump high enough.'

'Well, you kept bleeding on them. It was like hanging sausages above Brutus's head.'

Brutus thumped his tail at that.

Kael said, 'Ishtaer, was that a joke?'

'I don't know. I don't think I have a sense of humour.'

'Trust me, you do.'

His hand was warm where it wrapped around hers. When she'd first woken Verak had explained, briefly, about Kael's Viscus powers, and she could feel his strength flowing quietly, steadily, into her.

She tried to pull her hand away. 'You're still recovering.'

'It's fine. It doesn't make any difference.'

'You still need more healing.'

'It's nothing that won't sort itself out. The Healers I brought with me are run off their feet, and I don't want more crystal-debt to fix.' He sighed. 'Remember when I told you I'd never take more from you than you wanted to give?'

She nodded shakily, the memory indistinct.

'I meant it. Just trust me, all right?'

Ishtaer licked her dry lips. 'What happened to Sir Karnos?'

'You don't want to know.'

'I do. It's thanks to him I can walk normally.'

Kael cleared his throat and said in a voice that was nearly normal, 'He was right behind us, waiting for casualties. Too close as it turns out. Those rotten scurvy bastards didn't care he was a Healer, they killed him anyway. Used him to send a message back to my camp.'

'Your ransom?'

'Yes.'

'What did they want?'

'For the Empire to leave and never come back.'

'I don't suppose they'll be getting that.'

'No.' He cleared his throat again. 'We've done well uniting most of the people here. Empire'll probably send in a governor after this to oversee the running of the place. Opposite of what they wanted, but an attack like that can't go unanswered.'

'Will you stay here? In Palavio? Will they need a military presence?'

'Aye, but not mine. We'll march south, meet the Imperial army. They can do the peacekeeping. I've had enough here. I'm going home.'

It was a much slower journey back to Ilanium than it had been on the way out. Ishtaer discovered that while two people could travel pretty fast by mail boat and horseback, an army convoy travelled at the pace of its slowest member. A man could march three miles in an hour, but the oxen pulling the heavy wagons carrying tents, armour and provisions barely managed ten miles in a day. Even once they'd reached the Imperial River and loaded up several huge barges, the journey was slow-going. High summer arrived in Ilanium before they did.

By this time, both Ishtaer and Kael were as well recovered as they were going to be. She knew his foot and ankle bore a few ugly scars, not least of which was that one of his toes was significantly shorter than it used to be. Kael insisted that none of this was a problem, and that he'd rather keep the scars as a reminder.

'A reminder of what?' she asked on their last evening, prodding his foreshortened toe rather harder than necessary to get some reaction out of him. But all he did was wince.

'How bloody stupid I was to discount those darts.'

She ran her fingers up the knotted scar that wound around his ankle. The flesh here was still new and tender, and although she'd applied salves and bandages to it, Kael wouldn't let her use her Gift on it any more.

They sat on the deck of the lead barge, which was where Ishtaer felt more comfortable. Some of the men rode or marched along the riverbank, but without anyone to hold her on a horse, Ishtaer had a habit of falling off, and Kael was still resting his foot.

Being below decks on a boat, any boat, still set her teeth on edge. Without asking, Kael had set up a tent for her on the deck.

'You couldn't have known about the darts.'

'I should have planned for it. How come you did?'

She shrugged and began binding his foot again. 'I saw it in a vision.'

'Maybe you should come with me whenever I plan a campaign.'

'Yes, everyone needs a blind strategist.'

'Was that another joke, Ishtaer? And when did you stop calling me *my lord*?'

'I'm sorry. My lord.' She was proud of herself for not flinching. Tomorrow they'd reach Ilanium, and Kael had warned her they'd have to meet the Emperor and report on what had happened. She had to keep pretending she wasn't afraid.

'No, you don't need to. I'd prefer you to call me Kael. After all, we're of equal rank, aren't we now?'

'Aren't we, now,' said Ishtaer.

There was a smile in Kael's voice when he said, 'You're different, you know that? Bolder. Brighter. It's like you've … I don't know …'

'Come alive,' Ishtaer said. She finished tying the bandage

and tilted her head so she'd be looking up at him from where she knelt on the deck. 'I wasn't really, before, was I? Not when you found me, and not for a long while after that.'

She took a deep breath, felt the air fill her lungs. Tasted it. Listened to the cicadas and birds and the lap of the water against the moored boat. Someone was cooking crayfish and her stomach rumbled with the happy knowledge that it would soon be full.

Kael cleared his throat. 'Did you get my letter?'

'I did. Thank you.' She chewed her lip. 'I, uh. Haven't quite got around to contacting my family yet.'

'I suppose it'll take a while to get used to having one.'

'Yes.' She faltered, unsure if she should even voice her next thought, let alone how to say it. She busied herself tidying away her medical supplies.

'What's wrong?' Kael asked, his voice gentle. She couldn't quite get used to him being this ... well, kind. The reason why he was suddenly being so nice to her squirmed in her gut. *He knows. All the things I never wanted anyone to know ... he knows.*

'How would you feel if you suddenly turned out to have a long-lost niece and she ... she was ... like me.'

Kael took a breath and let it out. The bench he sat on creaked as he shifted.

'First of all, there is no one like you.'

'Thank the gods for that.'

'I don't mean it like that. How many other people could have survived what you did?'

'That's exactly it. I don't want them to know about it. Any of it. I want to be normal. I don't want to be the ex-slave, I don't want to be the blind girl, I don't even want to be Chosen. I wish I'd just grown up with my family and done normal things and never even heard of the New Lands. And I can't ever have that. Not even if I meet my uncle and my cousin and they're lovely and friendly and nice to me, they'll always know. Just like you know.'

Her eyes stung. Kael's hand touched her chin and tilted her face upwards. His thumb brushed away a tear.

'I won't tell them,' he said.

'Not all of it,' she hiccuped, 'but the rest, the blindness and the slave thing, they'll know. Everyone knows.'

'So what? So what if everyone knows? If anyone thinks any the less of you for it, then they're not worth your attention. Ish, you rode through the night to rescue a man – who you have every right to loathe – very nearly single-handed, and succeeded. Because of you, the worst of the Palavian insurgents have been neutralised, the people have some proper respect for what the Empire can do, and they have some chance at stability. What you did was amazing, and not just because of the effects in Palavio. Because not many people could do what you did, male or female, Chosen or blind or whatever. And I'll tell you something for nothing. If you'd been that nice girl who grew up with a normal family, you'd have stayed at home and read about the grisly death of Krull the Warlord in the gossip sheets, and watched from a distance as the Palavians destroyed themselves.'

His hand was very warm against her face. 'Anyone could have done it,' she whispered.

'But you're the one who did. I think you're amazing, Ishtaer.'

'I think that snake venom addled your brain,' she sniffed, and he laughed softly and took her hand.

'Come on. Big day tomorrow. Let's get something to eat.'

Chapter Fifteen

Good news travelled fast. It certainly did, Kael thought with some satisfaction, when you hired a Viator to spread it around. The Emperor sent a yacht out to meet them, decked out in multicoloured bunting and hung with flags. The Emperor's own standard, of course, flying above all the others. And Karnos's much-despised ass and beaver, at a respectful half mast. Then Kael's own familiar black and red emblem, and Verak's golden cockerel, and—

'What's that one?' he said, peering at the yacht.

Verak squinted. 'Don't know it,' he said.

'What does it look like?' Ishtaer asked.

'Party per pall, azure, gules, and argent; a raguly—'

'In Common, Verak?' Kael said.

'Didn't you go to Sir Flavius's classes on heraldry when you were at the Academy?'

'No, I fought people and then had sex when I was at the Academy. Ishtaer, it's a shield divided into three with a yellow bar across the top. Top left third is blue, with – what're they called? Like brackets on the sides. A silver cross and a caduceus. Top right is red with three spotted cats. Bottom third is silver with what looks like an eye with wings coming out of it. In the middle is an oval with a sphinx and a couple of bears.'

'I've never seen it before,' Verak said.

'Me neither.'

Ishtaer's forehead winkled as she thought. The sun had turned her dusky skin a rich brown, brought out the highlights in her dark hair, and made her pale eyes shine. She wore breeches and shirt, pressed against her body by the light breeze. She looked beautiful.

'It looks good,' said Eirenn, sauntering up behind them. 'The details can be changed, of course, but I thought this was the best design.'

'What are you talking about?' Verak said, but as Kael glanced back at the shield he realised.

'The field is split in three,' he said. 'The caduceus is a Healer's symbol, and the eye is for a Seer. Those cats, what are they—?'

'Leopards. Big cats are often used by Warriors,' Eirenn said, 'and leopards are considered a feminine symbol.'

'The lozenge in the middle,' Verak said. 'That was Saria Secunda's. The bears are on Sarius's arms.'

'And the blue shield with the silver cross. That was Rellan Mallus's. I remember now. The thing across the top—'

'The chief,' Eirenn supplied, 'and notched like that it's embattled, to show—'

'Difficulties overcome,' Ishtaer said quietly. 'It's my shield, isn't it?'

They all stared at the fluttering banner as it drew closer.

'I wanted it to be a surprise,' Eirenn said uncertainly. 'It's not finished yet. I didn't know they were going to put it on the yacht like that.'

'The Empire is welcoming home a new hero,' Verak said.

'Heroine,' Kael said. Ishtaer's face was unreadable. 'Are you all right?'

She smiled suddenly. 'I'm fine. Thank you, Eirenn.'

The boy looked hugely relieved. 'I did send a note to Malika with one of the Viators, for her to make you something to wear. I thought if you were going to meet the Emperor you should have something new.'

'I have two perfectly nice dresses—' Ishtaer began, and Kael laughed.

'Lass, you have one frock for a Midwinter temple visit and one you wore as a Tyro at the Imperial Ball. You'll need new stuff now, for state occasions. We'll have to commission you some armour.'

'I don't need—'

'You do. Remember what I told you all those months ago?'

She was silent a moment. 'It's all a show.'

'Right. Chin up.'

'Shoulders back,' Verak added, laughing.

'Eyes right ahead. There. Quite the heroine. Now, Eirenn, where's this frock?'

They came ashore at the Imperial Dock, reserved for the Emperor and his guests, and mounted horses caparisoned in their own colours. Eirenn helped Ishtaer onto her horse, and although he seemed to have done it many times before, this was different, since she was trying to climb into a side saddle, and in a long silk dress too.

Malika had come aboard the barge with the dress, helped Ishtaer dress and styled her hair, which was considerably longer than it had been at the Imperial Ball. She wore a circlet of red, blue and white flowers on her head, a silk cloak divided into three just like her shield, and a flowing silk dress that was silver on one side and pale blue on the other.

Over it, she wore a corset of blood-red silk, open laced at the sides. On her forearms were matching laced panels. The effect was of red silk armour. Ishtaer looked like a warrior queen.

'My congratulations to your dressmaker,' Kael said as she settled herself in the saddle.

'She's very talented. Apparently she's been getting lots of commissions since the Ball.'

'Good for her.' He paused. 'You look beautiful.'

Ishtaer ducked her head uncomfortably. Eirenn, holding her horse's decorated reins, gazed up at her as worshipfully as Brutus. The dog walked at her right, wearing the same ribboned lead he'd had at the Ball.

Ahead of them, the yacht's banners had been transferred to tall poles, and there had been an unexpected tussle on the barge as to who would get to carry Ishtaer's.

'I notice no one's fighting to be my signifer,' Verak grumbled.

'You aren't a beautiful young heroine,' Kael told him. 'Everyone ready? Off we go, then.'

He had a century of his men in full armour, following behind the three horses. To his left Eirenn, wearing the white of a Tyro, led Ishtaer's horse at a steady walk, up the path taking them from the docks to the Processional Way. People lined the streets, the enamelled bas reliefs hung with bunting. There was a lot of cheering going on. Ishtaer seemed oblivious, but he saw the way her white-knuckled fingers gripped the reins.

Verak waved to the crowd, his mood festive. Kael, who'd spent most of his life convincing people he was a cold-hearted killer, kept his eyes right ahead. But when Eirenn said, 'Will you look at Gloria's face? He looks sick as a parrot,' Kael couldn't resist.

There was the Glorius family, daughters waving happily, mother smiling weakly, father and son looking like thunder.

'He is so jealous,' Eirenn laughed, waving at the girls and blowing them kisses. Marcus's scowl intensified.

'Next time your life is in danger, it'll be Marcus riding to your rescue,' Verak said.

'Not if I can help it. I might seduce one of his sisters, just for the hell of it.'

Ishtaer's lips thinned. If Kael didn't know better he might have thought she was jealous. He almost smiled at that, and then he remembered why she wouldn't be jealous, why she'd never be jealous, why she'd never be with him, and after that it wasn't hard at all to look dark and forbidding.

The roadway winding around the Turris Imperio had also

been decked with bunting. It was pretty obvious which way they were to go. The sun beat down on them, and Kael's shirt stuck to him under his armour. Sweat trickled down Verak's brow, and he knew that even though they'd never show it, his men were roasting in their armour. Ishtaer remained cool, upright, an ice queen in her blue and silver.

The flags and bunting led them to an audience chamber and an applauding court. Kael dismounted on the roadway and handed Ishtaer down from her horse. 'Take my arm,' he told her quietly. 'When we get to the throne, a very small curtsey. Understand?' She nodded. 'Eirenn, take the dog. You're on her left, half a pace behind.'

'He should be beside me,' she said. 'He rescued you too—'

'He's a Tyro, and you're a Lady, and you were the one who set the camp on fire and risked your life to heal me.'

'It's all right,' Eirenn said. 'I don't mind.'

But he did, and Kael felt unfamiliar doubt ripple through him. Nevertheless, Eirenn stuck to his half-pace behind, and Ishtaer placed her hand on Kael's left arm, and with Verak at his right they entered the audience chamber, filled with bright colours and cheering people.

As they walked down the central aisle towards the Emperor's throne, Kael had the strangest sensation of walking towards the altar in a temple with his bride beside him.

Not that Ishtaer would ever marry you, said his conscience, and he cringed away from it.

'Imperial Majesty,' Kael said, bowing his head. Beside him, Ishtaer dropped a graceful inch, inclining her head as she did. Clearly, she'd learned about more than heraldry from Sir Flavius.

'Lord Krull,' replied the Emperor. 'Lady Ishtaer. The Empire welcomes you back.'

* * *

Afterwards, Ishtaer couldn't remember much of the meeting with the Emperor. Kael told a wildly embellished version of the rescue, most of which she was pretty sure he had no recollection of at all. She'd wondered how much he would admit to, whether he'd tell the court – and therefore the whole Empire – of his own mistakes, of his near-death state. She half expected her own part to be reduced to a bit of healing, because after all, why would the great Krull the Warlord admit to needing to be rescued at all?

But by the time he was done, Lady Ishtaer, warrior queen, was part of the Krull myth. The assembled spectators applauded so loudly they sent Brutus into a barking frenzy, which in turn made everyone laugh. She was reasonably sure Eirenn was clowning around with the dog too, happier since Kael had praised his archery skills, endurance and bravery throughout the whole escapade.

They walked back out into the sunshine, and Kael said to her, 'Right then, heroine of the hour. How do you want to celebrate?'

Her back ached from standing so straight for so long. Under the corset she was sweating more than she'd let on. The combined perfumes of the court had risen in the heat to make her feel quite dizzy. All she really wanted to do was lie down somewhere cool for a while.

But she'd endured worse.

'I don't know. How do you usually celebrate?'

There was a slight pause, during which Verak cleared his throat, and Ishtaer felt her colour rise as she realised how an oversexed young lord like Kael was likely to celebrate.

'With drink,' he said smoothly. 'Expensive food and drink. Where's the poshest eating house in the city, Eirenn?'

'You're asking like I frequent posh eating houses? I hear Bibalacus is popular with the more-money-than-sense brigade.'

'Bibalacus it is, then. Lead on, lad.'

'Of course, you usually have to book well in advance, and I doubt they'll allow dogs, but ... What am I saying?'

'I'm Krull the Warlord, lad, and this is Lady Ishtaer, the ... hmm. We'll have to think of a name for you.'

'Just Ishtaer does me fine,' she said, and Kael laughed.

'As you say, Just Ishtaer.'

He was teasing her, and it felt nice. Ever since she'd scooped him out of reach of the crocogators he'd been nothing but polite and friendly to her. No suggestive comments at all. Not a single one of his men had made any either.

She wondered what he'd said to them. She wasn't sure she wanted to know.

Kael handed her back up to the horse, Eirenn took the leading reins, and the hundred men who'd followed them through the city fell in behind them.

'Er, how big is this restaurant?' she asked. 'Can it take a hundred soldiers?'

Kael laughed. 'Doubt it. Back to the boats for you, lads. Have a swim, get your lunch and then bring the *Ghost* out of dock and kit her out. We'll be sailing for home in the next few days.'

The clang of a hundred fists on a hundred breastplates answered him.

They rode in silence for a bit, and then Kael said, 'Don't suppose you want to come with us, do you?'

Ishtaer, who'd been wondering what a posh restaurant was like, blinked. 'Where?'

'Krulland.' When she did nothing but stare in stupefaction at the blackness behind her own eyes, he added, 'As my Healer. Now Karnos is ... gone, I find myself in need of someone who can fix bones and mend cuts and cure fevers. One who'll do whatever it takes to cure a patient. A Warrior Healer is just what I need.'

'But ...' Ishtaer said, too stunned to think. 'But Madam Julia needs me.'

'Madam Julia wouldn't have graduated you from the Academy if she wasn't ready to let you go. She's not a fool. She can't keep you forever.'

She swallowed and clutched the reins tighter.

'Think about it,' Kael said, his tone deceptively casual. 'We won't be going straight away. It's a hell of an opportunity, Ishtaer.'

She just about managed to nod.

As they neared street level the noise of the crowd drifted up, cheers rising as they came into view.

'Get used to it, kid,' Kael told her, and Brutus barked excitedly.

They passed under the King's Gate, out into the crowd, and Ishtaer steeled herself for the wall of noise from all sides. She was used to listening hard to work out where she was going, what obstacles were in her way, who was approaching, but in this melee of sound she could have been riding straight into the ocean for all she knew. She gripped the reins hard and hoped Eirenn knew what he was doing. He'd suddenly gone very quiet.

If she hadn't been listening so hard, she might have missed the voice calling, 'Cousin Ishtaer!'

Her head snapped around. A young female voice, excited and slightly desperate.

'Cousin Ishtaer! Over here!'

On the other side of Kael, Verak's horse slowed.

'Kael,' he called above the noise. 'Look at this ...'

Kael's horse stopped. Eirenn pulled hers up too.

'My gods,' she heard Kael say.

'If Rellan were ten years older ...' Verak said.

Kael cleared his throat and called loudly to someone, 'Let them through!'

'What's going on?' Ishtaer asked Eirenn, her horse prancing a little at the interruption.

'Well, I'm not sure, but there's a girl there who looks just like you, and a man his lordship thinks looks just like your father. At a guess, Ishtaer, you're about to meet your family.'

The Academy was quiet at night, the students either out enjoying the day's celebrations or already in bed. Tomorrow there would be a feast in Ishtaer's honour, and Kael could already tell it was going to be hell for her. He'd spent the evening in Bibalacus with Ishtaer's new family, watching her listen to their stories and gossip and giving the barest version of her own life, pausing at the worst bits, which Kael found himself filling in with glib white lies.

Citizen Garados Mallus wasn't quite as tall as his brother had been, and his dark hair lacked the grey that had come too early to Rellan. But he had the same features, warm and smiling, and the pale blue eyes that were so startling in skin the colour of clear honey. His wife, Nima, was dark-haired, dark-eyed, and elegant.

Their daughter, Poppia, was an eerie mirror of Ishtaer, if she'd been that nice girl who'd grown up with her family and done normal things and never even heard of the New Lands. She was sweetly rounded, her eyes bright with youth and hope, bounding around her new cousin like an excited puppy. They were near each other in age, but in Ishtaer's eyes he saw whole lives lived and used and wasted.

He found her in the dining hall, on a bench pushed back against the wall. Brutus slept at her feet and Eirenn snored with his head on the table. Ishtaer had a flask of wine, which was nearly empty.

'Mind if I join you?' Kael asked, sitting down without waiting for a reply.

'Help yourself,' Ishtaer gestured to the wine, and he

poured some out. It wasn't exactly quality stuff, but he drank it anyway.

'Court celebrations don't appeal to you?'

Ishtaer wrinkled her nose. 'Too many people. Will they all be at the feast tomorrow?'

'Sure. And more. All of the Citizenry, every Chosen, dignitaries from every corner of the Empire. It's a state occasion.'

She looked pained. 'I don't suppose anyone will believe I'm ill?'

Kael smiled. 'I don't suppose they will.'

She glanced at Eirenn. 'Why do they celebrate me, and not him? And don't say it's because I've defied the odds, or whatever. It's not exactly been easy for him.'

'No, but it's not been as hard as it has for you. You've come from worse and done more. Ish, the storybooks are full of young Tyros doing feats of derring-do. But you ... you're something special.'

Ishtaer picked up the flask, held her cup steady, and poured. She didn't spill a drop.

'How do you do that? How do you do all of it?'

She shrugged. 'I concentrate. I listen. I remember details very clearly.'

'Every detail? Of everything?'

Her hand gripped the horn cup so tightly it creaked. 'Some I try to forget.'

In the dull light, there was no hint of the wretched slave. If he squinted hard, he could make out the faint scarring on her Seer's mark. She'd evidently worked on healing that, but not the S brand on her arm.

He reached out and traced it, and Ishtaer jumped a little. 'Why haven't you faded this? I know you could if you tried.'

'Like you said. Some scars are useful as a reminder.'

'Of what? I notice you gave your family a bit of a potted history this evening.'

'You've already told the world I was a slave, so there doesn't seem much point in denying it, does there?'

There, that right there, that looked like anger. Defiance. Kael smiled. He rather liked people who defied him.

'Your uncle told me,' he said casually, pouring out more wine, 'that you would be made very welcome in Draxos, as a family Healer.'

Her face gave away nothing. 'He said the same to me.'

'Does that sound like something you want to do?'

She sipped her wine. Her foot absently rubbed Brutus's back. 'I don't know.'

'It'd be a damn sight more pleasant than being my Healer. Draxos is warm most of the year, people are friendly, countryside is – well, I don't suppose it matters to you what the countryside is like, but it's gorgeous anyway.' Casually, he added, 'The rebellion was an isolated incident. More or less. Most of the stories are exaggerated.'

'By you?'

'By me. I was there. I saw the blood and misery and fire and anger. But I'm sure it's all in the past now.'

'If you're trying to scare me, it's not working. I know all about the rebellion. It really did end years ago. The country is more or less stable.'

'If poor.'

'Yes. Maybe I could do something about that. A clinic for the poor.'

'Maybe.' Dishing out free treatment to those who couldn't afford it. The sick children and exhausted widows, all those unsavoury hangovers of a rebellion so bloody the Empire had sent Kael in to sort it out. 'Or just spend your days looking after your family and their rich friends.'

'I could think of worse ways to spend my life.'

And she deserved it; the gods alone knew how she deserved it. A comfortable house, servants, good food and a family who loved her.

'You might even marry. A son of the Citizenry, perhaps, or a young merchant.'

'I will never marry.'

She said it simply. Not as a vow, not in self-pity. As a simple statement of fact.

'Sure, you say that, but surely someday you'll meet someone who gets your heart beating fast.'

'I like the way it beats now.'

Kael smiled. 'You're a very attractive girl, Ishtaer. And you could be very wealthy indeed. Garados wants to settle some money on you, and a Thrice-Marked, well, you could ask whatever fees you wanted and people would pay them. You'll be fighting men off.'

Her lips thinned, and Kael cursed himself for his choice of words.

'Sorry. Didn't mean … too much wine. You know what I meant.'

'That a young, attractive, well-connected Child of Two Marks is an irresistible prospect as a bride, even if she is damaged goods.'

'Ish —'

'My gods, Kael, I'm Thrice-Marked. If I married a Twice-Marked, I would bear Children of Five Marks. What a coup that would be.'

Her voice was flat. Kael wondered how much wine she'd had.

'Don't you want children?' he asked gently.

'No. I … I don't know.' She sat up straight. 'Do you know how many babies I've delivered? Can you imagine how many are conceived in a place like Samara's?'

Kael winced. 'Er, quite a few,' he said.

'I diagnosed somewhere around a hundred pregnancies. Around half of them were miscarriages. About a quarter were stillborn. I delivered twenty-three living babies in five years. Twelve of them died before they were a month old. Eight before six months. Of the remaining three, only one survived his fifth birthday. He died a month later. Samara invited him to her chamber to play with her dogs. They mauled him to death. The rest starved or froze. At least two were murdered by their own mothers so they wouldn't have to starve or freeze.'

Kael could only stare in horror. If Durran and Garik had been here he'd have held onto them so tight he didn't think he'd ever let go.

'The first ever potion I made was to abort a foetus. The second to prevent conception. I was taught by an eastern woman on the slave ship. She made me take both of them. Over the next five years I kept a constant supply of them, and I offered them to every woman in the compound. I was always amazed how many chose not to take them. As if they thought they'd be any different, that they'd survive and so would their baby, that Samara would be merciful. But then, she'd fooled me into thinking she was merciful years before. One little flash of kindness, and you'd beg like a dog for more, even as she beat you, and starved you, and gave you to her men for their entertainment. That any woman could want a child conceived in circumstances like that has always been beyond me, even when Samara turned me into so much of her creature that I could barely think for myself.'

Her voice was calm. Her face was impassive. If it wasn't for the trickle of wine from her cracked cup Kael might have thought she was simply relaying a story she'd read somewhere.

He took the cup from her, poured its contents into his own, and pushed it into her hand. She held it a moment, and said, 'Forgive me for not wanting to bring a child into that world.'

He couldn't speak for a moment. Picked up the flask and drank directly from it.

'You're not in that world any more,' he said hoarsely.

'Part of me always will be.' She cleared her throat. 'So, no, I don't think I will marry and have children.'

Kael couldn't think of anything to say to that.

Chapter Sixteen

Out from the darkness of sleep a huge red cat loomed.

It reared huge and fearsome, all fangs and claws, a crowned cat of blood red, but she wasn't afraid. She lay on a soft bed, a man sleeping beside her. A handsome man, a strong man. A man who opened his eyes and smiled at her.

She smiled back, and then he reached for his sword and plunged it into her belly.

Ishtaer once again woke up screaming.

The next day, she once more put on the silk dress and corset armour, allowed Malika to mess with her hair and to put cosmetics on her face, and paraded through the streets with Kael, Eirenn and Verak to the Imperial Tower. They were led to a different room – she had no idea how many the Tower had, but if it was meant to reach up to the heavens then she expected they probably never had to use the same room twice – where they were presented and applauded and given places of honour at the Emperor's table. Speeches were made, most of them very long and very boring. Ishtaer clapped until her palms felt bruised. Course after course of complicated food was served, drawing more astonished comments from Eirenn with every new concoction.

After what felt like days, they were released.

'Dear fecking gods, if that's what they do to people they're proud of, I should hate to see what they do to traitors!' Eirenn gasped as soon as they'd left the Tower.

'Do us a favour, Kael. Don't do anything heroic for a while, would you?' Verak said.

'Hey, it ain't my fault. Most I usually get is a medal.'

They all had medals now, hanging from silk ribbons

around their necks, and new victory names – even, to his surprise, Eirenn. It wasn't unprecedented for a Tyro to be given such an honour, although it was extremely unusual.

'I get any more names added to this one, I'll have to start using initials,' Kael said.

'Not a bad idea. LKVeKMVSDP,' Verak rattled off. 'We could call you Lekvekem Vusdup.'

'It has a ring to it,' Eirenn said, laughing.

'You okay, Ishtaer?' Kael said. He was riding beside her. He always rode beside her.

'Just a little …'

'Overwhelmed? Exhausted? Bored to tears?'

'Yes,' she said, smiling.

'Plans for later?' he asked casually. Too casually. After her outburst last night she'd stumbled off to bed, cursing herself for giving too much away. Again. If she'd been able to see she wouldn't have been able to look at him today.

'I'm meeting my family for dinner. That is, I don't think I need to eat for the rest of the week, but I'm meeting them anyway.'

Her uncle, as a member of the Citizenry, had been invited to the feast and given a much more prestigious position than a merchant from Draxos would usually get. He'd told Ishtaer over and over how very proud of her he was, and so had her aunt, and they'd both impressed upon her how much Poppia was looking forward to seeing her that evening.

'She didn't get a chance to tell you about her fiancé last night,' Aunt Nima said, and added, laughing, 'although once she starts she can be hard to stop.'

You might marry, you know.

'They seem very pleasant,' Verak said now, as they rode through the warm night down the Processional Way.

'Yes. They've been very kind.'

'Kael tells me you're thinking of moving to Draxos with them.'

Ahead of her, Eirenn stumbled a bit.

'No, I mean yes, but, it's … they … I'm thinking about it.' *My own house, with servants, and a chef to cook whatever I want, and rich people who will pay me a fortune to treat their gout …*

… while Kael bounds around all over the Empire, fighting river savages and throwing pots of devil's fire …

She gave herself a mental shake. Safety was what she wanted, wasn't it? Not just safety from people trying to hurt her, but from poverty, from hunger, from desperate deeds.

Servants who would do whatever I wanted. How long might it be until she started wanting what Samara wanted?

That night, as Kael was changing to go out, in the same double room he'd been given when he first arrived with Ishtaer, someone knocked at his door.

Shirtless, he opened it, and stood gaping for a few moments at Ishtaer. She wore a dark blue gown and had Brutus sitting at her side. He thumped his tail at Kael by way of greeting.

'Have I disturbed you?' she asked politely.

'No, I was just … just …' Just getting changed to go out and pick up a girl, but he couldn't say that to her.

He didn't know why.

'I can come back later. I didn't know when you were leaving the city.'

'Day after tomorrow. Tide turns around midday.' He tried to read her expression but it was as inscrutable as ever. 'We can talk now, if you wanted. I'm in no hurry.'

She nodded. 'Good. I … I wanted to know if your offer was still open. To come with you. To Krulland.'

His heart leapt. 'It is.'

She stood for a moment, as if considering what to say next.

'You don't want to go to Draxos?'

Ishtaer took a breath and let it out. 'I … would like to get to know my family better,' she said. 'But moving hundreds of miles to a foreign country when I barely know them …'

'You'd be moving hundreds of miles to a foreign country with me,' Kael said.

'Will you talk about your fiancé all evening and then list all his eligible friends who'd just love to marry a Chosen girl?'

He winced. 'Poppia?'

'I know she's just excited, and she's a really lovely girl, but …'

He waited.

'But all her friends are married, and all my aunt and uncle's friends' daughters are married, and I'm not sure I can face that conversation round the dinner table every night.'

Kael laughed. He couldn't help it. 'If I promise that nobody in Krulland will ever ask you when you're getting married, will you come with me?'

'Nobody? In the whole country?'

He propped himself in the doorway, folding his arms and smiling. 'I'm a very influential man.'

'I'll want to bring Brutus.'

'Naturally.'

'And Eirenn.'

'What's one pet without another?'

'That's not funny. Without him, you'd still be getting chewed on by crocogators.'

'All right, I take your point. Besides, wasn't that long ago Verak said I could train him better than Sir Scipius. Care to make a bet with me that I can get him to graduate as a Militis?'

There was a pause, then Ishtaer shook her head. 'I don't have anything to bet,' she said softly.

With any other girl he'd have made a saucy comment. With Ishtaer, he said, 'I'll pay you what I paid Karnos.'

'No.'

His eyebrows went up. 'No?'

'Karnos was just a Healer. A good one, but still just a Healer.' She took another deep breath. Kael tried not to watch the movement of her chest. 'I'm a Seer. And I might not be much of a Warrior, but I can defend myself. I'm much stronger and faster than someone without Militis powers. I've spent two days being feted by the Empire.' Her fingers flexed as if she was about to make a fist. 'I'm worth something.'

He regarded her, standing there in his doorway, probably the only woman he'd met who didn't react to him with his shirt off. He had no idea how the Horde would react to a female Healer. Sure, they'd been perfectly respectful to her in Palavio and on the ship, but at home? Every day? And everyone else at Skjultfjell? Would Mags ever accept her, Mags who thought girls who didn't stand up for themselves got what they deserved?

It was a pretty damn big risk he was taking.

She's worth something. Was she worth this?

'Twice his pay then,' he said, and when she opened her mouth, added, 'and don't you ask for three times that, you're only a half-trained Warrior and unless you can predict the future on demand you're getting paid over the odds to be a Seer.'

She paused. 'Room and board?'

'You eat what we eat. Plenty of it, especially in summer, and especially if you like fish. Leaner in the winter. But you won't starve. I promise that. Your own room. With a key. You work hard, you train with me and the lads, and you heal not just the Horde but everyone else in Skjultfjell. Women, children, fishermen, the lads who look after the horses. Eirenn works too. No freeloading.'

Her eyes narrowed in concentration. Eventually she said, 'Skjultfjell?'

'My stronghold. There's a village too.'

A glimmer of a smile touched her lips. 'They call it Skullfell here.'

Kael grinned. 'I know.'

She licked her lips. Then she put out her hand. 'Deal.'

Kael shook it, held it, and said, 'Just so you know, I'd have given you three times Karnos's pay.'

She smiled. 'Just so you know, I'd have taken one and a half.'

'Just so long as there are no more fecking processions,' was Eirenn's response to Ishtaer's news.

'You don't have to come,' she said, suddenly anxious she was pushing him into something he didn't want to do.

'Are you kidding? Join Krull the Warlord's Horde? Ishtaer, I can't believe you're giving me this opportunity.' He gave her a brief hug, startling them both, then ran off to pack.

Ishtaer's own preparations didn't take long. She had few clothes and not many other possessions. It took a while to get up the courage to tell Madam Julia she was leaving, but the older woman just said, 'I did without you before, I'll do without you again.'

Well, that's put me in my place, Ishtaer thought.

Julia's voice softened. 'I will miss you, though.'

And that was it. Ishtaer counted the months since she'd arrived in Ilanium as she made her way back to her room and passed Marcus Glorius on the way.

'My lady,' he said mockingly, and she heard his feet scrape in what sounded like an exaggerated bow.

She inclined her head, the way Sir Flavius had taught her. 'Tyro,' she said, and swept past.

Eight months ago, she wouldn't have done that.

The seas were calm, the wind brisk, and a week later they were rounding the headland, its contours so familiar to

Kael he could see them with his eyes closed. His scouts would already have seen the ship approaching, and by the time they'd negotiated the narrow harbour there would be donkeys and carts waiting on the shore and men rowing out in boats to unload the ship.

He stood beside Eirenn and Ishtaer at the prow, and pointed to the rock formation on top of the headland. 'See that, Eirenn? I always tell the boys, if they've not left the yard by the time we've rounded Big Cat Rock, they'll be late meeting the ship.'

'Big Cat Rock?' said Ishtaer.

'Looks like a lion or something, lying down and looking out to sea.' Kael paused and added, 'My sons named it that.'

Both of them went very still. No one on the deck paid them the blindest bit of notice. They were all his men, all of them sworn not to Krull the Warlord, but to Kaelnar Vapensigsson. The sailors he'd taken on in Ilanium had disembarked two days ago. There was no one on this ship who didn't live in Skjultfjell. No one he didn't trust.

'Durran is nearly seven. Garik is five. They're fine boys, but no one outside Skjultfjell knows they exist. A man like me makes plenty of enemies. Children are vulnerable. I can't risk … Imagine if those evil bastards in Palavio knew I had children?'

'They're not in the Book of Names,' Eirenn said. 'I mean, there's no one who doesn't know your entry into the Book.'

'No.'

'And your wife?' Ishtaer asked. Her face was still. He'd believe she was staring out at the rocks if he didn't know better. 'You never entered her name, either.'

'No. I don't have a wife. Never did. It's complicated.'

'Not that complicated,' Eirenn said, his cheeks pink. 'We all know how the biology of it works. They must have had a mother.'

Kael ran his hands through his hair. 'Ilse died just after Garik was born. We were away fighting in the Saranos. As for Durran, his mother is alive and well and rules my household with an iron fist in a velvet glove. Her name is Margit. Mags to everyone. Her husband was my best friend. He died before Durran was born. A rockfall. Mags and I raised both boys together.'

'So they're not true brothers?'

'Not by blood. But they both call me Papa and think of Mags as their mother. That's brother enough for me.'

He waited. Eirenn eyed him with a look that mixed distrust with disbelief. 'You want us to keep this secret?'

'Everyone has secrets, Eirenn,' Ishtaer said. To Kael, she said, 'I understand. I'll tell no one.'

'And nor will I,' Eirenn sighed. 'Cross my heart and hope to die.'

'Good, 'cos that's what'll happen if you breathe a word to anyone.' He glanced at the cliff path, where the boys were scrambling down towards the harbour. Improbably, they seemed to have grown since he left. Garik appeared to be wearing Durran's clothes, although whether that was because Durran had grown out of them or just because it was what they were doing these days, he had no idea.

I spend too much time away.

But hanging around at home wasn't going to bring in the gold. And without gold Krulland had very little to trade with when crops failed or animals died or new ships were needed. And without people being constantly reminded that this tiny country was protected by Krull the Warlord, there was no telling what might happen to it.

Palavio, that's what might happen.

Kael shuddered and made himself focus on the boys as they exploded into the harbour, running along, leaping over lobsterpots and fishing nets and moorings. The men on the platt, preparing boats to row out to the *Grey Ghost*, shouted after them, but Kael knew as well as anyone else that if either of the boys fell, any of the men there would leap after him without a thought.

'Papa, Papa!' Durran yelled, jumping up and down as he reached the end of the harbour wall. The *Ghost* couldn't moor in the shallow water of the harbour, so he'd have to wait for a boat to be lowered before he could row across to them. Or ...

'Papa, can you see us?' Garik shouted.

Oh, the hell with it.

He stripped off his leather jerkin, toed off his boots, handed his sword to Eirenn. 'Look after these,' he said, and dived over the side of the ship.

The water was deep and shockingly cold, even in summer, and Kael gasped as he came back up to the surface. He dimly heard Ishtaer say, 'What happened? Is he all right?' before he struck out to the shore.

About ten seconds later he heard a splash, and Ishtaer shouted, 'Brutus, no!', and he turned to see the creature doggy-paddling towards him, tongue lolling out.

Kael started laughing, and when the animal came near he ruffled its ears. 'Well, wolfie, you certainly behave like a dog,' he said, and swam on, towards the shallower water. Durran raced back to the beach and towards the water before anyone could stop him, followed by his brother, and the two of them splashed out towards him. He wasn't concerned. They could swim. Everyone in Krulland could swim.

The water was knee-deep on Kael by the time he reached them, hugging them close and breathing them in. Their voices tripped over each other, babbling about boats and ponies and pirates and a whole incoherent bunch of stuff he'd get Mags to explain later. For now, he just held on to them, his boys, and silently promised he wouldn't leave them for so long next time.

'Look, a dog!'

'You brought us a dog!'

Brutus pounded onto the pebbly shore and shook himself vigorously.

'No, not quite. He belongs to a friend of mine. But I'm sure she'll let you pet him, if you're very careful.' Brutus seemed so far to be a friendly soul, but if he hurt either of the boys Kael would make a fur coat out of him.

They ran off to play with Brutus, their father forgotten, and he waded ashore, where Mags stood, hands on hips, shaking her head at him.

'You really are the most ridiculous man.'

He grinned at her. 'I'm glad to see you too.'

She rolled her eyes, kissed his cheek and flicked a gesture at Brutus.

'Why are my boys playing fetch with a wolf?'

'He's not a wolf, why would I bring a wolf home?'

'I know wolves when I see 'em, Kael.'

'He's just a dog who looks like a wolf,' he said. 'The boys like him.'

'Hmm. Who's this friend he belongs to? What sort of reprobates are you bringing home now?'

'Our new Healer,' Kael said, watching Brutus trip up a man carrying a bunch of fishing nets. The boys fell about laughing.

'Ah yes,' Mags said, her voice quieter. She put her hand on his arm. 'We got your letter. I'm sorry, Kael. He was a good man, a good Healer.'

'A damned good Healer,' Kael said, proud of his voice for not shaking.

'What happened to him?' Mags asked, but Kael could only shake his head.

The splash of oars created a welcome distraction, and he turned to see Ishtaer and Eirenn in one of the boats coming ashore. Since he was already sodden, he waded out to pull them up onto the beach, and as everyone else leapt out, he leaned in and took Ishtaer's arm.

'It's dry,' he said, 'just step out, I've got you.'

She did, and he marvelled once more at the way she seemed able to move with such grace and ease when she could see nothing. Beneath his hand, however, her arm was tense as an iron rod. When a seagull screamed loudly overhead, her hand went to her hip where her sword was carried.

'It's just a gull. You'll have to get used to them, I'm afraid.'

He led her over to Mags, who was watching Brutus and the boys zip about the beach after the sticks Eirenn threw. The boy might not be much cop at running, but he could throw like nobody's business.

'Mags,' he said as Brutus and Eirenn bounded up, 'this is Ishtaer Lakaresdottir Vapendam, our new Healer. And this is her dog. And this is Brutus.'

'*Thanks*,' said Eirenn.

Kael grinned. 'Eirenn – what did your father do?'

'Uh, he was a shepherd,' Eirenn said, clearly confused.

'Eirenn Herdesson Krigare, then,' Kael introduced him.

Both Eirenn and Ishtaer looked confused as Mags held out her hand and said, 'Margit Herdesdottir. My father was a shepherd too.'

Eirenn shook her hand, and after Kael held out Ishtaer's hand, she did the same, which garnered a few curious looks from the others on the beach. Kael ignored them and began to lead Ishtaer towards the platt, the stone-built embankment above tide level where the contents of the boats were being unloaded. He was pretty aware of plenty of people staring, but whether this was at the Seer's mark on Ishtaer's face, or the fact that he'd had to put her hand in Mags's in order for her to shake it, he wasn't sure. Maybe they were staring because she was wearing breeches and a jerkin. Or because she looked pretty good in the breeches and jerkin.

Or maybe it was because he still had hold of her arm, in the sort of hold one would usually use on a lover.

He wondered if Ishtaer was aware of any of this.

He introduced her to Durran and Garik, who startled her by throwing their arms around her. And then Ishtaer startled him by kneeling down and hugging them back. For all that she'd told him she never wanted children, there was a shade of longing on her face as she held his sons.

'Ishtaer is going to be our Healer. I want you to treat her with respect, and help her if she asks you to. And even if she doesn't. Ishtaer can't see, so she might find things a bit difficult to begin with. So no racing around without looking where you're going, all right?'

They peered at Ishtaer's eyes, and she let them.

He walked her up the steep, meandering cliff path, counting off steps and warning her of uneven ground. Brutus padded along beside her, Eirenn just behind, while ahead the boys ran, pinging around with endless energy. Every small terrace and courtyard they passed was full of people and animals, donkeys and mules carrying goods up to the main house, dogs chasing each other around, cats leaping after seagulls, people passing sacks and baskets of goods along.

Nearly everyone they passed nodded or called out to Kael. Most of them peered curiously at Ishtaer, but not a single person stared in a way he'd have found offensive. And Kael was suddenly aware that he would have been offended. That he was proud to walk alongside this strange woman with her odd abilities and her scars and marks and her wolf.

'I'm really glad you're here,' he said, and her smile was puzzled, but genuine.

Chapter Seventeen

'This place is mental,' Eirenn said, poking at something that rattled. 'I got so lost on the way here, I'm going to have to start tying bits of string to doorknobs so I've got something to follow.'

'Great, something else to trip over,' said Ishtaer, opening a jar of something that smelled like it could strip paint. 'Here, what does this label say?'

'Fire ointment.' Eirenn peered closer. 'He's written that it removes foreign bodies, and there's a list. Dirt, cloth, insects – ugh.'

'He?'

'Sir Karnos, I guess. This was all his. Well – but some of the handwriting is different. I suppose he must have inherited the place from someone.'

Ishtaer replaced the jar and made a mental note of it. Karnos's workshop was huge, filled with shelves and drawers and racks. She'd found fresh herbs, dried herbs, macerated and distilled herbs, potion after potion and every type of dressing. There was a mattress and a couple of chairs for patients, and a small cubbyhole with a further bed for anyone she needed to keep an eye on. Next to that was a larger bedroom which contained every convenience of her room at the Academy, and then some.

'Fire ointment, fire ointment … blimey, would you look at this list?'

'List?'

'He has a recipe book here, sort of. Notes on what works and what doesn't. This has got all sorts of stuff in it I've never even heard of. He says for a severe infection, you can set it alight. Alight!'

Ishtaer considered the smell of the fire ointment. It seemed to be a common attribute of Healers to have an instinct for herbal remedies and to know what a potion or ointment might contain. She sorted the ingredients of the fire ointment in her head and said, 'Yes. It would burn very quickly like a ... like a firework, I suppose. Enough to kill an infection. But it would do some damage. Not to be used often, I expect.'

'Yes, that's what he notes.' Eirenn peered at the label again. 'Kills infections. From the smell of it I'd say it'd kill most things.'

Ishtaer unscrewed the jar again and dabbed some onto her finger. It tingled with heat. 'Yes, but I think it will work.'

'Sure, but you can try it out on someone else.'

Bit by bit, the realisation kept stealing up on Ishtaer that this was her domain now. She wasn't a student any more, she wasn't working under Madam Julia, she was responsible for everyone at Skjultfjell. No one could tell her what to do, which was both liberating and terrifying.

'Ish?'

'Hmm?' She carefully slotted the jar back into place.

'Do you think it's weird? I mean, Lord Krull, here?'

'What do you mean? You didn't actually expect him to live in a castle of bones, did you?'

'No, of course not,' said Eirenn, in a tone that said he did. 'It's just ... well, this place is kind of like ... like generations have lived here, and everyone's someone's cousin, and they all just muck in, and ...'

'... it's not how you expected a warlord would live?' came a voice from the doorway, which made Eirenn jump and Ishtaer smile. She'd heard Kael's footsteps and smelled his soap, the same sage scent he usually smelled of, but stronger now, as if he'd just bathed, and his clothes had been washed in the same stuff.

'Look, basically I'm just a feudal lord, and I spend most of my time here sorting out little disputes and making sure everyone's got enough food for winter. The warlord stuff is just …'

'A show?' Ishtaer said, remembering what he'd said to her all that time ago.

'Yes, exactly that. I work hard and I love my kids, just like everyone else. Of course, I am still in charge, just in case you were wondering if we run this place as a democracy.'

'They seemed to be trying democracy in Palavio,' Eirenn said. 'I wasn't a fan.'

'They were trying anarchy in Palavio,' Kael said. 'That's by the by.' She heard his boots creak as he shifted his weight. His foot still pained him, not that he'd ever let it slip. But every time he touched her she felt the ache, the occasional sharp pain, shooting through him.

He led them through the maze of corridors and rooms and what Ishtaer thought might actually be tunnels, until they reached the doors to the longhouse. The noise of dozens of people and the scent of food got stronger, roasted meats and vegetables and wine, making her stomach rumble.

Kael laughed. 'I'll warn you not to expect a feast like this every day,' he said. 'This is special because we've come home, and also to welcome you. But I meant what I said back at the Academy. You won't starve here.'

'Glad to hear it, if what the lads on the ship said about the winter is true,' Eirenn said.

'Well, it is and it isn't. Winter gets pretty swiving harsh here, I won't lie about it. Mags will probably already have started preparing for it. In the Dark – the deepest part of winter – often no one goes outside. The villagers winter up here with us. It's one of the reason the castle is so big. We bring the livestock into the barn or they'd just freeze to death. The boats come up onto the platt, else the storms would turn them to matchsticks. Even the *Grey Ghost* goes into hibernation. We take the masts off and winter her in a cave above the shoreline. But when they come to tell you about the Huntsmen and the—Whoa! Boys! Remember what I said about Ishtaer not being able to see where you were?'

But Ishtaer had heard Durran and Garik come thundering around the corner. All right, so she couldn't tell them apart from other children the same size and age, not yet, but she'd known enough to step back.

'Sorry, my lady,' Durran said, and his brother echoed him a second later.

'Just Ishtaer,' she said, 'not lady. And it's all right. No harm done.'

'Can we play with Brutus?'

'No,' Kael said before she could respond. 'You can go and wash your hands and help your mother bring in dinner. Go on, go.'

They made disappointed noises but sped off, and Kael took Ishtaer's arm once more, leading her through a doorway and into the longhouse. The noise was huge, but not as bad as the feasts at the Imperial Tower. There was no fancy music, just people talking and laughing. Occasionally, the cry of a baby rose above the rest of it. Under the scent of food she smelled old woodsmoke and decades of spilled beer. Her fingers trailed over a wall of stone and wood, her boots stepping on flagstones that had worn into dents through sheer use.

'This place is old,' she murmured.

'We have no idea how old. My ancestors weren't great record keepers, and quite a lot of what they did write down is in runes. Which reminds me, Karnos was a meticulous record keeper, but I can't say I ever understood his system. If you want me to read some stuff to you, just ask, all right?'

'All right,' Ishtaer said slowly.

'And I'll make notes for you too, if you want. We reckon this is the oldest part of the place,' he continued, as if he hadn't just offered to be her secretary. 'Bit by bit other outbuildings and walkways got added, then turned into rooms and corridors, until you have this absolute warren. Don't worry. You'll get used to it eventually.'

'From the sea, you'd never know this was all here,' Eirenn marvelled.

'No, and that's sort of the point. The whole place is roofed with turf, and there are whole rooms carved right out of the rock. They're actually great for keeping food stored.'

He led Ishtaer onto a small dais and to a high-backed chair. For a moment he paused, then said softly to her, 'This was Karnos's chair. He was hugely well respected here, even if everyone thought he was a miserable old bugger. They'll miss him a lot. Try ... try not to replace him, if you know what I mean.'

'I'm not sure I do.'

'Just be yourself. Don't compare yourself to him.' He patted her shoulder. 'This chair is yours now. The carving is unique, see? You'll sit here for all meals. We take most of them together.'

Ishtaer nodded and sat, Brutus flopping to the ground beside her with a sigh.

And the huge room went ... quiet.

There were still some children squabbling, some chairs scraping, a baby crying, but everyone else seemed to have watched her take Karnos's place, and they were waiting for something.

Beside her, Kael's seat scraped loudly and heavily.

'Right,' he said loudly. 'We're back, mostly safe and mostly sound. But there's one face missing, as I'm sure you've noticed. Karnos hasn't turned into an attractive young woman on our trip. If that were the case I'd have done the same to all my men.'

A few people laughed, but they all seemed to know what was coming.

'I know you received my letter about Karnos. I know you'll all miss him. He was a good man, a good Healer, and a good friend. No one will miss him more than me. No one will regret his death more than me. So I ask you to raise a drink to Sir Karnos Atrius Medicus Saraneus, or as he was privileged to be known in Krulland, Karnos Simmareson Lakare. Or as many of us knew him, That Miserable Old Bugger.'

A chorus of voices called out what Ishtaer thought was some combination of all those things. Verak's voice, she noticed, was one of the ones calling him a Miserable Old Bugger, but she clearly heard the tears in it.

'We will miss him,' Kael said. 'And we can never replace him. But we are in need of a Healer, which is why I have brought this young lady home with me.' His hand rested on Ishtaer's shoulder. 'She is Chosen, and has practiced medicine for many years, even before she attended the Academy. This may be why she graduated in what might be record time. Eirenn, did you check?'

'Third fastest,' Eirenn said from her other side.

'Not bad at all. She's also a Seer who can predict some remarkable things, and a Warrior in training. The Empire has given her some bloody stupid long name, but here in Krulland I think we should call her Ishtaer Lakaresdottir Vapendam. Welcome her.'

People yelled out variations of this name.

'Oh, and this is Eirenn. Right. That done, I'm bloody famished, so let's eat.'

This got a bigger cheer than anything he'd said so far.

'At least he didn't call you a dog this time,' Ishtaer said.

'I feel he's warming to me.'

Chairs scraped, conversation resumed, and Mags asked Ishtaer if she'd like some soup. While she ate, Ishtaer tried to work out who was sitting around her, but aside from Eirenn on one side and Kael on the other, she was lost. Mags and the boys sat opposite, with Verak close by, and several more children who all called him Papa. Various strange voices mingled around her, over and under the hubbub.

'You okay?' Kael asked, nudging her. 'You're quiet.'

'What was the name you gave me? Ishtaer Laka—Larak—'

'Lakaresdottir Vapendam. We have a much simpler naming structure here than in the Empire, which, let's face it, wouldn't be difficult. Verak took up a Krullish name when he married Klara, a local woman, and Karnos used one, too. Your second name is your father's name or profession, with son or daughter on the end. Changes every generation. Lakare is the Krullish word for doctor.'

Her brain whirred. Kael's second name in either language was Vapensigsson; her new name was Vapendam. 'What does Vapen mean?'

'Weapon. My father was known as Vapensig – Man of Weapons, literally – so I'm Vapensigsson. You're Lady of Weapons, Vapendam. It's a sort of honorific, like the victory titles the Empire gives.'

'Do you have one?'

'Kriglord. Means warlord. We're pretty literal around here.'

Ishtaer absorbed that, and finished her soup as Eirenn chatted to Mags about the differences in shepherding up here in the cold compared to out west in the wet. A large plate of beef was plonked in front of her without ceremony.

'Do I have to learn Krullish?' she asked.

'If you want to. Most people here speak Common. They'll respect you enough to speak it to you.'

Will they?

Kael touched her arm. His hand was warm, the touch reassuring. 'You'll be fine.'

He had faith in her. It was baffling. And even worse, she

kind of liked him touching her, which was confusing beyond belief. She ate a bit of beef to cover her embarrassment. 'I'll never figure out who everyone is.'

'There's a few hundred here, so I'd try and do it gradually if I were you. Up here on the top table we've me, Mags and the boys, and Verak, Klara and their kids. He has dozens of them, so they take up quite a bit of room.'

'I have seven,' Verak said, 'or have you forgotten how to count that high?'

'Ursula, Ture, Solvig, Lise, Alva, Goran and Hedda,' Kael reeled off. 'You think I'd forget? Or more to the point, that Klara would let me?' The rest of the table laughed. 'People tend mostly to sit where they want. I can't be bothered with all this formality. But some things you have to observe, and that means getting the people in charge up here and visible. That means me, and Verak, and Mags, and you.'

'And Eirenn?'

'Well, it seemed cruel to make him sit with the kids,' Kael said, a smile in his voice.

'You do know I'm not deaf?' Eirenn said.

'So long as you're not stupid either. Come on, eat up, busy day tomorrow.'

Kael wasn't kidding about it being a busy day. He had no interest in letting his men get fat and lazy, so he had them training immediately after breakfast, as usual. For five minutes Ishtaer and Eirenn stood to one side, both of them looking slightly shell-shocked.

'This ain't the Academy,' he told them.

A few yards away, Verak hefted his war axe and charged at Kennet Helgeson, whose shield blocked him with a mighty clang. The axe was made of wood, but it could still do a hell of a lot of damage.

'We use wooden swords here mostly, but every now and

then we break out the real stuff. And – Ishtaer, you still have that pouch of crystals?'

She nodded, touching it beneath her shirt.

'Eirenn, what do you do for crystals?'

The boy raised his right wrist, which bore a metal cuff studded with coloured crystals. It had a second-hand, battered look about it. Scholarship boy, Kael remembered. Most Chosen wore more than one piece of crystal jewellery, and those who'd been born to Chosen parents proudly displayed the necklaces given to them at birth.

Except Ishtaer. Hers was—lost.

'Right. You get your strength from them, we all know. And no one can take them from you, that we also know. But every now and then I'd like you to consider taking them off and fighting like a regular soldier. Build up your strength. Don't rely on them completely.'

Ishtaer's hand clutched at the pouch, her knuckles white.

'But only every now and then,' he added gently.

Ishtaer passed Brutus into the custody of Durran and Garik, who loved to watch the men practising, and told the dog, 'Sit. I'm safe. Safe, Brutus.'

Clearly this was something she'd trained him to understand, because he lay down with his nose on his paws and didn't attack anyone who waved a sword at her.

Kael gave Ishtaer and Eirenn both wooden swords and watched them spar for a while. Eirenn wasn't bad, except that his footwork let him down, and Kael could tell he'd never been up against a serious Chosen opponent. He might do okay against the regular lads, but if he tried to fight Kael or Verak or even the boys back at the Academy, he'd be mincemeat.

Ishtaer had a few good moves and her instincts were impeccable, but what Eirenn had said all those months ago still held true. She was a defensive fighter, always keeping herself from harm and never attacking. Yes, she had the major handicap of not being able to see what was coming, but Kael figured her timidity was her biggest problem.

'All right,' he said after a while. 'Eirenn, I want to see you against Rammlig. Go easy on him, Ramm.'

Rammlig, who looked like an ox but was as gentle as a lamb, grinned. Eirenn looked terrified but covered it well.

'Ish,' Kael said, 'fight me.'

She nodded and took up a fighting stance, but Kael knocked her feet out from under her, and she sprawled on the ground before his sword got anywhere near her.

'Get up,' he said. 'Don't expect me to fight politely.'

She got up, tensed for another attack. Too tense. Her grip on the practice sword was white-knuckled. Kael rapped her hand with his weapon, and she stifled a cry as she dropped it.

'Pick it up. Try again.'

This time he let her cross swords with him, just the once, before he sent her sprawling.

'Again.'

Another clash of swords. Another fall.

'Again. Again. We do this until I'm the one on the ground.'

Again and again she fell, and again and again she picked herself up and prepared to be knocked down. Kael's frustration grew.

'Stop letting me attack you. Fight back, girl.'

'I'm trying—'

'No, you're not.'

'You won't let me!'

'Let you?' He watched her hit the ground again. She'd be black and blue under her padded training gear. 'Enemies don't "let" you do anything, Ishtaer. Except die. Now get up, and forget about fighting fair.'

She got up, her chin jutting. He couldn't tell if it was with tears or determination.

Suddenly it hit him that he'd never seen her cry. He'd seen her angry, he'd seen her frightened, he'd seen her so tired she could barely speak, but he'd never seen her cry.

Before he worked out if he could use that to his advantage, Ishtaer's wooden sword hit him between the legs and he went down with a howl.

'How's that for not fighting fair?' she asked, and Kael nodded, his eyes watering, while all around them his men guffawed with laughter.

That afternoon, rather later than she'd planned due to Kael's relentless training, Ishtaer opened her little treatment room to the castle residents who'd been patiently waiting for the return of their Healer since Kael took him to Palavio. She dealt with a variety of everyday ailments, similar to the ones she'd treated at the Academy sickbay, the worst of which was a broken wrist which had been strapped up as 'a bit sore' two weeks ago.

'There really should be someone else here to treat these things,' she said after the patient had left, to what she thought was an empty room.

'Couldn't agree more,' Mags said, startling her. 'I often said the same to Karnos, but he was very, er, set in his ways.'

Ishtaer turned away to hide the flush in her cheeks and started tidying her implements. 'At the Academy we had non-Chosen learning herbology and surgery. It's considered quite a good career. Maybe ... if you know someone here who might be interested in learning, I could certainly use a hand. And it would be really helpful while I'm training.'

'Or when Kael carts you off to war.'

'Does he do that often?'

'If someone threatens Krulland he's there like a shot. But that doesn't happen often. People are scared of Krull the Warlord. If they saw him reading bedtime stories to his kids it'd be a different story, but I suppose that's why he doesn't take them with him.'

His child will die to save him.

'That's one reason,' Ishtaer said evenly.

'He buggers off to the Empire every now and then, just to remind people who he is and what he does. Goes off privateering sometimes, or gets hired to sort out a mess like in Palavio, but sometimes I think he just goes if he's bored, or thinks the men are getting lazy, or if he's got some loyalties there. But mostly it's because he gets paid.'

'He said he has a lot of gold.'

'Aye. Well, running a small country with a fearsome defensive force isn't cheap.' There was a creak as Mags took a seat. 'He's a generous man, but there isn't a lot of spare gold. Most of it's spoken for.'

'Winter food and things like that,' Ishtaer agreed.

'There's little call for fancy jewellery and rich clothing around here,' Mags went on, a strange note in her voice, 'and no call for socialising.'

Ishtaer frowned, and turned to face the other woman, wishing like hell she could read her expression.

'I wouldn't expect there is. Kael said the nearest town is a day's journey, and mostly he goes there for supplies or to hold a feudal court.'

'Utgangen, yes. Not a glamorous place.'

'I didn't come here looking for glamour,' Ishtaer said cautiously, and then realisation hit her. 'And I didn't come here looking for— for—I'm not interested in Kael. Not like that. Did you think that?' she babbled, words running into each other.

'He's a rich, powerful, handsome man,' Mags said.

'He spends most of his money on winter food, he does what the Emperor tells him, and I've no idea how handsome he is or isn't,' Ishtaer said. 'I'm really not interested in him. Trust me. I'm the last woman who would be.'

Mags was silent a moment, probably waiting for Ishtaer to burst out with something else. She turned away instead, her cheeks flaming once more.

'All right. He does get a lot of women sniffing around, that's all. I mean, what he does in the privacy of his bedchamber is his own concern, but if he were to marry it would affect us all.'

Especially you, Ishtaer thought, and wondered whether she should say anything.

'I don't want to marry him,' she said instead.

'Is there something between you and Eirenn?'

'No. He's a friend. A good friend, but just a friend.'

'He wants more than that, you know.'

Ishtaer closed her eyes, mostly to keep from rolling them. 'Less than a day and you can see that?'

'Anyone with eyes can see it.' Mags made an embarrassed noise. 'I didn't mean—'

'I'm used to it,' Ishtaer said, waving her hand dismissively.

'He's a handsome lad. Clever, funny, devoted to you.'

'Still not interested.'

Mags paused for a long time. Ishtaer ran out of things to tidy.

'Is it women you're interested in?'

She nearly choked. 'No. Really not. I'm not interested in anyone, Mags. I'm quite fine as I am.'

She listened to the tap of Brutus's claws on the stone floor as he wandered over to Mags, and the thump of his tail against the table legs as she said hello. Then Mags said, 'Are you running from someone?'

Constantly.

'I haven't left a husband behind, if that's what you're asking.'

'Neither had Ilse, but she was still running. I think from her father. You remind me of her. That is, she was very slight, and fair – Garik takes after her that way. But he doesn't have the same eyes. You do.'

Ishtaer finally turned around. 'What do you mean?'

'She always looked like she was poised to bolt. Or to crumble. You're not fragile like she was, but you still look as if you're only a few harsh words from falling apart.'

Ishtaer didn't know what to say to that.

'Kael didn't know the worst of it, I think,' Mags went on. 'He seemed to think that once he'd brought her here and given her safety, that she'd be all right. Then he buggered off to another war, and Ilse fell apart.'

'Did she love him?'

'I think she might have done. I think she idolised him. He rescued her. He was a knight in shining armour to her. And he didn't give her much more thought than … well, than a horse he once rescued from a beating.'

Ishtaer said nothing, her fingertips gripping the countertop behind her. *Like a horse he'd rescued from a beating.* Yes, that was it, that was how he'd treated her. As not quite human. At least, until she'd shown him …

'I do wonder, if he'd stayed, if he hadn't seemed to give up on her, if she'd still be alive. I think she thought Kael might marry her, and she might be mistress of Skjultfjell.'

'Like you?'

'Oh, I run the place, that's entirely different.'

Ishtaer straightened up and crossed to the small stove where she could boil water for sterilising instruments, mix potions or just make tea. She put the kettle on it.

'Tea?'

'Please.'

She busied herself making it, aware Mags was watching her, expecting the sort of comment she'd had all day, that she wasn't half as clumsy as people expected a blind girl to be. Instead, Mags said, 'Will you tell me what you're running from?'

I'm not running, Ishtaer wanted to say, but all she could do was shake her head.

'I can't. I'm sorry, I ...' She put down the teapot before she dropped it. 'I'm running from who I used to be. I'm not her any more. I'm trying really hard not to be her. And I don't want to think about who she was.'

Mags said, 'Was she dangerous? Was she a criminal?'

'No.' Although it could be considered a crime what happened to her.

'Does Kael know about this?'

Ishtaer nodded. 'But not Eirenn, and he's too good a friend to ask. Take it from me, he wouldn't like me half so well if he knew.'

'Maybe you should tell him, then.'

'No. Then I'd have no friends.'

'You know, that's rather up to you,' said Mags, and Ishtaer had the feeling she was failing some kind of test.

Chapter Eighteen

Mags continued to be polite to Ishtaer, but never quite as friendly as she was to everyone else. Eirenn charmed her, just as he charmed everyone, and whenever Kael released him from training duties he was usually found in the kitchen making the girls giggle helplessly with some outlandishly embellished tale. He also became a favourite with the children of the castle, and after dinner he often sat down in a corner of the longhouse by the fire and made up stories for them.

'Some people have the habit of making friends ever so easily, don't they?' Kael said to Ishtaer one evening after his sons had dragged Eirenn over to the fireplace.

'I don't think it's a habit so much as something he does out of ... I don't know. Self-preservation, maybe.'

'Very perspicacious of you,' Kael said, laughing. He poured more wine into her cup. 'Of course, for a Warrior the better self-preservation would be to learn how to use a sword.'

'He's getting better!'

'Sure. But I was talking about you too.'

She sighed. 'I thought I was getting better.'

'You are. But not good enough. Look. I know you graduated as a Healer ridiculously early, but in truth you'd been healing for years, just without crystals. I reckon you already had a pretty good handle on how to treat people, right?'

'Apart from myself,' Ishtaer said, thinking of her leg.

'And I know for years you never had the chance to defend yourself.' His voice was soft. They were alone at the table, and no one else in the longhouse was paying much attention. 'Listen. Ishtaer. I promised you when I met you that I would never … force you, and neither would any of my men. They have been treating you with respect, haven't they?'

'Yes, of course, everyone has.' She'd even endured some mild flirting from one or two of the men, but that had stopped so abruptly she suspected Kael had said something to them.

'But if they didn't? What if some man cornered you? What if no one was around to help?'

Ishtaer felt her fists form claws, her body tighten in on itself.

'I'd kill any man who hurt you,' Kael said softly, 'but I can't always be there. You have to fight for yourself.'

Her chair scraped loudly on the dais as she shoved it back.

'I've been fighting for myself every day of my life,' she said, and ran before he could say anything else. Brutus ran after her, apparently thinking this was a game, and it was only when she was safely back in her own room with the door locked that she slid down to the floor and he realised she was upset.

He wriggled close to her, licking her face anxiously, and when someone knocked on the door he growled at it.

'Ishtaer, let me talk to you,' Kael said, and she ignored him.

'I'll show you how I fight,' she muttered, and in the morning went out to the yard with battle in her eyes.

She was going to beat seven hells out of Kaelnar Vapensigsson, by fair means or foul.

Arriving in the yard, she called to Garik and Durran and told them to take Brutus for a walk. She wasn't worried the dog would intervene, but she didn't want the boys to see her humiliate their father. Because humiliate him she damn well would.

'Papa, can we go and play on the ice? Ingmar Bondeson said he was skating on it yesterday!'

'If you're very careful. Test it first. You know the drill.'

'Yes, Papa, thank you, Papa!'

She'd been at Skjultfjell for a couple of months, and every day the daylight got a little shorter and the weather got a little colder. Today the breeze was icy, and she hadn't been surprised to hear that several of the freshwater ponds had frozen over and the yards needed to be cleared of snow. It hadn't even got light until midmorning, which meant their training sessions started later and later.

'You okay?' Eirenn asked as she pulled on her gloves.

'I'm fine. Who am I fighting today?'

'Me,' said Kael, right behind her, and she made herself turn calmly.

'What a surprise.'

'And you won't need that,' he added, taking the sword from her.

'Unarmed it is then,' Ishtaer said, actually quite looking forward to punching him.

'No. Real steel today. Get your mail on.'

She realised that the sounds around her were subtly different. Yes, the movement of heavy mail shirts, the clash of metal on metal, the occasional indrawn breath as someone scored a hit.

'I'll be busy this afternoon,' she murmured, and took the mail shirt Eirenn was offering.

For once, Kael didn't try to ambush her before she was ready, but let her settle the long shirt in place, secure the cuffs at her wrists and don her gauntlets. She belted the shirt, which came to her knees and was split at the front and back to allow movement.

'Coif,' Kael said, handing her the mail hood and standing behind her to lace it so that it fit tightly around her neck. Ishtaer hated wearing a coif, which made hearing with precision pretty impossible, but the idea of a sword to the neck was less palatable.

'Shield,' he said, and fitted it to her left arm before handing her a sword.

Ishtaer had borrowed swords from the Academy when she rescued Kael, and once she'd handed them back he'd lent her one from his own stores to wear at her hip. It was more for the look of the thing than for any real defence, although it had given her some comfort to carry it on board the *Grey Ghost*.

'Anything else?' she enquired, testing the weight and feel of the sword.

'Yes. This,' Kael said, and swung his sword at her.

She'd got better since she arrived. Her reactions had improved, she was faster and more nimble – but even so, she only just stepped out of the way of a blow that would have turned her shoulder black and blue. She raised her own sword and thrust up, trying to catch him under the arm, but he slipped away and her sword just glanced off his mail.

She checked the movement and sliced back the other way, jabbing his ribs.

'Ow,' he said, and sounded pleased.

Just you wait, Ishtaer thought, and began to fight in earnest.

The mail was heavy, and despite the cold day sweat began to seep through her shirt as she drove Kael back, fury pushing her on. His sword clashed with hers again and again, sliding her blows away, but she was gaining on him, sending him backwards as she attacked relentlessly.

That blow was for every time he patronised her, and *that* was for telling her to fight harder when she'd been fighting all her life, and *that* was for every time he wandered around half naked in front of her and expected she didn't know, and *that*—

'All right, all right, yield!'

Like I'm falling for that, thought Ishtaer, who usually

ended up sprawled on the floor when Kael appeared to give in.

'Ishtaer, stop,' he gasped, and when she didn't he kicked her foot out from under her and she ended up on her back anyway.

Seething with anger, she hooked her foot around his ankle and brought him crashing down too. Unfortunately, where he crashed was right on top of her, his sword slamming down onto her right arm.

For a long moment she was too winded to think, and then pain began to radiate out from her arm.

'You're a lunatic today,' he said, and she shoved at him. Or at least she tried to. Her right arm didn't seem to be cooperating, and her left one was stuck behind its shield.

'You wanted me to fight,' she said, 'so here I am, fighting. Now will you get off me, please?'

'All right, so you're attacking, but you need a bit more common sense—'

He was chatting with her as if they were sharing a tankard of ale, not lying on top of her in a freezing training yard. 'Would you please get off me before I attack you again?'

'Oh.' Kael got to his knees, and as he did a jerking, tugging pain shot through Ishtaer's arm. 'Oh, *hells*.'

'Well, at least I'm wearing mail,' Ishtaer began, attempting to sit up and falling back with a gasp, her arm buckling the second she tried to put weight on it.

'Oh gods, I'm sorry. I didn't realise – here,' Kael abandoned his sword and grabbed for Ishtaer's injured arm. She cried out sharply.

'Look, just get this damn shield off me, would you?'

He quickly did, and she sat up cautiously, aware that the activity in the yard had quietened considerably. With her freed left hand she felt at her right arm. Kael's sword had slammed into it, and if she hadn't been wearing the mail shirt he'd probably have sliced it right off. As it was, the force of the blow had broken at least one of the bones in her forearm, and pounded several metal rings into her flesh. Already her arm was swelling up and her hand was utterly numb.

'I'm sorry, Ishtaer, that looks ... Let me help you—'

Irritated beyond belief, she snapped, 'You've done enough. For once in your life could you just leave me alone?'

Kael went silent. His hands fell away from her.

Ishtaer scrambled inelegantly to her feet. 'I'm going to sort this out and prepare my sickbay for a few more like it. Try not to kill anyone,' she snarled, and stalked off.

Anger propelled her back through the warren of corridors and rooms and she didn't even notice how well she knew her way around. Her rooms were at the far end of the complex from the training yard, next to a small herb garden that gave onto the kitchen gardens and fishponds. She was told the view was enchanting.

Her arm throbbed, but she was in no mood to be stopped by anyone with a concern or query, and marched right on without cradling the injury as instinct demanded. Adrenaline surged through her, keeping her upright as she rounded the corner into her little workroom and slammed the door shut.

Then she sagged against the wood, pain washing through her in waves.

The metal rings of the mail shirt had been mashed into the wound, although they at least hadn't been pushed as far as the bone. Ishtaer tugged off her gloves with her teeth and felt gingerly at her arm. A break to the radius ... and also to the ulna. Well, that was marvellous. Both would need to be reset, and she wasn't sure if she could do it by herself. Maybe Mags would help, because she certainly wasn't asking Kael. Or Eirenn might—

She broke off her train of thought as Brutus barked close by. A deep, angry, warning bark. Where had the boys taken him? Were they tormenting him? Anger surged through her, but she dismissed it. Durran and Garik weren't the sort of boys to torment a dog. They adored Brutus, and lately Garik had been pleading with his father for one of the stable kittens to come and sleep in his room.

She crossed to the door leading to the herb garden, wishing like anything that she could see out. The garden seemed empty, but there was Brutus's bark again, and the sound of a child crying.

Ishtaer set off at a run.

The boys had said something about playing on the ice. Chances were they were at the frozen fishponds, which several of the castle's children had been playing on yesterday. Ishtaer had listened to Mags discussing with the gamekeeper how best to break the ice so the fish could get some oxygen, and the children had begged them not to so they could continue skating.

The gamekeeper had said he was just going to make a few small holes. He assured everyone it would still be safe to play on. But as Ishtaer heard the crying get louder, she had a terrible feeling he'd been wrong.

She blundered into a bramble, getting snagged and yelping in frustration. 'Durran! Garik! Is that you? Can you hear me?'

Freeing herself from the bush, she ran on, hearing footsteps crunching through the snow towards her.

'Miss Ishtaer! You have to help!'

Durran ran into her, and Ishtaer hugged him tight with her good arm. 'What is it?'

'Garik! The ice cracked! I said he shouldn't let the dog on 'cos he was too heavy and the ice cracked, and I can't see him—'

'He fell in?' Ishtaer asked, horrified, pushing the boy ahead of her. 'Show me!'

Durran tugged her through the gate and up the slope to the ponds. Ishtaer hadn't been here before and had no idea at all how big or deep the ponds were.

'Can he swim?'

'Yes, he's Krullish,' Durran said, scorn overriding his fear. 'We can all swim!'

'Good, that's something. I need you to show me where he went in, and then run and fetch your papa, or Verak, or anyone. Can you do that?'

Brutus rushed up, whining anxiously. Ishtaer attempted to pet him with her injured arm, and failed. Durran didn't seem to notice.

'Will you be able to find him? You can't see!'

With a confidence she didn't feel, Ishtaer tapped the Seer's mark around her eye. 'I'll find him,' she promised. 'Where did he fall in?'

Durran led her to the edge of the pond and she stepped gingerly on the ice. It wobbled and creaked ominously.

'Now go and get help, and tell them to bring blankets,' she added as he ran away.

'Brutus, stay,' she said firmly. Then she stepped off the edge of the ice, and the shock of the water overwhelmed her.

Ishtaer had never had the luxury of swimming lessons with a doting father, as Durran and Garik no doubt had, but she'd grown up in a coastal town and occasionally been sent cockle-picking as a child. You learned to swim then, or the incoming tide could be a death sentence.

The waters of the Great Ocean surrounding the Saranos were cold. But not this cold. Nothing was this cold. For a few seconds she floated, numb with shock, as the cold drilled into her bones and bit at her skin. Then something brushed her arm, and she reached for it, only to find a fish slipping through her fingers.

If only I could see! she lamented fiercely, then told herself

227

it was probably so dark under here it wouldn't make any difference.

He'd float, she reasoned, and couldn't have gone far, so she swam as far as she could under the ice until she hit the bank, and turned back. She'd had to learn to orientate herself with precision, and it wasn't hard to find the hole in the ice where she could come up for air.

She ducked back under, and turned to her right to try again. Nothing. Back to the air. Again.

He can't hold his breath this long. He'll be drowning. And when he drowns he'll sink.

Panic pushed her on, out towards another bank. *I'm doing this wrong, I'm missing so much surface area, I don't know how to do it!*

And then she felt it. Something much bigger than a fish, something that felt like fabric. A sleeve. An arm. Garik. *Oh, thank the gods!*

She pulled his body to her. He wasn't moving, just floating eerily in the water. Ishtaer hooked her right arm under his chin and with her left, punched up at the ice. Her feet touched the ground, and she pushed her body up at the ceiling above her, feeling the ice crack and splinter as she shoved free.

She was near the bank. Heaving Garik's small body over her shoulder, she waded out, set him on the ground, and collapsed to her knees beside him. Brutus rushed over, whimpering and nuzzling her.

'Not now,' she told him, and pressed hands that were almost numb to the child's chest. His heart was still beating, although he wasn't breathing. She bent and began breathing into his mouth, pushing down on his chest, willing him to breathe, calling on every ounce of strength her crystals could give her to make his lungs work by themselves, to draw the water out, to make him live.

If I could breathe for you, I would, she promised him, and then Garik sucked in a great load of air and coughed up a great load of water and Ishtaer nearly sobbed in relief.

'Is he all right? Will he be all right?' Mags cried, and Ishtaer started, because she hadn't even realised anyone else had arrived. She pushed Garik to his side and he continued to cough up water, while Mags threw a blanket over him and rubbed his back before dragging him into her arms and hugging him tight.

'Oh, my precious boy,' she wept, and Ishtaer fell back. She heard Kael's deep voice, rough with pain, felt him kneel down and murmur to Garik. She thought she heard him sob a little.

Ishtaer wrapped her arms around Brutus, feeling his warmth seep into her, and tried to get her heartbeat under control. Someone draped a blanket over her shoulders. Eirenn said, 'Are you all right?'

She nodded. 'I'm fine.' And she felt fine, relief numbing her pain. 'We need to get Garik indoors, out of those wet clothes, warmed up. I need to check for infection, the pond water might—'

Then someone kissed her, and all her words disappeared.

It wasn't a tender kiss, or a lecherous kiss. It was a hard kiss, open-mouthed and fierce, and she felt hot tears on her cheeks that hadn't come from her own eyes.

'You saved him,' Kael gasped against her lips. 'You saved my boy. Oh gods, Ishtaer. Thank you.'

Ishtaer was too stunned to reply.

Kael carried his son back to the castle, feeling the small body shiver and shake in his arms, and cursed himself for being so blindsided by Ishtaer's anger that he hadn't checked the ice was safe. *If she hadn't been there, if she hadn't risked—*

'I think he's got rid of most of the water,' Ishtaer said, hurrying to keep pace with him, 'but I'll need to check he hasn't got any fluid on his lungs. First thing is to get him warm and dry, though.'

'And you,' he managed, looking at the dark hair plastered to her head, the coif carelessly pushed back around her neck.

'I'll be fine. I've been colder.'

He shouldered through the door to the room the boys shared and Mags bustled in behind him, shouting instructions for blankets and towels and hot stones for the bed. They were Krullish, they knew how to deal with the cold. Everyone knew how to take precautions, and everyone knew that sometimes precautions weren't enough.

They stripped Garik of his wet clothes, dressed him in the warmest ones he had, and wrapped him in blankets. Durran dived into the bed with his brother.

'I'll keep him warm,' he promised, and Kael's heart turned over.

'You were very brave,' he told Durran.

'I should have gone after him.'

'No, you absolutely shouldn't.'

'You could have drowned,' Mags scolded.

'Then I'd be dealing with two of you frozen to the bone,' Ishtaer said.

'But that means you're frozen instead,' Durran said. He looked miserable. 'And you're a lady. A lady shouldn't have to risk herself for a man.'

Kael touched his son's dark hair. *You're not a man, not even nearly.* 'Ishtaer is an intelligent adult who knew what she was doing. And she's a Warrior, so she's much stronger than any other lady.'

'And a lady who'd let a child drown isn't much of a lady,' Ishtaer added quietly.

Kael glanced at her, her face pale, her mail shirt miles too big for her. She was barely using her right arm, he noticed.

'You need to go and warm up,' he told her, 'and see to that arm. Do you want any help?'

She shook her head, and lifted her left hand from Garik's chest. 'I can't feel any signs of fluid on the lungs, and he seems to be free from fever, but he needs to be watched, all night. If he develops a temperature, or he's coughing up anything wet or frothy, or his breathing is noisy—'

'We'll come and get you. But you need to rest too,' Mags said. She took Ishtaer's hand and used it to pull her into a hug. 'Thank you,' she whispered.

'It's what anyone would do,' Ishtaer said, and disentangled herself. 'Come on, Brutus.'

She left, and Kael found himself sitting in his sons' bedroom, watching the two boys sleep. Tears burned behind his eyes, which was ridiculous, because they were safe, they were both safe, and fine. Crying now was pointless.

'He'll be fine,' Mags said. 'He wasn't under for long. And she is a good Healer.'

Kael nodded.

'If you want to get some sleep I'll sit up with them.'

He shook his head.

'Or my sister will come in. It's not a problem.'

Kael bit his own lip, and Mags slid her arm around his shoulders in a hug.

'I won't tell anyone if you cry a bit,' she said.

'I'm a swiving warlord, I don't cry,' he said, the words broken by a sob.

'Oh, come here,' Mags said, and pulled him into her arms. He pressed his face against her neck and cried great sobs of relief. Garik was safe, he was fine, and the dreadful, all-consuming fear that had been with him since Durran ran into the training yard, his face drip white, was ebbing.

'How could I have been so stupid?'

'It's not your fault, Kael.'

'I should have gone and checked the ice, they should have been supervised …'

'You can't supervise them every minute of every day.'

'Someone should.'

'Kael, they're smart boys, they know when something is dangerous. You saw the ice, it was thick enough to bear adult weight. They just got unlucky.'

'I'm never letting them play on ice again.'

'Quite probably Garik will never go near it again. Even you've fallen through thin ice, Kael. You told me.'

He lifted his head. 'I did? When?'

Mags glanced at the two sleeping boys. 'About eight years ago,' she said quietly.

Kael followed her gaze. Durran had his arms wrapped around his brother, his dark hair falling over his eyes. *He looks so much like his father.*

He straightened up. 'Last time I sat in a bedroom and sobbed on someone's shoulder,' he said.

'I recall I was doing a lot of sobbing too.'

'I recall we both had good reason.'

She squeezed his hand and smiled.

'Now look, with all this commotion neither of us has eaten since breakfast. You stay here and I'll go and fetch some food.'

'I can go,' Kael offered.

'Last time you looked for food you left half the cupboards open and one of the dogs got in.' She stood up. 'I'll send something on to Ishtaer too, she'll be in need of fuel. I doubt she'll have thought of it herself.'

'Harsh, Mags.'

'True though. That girl is incapable of doing anything for herself.'

Kael felt the bruise on his ribs from her sword and shook his head. 'Trust me,' he said, 'she's improving.'

Mags regarded him, head on one side. 'What *did* happen to her?'

He shuddered. He always did when he remembered Ishtaer's memories. 'You really don't want to know.'

Mags rolled her eyes and left the room, and Kael took the opportunity to offer a few very heartfelt prayers to whichever gods were listening. When Mags returned, it was with bowls of soup, chunks of bread and cheese, and a couple of tankards of ale.

'I sent Eirenn with some for Ishtaer,' she said. 'Didn't take much persuading.'

'I know. He's totally in love with her.'

'Not sure what he sees,' Mags mused, and Kael shot her a look. 'Don't be like that, she's perfectly pleasant, and I suppose she's quite pretty too, but she's so ... timid.'

'So timid she leapt into a frozen pond without even the benefit of sight, in order to save a child she'd known two months.'

Mags's hand tightened on her tankard. 'You're right, I'm sorry. Eat your soup before it gets cold. It's already dark out, did you realise?'

He hadn't. The shutters had been shut to keep the heat in, and he supposed they'd been here longer than they realised.

'I've asked Klara to take over dinner. Everyone knows what's happened, they won't mind us not showing our faces. Unless you want to – I'll stay here.'

'I'm staying too.'

Mags opened her mouth to reply to that, but the door banged open with such urgency that he never got to find out what she was going to say.

Eirenn stood there, eyes wide with panic. 'It's Ishtaer,' he said, and Kael's spoon fell into his bowl with a splash. He was halfway to his feet before Eirenn finished speaking.

'What?'

'She's just … sitting there, she's not saying anything, she's freezing cold and she won't get changed or eat anything, and her arm is a mess, and I don't – I don't know what to do.'

Kael turned to the door, stopped and turned back. The boys slept on, oblivious. Mags calmly set his food on the floor.

'Of course you must go,' she said.

'I said I'd stay—'

'And leave your Healer in a catatonic state? Kael, the boys will be fine. If there's any change I'll come and get you, but I think Ishtaer needs you more.' She gave him an unreadable look. 'You're the only one she pays attention to.'

Kael dashed back to the bed to give his sons a kiss, then hurried after Eirenn down the maze of corridors to Ishtaer's room.

'Did she say anything? Is she awake?'

'Yes, but she's just not … it's like she's entirely unaware of anything.'

'Shock,' Kael said. 'She's just overwhelmed and freezing cold, and I'm pretty sure that arm was broken. She'll have been running on adrenaline—'

He stopped dead as the realisation hit him. *Freezing cold and broken bones.*

'Oh gods,' he said, and set off at a run.

She sat on the treatment bed in her workshop, apparently staring at the far wall, her knees drawn up and her arms wrapped tight around them. Her face was whiter than the snow outside, her eyes huge and unfocused. The sleeve of her mail shirt was dark with blood and dented into her flesh. Brutus sat on the floor, nudging her with his nose and whining worriedly.

She wasn't even shivering.

'Ishtaer. Ish.' He shook her by the shoulder. She might have been made of ice. 'You're all right. You're going to be all right. We'll get you warmed up and treat that arm, and you need to eat something, and you'll be all right. Ishtaer, listen to me. Ishtaer!'

Her breathing was shallow and uneven.

'What do we do?' Eirenn asked, clattering into the room behind him.

I don't know. Kael tugged at her hand, which just made her clutch at herself harder. 'We need to get her warm. Get these clothes off her and warm up the room.' He was vaguely aware of Eirenn drawing curtains over the windows and clattering about with logs.

'Ishtaer, listen to me. No one's going to hurt you. We want to make you better. That's all. We want to help.'

Still nothing. Kael pressed his forehead against hers. She was frozen.

'Ishtaer, please, sweetheart. I know you're cold, and you're hurt. I know your bones feel like they've been turned to ice and your blood is full of stabbing little needles. I know your arm hurts so badly you can't even think about it. And I know that last time you felt like this very bad things happened and it never got any better. But it will this time. I promise you. I will make it better.'

Her breath hitched as if she was about to cry.

'I won't ever let anyone hurt you,' he whispered fiercely.

She moved her head against his.

'Just trust me, okay sweetheart? Trust me.'

She gave a tiny nod, and Kael let out his breath in a rapid sigh.

'Right, Eirenn,' he said. 'I need you to leave.'

'What?' The boy paused with a chunk of wood in his hand. 'No. She's my friend—'

'And you have no idea why she's in a catatonic state. I do. And I know she doesn't want anyone else knowing about it.'

'I won't tell—'

'But you'll know. Do as I say, Eirenn.'

Eirenn looked mutinous, but he put down the wood and walked over. 'Ishtaer. Do you want me to stay?'

For a moment she didn't react. Then she whispered, 'Go,' and Eirenn looked like he'd been slapped.

'I'll be back later,' he warned, and stumped out of the room, slamming the door behind him. The noise made Ishtaer jump. Good. At least she was reacting.

'You need to get out of these clothes, Ish. Can't warm you up otherwise. Now, are you going to do it, or do you need my help?'

Her throat worked a few times. He wasn't sure she could move.

Gently, he took her uninjured arm and prised the fingers from their death grip on her knee. That went well, so he straightened out her arm and tried not to notice it was like manipulating ice.

'This is going to hurt, just now, but then we'll fix it and the hurt will go away, okay? I just need to move your arm. Really carefully. All right? Here we go. See, not too bad, it'll be much better soon, you're doing so well. You're being so brave.'

Tears started trickling down her cheeks. Kael wasn't sure he could take that. His own eyes were burning again.

'Okay, now your feet. One by one, let's put them down on the ground. Just unbend your legs. That's it. There you are, much better, right?'

She was beginning to shiver, which Kael knew was actually a good sign.

'Now, I've just got to take this mail shirt off you, and you'll feel a lot better.' He stared despairingly at where it had been mashed into her arm. *I did that.* He turned away, hating himself, and swiped at his eyes. *She can't see you crying, idiot.*

He forced himself over to the cabinet where Karnos had always kept his heavy-duty instruments, the stuff he kept out of sight to avoid frightening people. Ishtaer appeared not to have changed the set-up, for among the saws and straps and plicrs, he found a pair of bolt cutters. Only he knew Karnos never used them for bolts.

Attempting not to shudder, he went back to Ishtaer, who sat exactly as he'd left her, and very carefully started to cut the mail shirt and coif off her. The heavy metal shirt began to slide away, and she flinched as it tugged on the wound in her arm.

'Sorry, sorry, I'll make it stop, just be brave a minute longer, you're doing so well,' he babbled, pulling carefully at the cold metal as she sobbed and shivered and he cursed himself with every breath.

When the shirt finally slithered to the floor he let out his breath and stripped off the sleeveless padded jerkin she wore underneath. Beneath this, instead of the corsets worn by fashionable ladies or the fabric breast band favoured by working women, she wore a tightly fitted leather vest over her shirt. It was fastened with buckles at the sides – dimly, he realised it must be one of Malika's creations – and getting ever tighter as it dried.

'Ishtaer. Ish.' He touched her shoulder. 'I have to take this off you. It's soaked through and freezing. I have to take all your clothes off but it's just so I can get new ones on you, understand? That's all.'

She quivered in response, so like the terrified slave he'd first met. She'd come so far and done so well, and now ...

He shook his head and made himself walk to her bedroom, retrieve a woollen nightgown and thick socks, and go back out. She hadn't moved.

Kael braced himself, and cut through the ties at the side of her vest. He peeled it away and simply tore her sodden shirt off her. Ishtaer shivered violently.

Her breasts were small and lovely and blue with cold. He dragged the nightgown over her head and carefully pulled her arms through the sleeves as if he were dressing a baby. Next he unfastened her breeches, said, 'I'm not looking at you, I won't look,' and pulled them off her as fast as he could, tugging the nightgown down over her legs and pushing socks onto her feet.

'There, isn't that better? Warmer? I'll get you a blanket,' he prattled inanely, going back to her bedroom and fetching one from the pristinely made bed. He wrapped it around her, then simply scooped her up and carried her over to the stove, sitting down on the floor with his back to the wall and Ishtaer in his lap. Her left arm was cradled by her right, which he figured was a good sign. There was no way he was going to try to fix it right now. She had to come back to herself first.

'Just rest, sweetheart. Just rest, and warm up. You'll be fine. You've been really brave.'

She rested her head against his chest, and said nothing.

Chapter Nineteen

Ishtaer woke to the sort of intense pain she thought she'd left behind, and a confusingly contrasting sensation of warmth and comfort. Someone held her close, a blanket covering them both. A large body. A male one. He smelled of sage soap and sweat and his heart beat strongly in his chest.

She lifted her head. 'Kael?'

'Yes, love?'

She tried to collect her thoughts, not entirely sure where she was or what she was doing in his arms. Again. Against her feet rested something large, warm and heavy. Something with a damp nose and a thumping tail. Brutus. Ishtaer smiled and tried to reach out to him, but her arms were tangled in the blanket and her right forearm throbbed abominably.

'You were freezing cold, sweetheart, and in shock. I had to warm you up. This seemed the best way.'

Of course. The pond. The fierce cold.

A shudder wracked her, memory clawing its way up from the darkness. *The crack of bone, the cold, the laughter—*

'Ishtaer?'

She held on tight to that voice.

'How's Garik?'

'He's fine. Mags is looking after him. We know how to deal with the cold.' He gently squeezed her shoulder. 'How are you feeling?'

Ishtaer considered this.

—the clawing pain, the crack of bone, the last time I fought back, the darkness—

—I'll never let anyone hurt you—

Her voice was hoarse when she replied, 'Exactly how

someone who jumped into a frozen pond with a broken arm ought to feel.'

He gave a soft laugh. 'Well, you've warmed up at any rate. I didn't want to treat that arm until you were out of the woods. And I … I don't think you should use your crystals to treat it, either. You're not strong enough. Not tonight.'

Ishtaer would have protested, but right now she wasn't sure she could keep her head up and her eyes open, let alone concentrate on healing broken bones. She forced herself to think, to concentrate on healing. Even when she'd been terrified, she could always find the best way to treat something.

Nearly always.

'There's a brace somewhere. Rods and straps and a sort of winch. For traction. That will do, if you'll help me.'

'Of course I will.' He paused. 'I've been on the receiving end of that brace. It's not pleasant.'

She held on tight to the conversation. 'Have you been on the receiving end of fire ointment? Karnos's notes said it dealt with foreign bodies and infections, and I think this wound has both. Gods only know what I picked up in that pond, and there's some metal still embedded.'

Kael sucked in a breath. 'Fire ointment. Evil stuff. I mean … yes, it'll remove anything that's not supposed to be there, but it feels … well, like you're on fire.'

'I suppose that's why he called it fire ointment. You'll have to strap my arm down, then,' she said matter-of-factly. 'I don't want to make it worse.'

For a long moment Kael held her a little bit tighter, and she thought she felt him brush something against her hair. *It was just the blanket*, she told herself as he stood up and carried her to a chair.

He clanked around with the contents of the chest containing the more heavy duty implements, and then he was back, taking careful hold of her right arm and laying it against the arm of the chair.

'You sure about this?'

The darkness loomed, memory tugging her down again. *The unbearable pain, too much to fight against, the helplessness, the apathy.*

Just don't hurt me any more.

'Just do it quickly, before I change my mind.'

He strapped her arm tightly to the chair, elbow and wrist, and Ishtaer braced herself. *He's doing it to help you.* The fire ointment had tingled on her finger, but that was nothing compared to the cold burn of it against her wounded flesh.

But it was bearable. It wasn't so bad.

She'd just opened her mouth to say so, when Kael lit a match.

The burn of the ointment alight was excruciating. The metal rings, the bits of cloth, the pond dirt, all flared into burning, hideous heat, and she screamed, shaking and thrashing. Hands held her down. She supposed they were Kael's. She kicked and sobbed and fought. Someone cried out, 'You won't hurt me again, you won't!' and she didn't know if it was herself or her memory.

By the time the burning had subsided to a level she could bear, she was back in Kael's lap again, his hands holding her arm away from her body, still attached to the chair arm.

'Told you it was horrible,' he said, and she gasped, pain throbbing through her. Her left hand clutched Kael's arm, her fingers digging into his flesh, holding on tight. If he was here, he was real, solid, not a memory – then she was here too, and her memories couldn't hurt her any more.

She forced her fingers to unbend, to touch her injured arm. The wound was clean. The flesh was hot from the fire, but not from infection. And even as she felt at it with her free hand, it seemed to be closing over.

'Right,' she said shakily. 'That's the first bit done with.'

This time she didn't imagine it. He kissed the top of her head. 'Well done. Now we just have to set the bone.'

'Bones. They're both broken.'

A ragged sigh escaped him. 'Ishtaer, I'm so sorry—'

I won't ever let anyone hurt you.

'It's not your fault. Well, I mean it is your fault, but it's … it's all right. Accidents don't count.'

He took in a deep breath and let it out. 'Nonetheless, I'm still sorry.'

She found a smile from somewhere. 'You can make it up to me by helping reset my arm.'

'Any time,' he said, helping her back up, supporting her injured arm very carefully.

He strapped her to the chair again, this time her torso and upper arm, and moved her forearm into the contraption she'd found when she first arrived, and grimly deduced the purpose of. To reset the bones, he'd need to pull them into alignment, and then keep the traction on until the bones had set. This meant an extra set of hands to apply the splints before traction was removed. With a mechanical device to hold the limb in place, one person could treat a broken bone by himself.

Only not, Ishtaer knew from bitter experience, if the person treating the broken bone was also the patient.

Concentrate. Hold on tight to the here and now. Don't let the memory take you.

'Do you have the splints ready? There are some ready formed—'

'I've got it sorted. Just brace yourself, okay?'

'Maybe I should—'

'Stay exactly where you are, and trust me. I've done this before.'

Ishtaer squeezed her eyes shut out of pure reflex.

Kael turned the wheel that would stretch her wrist away

from the elbow and she forced herself to keep her breathing even as the broken bones shifted.

Briefly she considered knocking herself out, but that would be no good as it could be hours before she came round and she needed to check the bones really had aligned properly. Numbing only one part of the body was something many Healers found very difficult to do, and it required immense concentration. Ishtaer was currently having problems remembering her own name. If she tried to numb her arm it would probably fall off.

'Keep talking,' she gasped. 'Keep me here and now.'

'Ishtaer?'

'I won't go back there. I won't.'

He let out a harsh breath. 'No. You won't. I'm here. I'll always be here when you need me.'

Kael's strong fingers probed gently at the site of the break, and she gasped out a sob.

'Nearly there,' he soothed. 'Just a little more. You're doing so well.'

'I'm having my arm reset,' she ground out, 'not giving birth.'

'I'm aware of the difference,' Kael said, a touch of laughter in his voice. He turned the wheel a fraction more. 'When Mags had Durran she screamed the place down.'

'You were … there?'

'Aye. She needed someone's hand to break.'

'I'm glad you were there when … your son was born,' Ishtaer panted, and Kael gave the wheel one last turn, popping the bones into place.

Ishtaer's breath whooshed out of her in one huge gasp.

'I had to be there,' Kael said slowly, feeling at the break again. 'His real father couldn't.'

'You don't,' she drew in a shaky breath, 'have to lie to me. Healer, remember?'

Kael's fingers went still.

'Durran is your son. And Garik isn't. Not biologically. You let Eirenn and me think it was the other way around.' Ishtaer made her fingers move. 'Good. That's good.'

'Good?'

'There's very little nerve damage. Do you have a dressing for this wound, before the splint goes on?'

She heard him draw in a breath as if he was about to speak, then he let it out and muttered, 'Of course.'

He was silent as he prepared the dressing, and Ishtaer felt the memory tugging at her again. 'Keep talking.'

'I don't know what to say.'

'Say, "Ishtaer, I'm going to talk about anything to distract you from the memories of the last time you woke up in darkness with a broken bone, because even though you're holding on really tight to the present and the knowledge it'll be all right, I can see you're slipping back into a terrible place," and I need—I need—'

'All right, all right.' His fingers curled around hers. 'I'm here. I'll help. I—what do you want to know? About Durran?'

She concentrated hard on breathing, on the feel of his hand on hers. 'No one else knows he's your son?'

'It didn't seem right or fair to Hasse. Mags's husband. They were childhood sweethearts. Hasse and I grew up together, like brothers. Mags was a sister to me. But they couldn't have children. I don't know why. Karnos did, but he never said.'

'So you ... what? Offered your services?'

'No!' He pressed the bandage a little too hard against her arm and she flinched. 'Sorry. But no, it wasn't like that. It was after Hasse died. A rockfall, I think I told you. I was about your age. Mags was ... she was just destroyed. She loved Hasse more than anything. And I did too. We tried to comfort each other. Had too much to drink. It ...' His hands stilled in the act of placing the splints. 'It was an act of desperation, I think, for both of us. And when she found she was pregnant, only she and I knew the real truth. Everyone assumed it had happened just before Hasse died, and talked about how tragic it was. I couldn't dishonour my best friend like that. Or Mags. So we just agreed to … let people think what they thought. Hasse and I have – had – similar colouring. Everyone says Durran looks like his father.'

'And when he grows up, and looks like you?'

Kael sighed. 'I don't know. Maybe we'll tell him. I don't know.'

Ishtaer adjusted one of the splints, and nodded to him to start binding her arm.

'And Garik?'

'Hah. Garik I was never sure about, until now. Are you sure?'

'There's nothing of you in him. Durran, I can feel your blood in him.'

'That's a little creepy, Ishtaer.'

'Sorry. But … did you know he wasn't yours?'

'If he was, he was born very early and rather large for a premature baby.' Kael sighed. 'Ilse seduced me with rather alarming impatience. When she told me she was pregnant I had no choice but to take care of her. But I was never quite sure …'

'I'm sorry.'

'Aye, well. I ended up with Garik, and I'd never deny him. Even after all that happened to Ilse.'

'Do you think it was very terrible?'

Kael was silent a moment, then he said, 'Terrible enough that the day after the birth she walked down to the shore and into the water and never came back.'

Shock ran through her. 'I thought she died in the birth?'

'I think she wished she had.'

Ishtaer felt hollow. 'I'm so sorry. I shouldn't have said anything.'

'So long as you don't say anything to anyone else. Whoever Garik's biological father is, I don't think he was a very nice guy. Ilse was running from something, and my bet is a man.'

'Mags said the same thing. She said I look like I'm running, too.'

'You do. But you're not running as fast, these days.'

Ishtaer didn't know what to say to that. Kael finished binding her arm and carefully released it from the traction device. 'How does that feel?'

She flexed her fingers cautiously. 'Good. Fine. Well, not fine – but better. I mean it won't get any worse overnight, and I can heal it properly when I'm feeling ... better.'

He ruffled her hair affectionately. 'You should eat something. Mags said she sent Eirenn with something ... Oh yes, there it is. I'll heat up the soup for you.'

She nodded mechanically and stood up, pushing the chair towards the table and sitting back down again. She was tired, but she was functioning, and she'd stayed in the present, in this clean warm room with a good man who was taking care of her—

A good man? Where had that thought come from? He was Krull the Swiving Warlord, he was famous for ...

... for a lot of things she'd never actually experienced him doing. Showboating seemed to be the worst she could lay against him. Pretending to be wicked. Krull the Warlord would never spend half the night bringing a catatonic girl back into the real world. Kaelnar Vapensigsson, it appeared, would.

'You eat that while I go and sort your bed out,' he said. 'The fire's not lit, and you need to stay warm. Do you have a warming pan?'

She did, although she'd never used it. Now would not be

the time to tell Kael she'd still never got up the courage to sleep in her bed.

But when she'd finished eating and tiredness made her shiver, Kael said, 'Right, no arguments, I'm staying in your bed tonight. You need me to keep you warm.'

'I'll be fine,' she protested, getting to her feet.

'Yeah, you said that earlier and I found you slowly turning to ice.' He pulled her against his body, his strong, hard, warm body, and for the first time Ishtaer could remember, she wasn't frightened. He wasn't going to hurt her, or force her, or do anything but hold her, as if he cared for her and wanted to keep her safe.

It was very seductive. But Ishtaer had listened to Samara promising to keep her safe, usually shortly before beating her half to death.

The memory slithered up around her again, cold and dark.

'I wish you'd trust me, Ishtaer,' Kael murmured, and she took a deep breath.

'I do.'

Kael woke with a soft, warm woman in his arms, her head tucked against his shoulder, and for a long moment allowed himself to indulge in the sheer pleasure of holding her.

Then for an even longer moment he indulged in the fantasy of kissing Ishtaer awake, sliding off her woollen nightgown, pressing her strong, supple body against his – and probably getting eviscerated for his trouble.

Sighing, he eased away from her before she discovered the effect she had on his body, and slid out of bed, nearly stepping on Brutus as he did. Her very own furry chaperone. Brutus seemed to like him well enough now, but if he tried something Ishtaer didn't like he could well imagine the wolf enjoying a meal made of warlord entrails.

He stood and watched Ishtaer for a while, her chest rising

and falling beneath the covers, her cheeks pink with sleep. Her splinted arm lay outside the blankets, and he reached down to touch her fingers to check they hadn't gone numb or cold.

Her eyes fluttered open as he did.

'Hey,' he said, and the longing for this to be something he did every morning nearly overwhelmed him.

This is ridiculous. You've never wanted to be tied to one woman, and as for that moony fantasy you've just had about seeing your betrothal necklace on that pretty collarbone, you can go and stick your head under the pump until it goes away.

'Hey,' Ishtaer murmured, stretching like a cat. Beautiful.

'How're you feeling?'

'Better. Much better. I'll get this fixed today.'

'Take it easy. Give yourself time off. No training today, that goes without saying, and I'll warn everyone not to come for healing—'

'That's silly. What if it's something urgent?'

He prevaricated. 'Urgent stuff only. But I'll be here to help.'

She smiled. 'You had a hard day yesterday, too. You should rest. Healer's orders.'

'If my lady insists.'

'She does.' Ishtaer pushed back the covers. Her nightgown had tangled up around her thighs, and Kael let himself gaze at her long, strong limbs, the colour of honey, *and would they taste as good—*

Good gods, Kael, stop it!

'I, er. Breakfast. Will be soon. I'm sure. Can you get dressed? Do you need me?'

She sat up and swung her legs around, covering them with the thick wool. 'I'll manage, thanks. You should go and see Garik.'

'Yes. Garik. Definitely. I should.'

Ishtaer gave him a strange look, but nodded. 'I need to thank you for yesterday,' she said, her tone quieter.

'You really don't.'

'I really do. You saved my soul last night. And it's not the first time.'

'You saved my son. And no, I don't care about what we said last night. He is my son, biology be damned.'

She smiled, a tired smile. 'I wouldn't expect you to say anything else.'

Kael turned for the door, then turned back and cupped her cheek. 'I'm glad you're okay,' he said, before brushing a light kiss over her skin, and leaving before he did anything to ruin it.

Chapter Twenty

He found some plate armour for her after that, ill-fitting but enough to protect her from more broken bones. Ishtaer hated wearing it, heavy and hot, but she had to admit she came away with far fewer bruises after training in it.

The days grew shorter and colder, and more of the villagers came up to the castle for the winter. The yards were full of animals, cows and goats and chickens milling about during the short hours of daylight before they were shut up in one of the turf-roofed barns so they wouldn't freeze.

Ishtaer's arm healed perfectly, aside from the small scar which she elected to keep, as a reminder. When she told Kael this he touched the uneven skin gently, and said, 'As if I'd ever forget.'

He rarely spoke about the night he'd played her angel, except to joke lightly about 'how I set you on fire that time.' He trained with her, rarely pushing her too far, getting her to repeat drills over and over, even if it meant hitting him repeatedly with her wooden sword. He encouraged her.

Ishtaer realised that he was behaving like her friend.

When they went down to the village to bring up the last of the boats for the winter, it was Kael who partnered with her, not Eirenn or Verak, or any of the teams of men who'd turned out to help. And when a storm hit before the last of the families could move out of their cottage by the shore, it was Kael who grabbed Ishtaer's medical bag before she could and raced down to the village with her.

A cottage had partly collapsed, and while most of the family had escaped with minor injuries, a girl of about fifteen called Ailsa had been caught by a falling chimney which had broken most of her ribs and caused severe internal damage.

'I can heal her, but I need you,' Ishtaer said to Kael as she knelt in the rubble, freezing rain pelting down on her. 'I'll go into crystal-debt.'

'Whatever you need,' he said, hand on her shoulder, and she felt his strength spreading through her like sunshine.

By the time she was done she lifted her head to find they'd been there hours, and that a tent had been erected around them, with a brazier, and that Kael still sat beside her, quietly lending her strength. When she judged Ailsa stable enough to be moved, he helped carry the stretcher up to the castle and brought Ishtaer food and drink throughout the night.

He breakfasted with her in the mornings, trained with her until they ate lunch together, and often wandered in to chat while she held her afternoon surgery. He sat beside her at dinner, topped up her glass and laughed with her about the day's events. He spent more time with her than anyone other than Brutus, who worshipped him.

And Ishtaer liked it.

When she went to bed at the end of the day, she climbed between the sheets – because it was, after all, just a bed, and nothing bad was going to happen to her in it – and thought about how it had felt to go to sleep in his arms, feeling safe.

Shortly before the Dark, Kael leaned towards her at dinner and said, 'I'm taking the sled to Utgangen tomorrow. Time to hold court. Do you want to come? There's an armourer there who can make you something that fits properly. Old Smed is great at repairs, but a whole new suit is beyond him.'

'My own armour?' She bit her lip. 'Will it be expensive? I don't know how much things cost.' He'd paid her periodically, a small pile of coins in a jar that slowly grew.

'My treat.'

'Kael, you can't buy me armour.'

'You're part of my horde. I'll buy you whatever the hell I want.'

'I thought all your money went on winter food.'

'That's just what I tell fortune hunters. Some of it goes on presents for friends.'

She sighed. 'I can't accept that. But thank you for the offer.'

In the morning, instead of dressing in her borrowed armour, she dressed in the thickest furs she had and carried a small bag of clothes and toiletries out to the sled, which rested in the uppermost yard of the castle, the one which led to the Utgangen road and the only one which was guarded.

'Are you sure you'll be all right?' she asked Mags anxiously. 'I've left out all the most common things people might need and Eirenn's labelled them all, he knows what's what, and I've put extra doses of Ailsa's painkillers in her mother's room, just in case we're late a day, and—'

'We'll be fine,' Mags said. 'We've coped for months without a Healer before. We'll manage for two days.'

'If Marta's baby comes early—'

'It's not due for three months, she's had no complications and she has done it three times before. Midwifery we can do, Ishtaer. Get yourself off to Utgangen and stop worrying.'

Kael took her bag from her, laughing, and went to stow it in the troika.

'Will you be all right?' Eirenn asked quietly.

'I'll be fine. We've enough furs to keep a village warm, and plenty of food for the journey, and dry wood and even some kind of tent affair, Kael tells me, which means we can sleep in the sled if we get stuck in the snow—'

'I don't mean on the journey. I mean you're spending two days with just him. I don't want him to … to try anything.'

He was shuffling his feet, she realised. He was embarrassed.

'Kael isn't going to try anything,' she assured him. 'I trust him.'

'He used to try it on with you all the time,' Eirenn said.

'Well, he doesn't any more. He's not interested in me and I'm not in him. Frankly, I suspect as soon as we get to the inn he'll be out looking for a girl.'

'I'd rather have a woman than a girl,' said Kael from behind her, making her jump. 'Now, if you're done predicting my actions, are you ready to go? Good.'

Durran and Garik ran up to give them hugs, Eirenn helped her into the sled and pulled the furs over her, then the sled was gliding out of the courtyard and across the snow.

Silence fell very quickly, Skjultfjell with all its noise and warmth falling rapidly behind, and Ishtaer could hear nothing but the crunch of snow under the sled's runners and Brutus's sigh as he settled by her feet. The ponies pulling the troika were almost silent on the snow, which seemed to deaden all other sound.

'How long will it take?' she asked, although she already knew.

'We'll be there by supper. The Dark is still a week off, but people tend to travel less this time of year anyway.'

'What is the Dark?' Ishtaer asked. 'Everyone at Skjultfjell seems so frightened by it.'

'It's the darkest week of the year. Barely gets light for an hour a day, and it's freezing. Really, really freezing. You've got to prepare for it or you will die. Every year we lose a few animals, no matter how careful we are. For the most part, hardly anyone goes outside at Skjultfjell. It's one of the reasons there are so many corridors and tunnels.'

'Mags said you have some sort of festival in the middle of it.'

'Yeah. It's a bit like the Midwinter events in the Empire. Something to look forward to, to liven up what might otherwise be a long, slow period. We exchange gifts too. Just small tokens, for family usually. If you got the boys something small they'd love it.'

'I'll have a look when we reach town. I suppose the presents are what the children look forward to the most?'

'Usually,' he said with a laugh. 'And the late night storytelling, and the candies Mags has been making in secret for ages. Everyone looks forward to it. Also it keeps people's minds off the Hunt.'

'All right, what's the Hunt?'

'The Wild Hunt. Supposedly this demonic bunch of huntsmen with hellhounds and horses made of bones or some rubbish. Mostly it's a story told to kids. If you see the Wild Hunt, then they'll chase you until you die. So they stay inside.'

'Ah. Whereas if you told them it was just too cold, they might risk it?'

'You're smarter than you look, you know.'

He was teasing her. 'For all I know, I might look like a genius.'

'I don't know what geniuses look like. Aren't they all beardy old men?'

Ishtaer pulled down the scarf covering her chin. 'No, no beard there.'

Kael laughed. 'Do you know, it wasn't that long ago you told me you didn't think you had a sense of humour.'

She frowned. 'In the summer. On the river barge.'

'You were wrong. You do, and I like it.'

Thoughtfully, she rewound the scarf. 'This time last year, I was sitting in Madam Julia's sickbay, healing Malika's hands.'

'The seamstress?'

She was surprised he remembered. 'Yes. I was so frightened Madam Julia would find out, and punish me.'

'Why would she punish you for doing your job?'

'I don't know. I think I was just so used to being punished.'

He shifted on the seat next to her, and put his arm around her shoulders. Ishtaer leaned against him.

'You said on the barge that you felt like you'd come alive. That ... person I met, last year, she seems like a ghost now.'

'She was,' Ishtaer said. 'She still haunts me sometimes.'

His gloved hand squeezed her shoulder.

'You know, you've come a long way,' he said. 'A year ago you'd never have rested your head on my shoulder like this.'

She shifted and realised he was right. She didn't even remember laying her head there.

'I don't suppose I would.'

They drove on through the sharp, cold air. Kael said rather abruptly, 'I'm not going out to find a girl once we arrive, you know.'

'A woman, then?' Ishtaer said, wondering why the thought of it hurt. What Kael did with a woman was his own business.

'No. Not anyone. I'll stay with you. I don't want to leave you by yourself.'

'I'll be fine—'

'I'm still not looking for a woman.'

'I don't mind—'

'I don't want one, all right?'

She bit her lip, and nodded. He was tense under all those furs.

'All right. I was only joking with Eirenn anyway. He thought you'd try something with me.'

'I've told you before—'

'Yes, I know, you don't want me.'

'Don't want you? Ishtaer – how could I not want you? You're brave and funny and clever and – did I mention brave? And you're beautiful. Any man would want you.'

'Stop it,' she said, straightening up, away from him.

'No. Look, just because I want you doesn't mean I have to have you. I told you I'd never make you do something you didn't want to, and I mean to hold to that. I will never force

255

you; I won't "try anything" with you. I respect you, and I like you, far too much to mess things up.'

Ishtaer said nothing. She couldn't think of anything to say.

'The reason I'm not rushing out to find another woman isn't so I can stay in and seduce you. It's just that I don't want another woman.'

Her hands gripped each other as best they could in their leather mittens. The sound of the crunching snow was deafening.

Kael swore. 'I should never have said that about wanting you. I meant it as a compliment. It was a stupid thing to say. I'm sorry.'

'It's all right,' she managed.

'It's not all right. Can you forget I said that?'

Ishtaer swallowed. 'Yes,' she said, but it was a lie.

Kael cursed himself for the rest of the drive, he cursed himself as they checked into the inn, he cursed himself throughout a polite but distant supper with Ishtaer. When he saw her up to her room that night, he hesitated for an agonisingly long time over whether to kiss her cheek or touch her hand or do anything at all, but she took the decision out of his hands by murmuring, 'Good night, then,' and disappearing into her room.

The click of the key turning in the lock had never been louder.

What was wrong with him? Impassioned speeches, babbling explanations? He was Krull the Swiving Warlord! He didn't witter, he didn't stumble over apologies, he didn't behave like a lovesick fool over a woman!

He didn't—

Oh, hell. He didn't have feelings like this.

He continued to curse himself throughout most of the night, and woke thoroughly grumpy after not nearly enough sleep. Worse, today he was holding court at the town hall, an opportunity for people to come and air their grievances or ask for help. It had to be done, but he could rarely say he enjoyed it.

Last time it had been mostly border disputes and three men who all believed they were the father of the same woman's unborn child. He'd drawn a chalk circle, placed the woman in the middle of it, and told the three men that the true father could pull her out. When two started pulling in opposite directions and she started screaming, the third stood back and said he couldn't hurt her. Kael had sent her home with him, and told her not to be so profligate with her affections next time.

The irony of this was not lost on him.

'Gaspar is the smith we're going to see,' he said to Ishtaer over breakfast in the inn's common room. 'I'm not sure where he's from, but he makes very fine armour. He'll need to measure you quite carefully, though. I don't expect he'll take any liberties, but I'll stay with you.'

'There's no need, I'm sure you're busy—'

'I'll stay with you,' he said firmly, and she shrugged, all camaraderie gone.

Kael cursed himself again.

Gaspar seemed a little put out when he discovered he was to make armour for a woman, but when Kael took him aside and told him the full extent of the order and how much he was going to get paid, he quickly shut up.

'And don't tell her how much it costs,' Kael added. 'She thinks she's just paying for the one set.'

'Anything you say, my lord,' Gaspar said, and Kael could almost see the flash of gold in his eyes.

Afterwards, despite Kael offering to escort her back to the inn, Ishtaer accompanied him to the town hall. It wasn't large or grand, but then neither was Krulland, and that was what Kael represented when he fastened on his lord's mantle and took his seat on the dais.

Ishtaer sat beside him, facing the court, and Kael tried not to enjoy her presence there too much.

'Let 'em in,' he said to the mayor, and braced himself to dispense justice.

As usual, most of the plaintiffs had minor disputes. A few had lost crops or livestock to the cold or to disease, and Kael had the town clerk assign them enough to see them through the winter, with the promise that his men would be out to check they weren't lying about their hardship. Even in his own lands, the horde of Krull the Warlord was feared.

Two men had the most banal dispute he'd seen in years, arguing pedantically for hours over a patch of land Kael was sorely tempted to claim for himself, until he learned it was too small to graze a horse on.

'I declare it common land for your community. They're to have full access over both your properties. Now go away. You're both ridiculous.'

One woman was brought forward in chains, thin and dirty, her face bruised and crusted with blood. The magistrate accompanying her told Kael she faced execution for murder but protested her innocence so strenuously that he thought it best to seek his lordship's judgement.

Beside him, Ishtaer tensed.

'Who did she kill?'

'Her husband. Stabbed him.'

'Do you deny the accusation?'

'Oh no,' the woman said. 'I stabbed him. After he beat me, drugged me, locked me in the cellar and forced himself on me.'

Kael glanced at Ishtaer, who had gone very still.

'Drugged you?' he asked.

'The ...' the woman looked uncomfortable. 'The drug that makes you ... it makes you want ...'

Realisation dawned. 'An aphrodisiac? He gave you Venerin?'

She nodded, looking miserable. 'He said I was frigid. I just didn't want him.'

Kael was glad she'd stabbed the bastard.

'A husband cannot force himself on his wife,' the magistrate said patronisingly.

'You're an idiot,' Kael said, and the man stared in astonishment. 'Rape is rape whether it's by someone you're married to or a complete stranger. And the last time I checked, false imprisonment and bodily harm weren't legal in Krulland either. Venerin certainly isn't.'

'But the law says a husband may discipline his wife,' the man protested.

'What? No, it doesn't, we repealed that. Didn't we?' Kael stared at the Utgangen mayor and magistrate. 'Go and find wherever it's written down and scratch it out. And then take this magistrate and lock him in his own cells for a week so he can learn the value of compassion.'

The clerk and the guards looked surprised, but they did as he said. Kael scrubbed his hand over his face. He was queasily aware that he'd never given much thought to the idea that the law could be used against people.

Not all weapons are swords, you idiot.

Beside him, Ishtaer stirred. Her hand moved to Brutus's collar, and every eye in the place watched it. Brutus stared back at them, looking more wolflike than ever.

'Do you have somewhere to go?' she asked the woman whose chains were being struck off.

'My sister. She offered to take me in before when — when he started —'

'How far away is she?'

'Two days' travel.'

'You came here in the magistrate's sled? Did he bring guards? Good. Stay here at the posting inn tonight and rest.

Take a knife with you when you travel back. If your guards attack you, use it. Are you hurt?'

The woman gaped at her. 'She is,' Kael said quietly.

'Then come with me.' Ishtaer rose to her feet and held out her hand.

The woman followed her without question.

Everyone in the town hall stared after them, including Kael.

'Ishtaer Lakaresdottir Vapendam,' he said into the silence. 'Rather magnificent, isn't she?'

Ishtaer busied herself taking care of Aune, the woman who had stabbed her husband, taking her to the inn and requesting a bath to be brought up. She healed the worst of Aune's wounds, found clean clothes while the woman bathed, and then ordered food.

'You're being far too kind, my lady,' Aune said.

'No, I'm not. I'm doing what any decent person would do,' Ishtaer said, and then she sat back in her chair and felt her mouth drop open.

'My lady?'

A year ago, I was you. But worse. Or did it all become the same below a certain level?

The thought knocked her off balance. A year, was that all it had been? Since someone had to bathe her and heal her and dress her. She'd just swept out of a feudal court and given orders which were fully carried out.

The world was turning in a very different direction for her these days.

Supper that evening was less constrained than it had been the night before, but Ishtaer felt that it was only Aune's presence that kept it from being so taut. She could feel the tension between Kael and herself every time he spoke, or accidentally touched her, and she hated it.

I want you. Why did that disconcert her so much? She knew he wasn't going to do anything about it. Why did it make the blindest bit of difference?

Halfway through their return journey snow started falling. By the time they were an hour from home, it had turned into a blizzard.

'We could stop and tent up,' Kael said to Ishtaer, who was bundled up with so many scarves and fur coats she looked like a rather adorable mole, 'or push on through. Risk is if we stop, the snow could build up around us, and we'd never get out.'

'Whatever you think is best,' she said, which annoyed Kael. Where was the woman who'd rested her head on his shoulder and bickered with him?

'Your opinion, Ishtaer. I want to hear it.'

She shrugged. 'I don't want to get caught in a snowdrift, and if we stop it'll probably kill the horses. But you know this terrain much better than I do. If you can't see where you're going, I might as well be driving.'

She had him there. 'We'll go on,' he said, 'but slowly. Hopefully it'll clear.'

It didn't, of course, and the hour it should have taken them stretched into three. By the time he finally saw the lights of Skjultfjell through the thick, solid snow, Kael felt like he was made of ice and he'd never be warm again.

He glanced at Ishtaer. She hadn't complained once about the cold.

He steered into the courtyard, which was deserted. 'If you hold the horses, I'll go and find someone to help us unload,' he said, and she nodded and climbed down stiffly, feeling her way along the thickly furred flank of a stocky pony until she reached the head of the shaft horse. Brutus slunk along beside her, looking miserable, and the horses were too tired to even react to his presence.

Kael made his way in through the nearest door, stamped the snow from his boots and tried to adjust to the gloom. Up here was mostly storage and summer stabling, deserted this time of year, but with access to better-used parts of the castle that didn't involve going back outside.

He climbed down a ladder, wove past tightly bound hay bales and made his way through the dark and dusty parts of the castle to the longhouse. Dinner was clearly over, but the place was still full of people talking, laughing, finishing drinks and generally being bright and warm and alive. He stood in the doorway for a moment, enjoying the warmth before guiltily recalling Ishtaer standing alone in the snow, and bellowed for attention.

By the time he'd organised a dozen or so men to assist with unloading the troika's goods and stabling the horses, Ishtaer had been alone for maybe a quarter hour. The courtyard was sheltered, but the blizzard raged on. He poured a cup of hot wine for her and led the men back up to the top courtyard.

And heard the shouting before he even got to the door.

'... my horses or my dog! This is not your domain!'

The hot wine spilled on his boots as he dropped it and ran.

'You can have no one here! Go! Be gone!'

Kael shoved open the door and burst into the courtyard, a dozen men bearing torches behind him. They spilled into the dark yard, gasping at the cold, light spreading and guttering in the fierce snow.

Ishtaer stood with her sword in her hand, ready in a fighting crouch, Brutus snarling beside her and the horses squealing with terror.

There was no one else there.

'Where did they go?' Kael demanded, rushing over to her as his men spread out into the yard. 'Are you all right?'

'Kael? There were more than a dozen, maybe two, big

horses, dogs, armour and blood and—' She collected herself. 'You must have frightened them away.'

'Two dozen men?' He glanced around wildly. The courtyard held nothing but the troika, his men and snow. 'They can't just vanish! Who has the sharpest eyes? Can you see through the snow?'

Ishtaer glared around the courtyard, as if straining to see her attackers.

'Did they speak to you? What did they want?' How had they got here? Where had they gone? 'Maybe they followed us.'

'We would have heard! They were blowing horns, and the horses were huge, they made such a noise on the ground, and the hounds were baying, and—' she faltered. Her foot stubbed at the snow. 'I didn't think the yard had been cleared.'

'Not in this blizzard,' Kael said slowly. He looked at the thick snow on the ground. Even the hugest stallion wouldn't make much of a noise on it. And any hoofprints would be eliminated by the falling snow.

'Ishtaer, did you say hounds?'

'Yes. Barking and howling.' She looked confused. 'I heard them coming ...'

'It's the Wild Hunt!' gasped one of the men.

'It's not the swiving Wild Hunt,' Kael snapped, even as the rumour spread. 'What are you, seven? There's no such thing.'

'I've heard 'em,' said one of the younger lads defensively. 'When I was a kid.'

'Heard what? Horses? Men in armour? Dogs? Place is full of 'em, lad. Now stop all this nonsense and unload the sled. It's perishing out here.'

Nobody wanted to be out in the blizzard a few days before the Dark, Huntsmen or no Huntsmen. The sled was unloaded pretty sharpish, the goods stored, and Kael led Ishtaer inside to the warmth and light of the longhouse.

'I know what I heard,' she said as he hustled her along the corridor.

'We have dogs here, and the wind can sound just like a hunting horn when it whistles through the—'

'And the horses? I didn't just hear them, Kael; I felt them. I could smell them, and feel their hot breath. The men smelled of blood and slaughter. The horses of sweat and manure and leather. I heard the clank of armour.'

'Well, the stables,' Kael began, somewhat feebly.

'And the voice talking to me? I suppose that was just the creak of a door, was it?'

She has very accurate hearing, he told himself, then overrode it with, *But who could hear properly in that blizzard?*

'What did it say?'

She gave a bitter laugh. 'He said he was looking for a maiden to bear away. I told him he hadn't found one.'

His fingers tightened on her elbow. The Huntsmen were said to bear away maidens. But probably someone had told her this. Talk in the inn had turned occasionally to the Hunt. 'Anything else?'

'He said he'd take my hound and my horses to join his hunt and slaughter me if I didn't run. So I got my sword out.'

Pride swelled in him. 'Good girl,' he said automatically.

'I told him he couldn't have anything here, or anyone, and then you came and ... I don't really know what happened then.'

Kael paused with her just outside the longhouse. 'Are you all right?'

'I'm fine. I just ... it felt so real. Do you really think it was the Hunt? I thought that was just a myth.'

'It is just a myth.'

'Then I was just challenged by some madman on a big horse who vanished without a trace. Were there hoofprints?'

'No, but that doesn't mean anything, the snow was falling

too fast. Even the troika's tracks were disappearing.' He frowned. 'It could have been a vision. You've seen the future before.'

'Yes, but not like that. I could *smell* them, Kael. They were *there*.'

Nevertheless ... 'I'm going to station some guards up there, wherever there's a window. If they come back, we'll catch them. Right now, it's probably best to keep quiet about this. I'll tell the lads, too. No point in scaring people.'

She nodded uncertainly.

'Come on, there's probably some food around somewhere, we both need to eat after that journey.'

Ishtaer agreed, reluctantly, and he took her in to dinner.

But later in the evening after they'd eaten, put Durran and Garik to bed and admired the kittens they'd chosen from one of the stable cats' litters, after Kael had gone to his room to bathe the last of the chill away, he still didn't feel easy. He'd posted guards, all of them brave and intelligent soldiers who knew the difference between wind howling and a huntsman's horn, and he didn't seriously expect anything to happen.

But he still found his feet taking him towards Ishtaer's room, tapping on her door and hoping she was still awake.

She answered the door in her nightgown, a shawl around her shoulders. Her hair was damp, dark strands brushing her shoulders, and her cheeks were pink.

'Yes?' He watched her inhale. 'Kael?'

'You always know when it's me.' He leaned in the doorway, smiling.

'Are you all right? Can I help you with anything?'

Her voice was a little chilly. Kael tried to make his sound warmer. 'I want to talk to you. Can I come in? No sense wasting the heat.'

She stood back to allow him in. Brutus thumped his tail but didn't get up from his bed by the stove.

Kael shut the door and leaned against it, hands in his pockets. He'd dressed after his bath, but it looked like she'd just got out of hers.

'You're a Seer.'

'Yes?' she said, as if waiting for something less obvious.

'But you can't see.'

She folded her arms. 'Is this going somewhere?'

You're making a mess of this, Kael told himself. *Didn't you used to be cool with women?*

'I mean – you don't talk much about being a Seer. You see visions.'

'Yes.'

'You see what's not there. Or maybe, what is there but no one else can see. I ... I wonder if you'd have known if you could see? If you'd have seen the Wild Hunt today instead of just hearing them?'

'Are you saying you believe me?' she asked cautiously.

'I'm saying it's a damn sight more plausible than a bunch of mortal huntsmen appearing from nowhere and then vanishing again instantly. Maybe only certain people can see them, I don't know. But I'm not calling you a liar.'

She rolled her shoulders. 'Thank you.'

He didn't think that meant he was forgiven. 'And the other thing ...'

Those shoulders tensed right up again. She was so easy to read.

'About what I said on the sled. I don't want to spoil things between us—'

'It's fine.'

'You keep saying that, and yet you're behaving like—like—'

'Like I did the last time you tried to seduce me?'

She said it coolly, but he saw the tension in her face. Kael squirmed.

266

'Well, er … yes.'

'You know what?' Ishtaer said, leaning back against the counter and looking wearier than he'd ever seen her. 'I am so tired of being afraid. I hate it. I hate it that when a man touches me I want to cringe or run away or beat him to death.'

'It's an improvement on just cringing,' Kael offered, trying for levity.

'I shouldn't feel like that. I don't want to. But it's so hard, I just …' She scrubbed her hands over her face. 'Have you ever stood at the top of a cliff, or a high building, and felt the drop pulling at you? And just staying up there is so hard?'

Kael nodded. Then, remembering himself, said quietly, 'Yes.'

'It's more like clinging to a cliff,' she said. 'A cliff above a volcano or, or a pit of monsters. You know if you let go you'll suffer a world of pain and you'll never come back, and there will be nothing left of you, but just holding on is so hard. And climbing up is almost impossible.'

She stood three feet away. He wanted to go to her so badly, to hold her and tell her everything would be all right.

But you can't make it all right, can you, Kael?

'When the Hunt rode into the yard today I thought first about defending Brutus, then the horses, and it never occurred to me that I deserved defending too. I get so angry with myself. It took me *how long* to be comfortable with you? And then one comment and we're back to the start again.'

'I'm sorry. You have no idea how sorry.'

'Yes, so am I.' She straightened up. 'I don't think I'm fit company tonight. You should go and get some sleep after that drive. I'll see you tomorrow.'

She stood there, tall and strong and resolute, and fragile and vulnerable and hurting so badly he'd have done anything to make her better.

'What can I do?' he asked softly.

She stared out at nothing. 'Damned if I know.'

He raised a hand, and let it drop futilely. Then he screwed up his courage, walked over and brushed her cheek with the back of his hand.

'You're not damned at all,' he said, and left.

After he'd gone she stood for a long while, leaning against the counter in her workroom. *You're not damned at all.* Yeah, that was all right for him to say.

I can't see. I can't bear to be touched. I talk to ghosts and mythical beings. I spend half my time trying desperately not to be a terrible wretch.

I feel pretty well damned.

But Kael didn't treat her like that. No one in Skjultfjell treated her like that, and as for the people she'd met in Utgangen, they seemed to be pretty in awe of her. All right, so this place wasn't exactly a microcosm of the real world, and if she went back to the Empire she'd be back at the bottom of the heap, raised up only by her connection with Kael and these bloody marks all over her skin. Lady this or that didn't matter when everyone remembered you as the skinny, pathetic slave and they'd seen you beaten every day in the training ring.

You could just never go back.

But what good would that do? Hiding away here forever, like a coward? Ishtaer was well aware that she was a coward, but she was never going to face down her demons if she ran so far from them that the only safe place was this castle on the edge of the world.

And that worst demon, the one that crawled over her skin whenever anyone spoke of sex or lust, she was never going to conquer it by pretending it didn't exist. She dealt with its consequences daily, for heaven's sake; every pregnant woman in the castle came to her at some point. She played with their children and listened to them brag and moan about their husbands.

Just because I want you doesn't mean I have to have you. It's just that I don't want another woman.

She ate with Verak and Klara every day and their affection for each other was palpable even from the other end of the table. Once or twice their older children had cried, 'Eurgh, Mamma, stop kissing Papa, that's disgusting!' and Klara had replied, 'When you fall in love like I have, you'll do a lot of kissing too.'

Klara had found a good man, who loved her and respected her, and clearly they found a lot of pleasure in each other. And for the first time in Ishtaer's life, she was jealous.

Chapter Twenty-One

Despite Kael's best efforts, the story of Ishtaer and the Wild Hunt spread through the castle quicker than a forest fire. As with every other story he'd heard about her, it soon became wildly exaggerated, with fire-breathing giant Huntsmen and hellhounds the size of stallions. Ishtaer had, according to rumour, screamed some exciting, inspirational and snappy lines at the invaders, his favourite of which was, 'You shall not take this place! It! Is! Defended!'

'I never said that,' Ishtaer muttered as they passed a family retelling the story amongst themselves.

'No, I think Eirenn was responsible for that. Don't worry about it. It makes people feel safer that there's someone here who frightened off the Wild Hunt.'

She frowned at him, but said nothing. Three days into the Dark, and everyone was getting bored and fractious. Stories were one of the best ways to pass the time, and Eirenn was pretty good at telling them.

'Are you looking forward to Midwinter?'

'Yes,' she said, and added, 'although I don't really know what to expect. In Ilanium it was all visits to the Temple and prayers and readings I didn't understand.'

'Well, here we have visits to the longhouse for feast food and stories even the kids can understand. Uh. I did mention to you about Midwinter gifts, right?'

She smiled. 'Yes, you did, and I went shopping in Utgangen with Aune.' She hesitated. 'We must write and find out how she's doing, after the Dark.'

He smiled at the 'we'. 'Absolutely. But I did enquire about her sister and it seems she's a stout farmer's wife who has been known to intervene in fights between full grown men and come out the champion.'

'A fierce pair of sisters.'

'Yeah. I think she'll be all right.'

'I hope so,' Ishtaer said quietly.

'You can't save everyone, Ishtaer.'

'Neither can you,' she said, and his heart clutched.

He thought again about the gift he'd bought, totally on impulse, walking back from the town hall in Utgangen. The covered market, the only way to shop in such frigid temperatures, was warm and glowing and he'd wandered through, looking for trinkets for the boys for Midwinter. What he hadn't expected was something calling out to him from one small stall, crying like a siren that it would be perfect for Ishtaer.

He hoped she wouldn't take it the wrong way. And then again, a small secret part of him hoped she would.

That night they sat around the huge fire in the longhouse, a fire that would burn continuously throughout the Dark, and told stories. Eirenn told once more his very popular and heavily embellished version of Ishtaer's encounter with the Wild Hunt, and she sat there smiling, saying nothing. Between them sat Garik and Durran, the younger boy curled up against Ishtaer's side. She put her arm around him, whispered something in his ear that made him smile, and turned her attention back to Eirenn.

Kael's heart ached at that, even worse when Mags caught his eye and sent him a very speaking glance. *We look like a family*, he thought, and wished painfully that they were.

When Durran finally drifted off, halfway through Old Alvar's traditional tale of how the Wild Hunt came to be – traditional in that he traditionally never told it the same way twice – Kael glanced over and saw that Garik was fast asleep, and Ishtaer was about to nod off too.

He nudged her gently, and to his delight she barely flinched. 'The boys are asleep,' he said. 'We should get them to bed.'

She nodded and rose gracefully with Garik already in her arms. But when she headed towards the door leading to the part of the castle where they slept, Kael stopped her. 'No. In here.'

'Here?'

'Yes. It's traditional to spend Midwinter night all in the same room. Some people even spend the whole Dark in their longhouses. I guess it goes back to when the longhouse was the only room there was.'

'But, the beds …'

'Follow me.'

The benches around the edge of the longhouse were used for storage, and tonight they'd been packed with bedrolls and blankets. He made up a couple for the boys, close by each other, then another for himself and, casually, one for Ishtaer too.

'It'll tickle them no end to wake up with Brutus next to them,' he added, and Ishtaer nodded, looking slightly uncertain. 'You don't have to stay here. You can go somewhere else, or back to your room if you like.'

She bit her lip and turned her head back to the huge central fire and the group of rapt listeners. Ishtaer was the only castle resident who hadn't gone chalky white in the dark of the midwinter, where the weak sun showed for less than twenty minutes a day, and her bronze complexion turned golden in the firelight. Her hair shone like a crown.

I love you, Ishtaer, he thought, and wasn't even surprised by the idea.

'I'll stay,' she said, and he smiled.

In the morning, he woke to the excited chatter of children and the equally excited deep bark of a big dog. Durran was teasing Brutus with a lamb bone, and the dog was feinting cleverly from left to right, before leaping on the boy and licking his face.

'Eurgh!' Durran laughed, and Kael grinned.

'Teach you right for teasing him, lad,' he said.

'Mamma gave Brutus the bone as a Midwinter present!' Garik cried. 'I didn't know dogs got Midwinter presents!'

'Everyone you love gets Midwinter presents,' Ishtaer said, and he turned to see her sitting up in her pallet, looking tousled and flushed and so incredibly desirable Kael was very glad of the blankets covering his lap. He sat up hastily, rearranging folds of fabric.

'Yes, they do. Go and fetch your shoes, and bring mine and Ishtaer's too,' Kael said, and the boys hared off through the busy longhouse, half full of people sleeping, the other half groups sitting around exclaiming over small gifts.

'Shoes?' said Ishtaer. Her own were nearby as she, like most people in the longhouse, had slept in her clothes.

'It's more of an expression. The tradition is that gifts are left in your shoes. I don't know why. It really only works for very small items, and since often a lot of people receive new shoes for Midwinter, it's sort of evolved to a small bag or pile of gifts. We still call it the Midwinter Shoe.'

He glanced around. 'Mags looks like she's opened hers with her sister's family.' He frowned. Mags always stayed with the boys at Midwinter. He'd expected her to lay a pallet down near his, but he'd fallen asleep thinking of Ishtaer nearby, and this morning …

What was she playing at?

'Papa, Papa,' cried Durran, giddy with excitement as he ran back carrying two cloth bags and reverently placed one of them by Ishtaer's pallet. His heart started beating faster.

'Thank you, Durran,' Ishtaer said, giving him a hug.

'You're welcome,' the boy beamed, and Kael smiled at his excitement.

Garik ran up with his own bag and Kael's. 'Look how many gifts!'

'Because you've been a good boy this year,' Kael told him with a hug, 'and I told you if you learned your letters you'd be rewarded. Show me what you've got?'

The two boys eagerly pulled out small toys and gifts of clothing from the bag. Ishtaer had bought them small wooden animals, and his heart constricted at her worried expression before she realised they liked them. Mags had made them new mittens and Kael wooden swords and shields. Even Eirenn had contributed, with small handmade wooden flutes which, he explained when he sauntered over, were traditional in his part of the world.

Small boys with noisy toys. Kael gave Eirenn a look, which was returned with far too much innocence.

'Now you, Papa, now you!'

Mags always gave him the same gift of a scarf, and Verak of a knife or other small weapon, and this year was no different. Durran and Garik had made him pepparkakor with wonky icing decorations, which he praised profusely. Ishtaer had given him a small dagger with crystals in the handle, which he was pleased with until Eirenn said, 'Hey, just like mine,' and produced a slightly different one.

His heart plummeted.

She thinks of the two of you the same. Kael glanced over at Verak and Klara. Verak held a similar dagger in his hands.

'I'm sorry, I didn't know what to get you,' Ishtaer apologised.

'A man can never have too many weapons,' he said lightly. 'It's perfect. Thank you.'

Now I feel really *stupid.*

Because next the boys urged Ishtaer to pull out her presents, while Kael calculated the chances of ripping the bag out of her hands, extracting his gift, and handing it back while pretending to have just, say, tripped over. Slim.

She took out the pepparkakor shaped like animals which, his sons explained eagerly, were wolves, 'You know, like Brutus!' Ishtaer gracefully said she was sure they did, and Kael hid a wobbly smile because he was sure they didn't.

Eirenn said, 'My present was too big,' and handed her a bow the perfect size for her height, complete with a quiver of arrows. 'So we can practise together,' he said, and got a hug for his troubles. Kael wanted to howl.

By now Mags and Verak had wandered over to thank Ishtaer for their gifts, and they watched as she opened Kael's gift.

He wanted to pull his pillow over his head.

'It's crystal,' Ishtaer said, even before she'd taken it from its velvet wrapping. 'Jewellery?'

He looked at the stones in their silver setting, a glittering rainbow with a large pale blue stone at the centre, the colour of her eyes.

'A necklace,' Mags said. 'Here, let me help you put it on.'

Eirenn cottoned on first, his sharp gaze swinging to Kael, who pretended to ignore it.

'You can't go about with that scruffy bag around your neck any longer,' he said.

'Hey, I made that scruffy bag,' Verak said, but the jocularity in his voice seemed strained too.

'It's lovely. You're too generous,' Ishtaer said, caressing the crystals with her fingertips. He could remember their warmth, the way they'd sung to him softly as he'd picked them up off the stall in Utgangen.

'It's very … Ilani,' Mags said slowly, glancing from the necklace to Kael and back again. He swallowed.

'Yes, right. Ishtaer has a place in Ilani society. Whenever she goes back she'll want to look the part. Right, Ish?'

She was still caressing the necklace, feeling how it was made of one smaller chain fastened to a larger one. 'Yes. Thank you. I love it,' she said, smiling in his direction.

'*Promise* you love it?' asked Eirenn with a look of loathing in Kael's direction.

Ishtaer looked puzzled. 'Yes. I—why? Does it look wrong on me?'

'No, it *engages* with your skin tone very well.'

'Eirenn,' Mags said sharply, shaking her head. He opened his mouth to speak, then shook his head and clenched his fists.

'Why don't you boys come to the kitchen and help me with some of the vegetables?' Mags said, grabbing Eirenn and pulling him along too. Verak excused himself to go back to his family.

Kael sat on his pallet and watched the woman he loved wearing his betrothal necklace, and felt like the world's biggest fool.

The people of Skjultfjell didn't usually go quiet when Ishtaer walked by, but all throughout Midwinter she was uncomfortably aware of their scrutiny. By the time they sat down for the feast half the castle had been preparing, she felt as if every eye were turned on her.

'Do I have something on my face?' she whispered to Kael. 'People are staring.'

'Because you look beautiful. I mean, how can you tell people are staring?'

'I can feel it. And they've been going quiet too. Did I do something wrong? Were my gifts not ... appropriate?'

'They were fine,' he said. 'We all liked our daggers.'

And then it hit her. What an idiot! He'd bought her this beautiful necklace and all she'd got him was a knife, of which he probably had hundreds, and which certainly wasn't any different to the ones she'd bought Verak and Eirenn.

She wanted to put her head in her hands and groan, but she forced herself to keep eating and chatting, listening to the boys prattle excitedly about their presents and how fun it had been to sleep in the hall and how cool Brutus was …

… and thought, this is a man who has saved my life and my soul and seen me at my very, very worst, more than once, and still likes me, still wants to spend time with me, still tries to help me. He's kind and funny and strong and loves his children and he respects me, and he bought me beautiful jewellery and all I got him was a knife and …

Kael touched her arm and she jumped, nearly stabbing him with her fork.

'Are you all right?'

'Yes, fine, just thinking, you startled me, nothing bad, just thinking,' she babbled.

'Okay,' he said, but he didn't sound as amused as he usually did when she babbled. 'Listen. I want to talk to you about something. But later. In private.'

'Oh?' Ishtaer said, her voice much higher than usual.

'Yeah. Uh. After we're done here. I have some aquavit. We'll probably need some. After all this food.'

'Yes, probably.' She was talking as fast as him. 'Shall I meet you—'

'Come to my room.'

'Your room?' she squeaked.

'Or your room. Or my office. Wherever you like. Doesn't matter.'

'Right, your room. Why not, I don't mind.'

'Sure.'

'Right.'

Ishtaer wondered if she could dive into her soup, and never come back out again.

For the rest of the feast, which went on for hours and consisted of every kind of meat and fish and preserve she could think of, she was acutely aware of Kael sitting there beside her.

She was always aware of him. Always knew when he was near, what he was wearing, how he was feeling. When she walked beside him it felt entirely natural to tuck her hand into his elbow, even when she knew perfectly well where she was going and there were no obstacles. When she'd woken beside him that morning in her bed she hadn't been frightened or uncomfortable. She'd felt safe. Warm.

She trusted him. She liked him. Ishtaer had no frame of reference, but she was beginning to wonder if she actually loved him.

His thigh brushed hers beneath the table. It felt … nice. What would it feel like to touch more of him? She'd had her hands all over him when treating him for various injuries, not least the ones inflicted in Palavio, but that was in a medical context. What if she touched him all over just to see what he felt like? To feel his naked body against hers? To kiss him, more than that fierce brush of lips so long ago … which she had, if she was honest with herself, liked?

Her hand went up to the large central stone in the necklace he'd given her. Such a gift, from such a man, and she'd misjudged him badly.

I know what gift to give him, she thought, with sudden perfect clarity. I know the right thing to do.

Kael found himself pacing. He'd said goodnight to the rest of the well-fed, boozed-up inhabitants of the longhouse and put the boys to bed, then he'd gone to his room and fussed around making sure it was warm and bright and welcoming. Not that Ishtaer would be able to see that he'd lit candles and tidied things up, but it made him feel like he was making an effort.

He poured out a glass of aquavit and downed it in one. His heart was still thumping.

Just think about how to say it, he told himself, pacing.

Ishtaer, that necklace isn't what you think it is. What is it then, a type of biscuit? *Ishtaer, that necklace has a meaning.* Ugh, like moonstruck youngsters assigning meanings to flowers. *Ishtaer, I shouldn't have given it to you.* Yeah, she'd love that rejection.

Ishtaer, I love you. She'd run screaming.

He ran his hands over his face and moaned. 'This is going to be a disaster.'

'What is?'

Bollocks. He spun around, realising he hadn't shut the door properly. Eirenn stood there, looking unhappy.

'I'm going to tell her,' Kael said pre-emptively.

'So you bloody should. She has no idea what that thing symbolises.'

'I know, which is why I'm going to tell her.'

'Did you not think of this before? What it would look like? "By the way, Ish, wearing that means you're engaged to me."'

'No, clearly I didn't,' Kael snapped. 'When it comes to her I can't think at all. I saw that necklace and I knew she had to have it and I knew I wanted it to be—I wanted her to be—'

He broke off helplessly.

Eirenn straightened up, his expression unreadable. Kael made an angry gesture at him.

'You want her to be your wife?'

Wordless, he nodded.

'You love her?' Eirenn's voice sounded hollow.

Kael nodded again.

'I see. Well, I … I see.'

And he did, Kael thought, looking at the boy's face. Only he didn't look like a boy standing there, he looked like a man who'd just had his heart broken.

'Right then,' Eirenn said, squaring his shoulders. 'Good luck,' and he walked away rapidly.

Kael was about to go after him when he heard Ishtaer say, 'Eirenn, are you all right?'

'Sure. Just too much food and wine. Bed for me, I think. Night, Ishtaer.'

'Night,' she said, and appeared at his door a moment later. 'What on earth did you say to Eirenn?'

'I, uh.' Kael stared at her, taking in the sight of her. She'd bathed and changed and wore a green gown with a fur trim, her hair loose about her shoulders, her skin glowing with warmth and vitality. The crystal necklace lay against her collarbone, twinkling in the light of the candles.

He wanted to close his eyes and keep the image of her there so he could look at it whenever he wanted. She was magnificent.

'Kael?' She took a step into the room, closing the door behind her. For once she was alone.

'Where's Brutus?'

'Oh, he was tired. I left him in my room.' She smiled at him, but there was a tightness around her eyes that worried him.

'Someone told you,' he said heavily, all his practised words fleeing hopelessly.

'Told me what?'

'About the necklace. That it means we're engaged.'

Ishtaer went very still.

Kael wanted to kill himself.

'We're engaged?' she said carefully. 'To be married?'

'Well, not in a duel,' Kael said helplessly, and regretted it before he'd even finished saying it.

'That's what this necklace means? That's why everyone's been looking at me strangely?' Horror came over her face. 'That's what Eirenn meant about promises and engagements! Does everyone know?'

'Uh, no, not everyone. It's a Chosen thing, not a Krullish thing as such—'

'But everyone here knows about the Chosen. You're part of the Empire. Even in Utgangen people knew what my marks meant,' Ishtaer said, anger rising in her voice.

Panic swamped him. 'Yes, I know, but—'

'Did you think I wouldn't notice? What's next? Will you buy me a ring and forget to tell me we're married? What about children? Am I supposed to notice when I've had those?'

Her face was flushed. She'd never looked more lovely or more angry.

'What were you thinking, Kael?'

'I wasn't thinking. I can't think,' he said, trying to remember how he'd explained it to Eirenn.

'No, that's obvious! How could you make such a fool of me? When you know how hard I try, all the time, not to be an object of mirth or hate, how—I thought you liked me, I thought—'

'I do like you,' he burst out desperately. 'Ishtaer—'

'I came here tonight,' she said, trembling, 'because I wanted to give you something. Something I've never given anyone before. Not willingly. I wanted to show you how I felt. And now – now I feel like a fool, and what's worse is I feel like a possession. Like you can marry me and lock me away in your castle, like you lock away your sons—'

'Hey, you leave my sons out of this.'

'What? Even though this morning you proclaimed to all of Skjultfjell that I was going to be their stepmother? My gods, Kael, I actually thought you had some respect for me.'

'I do. I do respect you.'

'Well it doesn't bloody feel like it!' she yelled.

For a long moment they faced each other, her eyes blazing like the stone at her throat. Then she reached up and unclasped the necklace.

'Here.' She held it out to him. 'Give this to someone who

doesn't mind being treated like something you own. I've already wasted enough of my life like that.'

His heart breaking, Kael couldn't take it from her. She waited for a long moment, then dropped it on the floor and walked out.

Chapter Twenty-Two

No one said anything to Ishtaer about the absence of her necklace the next day. Or the day after that. Even Eirenn held his tongue. She stormed about the castle in a filthy mood and reversed course if she so much as heard Kael's voice. At mealtimes she sat stonily beside him and turned her head away to talk to Eirenn and Mags, both of whom seemed increasingly uncomfortable with the situation.

At night she tossed and turned in her bed, crying hot angry tears into her pillow. Angry at him, yes, but so damn angry with herself for being so damn stupid. How could she have misjudged him that badly? She'd thought he understood her, and all the time he was just blithely marching down his own path and expecting her to fall in beside him.

Well, no more! When spring came she was leaving, going back to the Empire, going back to … All right, she didn't know yet, but she'd work something out. Kael was as bad as all those fortune seekers in the Empire, all the Citizens who wanted to breed more Chosen. A Twice-Marked marrying a Thrice-Marked! They'd have the world's first Child of Five Marks.

A treacherous vision came to her of a little girl, dark-haired and blue-eyed, laughing and waving a wooden sword with her chubby arm at her doting brothers.

No! It wasn't going to happen. Ishtaer had sworn she would never raise a child created by an act of hate, and she was damn sure unlikely to have one created in love. Because no matter how much she loved Kael, he thought of her as just something else to own. Not even important enough to be consulted on her own marriage. Someone who could be kept, who owned nothing, not even her own mind. A slave.

Two days after the Dark found her in the high courtyard dragging out archery butts and firing savagely again and again with Eirenn's bow. If the damn Wild Hunt came back now she'd shoot them all. So she couldn't see the target, she still knew where it was, she could still—

'Ishtaer. Come inside. You'll freeze.'

She stiffened, and fired another arrow. 'You. Go away.'

Kael sighed. 'No. We need to talk.'

'We really don't.'

'Ishtaer—'

She swung around and aimed her arrow at the sound of his voice. 'You have humiliated me in front of your family and my friends, and you want to *talk*? I want to *kill* you! You of all people know why this is so hard for me, and to try and make me some kind of *possession*—'

She broke off, tears stinging her eyes and stealing her breath.

'Ishtaer,' said Kael, and to his credit he sounded appalled. The snow crunched as he took a step forward. Brutus growled at him. 'Don't cry. You never cry.'

'I know I don't,' gulped Ishtaer, who'd been doing little else all week when no one could see her.

'Will you listen to me? Just at least listen to what I've got to say?'

She sniffed loudly and kept the bow up. 'I don't see how you could make it any worse.'

'I love you,' he said, and her fingers tightened on the bow. 'That's why I bought the necklace. Because I couldn't see it on anyone but you. Because I want to marry you. I love you. I don't want to possess you. I just want to be with you.'

Her aim wavered. She told herself it was because of the cold.

'I know I did this all wrong. I got … confused. I wasn't thinking. I've never done this before.'

'Obviously,' she spat. 'If you had someone would have shot you already.'

'Touché,' he said. 'Look. I'm really sorry about the way I handled things. I wanted to tell you, that night – and I know I should have done it before, I should have explained, I'm sorry, I'm an idiot. I can't think straight when I'm around you. Or even not around you. I did this all wrong. And I'm sorry.'

Ishtaer said nothing. But she didn't lower the bow.

'I wish you could see yourself,' he said softly. 'You look like a warrior queen. You're magnificent. I could never possess you. No one could.'

'But they did,' she whispered, another hot tear rolling down her cold cheek.

'Not all of you. Not right down to the heart of you. Or you wouldn't be here. With me.'

But I was, you don't understand, I was hers ...

'You belong to yourself. Always have. Even then. Soon as I called you by your name you remembered that.' He sighed. 'I'm not asking you to be mine. I'm asking you to call me yours. Because I am. Even if you never speak to me again. You don't have to wear the necklace. You don't have to marry me. You don't have to bear my children. You just have to be your magnificent self.'

The bow wobbled in her hand.

'I love you, Ishtaer.'

Her hands shook too badly to hold her aim. She dropped her hands to her side and marched past Kael, back inside the castle, away from all the confusion he was creating in her.

But it didn't go away. She locked herself in her room and cried, and then she busied herself restocking ointments and potions, and then she sat and wound bandages, and all the time she heard his voice, over and over. *I couldn't see it on anyone but you. I want to be with you. I could never possess you. I love you.*

She wiped more tears from her eyes.

What *are* you afraid of, Ishtaer? Did you really think he was going to lock you away like chattel? Don't you know him by now? Don't you know yourself?

What do you want?

'I want to be with him,' she said, and realised it was true.

Every shutter had been closed for weeks, and the longhouse was starting to suffer the effects of a large fire and lots of people. Dark, hot, stifling after the stark fresh air of the courtyard—air so cold you could slice it, air so cold it hurt.

Kael barely noticed any of it.

He stared out at the hall blankly, at a jumble of people laughing and talking and eating. The seat beside him was empty. Mags said something and he replied, although even if put to swordpoint he couldn't have said what the conversation was about. The seat beside him remained empty. Durran splashed his toy animals through his soup on some sort of epic journey, and Mags scolded him, and the seat beside Kael was still empty.

He'd told Ishtaer he loved her, and she'd walked away.

Someone nudged his arm. Then someone hit his arm. 'You need to talk to her,' said Eirenn, and everything inside Kael hurt.

'I did. I did talk.'

'And?'

And? He wanted to weep. He'd ruined everything, completely destroyed forever the chance of happiness with the one woman he'd ever really loved through his own arrogance and stupidity, and—

'Huh,' said Eirenn, but Kael was too mired in self-pity to notice. Until the lad added, 'Well, it's certainly had some effect.'

His head came up. Causing a stir as she walked the length

of the longhouse, her wolf at her side, was Ishtaer. She wore her green gown with the fur trim, cut wide on the shoulders, her sword belt an embellished gold affair. Her hair drifted loose around her bare shoulders. Her face was serene, and so lovely it hurt to look at.

Kael stared like the lovestruck fool he was, trying to commit every detail to his memory to save forever, so he could see her when his eyes closed. He watched her sweep up to the dais, cross it towards him and take her carved seat with the grace of a queen.

Preparing for her to ignore him as she had all week, Kael clenched his fist so hard blood trickled from his palm.

And Ishtaer turned to him, cupped his unshaven cheek in her palm, and kissed him.

Kael couldn't have been more astonished if she'd stripped naked and performed a circus act.

Her kiss was hesitant, nervous, betraying the sangfroid of her appearance, and after the first astonished second, when she seemed like she might be about to pull away, Kael reached up to touch that vulnerable skin between her shoulder and neck and held her where she was, kissing her back.

And Ishtaer, strong, brave Ishtaer who could cut a man to ribbons if he did something she didn't want, simply pressed herself closer with a soft sigh, allowing him to take charge and kiss her. Her lips were soft, her tongue hesitant, as if she wanted to please but didn't know how to go about it. It was nearly too much for Kael to take. Tenderness overwhelmed him and he urged her closer, half off her chair, half onto his lap, his hand sliding to her back and holding her against him as her arm went around his shoulders and she pulled herself closer still.

He might have kissed her for hours, had it not been for the high-pitched, shocked, 'Papa!' and the childish giggle that followed it.

Guiltily, he recalled that this act of foreplay was being performed not just in front of the whole castle, but his children in particular.

He pulled back from Ishtaer, whose eyes were closed, cheeks flushed and lips red with desire. If not for their surroundings he could have taken her there on the table.

Except, he realised as he held her in his arms, that he'd never take her anywhere at all. Even if this was all she was willing to give, he was nothing more than a grateful recipient.

Now who's the slave, my lord?

'Kael, really, at the dinner table?' said Mags briskly, but he heard the laughter in her voice.

'Yes, really, at the dinner table,' he said, and on his other side Verak snorted with laughter.

Ishtaer pressed her face against his neck, breathing hard, and her heart hammered against him.

'Not that I'm complaining,' he murmured in her ear, 'but what was that about?'

'I don't,' she began, her voice muffled, then she lifted her head to whisper in his ear, her hot breath doing lurid things to his imagination. 'I want—I want you. What you said – I want …'

He waited, his entire body strung painfully on the knifepoint of desire.

'I *want*,' Ishtaer said, and Kael very nearly forgot his children were sitting opposite him as he kissed her until neither of them could breathe.

'All right, all right, you've made your point,' said Eirenn, sounding as if he'd eaten a toad. 'Could you do that away from the dinner table, please?'

'Yes,' Kael said, breathing in the scent of her. 'Let's.'

'After dinner,' Mags said sharply. 'Or you can explain to the boys exactly what you're sloping away to do.'

Durran and Garik looked at him with bright, inquisitive

eyes. Kael felt his cheeks heat with a blush he didn't think he'd displayed since … well, ever.

'Yes, good point,' he said, and tipped an equally blushing Ishtaer back into her seat, holding onto her hand with lightheaded joy. 'After dinner,' he whispered to her. 'We'll … we'll … we'll talk, is what we'll do, and then we'll, you know, we'll—'

'Yes,' she whispered back, and Kael knew he wasn't going to get much eating done that night.

After a dinner she was too nervous to eat, after walking together to Durran and Garik's room to tuck them in rather distractedly, after asking Eirenn, her face scarlet, if he'd take care of Brutus tonight, Ishtaer walked hand in hand with Kael to his room. Neither of them said anything.

When they were inside, he shut the door, turned the key, and said, 'I'm leaving the key in. You can leave any time you want. I just don't want to be interrupted.'

'I think everyone knows we don't want to be interrupted,' Ishtaer whispered. It seemed very hard to find her voice.

'Look, we don't have to do anything you don't want to,' Kael said, and her courage came flooding back.

'But I want to do everything,' she said.

Kael let out a ragged breath.

'I don't want to be afraid any more,' she said, and he was there, kissing her.

For something she'd never done before, Ishtaer was finding it surprisingly easy to kiss Kael. Her body moulded itself against his, her hands sliding over his back, her arms holding him to her. He held her as if she was something precious, as if he couldn't stop touching her, as if he loved her.

He drew back, breathing hard, and said, 'We should take this slowly.'

'Yes. Maybe. I think.'

He laughed softly. 'And we can stop any time you want to,' he said caressing her cheek in a manner guaranteed to make her never want to stop.

She nodded, wordless, and Kael kissed her softly again before moving away. She heard the clank of buckets, the splash of water, and frowned.

'Um, what are you doing?'

'I had an idea. I had to think of something during dinner, after all. Was it just me or did it go on for years?'

'It wasn't just you,' said Ishtaer, who'd barely eaten anything because she was trembling too much to pick up a fork.

'Good. I thought, why don't I ask Verak to nip back here and heat up some water for a bath?'

'I bathed before I came to dinner,' she said uncertainly. Was this some custom she didn't understand?

'Sure, but ... look, my thinking is this.' He came to stand before her again, taking her hands in his. 'This will be the first time you've ever made love with anyone, won't it?'

She nodded, her fingers tightening around his.

'Well then.' He kissed her fingers. 'Then you should start anew. Wash away the past.'

Her heart swelled. He *did* understand.

'This is a fresh start. A brand new day.' His lips brushed hers. 'Do you trust me?'

She nodded, too emotional to speak.

Kael undressed her, unlacing the finest dress she owned and laying it with her sword belt across a chest.

'I have to ask,' he said, toying with the edges of her chemise, 'the sword?'

'Just in case you turned out to have been messing me around,' she said as lightly as she could.

'I'll never do that,' he promised.

'I know,' Ishtaer gulped, on the edge of tears again. Kael

kissed her until they went away, then he raised her chemise over her head and the warmth of the fire and his body breathed against her bare skin.

'Oh, Ishtaer. You are so beautiful,' he said, his fingertips tracing a line from her shoulders to her hands, and listening to the reverence in his voice, she felt beautiful. He removed her undergarments so gently he might have been unwrapping a priceless artefact. Ishtaer felt no shame, no embarrassment, but instead a kind of power.

'I'm not made of glass,' she said, smiling as he rolled down one stocking. 'And you have seen me naked before.'

'Yes, but I was trying not to notice,' he said, and her smile widened.

He led her to the bath, which steamed fragrantly with the scent of sage, and handed her in as if she were stepping into a carriage. When she lay back she felt fine linen against her skin. He'd draped the bath with cloth for her.

She heard the rustle of cloth and smelled the clean hot skin that meant he'd at least partially undressed, and then he was beside the bath, taking her hand and washing her arm.

'This bath smells of you,' she said dreamily.

'It's the soap I use.' He sounded stilted, unsure what to say. 'Mags makes different kinds. I like this one.'

'I like it too.'

The cloth he used dipped across the top of her chest to her other arm. Then he leaned her forward and washed her back. When he was done and she reclined against the linens like a queen, she reached out and stroked her hand up his arm, feeling the formidable muscles there tremble.

'Is this all right?' he asked. 'Is this okay?'

'It's wonderful,' Ishtaer breathed, and he leaned forward to kiss her gently, his bare chest against her arm, as the washcloth caressed her breasts. Ishtaer let out a ragged breath against his cheek, but she didn't tell him to stop and he continued on, gently caressing her, cupping the slight weight in his hand and stroking his thumb over her nipple, all with the fine cloth between them.

And just as heat started to gather inside her he slid the cloth away under the water, over her stomach and her hips, sliding over her thigh. He washed her right leg, then the left, each time stroking up the inside of her thigh and stopping just before the top. By the time the cloth touched her hips and buttocks, Ishtaer was panting, wanting something she couldn't name.

No man had ever touched her and made her enjoy it. No one had ever teased her, stroked her, excited her like this. She wanted his hands everywhere, not through the barrier of the cloth or the water but everywhere, touching her and inciting the fire under her skin.

When he finally slipped the cloth between her legs his arm was around her shoulders as she pressed her breasts against his chest, kissing him desperately. The fine linen caressed her tender flesh, and just when she didn't think she could stand it any more, the cloth disappeared and his fingers were there, stroking her, exploring her, finding ways to touch her that had hot streaks of pleasure shooting through her veins.

'Kael,' she gasped against his mouth, and then he found a spot that made her arch against him and shudder, and he caressed it over and over until the heat and pressure inside her exploded and she cried out in shock and delight as pleasure shook her, convulsing in his arms.

Kael lifted her gently from the bath, her body still trembling with the aftershocks of her orgasm. *I did that*, he thought, pride making him grin like an idiot. Ishtaer clung to him as if he were a raft in a storm, and he kissed her forehead, her closed eyelids, the tip of her nose.

Gently he slid her down to stand on the hearthrug, steadying her as she stumbled. 'Easy. I've got you.'

Ishtaer clung to him, her eyes opening huge and dazed. Unable to help himself, he kissed her, tasting her desire and wonderment, before reaching for the towel and carefully drying her.

She was flushed, and not just from the heat. Her hair clung to her in damp tendrils, her lips were red and swollen, her nipples hard and tight. His whole body ached with wanting her, but he told it to shut up and wait, and instead gently led her to the bed.

This time it wasn't his hands that caressed her but his mouth, tasting that golden skin, his lips and tongue exploring the satin smoothness of her. He kissed her chest, made love to her breasts, and then rolled her gently over to map the muscles of her back.

There were scars here, old marks, the skin puckered and rough. He kissed those too, every inch of them, where someone had beaten her, whipped her, thrown her against hard ground and done unspeakable things to her. He'd seen their full extent when he washed her back and for a moment anger had eclipsed desire, before he'd renewed his promise to obliterate every bad thing that had been done to her.

He kissed her firm, round buttocks, enjoying the way her muscles quivered as he licked a path down her thigh, and ascertained that the back of her knee was ticklish.

'Stop!' she gasped, and he grinned.

'Sorry. I'll make it up to you,' he said, flipping her over and licking his way up her other thigh until he was settled between her legs, tasting a sweetness he was pretty sure no one else had ever tried.

Her response was so gratifying, from the quiver of muscles under her skin to the gasp of his name as she shook and trembled and finally shuddered in pure pleasure, moaning what might have been his name spoken by someone with no breath left.

He kissed his way back up her body as she trembled and clutched at him, and when he licked into her mouth she made an animalistic sound as she tasted herself on him. Kael slid into her slick heat as if he'd done it a hundred times before, and she wrapped her arms and legs around him as he moved inside her.

'Ishtaer,' he said, and ran out of words.

'Don't stop,' she breathed, and he didn't, finding a rhythm that she matched and surging with her into heat and light and love so blinding he blacked out as the pleasure took him.

When he came back to himself he was lying heavy on Ishtaer and her face was buried in his neck, hot tears burning his skin.

The delight dropped away and horror overtook it. 'Ishtaer? Ish! What's wrong? What did I do? I'm sorry, Ishtaer, I'm sorry …'

'No,' she gasped. 'No. I just – I didn't know, I didn't know …'

She lifted her head and took a deep breath. And thank all the gods, she was smiling at him.

'I didn't know it could be like that,' she said, and relief overwhelmed Kael. He kissed her, long and deep, and fell into a contented sleep in the arms of the woman he loved.

Out from the darkness of sleep a huge red cat loomed.

It reared huge and fearsome, all fangs and claws, a crowned cat of blood red, but she wasn't afraid. She lay on a soft bed, a man sleeping beside her. A handsome man, a strong man, who opened his eyes and had the face of the pirate king who'd laughed like a god as he whirled in a storm of slaughter until the deck ran red with blood.

'Ishtaer?' said the pirate king with Kael's voice, and Ishtaer screamed and ran.

Chapter Twenty-Three

'Where'd she go? Where'd she go?'

Trousers barely fastened, Kael raced barefoot along the corridor after Ishtaer, trying to work out what the hell had gone wrong. Last night they'd made love explosively and she'd fallen asleep smiling in his arms. This morning he'd woken up to find a madwoman screaming and bolting, stark naked, from the room.

So he ran after her.

A few shocked onlookers pointed dazedly and he ran on, in what he realised with a sinking heart was the direction of Ishtaer's own room. Why had she run? What sudden change of heart had hit her this morning that hadn't occurred last night? Had he been totally mistaken in her reaction to him? No, he couldn't have been. Nobody could have misunderstood that bone-shaking pleasure.

He reached the door to her workroom at the same time as Brutus, the dog whipping in ahead of him, closely followed by Eirenn. Skidding inside, he saw the door to her bedroom slam so hard it banged back on its hinges, revealing Ishtaer huddled naked on the floor, shaking and sobbing.

'Ish,' he started across the room, but Brutus blocked his way, snarling and baring his very large teeth.

'Brutus, back off, good dog,' he said, but before he got any further someone slammed into him, bearing him to the ground with a painful thud and laying a cold steel blade against his throat.

'What,' Eirenn growled, 'did you do to her?'

'Me? Nothing! I didn't do anything! Ishtaer, what is going on?'

'She is sobbing her heart out after spending the night with

you, that's what's going on,' Eirenn said. His knees pressed painfully into Kael's armpits, effectively trapping him. *Damn, I taught him that move.* 'I'm only going to ask once more: What. Did. You. Do?'

'I. Don't. Know!' Kael yelled in sheer frustration. 'She was fine last night, she just woke up and screamed and ran. Eirenn, you saw her last night. Did she look like a woman doing something she didn't want to?'

Eirenn's face was thunderous. Kael had never seen him so angry. 'No,' he ground out.

'And do you really think I'd do anything to hurt her? After all this time, do you really think that of me?'

Eirenn's gaze flicked past him towards Ishtaer's bedroom, where her sobs seemed to have subsided.

'Well, something's upset her, and you're the one she spent the night with. What happened?'

'I am not giving you a detailed account of what we did last night. Just let me up, all right? It's not like her dog will let me past anyway.'

'Wolf,' came Ishtaer's voice, and they both turned their heads towards it. Eirenn climbed reluctantly off him. 'He really is a wolf.'

They looked at Brutus, crouched in the doorway like a coiled spring, lips peeled back over huge, sharp fangs.

'That's what I've been telling you,' Eirenn said cautiously as Kael got to his feet.

'But why are you telling us that now? Why suddenly … Ishtaer, did you have a vision?'

'Yes,' she said, and took in a ragged breath, 'but not last night.'

Slowly she uncurled and, seeming to realise she was utterly naked, pulled her nightgown from the bed and over her head.

Then she faced them, and her eyes met his.

'I can see you,' she said quietly. 'I can see everything.'

Kael stared at her. She stared back, her eyes the same pale blue they'd always been, now focused directly on him.

'See?' Eirenn said beside him. 'As in … see?'

'You're wearing a blue shirt,' Ishtaer told him, 'and a brown jerkin, and brown trousers, and you have a red scarf around your neck. You have dark eyes and dark brown hair. Kael, you're wearing green trousers. They make your skin look very pale. Your eyes are almost black. Your hair is as dark as you told me that time. Black, in this light.'

They both gazed at her in stupefaction.

'And Brutus is grey and brown and white and most definitely not a dog. I think he must have come from the circus that was in town the night before we found him. He's not quite fully grown yet. He'll be huge when he is.'

'But—but—' Kael managed, and couldn't think of another word.

'And you,' she addressed him calmly, 'you are the pirate who stormed a merchant ship on the run from the Revenue and killed most of the crew. You threw the captain overboard, apparently without realising that he had in his pocket a crystal necklace belonging to the girl he'd kept locked in his cabin. You were surprised when she leapt overboard after it. She never found it, of course. It's at the bottom of the ocean.'

His shock turned to horror with every word. She delivered it as if telling someone else's story.

'You won't remember her, of course—'

—the rain lashed down on me as the pirates attacked, and I flew across the deck after the captain as he was thrown overboard with my necklace, my mother's necklace in his pocket, and the pirate king laughed like a god as he whirled in a storm of slaughter until the deck ran red with blood, never stopping me as I leapt into the cold dark sea—

She'd never shown him the pirate king's face. In Ishtaer's

memory he was an exaggeration, he was a nightmare, he was the devil. He was the devil and she chose the cold, dark sea.

'I never saw your face,' he said, as if that was some defence.

'I suppose a pirate king sees people running from him every day,' she said. 'Even when it means drowning.'

'Ever been in a sea battle? Half the damn crew leap overboard,' Kael said. 'It's chaos.'

Ishtaer was silent a moment. Her gaze slid away from his.

There had been so many ships that season, raiding the Saranos and their failing economy, and there were often girls, stowaways or whores, and after all he was Krull the Warlord and he'd made a name for himself as a real evil bastard, so people often ran, and jumped, and took their chances ... 'Look, if I'd seen you, I'd have tried to help—' he began desperately.

'From the bed of one captain to another? All she wanted was those crystals, and to get away from the slaughter on the deck. The wood ran red with blood. She remembered the hot spray of it on her skin for years afterwards.'

'Ishtaer—'

'So she jumped, and swam, and if you'd followed her, if you'd really tried to *help*,' her voice sharpened, 'you might have stopped her being picked up by a slave ship. You might have taken that ship and slaughtered the slavers there, who kept people, men and women and children, chained on a deck so filthy and cramped that even the healthy joined the piles of stinking corpses.'

Her eyes met his again, the blue of spring skies, and she said, 'I remembered the pirate king's face. I never thought I'd see it again.'

Kael opened his mouth and no sound came out. He stared at her beautiful, beloved face, at the cold blankness there, and didn't know what the hell to do.

'I'd like you to leave now, please,' she said. 'Just go.'

'But, Ishtaer,' said Eirenn. Kael had completely forgotten he was there.

'No. Just go. Both of you. I need … I need to have some time to think. Please.'

Eirenn grabbed his arm and tugged him out of the room, but not before Kael threw one last agonised glance over his shoulder at Ishtaer, standing there in her nightgown, a statue again.

Eirenn shut the door and glared at him.

'I don't need it from you too, kid.'

'All right. First of all, stop calling me "kid". I'm only a couple of years younger than you.' At Kael's frankly disbelieving look, he insisted, 'I've been a first-year Tyro for five years. That's not the issue. Did you really do those things she said?'

At least it wasn't an outright accusation.

'I'm a warlord and a pirate,' Kael said. 'I've done a lot of things. Emperor sanctioned me to raid ships carrying illegal cargo. That merchantman was running from the Revenue, and legal ships don't do that.'

'So you killed everyone on board?'

'When they started firing on us we fired back.' He leaned against the wall, head back, exhausted. How many short hours had it been since that blissful night with Ishtaer? It seemed like another lifetime.

'Yeah, but slaughter—'

He rolled his head to fix Eirenn with a look. 'You've never been in the middle of a pitched battle, lad, so I'm going to ignore that.' He scrubbed his hands over his face. It wasn't much of an excuse. None of it was.

None of it ever was, when it came to Ishtaer.

'Do you remember her?'

'I remember the ship we took in the storm.' A fight like

299

that, in the howling wind and rain, the ship bucking like a maddened bull, the adrenaline pumping like a jackhammer ... How was he supposed to notice one girl in all that? *Excuses, Kael.* 'Five years – no, six now. The Saranos. Just before the war. There were a lot of ships.'

'The Saranos war? But—how come Ishtaer wasn't caught up in that?'

Because a war was kicking off, so the gods sent Ishtaer a Militis mark. And instead of being feted as a Warrior – dear gods, did you expect her to save them all? – she got thrown out of the relative safety of the Manor House, and when a stupid boy tried to rape her she used that gods-given strength and skill to kill him. And then she had to run.

He saw it as clearly as if she'd sent him another horrific vision, and the irony tasted like bile in his mouth.

He cleared his throat and said, 'Reckon she left just before it kicked off.' *Days before I arrived. Days.* 'Let's see – we were about ten days out of port, chasing down illegal Saranean exports. Can you believe that's what started the whole swiving mess? Illegal exports. They refused to bide by any of the Empire's rules, Empire sent in governors and peacekeepers, people rioted, Empire sent troops ...'

'And eventually they sent you.'

'I'm a last resort. We'd only just got back to the Empire from the mess in Draxos when we were sent back out to the Islands. Whole conflict lasted a few weeks. Didn't take much to subdue 'em. Do you know what did it? When we found the workhouses. People there had no idea what really went on in them. They were so disgusted with their own government they lay down arms and let the Empire take over. I remember we had a load of orphans from the workhouses on the ship. There were charities in the Empire to reunite them with their families or find them new ones.'

He remembered the huddle of shocked, frightened kids,

none of them older than about twelve. The workhouse wouldn't look after a kid past twelve. They were sent out to work, which for a lot of them was a step up.

None of them knew a thing about the Empire. Despite the Saranos being on a key trading route between the Empire and the New Lands, they'd been so insulated, so wilfully ignorant of the world outside. Hell, they hadn't even known what the marks of the Chosen meant. They'd thought he and Verak were some kind of warlocks.

'Did any of them succeed?' Eirenn asked, and Kael opened eyes he hadn't recalled closing.

'I doubt it. War's a swiving awful thing, lad. Probably Ishtaer's story isn't even all that unusual.'

Eirenn regarded him with intelligent eyes. 'What is her story?'

'Trust me, you don't want to know. And I certainly ain't telling you.' He straightened away from the wall. 'Right. Anyway. Rumour mill's probably going at the speed of light after her naked dash this morning, so we should probably go and stop it.'

'By saying what?'

'Hey, you're the storyteller, kid.'

'Stop calling me kid.'

'It's a sign of affection,' Kael said.

'Yeah, right.'

But they hadn't even reached the longhouse before Verak intercepted them, his face grey.

'What?' Kael said.

Verak held out a letter. It had the Emperor's seal on it.

Kael grabbed it. A letter arriving three days after the Dark had to have been sent by Viator. And that meant it had to be urgent. More than urgent.

The letter was brief, and in the Emperor's own hand.

'Lady Samara has stolen my nephew. Come to the Empire immediately. My army is waiting.'

He stared at it in shock, reread it, and stared some more.

'It can't be,' he said.

'It is,' said a voice, and a woman he hadn't even noticed standing behind Verak stepped forward. Lady Aquilinia. 'I saw it myself.'

'And you didn't stop it?'

'I wasn't there.' She tapped her Seer's mark. 'My visions are extremely reliable. In any case, by the time I'd reached the Emperor so had Samara's ransom demand.'

'Fuck,' said Kael.

'Precisely. He wants you there as fast as possible.'

'He does know what time of year it is?'

Aquilinia gave him a steady look. 'Yes, he does, and he also knows what Samara may do with his nephew if he dallies too long. Where is your Seer? She should have some insights into Lady Samara for us.'

Kael winced, and so did Eirenn.

'She's, ah, not well.'

'She is a Healer. She can get well,' Aquilinia said crisply. 'Her presence is imperative.'

He exchanged a look with Eirenn.

'She can't,' Eirenn said.

'What's wrong with her?' Verak asked. 'What did you do, Kael?'

'Why does everyone assume it's my fault! Gods. Look, Ishtaer has just … she's just had a bit of a bad time and she's kind of … vulnerable, and I really don't think this is going to be something she'll be able to do—'

'What won't?' asked a cool voice from behind him, Ishtaer's voice, and he whirled around to see her standing there looking remarkably composed, Brutus at her side. Great. Two women he'd slept with, looking unimpressed with him. All he needed now was Mags and the nightmare would be complete. 'What won't be something I'll be able to do?'

Her eyes scanned their faces. Kael wondered if she realised who Verak was.

'Lady Ishtaer,' Aquilinia said. 'Do you remember me?'

Ishtaer glanced at the woman's Seer mark and, as if just recalling a chance meeting said, 'Lady Aquilinia. Of course.' The two women exchanged curtseys as if they were meeting in the Imperial Court. 'Are you here on business?'

'Unfortunately I am. The Emperor has sent me to summon Lord Krull and his men to what I fear will amount to war. He has also specially requested your presence.'

'Mine?' Ishtaer's brows went up. She seemed to be trying to read the other woman's face, but Kael knew she was hopelessly out of practice and besides, he'd bet good money Aquilinia never let slip an expression she didn't want to.

'Yes. The Emperor's nephew has been kidnapped by Lady Samara. She appears to have captured the ship he was travelling on. The boy is three. The Emperor is understandably distressed. He requests your advice on how to deal with her.'

Ishtaer froze. 'Samara?'

She looked like she was about to faint. Kael grabbed her arm without thinking. 'Are you all right?'

Ishtaer shook herself free. 'Yes. I'm fine.' She took a deep breath. 'Very well. When do we leave?'

She felt almost preternaturally calm. This morning when she woke up beside the man who had caused her to be sold into slavery, Ishtaer thought she couldn't be any more shocked. Now she found herself packing for a trip of indeterminate length, calmly sorting prescriptions and preparations for the castle inhabitants and watching Eirenn write down instructions for Mags.

'If Marta goes into labour before we return Mags should know what to do. And if there are complications send for old Moa from the village. Valtar's mother. She told me at Midwinter she's delivered twins and breech births and once performed a Caesarian. She can probably handle whatever happens.'

Eirenn dutifully wrote it down and Ishtaer closed her eyes and selected another jar from the shelf.

'Do you know you're doing that with your eyes closed?'

'Yes. I don't know what anything looks like. Now, this is for Smed's hip. He should have no more than one teaspoon daily, no matter how bad it gets. More could set off his heart problem. Tell Mags that, under no circumstances should he have more.'

'I'm sure she can handle this,' Eirenn said. 'She's looked after things in the absence of a Healer before.'

'I know,' said Ishtaer. 'I just need to ... do something. Occupy my mind. Feel in control.'

'Got it,' said Eirenn. He turned and looked at her from under his fringe of dark hair. He was a very handsome boy, she realised – and she also acknowledged that he wasn't a boy, any more than she was a girl.

And she was far too numb inside to think about it in terms any less dispassionate.

'Are you sure you're okay? I mean, you've had a pretty big shock. Two of them in fact.'

'I'm fine,' Ishtaer said automatically.

'Fine? 'Cos we're going off to fight the woman who had you starved and beaten for years.'

She shot him a glance. It still felt strange to be able to do so.

'What do you know about that?'

'Only what I've worked out. The state you were in. You were a skeleton when I met you. And you were terrified of everything.'

Ishtaer stared at the wall past his head. It was white. It

304

held a chart of human anatomy. It was flanked by shelves of jars and drawers. It was a wall she'd walked past countless times and yet had no idea what it looked like.

'Whatever you've imagined,' she said, 'it will be worse. Much, much worse. I promise you.'

They left the next day, after the *Grey Ghost* had been carefully brought out of her winter berth and refitted overnight. Most of the castle seemed to think they were insane, but Aquilinia assured them their journey would not be troubled by bad weather.

'Keep close to the coast,' she said. 'The icebergs rarely form there. I foresee no storms. Provisions can be taken on board in Ilanium. Just take what is necessary for the journey.'

'Are you not coming?' Ishtaer asked as she stepped into the row boat and Aquilinia remained on shore.

'No. His Lordship has engaged me on a further task. I will meet you in Ilanium. Take care, my lady.'

She curtseyed and Ishtaer did the same, and then the boat was being rowed towards the pirate ship with the human skin on its hull, away from Skjultfjell, away from Durran and Garik who leapt up and down waving, away from the only safety she'd ever known.

Chapter Twenty-Four

She stood at the rail, watching Skjultfjell disappear behind the cat's-paw rocks that shielded the harbour from the sea. Kael watched with her, and when there was nothing but rock to see, he said, 'Is it how you imagined?'

She glanced up at him. 'Skjultfjell? I'm not sure I did imagine it. I didn't expect it would be so hidden from view, though.'

'That's deliberate. Back when it was just a longhouse it was turf-roofed and set into the depression at the top of the hill. Until my great-grandfather built the lower courtyard all you could see of the whole place was an arrow slit or two, carefully disguised as a depression in the rock. The harbour seemed to shelter nothing more than a small fishing village.'

'Very ... defensive.' She stared at the rocks. 'You're the lord of all Krulland, aren't you?'

'I am.'

'Don't you want a big castle to show off to people? Why do you hide?'

He frowned, affronted. 'I don't hide. Lord Krull doesn't hide. I adopt a defensive position.'

'You hide,' she said, turning to face him. 'You hide your castle and you hide your family. Have your sons ever left Skjultfjell? Have they even been as far as Utgangen?'

'I told you,' he said, riled now, 'they're targets. I can't risk someone using them to hurt me.'

Your child will die to save you.

'So you pretend to the world that they don't even exist? You never listed them in the Book of Names. Mags told me your mother is still alive and living in a city the other side of Krulland. With your sister. And her children. And you haven't seen them since they left Skjultfjell. You've never even met your niece and nephew.'

'They're targets too! If my enemies knew who my mother was—'

'And what about me?'

Her question cut him off and he stared down at her, dark hair whipping across those pale eyes.

'You said you didn't want to possess me. If you married me would you keep me locked up in Skjultfjell?'

Every instinct in him screamed that yes, he damn well should, lock her away from anyone who ever wanted to hurt her. But every part of him knew he couldn't.

'We had this conversation—'

'Would you? Can I fight for myself, is that why I'm allowed out?'

'Well, yes of course you can, and the boys are just children—'

'Not forever. They'll grow up and want to know why they can't join your Horde and learn to fight and leave the castle and visit the world. What if they're Chosen? In a few years they could manifest marks of their own. Then what will you do?'

'I don't bloody know, Ishtaer, stop asking me questions like this!'

She tilted her head and gave him a knowing look. It irritated him beyond belief.

That was his excuse for saying what he said next.

'What does it have to do with you anyway? They're my sons, not yours.'

The shutters dropped down across her face and she stepped back. Damn, damn!

'I mean,' he caught her arm as she turned away, 'I didn't mean that. If you married me—'

Ishtaer shook herself free. 'Whatever makes you think I'd marry you?' she said coolly, and walked away.

For five days the journey was uneventful. They sailed down the coast of Krulland and across the channel to the Ilania mainland, suffering no worse than a thunderstorm. Ishtaer stayed on deck throughout, and Kael realised she was actually sleeping up there as well, in a hammock, and not in the cabin he'd given her. He'd have protested that it was too cold, but right now he didn't need reminding about Ishtaer and her feelings on ships' cabins.

Two days away from Ilanium the lookout spied a small boat with a curved prow and square sail. Nobody thought anything of it, until another boat joined it, and another.

And then a huge warship with two sails and three banks of oars and a prow shaped like a battering ram suddenly appeared from behind a small island off the north coast of Ilanium.

'What the *hell* is that?' said Eirenn, eyes wide.

Kael stared at the thing. 'A trireme.' At the kid's expression, he added, 'Old-fashioned galley. Three rows of oars. Fast in a straight line but hell over long distances. Unfortunately,' he added, unsheathing his sword and taking the stairs to the main deck two at a time, 'also terrific at ramming other ships.'

'Ramming? Did you say ramming? They're going to ram us?'

'Hard starboard! Battle stations!' Kael yelled, his crew already ahead of him. 'Archers ready!'

'But, hold on, how do you know they're going to ram us? They might just ... be sailing in that direction.'

'At that speed? Starboard, I said! Leave the cannons, we need to be head on! Face the buggers! We show them our side they'll tear a hole in it!'

He raced past the crew on the deck, nodding at Verak and leaping up to the quarterdeck where Ishtaer stood clutching Brutus's collar, her eyes wide, her face drip white.

'Ishtaer. Ish! Get the dog below decks. Do it! He'll be no damn use if it comes to fighting.'

She was staring past him at the rapidly approaching galley.

'Ishtaer, can you hear me?'

She pointed. 'The sail,' she said. 'Look at the sail.'

He glanced back impatiently. 'What about it?' Now the ship was a little closer he could see the design on the largest sail. A stylised S.

He whipped his head back to Ishtaer, who pushed back her sleeve and showed him her arm, where the same design had been branded into her skin.

'It can't be,' he said.

'It is. That's how they got the boy, isn't it?' He looked back at the boat. No one used galleys any more; they were slower than sailing ships and had a much smaller capacity for cargo. Where the hell had Samara got hers from? And who was crewing it?

'Burn them,' Kael said, turning to give the order to locate the carefully packed devil's fire.

'No! What if the Emperor's nephew is being held on that ship?'

'Two days from Ilanium? Why would they hang around?'

'They're here for some reason.'

'Yeah, to stop us following.'

Kael looked at Ishtaer, her colour returning, her hand on her sword hilt. She looked brave and terrified all at the same time.

'Right,' he said. 'Cannons ready!' he yelled. 'We go alongside and broadside them! Prepare for boarding!' To Ishtaer he said, 'You coming?'

She squared her shoulders and handed Brutus's collar to Eirenn. 'Of course.'

Samara's ship swerved too late to ram them, and Kael's archers took out quite a few men on deck. Ishtaer scanned the sailors, trying to catch a glimpse of a dark-haired woman, but if Samara was on board then she was well hidden.

Beside her, Eirenn fired off another volley of arrows. He was phenomenally quick and deadly accurate. She saw at least three men fall to his shots.

'I'll have to get practising with my new bow,' she said, attempting to conceal her jangling nerves.

'Sure, in a week you'll probably out-shoot me,' Eirenn said, taking a fourth man in the throat.

'Stick to the sword for now,' Kael said on her other side. A grapple hook lodged in the rail by his hand. He casually severed the rope with a single swipe. 'You're lethal close up.'

She wore no armour but the mail shirt she'd hurriedly pulled on. There had been no time to lace up a coif so she, like most of the men on board, was bareheaded. At her hip rode the sword she'd taken from Kael's armoury when she first arrived at Skjultfjell. It wasn't a magnificent jewelled longsword like Kael's, but it was strong and sharp and that was all that mattered.

Her heart was beating like a drum.

Below her, cannons were firing at the trireme, but the other ship lay so much lower in the water that they didn't do much good. Men from the trireme had begun to leap towards the *Grey Ghost*, shimmying up ropes and diving in through the gunwales when the cannons rocked back. She heard the yells and clash of steel from below. Brutus was locked in Kael's cabin, where no doubt he was going insane.

If she thought about that, she didn't have to think about

the fight on her hands or the very real possibility that Samara was mere feet away from her.

Beside her, Kael swung around and swore. 'Here we go,' he said, and his hand very briefly touched her shoulder before he leapt off towards the enemy soldiers starting to pour onto the deck.

Ishtaer gripped her sword tight and raised it to fight. She never saw the blow that hit the back of her head.

Kael was rather enjoying himself.

It had been a while since he'd had a good knock-down fight. These soldiers didn't fight politely or wait their turn to come at him one-on-one. They fought dirty, attacking like a swarm, hacking and slicing like madmen. Like, Kael thought with a fierce grin, he fought too.

He took out three before he had a chance to glance around for Ishtaer. He didn't see her. Eirenn was there, bow abandoned, fighting hand-to-hand with some brute twice his size. As Kael watched, the lad darted away from a heavy sword-thrust, spun on his wooden leg, and used the momentum to slice his sword deep into his enemy. The man screamed and fell.

Kael grinned at Eirenn, and Eirenn grinned back.

Ishtaer woke in darkness and for a hideous, panicked moment thought she'd gone blind again. But no, there was light filtering in through a badly-fitting door, enough to illuminate the small chamber she was held in. Her wrists were manacled to a chain attached to the wall. Her sword was gone.

She was chained in the belly of the enemy boat.

The volcano rose up to meet her, rock burning her fingers as she held on.

And held on.

And began to climb.

Anger replaced panic. This whole raid had been planned against the ship, against her! Samara had sent this ship to find her and capture her and – what? Bring her back to the New Lands? Starve and beat and torture her again?

The rumble of cannon fire filtered down. Dust fell from the wooden ceiling. The walls trembled and rocked. Ishtaer looked around her for escape, for weapons, but there was nothing. Only one door, out of reach, and the chain that held her to the wall.

The heavy chain.

She glanced up. It was not attached to the wall, but ran through a metal ring securely bolted to the old, hard wood.

She twisted, planted her feet against the wall, and pulled hard. The metal groaned. Her wrists burned. The wood would not give. She kicked hard against the wall and threw her whole body weight into it, every ounce of strength she had, but the metal had been bolted on so long ago it was practically part of the wood now.

Sobbing with frustration, she slumped against the wall. Her wrists were attached to either end of a long chain. If she could just get one hand free, she could pull the chain through the loop and be free of the wall.

Ishtaer looked at her hands, at the edge of her Warrior mark on the right and the delicate Healer mark on the left.

The right hand was the stronger. Left it would be.

She braced herself, and dragged the thick manacle slowly towards her fingers, taking skin with it, feeling her bones crack one by one.

Kael yanked his sword free from a fat man who'd tried to cut off his head and kicked the body away. The fighting was dying down now. There were far fewer men on deck, and the noise from below was getting less and less. The enemy, realising they were both outnumbered and outclassed, were shrinking back.

In fact, when he turned around there was no one left to fight. Three men up against the ship's rail. Two raised their hands in surrender. The third leapt overboard.

'Verak! Round 'em up. Tie 'em in the bilges. We'll let the Emperor decide what to do with them.'

Eirenn limped over beside him. He had a cut on his face but didn't seem badly hurt. In fact, he looked exhilarated. 'We won?'

'Aye lad, we won. Were you in any doubt?'

Eirenn grinned. 'I've never won a fight before.'

'You were never on my side before.' He clapped Eirenn on the shoulder. 'Not over yet, though. We've still to secure their ship. Have you seen Ishtaer?'

Eirenn shook his head. 'Bit busy trying to stop people killing me.' He glanced around the deck. 'She's probably gone below. Brutus is probably going mental.'

Kael frowned. Ishtaer hated going below decks. Even the great cabin, accessed directly from the deck, was too confined for her.

'She'll be fine,' Eirenn said, reading his face. 'She's a better fighter than I am. Than probably anyone else on the ship except you.'

'Yeah, I know she'll be fine,' said Kael. 'I'm just going to look for her ...'

She leaned against the wall, breathing hard, her hand a mass of throbbing agony. Flesh shredded, bones pulped, blood pouring over her.

Ishtaer forced herself to concentrate on stemming the blood. She couldn't heal it fully, not now. She had to get out first. She still had one good hand. And the chain would make a decent weapon until she could get a sword.

She was about to try the door when voices came from the other side of it.

'... it's her. How many other women have that mark on their face?'

'Reckon she's awake yet?'

'Maybe. Maybe not. We can still have fun with her if she's out cold.'

'Will Ladyship mind?'

'Nah, she told us to enjoy her.'

The last words came to Ishtaer through a red fog. The pain in her hand vanished, and every beat of her heart pumped fresh rage into her blood. Her right hand went up, gathering the chain with its loose, bloody manacle into a weapon to be swung.

When the door opened, she attacked.

She wasn't in the captain's cabin with her dog, who had shredded the bedclothes and nearly bit Kael's hand off when he opened the door.

'Where is she, boy? Where's Ishtaer?'

Brutus whined anxiously. Wolf or not, he behaved like a damn dog.

'Help me find her,' he said to Brutus, who might have understood or might not, but he bounded up onto the deck, sniffing at pools of blood, growling at enemy soldiers. Kael followed, but Ishtaer was nowhere to be seen.

He dragged Brutus away and down the companionway, shouting Ishtaer's name. 'Have you seen her?' he asked every one of his own men. No one had.

She wasn't on the spar deck. She wasn't on the gun deck. She wasn't on the berth deck. Kael started to panic.

She wouldn't have gone lower than this. Maybe if she'd been fighting a retreat, but he didn't think she would.

He went down to the orlop deck. The hold. She wasn't there. She wasn't anywhere.

Back up in the fresh air, he let Brutus go sniffing around corpses as they were heaved over the side. Dear gods, what if she'd gone over too? What if she'd been hurt and fallen in the sea? What if—

No. He couldn't let himself think like that. He couldn't.

If he ever got her back he was damn well locking her up in Skjultfjell with his sons, and to hell with what she wanted. She had to be safe.

'Still nothing?' Eirenn said, his expression worried. He glanced at the trireme, still anchored to the *Ghost* by ropes and hooks.

Verak strolled over, wiping blood from his sword and not looking particularly hard-worked. 'Still not found her? Maybe she went over to their ship.'

They all stared at the trireme's deck, plainer and flatter than that of the *Grey Ghost*, with very few places to hide. All it held was a few corpses. None of them were Ishtaer's.

'I'm going to check,' Kael said, striding towards the rail.

'There're probably still a few men there, I mean the ones who row it or whatever, they can't have all been up here and fighting …'

'I can handle them. Are you coming?'

Eirenn eyed the gap between the ships. 'Not sure I can make the leap,' he said, gesturing to his leg.

'I'm with you,' Verak said, and called over a couple more men. 'Safety in numbers. We don't know what we might find.'

A nightmarish image of the slave ship Ishtaer had burned into Kael's memory came flashing back. He shuddered. 'Let's go.'

He slung his bow over his shoulder, leapt onto the ship's rail, balanced for a second, then swung down onto the deck of the trireme. Verak and his men followed a second later.

The ship was eerily quiet.

'Trap?' Verak mouthed, and Kael frowned. It didn't feel like a trap. It felt … wrong.

Access below decks seemed to be through one hatch. It lay open, exposing a ladder stair and nothing else. Kael approached carefully, sliding an arrow from its quiver and aiming it at the hatch. Verak did the same.

Nothing emerged.

Kael dropped into a crouch, peering inside. It was duller down there, the light coming only from the oar holes. He saw the outflung arm of a corpse, red and bloody. Nothing moved. *Oh gods, if she's down there …*

He'd dropped through the hatch before he could even finish the thought, and the first thing he saw was that the outflung arm was actually a severed arm. And it was by no means the only one.

The reason nothing moved was because everyone was dead.

Kael stared in horror, unable to speak, as his men descended behind him and stood just as appalled as he was. There were bodies and parts of bodies everywhere. The floor and walls were red with blood. Someone had massacred them.

He heard a sound behind him, a growl, and wondered for an insane second if there had been some huge beast down here. But these men hadn't been bitten or clawed. They'd been hacked to death with a sharp blade, and in some cases, bludgeoned. People had done this.

He turned, and the source of the growl stared back at him.

Ishtaer had done this.

She stood with a curved sword in one hand and a length of chain looped over her arm. Her hair obscured her face in a dark tangle, her eyes seeming to glow through it. She was drenched with blood, breathing shallowly, and as he watched, her head came up and her gaze fixed on him.

'If that bitch wants me, she can come and get me.'

Chapter Twenty-Five

There was no parade, no glorious amble through the streets of the Empire's capital. Ishtaer watched the city come into view, a huge rock in the middle of the bay, surrounded by white cliffs, the Turris Imperio rising up to the sky. It wasn't as big as she'd expected, or as glittering. The docks looked like docks anywhere, like the docks on the island of Gurundi where she'd sneaked aboard that merchantman disguised as a boy, like the docks in Puerto Novo where she'd been herded into a corral at the slave market.

Kael didn't leap aground the way he had when she'd first arrived at the city. He set down the gangplank, wrapped his fur cloak around him, and glanced at her.

'Are you sure you're okay?'

'Better than ever,' Ishtaer said, and meant it.

'How's your hand?'

She glanced at it, still bandaged. Eirenn had helped her reset the bones, very pointedly not asking any questions about what had happened to it. She'd have told him if he'd asked. She'd have told anyone. *I broke my own hand to escape from my chains and have the freedom to fight the men who wanted to rape me.*

And then I killed them all.

'It's fine. Better,' she amended at his dubious look.

'You've been very … calm … since the fight with the trireme.'

The fight on the trireme, Ishtaer thought. She didn't remember it in detail, but flashes came back to her in unguarded moments. *I killed them all.*

She didn't feel calm. She felt invincible.

She'd stood on the deck of the *Grey Ghost* with her hand

a bloody wreck and watched the trireme being burnt and sunk with its grisly cargo. And she'd turned to look at the captives Kael's men had manacled on deck, ready to be sent to the Empire's prisons, and seen the fear in their eyes. They were afraid of her.

The power was immense.

'I'm not afraid any more,' she said.

Kael gave her a look that was hard to decipher, then turned and walked down the gangplank. She followed, with Verak and Eirenn, to the horses already waiting for them. She still wasn't much of a rider, but all she was required to do was stay sitting on the thing while the Emperor's men escorted them through the city.

She knew she should be thinking about what to say to the Emperor, but her attention was continually caught by the people and buildings of the city. They passed the high walls of the Academy, shining white even in the dull winter sunshine, and she was surprised to see how tall the buildings behind it were, and how richly decorated with painted columns and coloured panels. Rising above the rest of the buildings was a tall tower with a bell – the same bell, she realised, that had organised her days at the Academy.

The Turris Imperio loomed at the end of the Processional Way, a road lined with bright tiles and bas reliefs. Every gate they passed under was even more richly decorated than the walls, carved and painted and gilded. It was starting to give Ishtaer a headache.

They rode up the roadway around the tower to an audience chamber that was as carved and decorated as the Processional Way. 'One of the more restrained rooms,' Kael told her in an undertone, catching her stupefied expression. 'Practically cosy. I'd avoid the Mirrored Chamber at all costs if I were you.'

The Emperor was not as grand as she'd expected. In this

insanely over-decorated palace he seemed out of place, a soberly dressed man with a neat grey beard. Beside him stood the Empress, equally sober, and on a sofa nearby sat a drawn, tense-looking couple she guessed were the Emperor's younger sister and her husband, the parents of the missing nephew.

'Lord Krull, Lady Ishtaer. Sirs. Thank you for coming so quickly. Please sit down.'

His gaze fell on Ishtaer as she took her seat, then fluttered away again. He gestured to a servant, who brought forward a letter.

'The ransom demand?' Kael said.

'Indeed. It is … well. Take a look.'

Kael read it, and whatever was written there made him blanch. He glanced quickly at Ishtaer too.

'What is it? What does she want?'

Kael looked up at the Emperor, who nodded gravely before fixing his gaze on Ishtaer, and told her what she'd known since Aquilinia first brought the news.

'You,' said Kael. 'She wants you.'

The Imperial Army had been amassed, ships had been made ready, and Kael had work to do, a strategy to plan.

He kept thinking of Ishtaer instead.

The Emperor had agreed very smoothly that there was no way Ishtaer would be exchanged for his nephew, although Kael got the feeling that he'd damn well considered it.

'Might I ask why she wants you back, my lady?' he'd said solicitously.

'She doesn't like to lose,' Ishtaer said calmly. That terrible, dangerous calm she'd shown since the fight with the trireme. 'She might have only lost a useless slave, but it's still a loss. And since Lord Krull has been trying to make me famous, it seems probable he's succeeded and she's heard of the slave who got away and became a famous Warrior and Healer.'

She glanced at the marks on her arm, at the bandage on her hand. 'It is, after all, why she bought me.'

'She called you a witch,' Kael said, remembering.

'She thought that's what the marks were. She doesn't understand the Chosen. Just like they didn't in the Saranos,' she added. 'She'll be spitting mad that she could have had her own witch and it got away.'

'You're not an *it*,' Kael said hotly.

She gave him a look too calm to be true. 'I was to her,' she said. 'And I'm dangerous. I know her secret.'

'That she's a psychopath?' Kael said. 'I think we're all getting that.'

She looked at the Emperor for a moment, and then at Kael. 'What were you doing in the New Lands when you found me?'

'Is this relevant?' the Emperor said.

'You were looking for Venerin. Trying to find the source.'

She watched the realisation ripple over his face. 'Samara?'

'Yes. And no. I told you,' Ishtaer said measuredly, 'that I was good with herbs.'

Everyone stared at her.

'I wanted to please Ladyship,' she continued. 'I made what she wanted. It was mildly effective, and then she ordered it baked into cakes and sweetmeats. That's what makes it as potent as it is. She uses it as temptation and reward for her slaves. If you want to eat, that's what you get.'

Kael felt sick.

'It's exported inside the oil drums,' she added. 'In tiny sealed containers. I don't know what happens to it after that. But that's where it comes from.'

'Why,' Kael had to clear his throat and start again. 'Why didn't you tell me this before?'

Ishtaer looked at the Emperor, who was trying and failing to keep his calm.

'I didn't want to be punished.'

The Emperor found his voice. 'You won't be. Dear gods, Lady Ishtaer. Shut this woman down. Destroy all her Venerin. Burn her alive. Just bring back my nephew.'

The ships were loaded with supplies, with men from the Empire's regular troops, and with Healers to tend to them. Kael was surprised to see so many, both fully qualified and still in training, some of them Chosen and some trained by Madam Julia as lay healers. Still, the Empire was paying for it, and he supposed it was better to have too many than not enough.

And since Ishtaer was avoiding him, he had no way of asking her about it.

They'd been under sail for a few hours by the time he managed to corner her on the poop deck. 'Do we really need all these Healers?'

She paused in her contemplation of the sails and gave him a measured look. 'It rather depends on what you want to do when we get there,' she said.

'What do you mean? We fight. It's sort of what armies do.'

'Against other armies, yes. But—'

'She has ships, Ish. It's quite feasible she's been building an army.'

'All right, then.' She leaned back against the rail, looking up at him. 'Say she does. Will she have hired them and trained them herself? No. She'll have hired mercenaries. Professional killers. They'll do their best to kill everyone. So, you'll need Healers.'

He folded his arms, waiting. Ishtaer chewed her lip and gazed out over the sea at the admittedly fine sight of the fleet.

'And if she hasn't got an army?' Kael prompted eventually.

'Then you'll be fighting slaves. She doesn't have a lot of guards. But she has a lot of people who are utterly loyal to her. You saw me, I wouldn't leave even though she was killing me. You know everyone in that compound, no matter how weak, will pick up a weapon and fight for her.'

If anyone else had told him this he'd have said they were being ridiculous. But he was looking at Ishtaer, really looking at her for the first time in days, and he could see the fire burning behind that terrible calmness.

'They won't last long,' he said slowly.

'I know. Hence the Healers.'

'They're for the enemy?'

Ishtaer pursed her lips and looked away again. She didn't seem to have got the hang of eye contact. The wind blew her fine dark hair around, obscuring her face.

'What is your plan when we get there?' she asked.

'Reconnoitre until we know what we're dealing with. Be prepared to fight before we even land. Expect an army. Get to know the lay of the land.'

'And then what?'

'Fight.'

'And then what?'

'And then we get the kid and go.' He waved a hand. 'I'll work out the details later.'

'And then what?'

He scowled at her, annoyed. 'What do you mean, and then what? And then we return the boy to his family, Emperor pays us, we have a victory ceremony—'

'And in the New Lands? What happens there? Does Samara go on exactly as before?'

'No, because we'll kill her.'

'Right. And don't you think she might have some plan in place against that? Some method of escape? She might already be gone. This might be a trap.'

'I'm aware of that,' Kael said. 'If it is then we chase her. You forget,' he leaned in close, 'we have what she wants.'

Her eyes did meet his then. Painfully clear and bright, the blue of them burned into him.

'You're going to hand me over,' she said quietly.

He stared at her, first in astonishment and then in rage. After everything they'd been through, everything they'd done together, after finally believing that she could trust him, she still thought this of him?

'Do you even know me at all?'

'Yes,' she said calmly. 'I know you're a great warlord and strategist. And you'll listen to advice from someone who knows your enemy.'

'I am not handing you over,' he stormed. 'How could you think that?'

'Kael, please—'

'No! You do not sacrifice yourself for this!' He put his face right in close to hers, as close as he'd been when she was hot and naked and gasping in his arms, and said fiercely, 'I will see everyone here dead before I hand you over.'

She looked back at him calmly. 'Then that's what it'll come to,' she said, and pushed past him to walk away.

Ishtaer had finally taken a cabin on the ship, and it was there she retreated, heart thumping with anger, with frustration, with fear. Not, for the first time, fear for herself but for Kael, for everyone else on the ship and in the fleet.

She closed her eyes and saw herself walking towards Samara, passing the small figure of the Emperor's nephew toddling the other way, towards Kael, towards safety. It was going to happen. It had to.

Because the other vision she was seeing was of slaughter.

Footsteps sounded, and Ishtaer hurriedly wiped her eyes before turning to the door as it opened. A stranger stood there, a tall young man with fair hair and chiselled good looks. He wore a jerkin and breeches of a rather superior quality, a sword with a jewelled pommel at his hip and a necklace of crystals just showing beneath his collar.

'Can I help you?' she asked, and a small frown creased his pretty brow.

'You don't know who I am, do you?' he asked, and she felt her eyes widen as she recognised his voice.

'Marcus?'

He spread his hands as if to say 'here I am'.

'I heard you'd got your sight back. How'd that happen?'

I learned to trust a man. 'It's not very interesting.' She turned to fuss with the blanket on the bed. 'I didn't know you were aboard.'

'No, I was on the *Pride of the Empire*. I rowed across with my uncle. He's one of the commanders.'

'I see.'

Marcus let out a short laugh. 'Yes, I suppose you do.'

Ishtaer glanced at him over her shoulder. He was leaning in the doorframe now, his broad shoulders filling it. 'Was there something I could help you with?' she asked again, her voice cool.

'Where's your mutt?'

'I left him with Madam Julia.' Where he would be safe, and cared for, even if she never came back. She didn't need a guard dog. Not any more.

'There's a rumour flying around that you killed everyone on board Lady Samara's galley.'

'Not everyone. Quite a lot of them boarded the *Grey Ghost*.'

'So you just killed the ones who didn't board?' He didn't sound remotely like he believed her.

She turned around to face him. 'I killed the ones who knocked me out and tied me up on board the galley, yes. Their intentions were not ... pleasant. I'd had enough of being treated unpleasantly.'

Marcus had a very pretty Cupid's bow lip, but it became less pretty when he curled it in derision. 'So you're still frigid then.'

Anger flared in her. *I could cut you to ribbons before you even saw me move*, she thought, and knew it was true. But she pressed that down, and said instead, 'I don't want to fight with you, Marcus. We're supposed to be on the same side. When we get to the New Lands, you can see where I lived for five years and how I was treated for five years and maybe you can imagine what sort of a state you'd be in after that. And then you can tell me if you think "frigid" is the right way to describe me.'

Marcus opened his sneering mouth to reply, but the voice she heard was Kael's, coming from directly behind him.

'Not in the least,' he said, lightly shoving Marcus out of the way. 'Go away, Gloria, and stop harassing your superiors.'

'She is not—'

'Yes, she is, and you know it. She doesn't want you in her cabin, and the last time she found herself in a cabin with some men she didn't like we had to add up the limbs to count how many there had been. Go.'

Marcus went.

'I don't need you to rescue me,' Ishtaer said, anger rising again.

Kael shut the door. He looked tired. 'No, I know you don't. Look, Ish, we need to talk. I understand you've got some stuff you need to think about'—at this she snorted, and he carried on— 'and maybe you need a bit of space from me. But I'm here when you want to come back. If you want to come back,' he amended hastily.

She sat down heavily on the bunk, looking up at him. The pirate king who'd laughed as he slaughtered the men of the merchant ship. The friend who'd held her in his arms when she was too frightened to speak and pulled her back from the grip of her demons. The man who'd made love to her for the first time in her life.

'I think I can see again because I learned to trust you,' she said. 'I gave you everything that night. I mean I … I've never willingly given anyone my body, and certainly not my heart and soul too.'

The look on his face was heartbreaking. 'I know, and what that means is … it's incredible, Ishtaer, it's—'

She held up her hand. 'It's something that was very hard for me to do. And now I need you to do something just as hard. I need you to trust me.'

'What are you talking about? Of course I trust you!'

'Then why won't you listen to my advice about Samara?'

His face took on a shuttered, mulish look.

'She will have you all killed or enslaved. Everyone on this ship and all the rest. You, and Verak and Eirenn and everyone. Imagine her glee at reducing you to the state I was in. And when she's captured the fleet of the great Krull the Warlord, what's to stop her sailing it to Krulland and killing everyone there? Or maybe just enslaving them. She'd starve your boys to death, she'd beat and whip them, she'd have Mags raped and—'

'Stop,' Kael said quietly, forcefully.

'She won't fight fair, Kael. We have to stop her fighting all together.'

'Then what have I brought all these men for?'

'Do you really think the Emperor would have let you leave without them? Look. When we arrive, you send word, as quick as you can, that you'll agree to the exchange. That you'll meet her on the beach, with the boy, and as soon as you see he's safe, you'll send me over.'

He looked doubtful. 'You really think she'll fall for that?'

'We start walking at the same time, then.'

'You're actually going to do it? To swap yourself? To go back to her?'

Ishtaer sat down on the bunk with a sigh. 'She doesn't like to lose. She'll be furious I escaped her. She …' Ishtaer ran her hands over her face, trying to find the right words. 'She won't release the boy until she thinks she's got what she wants. You do understand that, don't you? You can't … intimidate her. She won't be afraid of Krull the Warlord. She'll get a hell of a thrill out of taking me away from you.'

He sat down beside her, took her hands in his and looked at her earnestly. 'Then we kill her. Soon as we see her. Arrow through the head. Eirenn could do it, or Benbow, he's almost as good as a Chosen, or …'

His enthusiasm faded as he took in her expression, and he sighed. 'And then her people would kill the boy.'

'She'll probably have them standing there with a knife at his throat just in case you turn on her.'

'Ishtaer, I can't just hand you over. I physically can't. She'll kill you. Slowly.'

'That's her intention, yes.' She squeezed his hands gently and smiled a bit. 'I told you to trust me. She will hurt me, as soon as she gets me. But I don't think she'll kill me, not just yet, not after all the trouble she's gone to getting me. But I can heal a hurt, I've done it before. Listen. How well do you recall the terrain of the beach?'

He looked baffled, but said, 'I recall it was a swiving awful place to be. Remains of ships and bleached bones.'

'How big were the remains of ships?' At his look of confusion, she added, 'Big enough to conceal an archer? High enough for him to have line of sight to Samara's head?'

His eyes narrowed. 'What are you planning?'

'Arrow in the head. Just as you said. But only after you've got the boy.'

'And after she's got you? Her people will kill you.'

Ishtaer shook her head. 'I don't think they will. They won't have been ordered to kill me straight away. They'll have relaxed. They'll be waiting for orders. Remember how everyone in that court lived and died at her command? They won't know what to do. And that's when you need to be fast. Overwhelm them. If there are mercenaries they'll know whose side they want to be on. A dead woman won't pay them.'

She held her breath and watched his face as he considered the scenario.

'She'll still hurt you,' he said.

'And I'll recover. Do you have a better idea?'

Kael let out a long breath, and Ishtaer did too. 'No. We'll ... we've got three weeks. We need to work out the kinks, plan for contingencies. And I'm not saying we might not use a better plan if someone thinks of one. We do have most of the finest strategists in the Empire sailing with us, you know.'

'Are any of them experts on murderous slave owners?'

He squeezed her hands again. 'No.' He looked at her for a long while, his eyes softening, and then he moved forward and she knew he was going to kiss her.

She drew back. 'No. I—I can't. Not now. Not while I've got Samara in my head.'

Kael grimaced. 'Fair enough. But, Ishtaer, when this is over ...?'

She looked at him, not as the pirate king or as her friend but as the man who'd made her melt with pleasure, and her blood ran a little hotter.

'When this is over,' she said. 'Maybe.'

Kael sighed and stood up. 'Maybe is better than never,' he said, and smiled, and Ishtaer smiled back.

After three weeks the coast of the New Lands loomed, waves

breaking over the coral reef that had broken so many of the ships in Samara's bay. The *Grey Ghost* steered around it, moving north, heading for the next bay to shelter for one last night before the confrontation.

Kael rowed a small boat ashore. It contained the messenger with Kael's offer, and it contained the three best archers the fleet had to offer. For three weeks they'd been firing from ship to ship, moving targets over extreme distances, until Kael was satisfied they could hit a jumping flea from half a mile away.

'Remember the plan,' Kael said to Eirenn, Benbow, and a Draxan Chosen named Ismail. 'Only once we have the boy, and she's already hurt Ishtaer.'

'Surely the point is to stop her hurting Ishtaer?' Eirenn said for the hundredth time since the idea had been explained.

'Surely the point is that her attention needs to be focused on Ishtaer and that you need to do what I tell you. Go. Good luck.'

He rowed back to the ship, climbed aboard while the boat was hauled up behind him, and went to his cabin before going in search of Ishtaer.

He found her on the main deck, staring out at the bleak shore.

'I never thought I'd see this sight again,' she said with a sigh, and turned to face him.

'It's still not too late to back out,' Kael said, and she gave a tight smile.

'Do you want me to share with you my vision of what happens if I don't go ahead with this?' she said.

Kael shuddered. 'No. No, I really don't.' *Your child will die to save you.* 'Look, I wanted to give you something, and don't argue about taking it, not … not now. Just take it.'

She frowned, but accepted the cloth-wrapped bundle he handed her.

'It's what Aquilinia was picking up for me. From the forge in Utgangen. Your armour isn't ready yet but it might be by the time we get home.'

She held the sword flat across both hands, stared down at the hilt with its patterns of crystals. It was good work, he knew. The smith in Utgangen had been making swords for Kael for years.

'Every Warrior should have a sword with crystals in the hilt,' he said, and she looked up at him.

'I'm not a Warrior. I still never graduated, remember?'

Kael laughed. 'Who cares about graduation? You've been training with Krull the Warlord, you could beat any of those kids from the Academy with your hands behind your back.'

'Or even attached to a chain?' Ishtaer said, smiling faintly. She flexed the hand she'd mangled on the trireme, which bore only the faintest of marks as a reminder. 'This is beautiful, Kael. Thank you. But you know I won't be able to wear it tomorrow? She'll not let me go armed. I doubt I'll even get away with a mail shirt.'

He nodded, and reached inside his jerkin for a second parcel, smaller and achingly familiar.

'Which is why I want you to take this. Wear it. She can't take it off you, you know that. And don't attach any significance to it,' he babbled, 'you can throw it back at me after tomorrow, but I can't let you do this without some crystals.'

She looked at the necklace for a long moment, the crystals twinkling in the fading sunlight. Kael could hardly bear it.

When she held it out to him he wanted to cry. Then she said, 'Help me put it on?' and relief surged through him.

She turned around so he could clasp the necklace at her nape, and then she turned back and put her arms around him and kissed him.

Kael was too astonished to do anything but kiss her back,

hold her slim, strong body in his arms and sink into her embrace.

And when her lips left his and she looked up, blue eyes uncertain and trusting, he said, 'I love you,' without knowing he was going to.

Her fingers stroked his hair. The corner of her lip twitched in what was almost a smile. But her eyes were full of fear, and her body trembled in his arms. 'After tonight,' she said, and seemed to run out of words. 'I don't know what will happen.'

'After tonight,' Kael told her, 'I'll still love you. Seas could rise and empires could fall and I'd still love you.'

'It may well happen,' she said on a gulp, and he realised she was near to tears. When he opened his mouth to tell her again that she could still back out, she said, 'No, don't say it. I have to do this. I have to.' She pressed her lips to his, then said, 'Kael, will you do something for me?'

'Anything,' said Kael, who would have brought her the moon if she'd asked for it.

'Will you come to my cabin and make love to me?'

Desire nearly overwhelmed him. Kael had never swooned in his life but he thought he was in real danger of it there on the deck.

'Good gods, Ish, don't say something like that without warning.'

She smiled tentatively. 'I've never made love with a man whose face I can see,' she said. 'And I want my last memory of a ship's cabin to be a good one.'

'As good as I can make it,' Kael promised, and scooped her up into his arms.

'Kael!'

'When all this is over,' he told her, carrying her down the companionway past Verak, who just laughed at them, 'I'm going to ask you to marry me.'

331

Her eyes were huge in her face. 'And when you do, I'll say yes,' she said, and Kael grinned and carried her to her cabin.

In the morning she left him sleeping, committing every part of the sight to memory. His dark hair on her pale pillow. The stubble shadowing his jaw. The formidable muscles of his torso where the blanket was flung back.

Then Ishtaer crept out of her cabin to be sick, as she had every morning that week, and prayed that Kael would forgive her for what she was going to do.

Chapter Twenty-Six

The Emperor's nephew was three years old, and his name was Otho. He appeared at sunset, cradled in Samara's arms in a litter heaped with pillows.

Ishtaer stood beside Kael on the godsforsaken beach, flanked by Verak and the rest of the Chosen Warriors who'd come with them. Behind them stood Kael's horde and the massed ranks of the Imperial Army. Banners snapped in the freezing wind.

Samara had, as Ishtaer predicted, hired mercenaries. Ranks of them poured forth over the dunes, men with no uniform and no apparent discipline. Men who did, nonetheless, make their living killing people.

Kael glanced at the woman he'd spent most of the night making love to, standing straight and tall beside him. Her chin was up, her shoulders were straight, and she could not have looked more different to the cowering slave she'd been the last time they were on this beach.

'Kael,' she said as the silk-draped litter drew closer.

'Ishtaer.'

'Whatever happens here today, remember I love you. Always remember that.'

His heart swelled. He wanted desperately to stop her going ahead with this terrible plan, and knew he never could.

'I will remember,' he said. 'Always.'

She nodded, her jaw tight, her gaze never moving from the litter.

'And, Kael?'

'Yes, Ishtaer?'

'Don't let that bitch off this beach alive.'

'I don't intend to.'

The litter was set down a hundred yards away. Kael pointedly did not look around at the bleached timbers of a hull sticking up from the sands, or the rock formations off to his right, or any of the other places his archers could be hidden. He focused instead on the man stumbling forward across the sand, lumbering blindly towards them.

He heard someone draw in a sharp breath at the same time he realised why the man stumbled. It wasn't just because he was terribly thin and had clearly been beaten. His eyes had been gouged out, leaving awful empty sockets in his face.

Then Verak said, 'My gods. I remember him.'

Kael peered closer, tried to see past the dreadful disfigurement, and his eyes widened. This had been the guard he and Verak had intercepted all that time ago, taking Ishtaer back to die in the cells. He'd disobeyed Samara's order. He'd lied.

And clearly she'd found out about it.

'My lady says send the girl,' he said, mumbling through a mouthful of broken teeth.

'The boy first,' Kael said.

The guard looked around in something like confusion. Clearly, this wasn't part of his script.

The litter was set down a hundred yards away. Samara unfolded herself from it, standing on the sand with her dress blowing in the wind. Kael felt his hand curl into a fist. She wore the red silk dress she'd sent Ishtaer to him in all that time ago.

She turned and said something to the nearest mercenary. He gave an order, and a dozen men suddenly had arrows pointing at the litter where Otho sat, looking confused and upset.

'She'll kill him if I don't go,' Ishtaer said.

'She might kill him anyway. Ishtaer—'

Her hand touched his. 'I'm going. I'm sorry, Kael.'

And she began walking.

He watched her walk straight and tall across the sand. The cold wind blew her fine dark hair about her face and rippled the mail shirt she wore. The weak sunlight glinted off the crystals at her neck.

Kael watched her walk away from him, and his heart broke into pieces.

You look old, Ishtaer thought, staring straight ahead at Samara. She'd always thought her mistress was young and beautiful, but that was pretty much because Samara had told her so. *Even when I could see I was blind!*

Halfway there she stopped, and called, 'Send the boy. I won't move until he's passed me.'

Samara gestured to her mercenaries, and to Ishtaer's horror one of them came forward with a torch to light the archers' arrows.

'Turn back and they'll fire,' Samara said.

'I understand.' *I understand you'd burn a child to death to get what you want.*

'Strip,' Samara said, her eyes glinting.

'I'm unarmed.'

'Strip.'

'Send the boy. Then I'll do what you want.'

Samara's lip curled, but she nodded. The men at the corners of the litter picked it up and began walking. Ishtaer's heart pounded faster and harder as they approached. It could still all go wrong. She could still just set the litter on fire for the hell of it.

When they'd gone twenty yards, she took off her mail shirt.

At thirty, she unfastened her jerkin and let it drop.

At forty, her boots came off, and then her breeches.

The cold wind whipped straight through her shirt, but she barely felt the chill.

'All of it,' Samara said.

The litter was a few yards away now. Ishtaer could see the wide-eyed fear of the small boy sitting amongst the cushions, his face streaked with tears.

From somewhere, she found a smile for him. 'It will be all right. These men will take you home where you'll be safe.'

'Back to Mama?' the boy asked, and Ishtaer nodded.

'Back to Mama. Just be brave a little longer, Otho.'

As the litter passed her, Otho started crying again. Ishtaer forced herself not to look.

She unbuckled her leather vest and pulled it over her head. Standing before Samara's leering mercenaries, her courtiers and her guards and her slaves, men who had violated her over and again, she stood in her undergarments and refused to show fear.

'All of it,' Samara said, painted lips curving in a cruel smile.

Behind Ishtaer, not one of Kael's men made a sound.

Ishtaer unlaced her shirt. Then her linen drawers. They dropped to the pile of clothes at her side.

She stood naked but for the necklace of crystals, and raised her chin in defiance.

'Now come here,' Samara said, and Ishtaer wondered if Otho had reached Kael yet. She began walking, slowly.

The mercenaries whistled and catcalled her.

'What is she paying you to watch naked women walking by?' Ishtaer asked.

'Call this a bonus!' one yelled back.

'Do you see the man back there in red and black? He gets to see this whenever he wants. Do you know why? He's Krull the Warlord. He'd pay you an awful lot more than Samara and you wouldn't have to threaten small children.'

'What if we like threatening small children?' called one, who had no teeth.

'Then he'll use your skin for a cloak,' Ishtaer said, walking ever closer to Samara and seeing the rage and madness in her eyes.

'Is that really Krull the Warlord?' piped up one youngish man.

'It is. And he's always looking out for new men to join the Horde. The Emperor pays him silly money for a job like this.'

They were muttering now, casting glances at Samara. Some of them probably didn't care that she starved and beat her slaves or instructed them to set fire to a small boy. But a lot looked like they'd rather be in the better-paid employ of a man whose actions were sanctioned by the Empire.

She met Samara's furious gaze, and smiled. 'You need to work harder at inspiring loyalty.'

'Stay with me and you can have her,' Samara said quickly to the men, who leered at Ishtaer.

'The last time a man tried to touch me without my consent I broke his neck,' Ishtaer said calmly, stopping a few feet from Samara. 'The one after that lost his arm below the elbow. Then I slit a few throats, and it got rather hard to tell whose blood was whose after that.'

A couple of the men laughed. Ishtaer did not.

'You never tried to find out what these marks meant,' she said to Samara, raising her arms. The beautiful script of her Healer's mark and the chasing blades that marked her as a Warrior. She'd finally seen the Seer's mark on her face, and it was the prettiest of them all, delicate feathery lines framing her eye.

'They mean you're a witch,' Samara spat, 'a useless and ugly one.'

'They mean I'm a Healer and a Warrior and a Seer,' Ishtaer said. 'They mean I'm a very useful person to have around. So long as you don't starve me, beat me, rape me and blind me.

Lord Krull,' she added for the benefit of the listening men, 'certainly finds me valuable.'

'Still handed you over, didn't he?' Samara said viciously. Then her expression changed as she saw something behind Ishtaer. 'Bastard!'

Ishtaer turned her head to look back across the beach to Kael for the first time since she'd walked away from him. He was stepping back from the litter with a torch in his hand as flames licked over the silk hangings.

He saluted them with the torch. Beside him, Verak stood with Otho in his arms.

'Unlike you, he got the child out first,' Ishtaer said, turning back to Samara, who slapped her suddenly, viciously. She reeled back, but kept her footing, and resettled her gaze on Samara's face.

She let her loathing show in her eyes, and for the first time, Samara looked a little afraid.

Ishtaer raised her voice and said, 'Walk across the sand and join Krull the Warlord. He will take whoever wants to travel to the Empire back with him.'

'Shut up,' Samara said, and gestured to the nearest soldier. 'Shut her up!'

The man hesitated, so Samara grabbed his pike and swung it at Ishtaer. She stepped back, but another man, less principled, grabbed her from behind and pushed her forward.

The point of the blade slid through her flesh, smooth as butter, and Ishtaer felt the tip push out through her back a second before the pain hit her.

As she fell to her knees, she tipped her face up to see Samara's vicious, gleeful face for the last time.

Then an arrow hit the back of Samara's head, another the side, and a third hit her eye.

She fell to the ground, dead, just as Ishtaer fell into blackness.

* * *

'I'm sorry.'

That was the first thing she said to him when she opened her eyes. Her hand was in his, her fingers cool and limp. Her face looked bloodless, her lips dry.

But she was alive, and she was recovering, and Kael promised to build temples to the gods who'd answered his prayers.

He lifted her hand to his lips and kissed it, very gently. 'What could you possibly be sorry for?' he asked.

Ishtaer turned her head away. 'For not telling you.'

'But ... you did tell me. You told me she'd try to hurt you. I didn't realise it would be so bad. But Hanna here can run almost as fast as I can. She got to you before you'd lost much blood and managed to repair most of the damage.'

He saw Ishtaer's tired blue eyes track to the young woman sitting nearby. Hanna's smile was tense.

'You should hire her,' Ishtaer said.

Alarmed, Kael said, 'Will it take you so long to recover? Hanna, you said the wound was clean and there was no major organ damage, you said—'

'It will heal well,' said Hanna. 'But there was ...' her gaze flickered back to Ishtaer, eyes troubled.

'There was what?' Kael demanded, clutching Ishtaer's hand.

'The baby,' said Ishtaer, turning her head back towards him. 'I lost the baby.'

For a long moment he just stared, not able to take in what she'd just said. Hanna slipped quietly from the tent, her eyes averted.

'I'm sorry,' Ishtaer whispered. 'I knew if I told you you wouldn't let me go, and then Samara would kill the boy, she'd enslave you, and—'

'You knew?' Kael said slowly. 'You knew you were pregnant? And you still did it?'

'I'm so sorry,' she said.

Kael felt rage rising up inside him, hot and hurt and all-consuming.

'You sacrificed our child, my child, and you didn't even consult me? How could you do it? My gods, Ishtaer, if you didn't want a baby you know better ways of getting rid of it than that! How could you? How *could* you?'

To his horror he felt tears burning his eyes.

'Kael, please. I did it for you. For everyone. She had to be stopped—'

'So this was a vendetta? You just wanted revenge on Samara? You let our child die because of your revenge?'

He was on his feet, throwing her hand back on the bed. She flinched.

'Remember what I said? No matter what, remember I love you,' she said, her big blue eyes pleading with him.

The pain that shot through him at her words was overwhelming. Kael reacted the way he always did when he was hurt. He fought back.

'Well, I don't swiving love you,' he snarled, and stormed out into the harsh sunlight.

There was Hanna, one of the Healers Ishtaer had hired herself. Did she know? Was she in on the plan?

'Get out of my sight,' he said, and she fled like a mouse from a tiger.

The camp spread around him for miles, rows of tents where all those extra Healers were working extra hours, caring not for men injured in a war but slaves dying of malnutrition. A corral held the mercenaries who hadn't joined Kael's forces. Graves were being dug for the small number of men who'd died in the short scuffle that followed Ishtaer's sacrifice.

He wanted to scream. He wanted to kill her. He wanted to cry. How could she do that? She'd met his sons, she'd seen how they were his world, she knew how hard he worked to protect them, and then she just threw away this baby as if it was nothing. How could she?

His feet took him through the camp to the shore, to the men loading boats to row out to the fleet. Verak stood pointing to bales of goods, handing out orders.

His face changed when he saw Kael.

'What's happened? How is she?'

'Don't even mention her,' Kael snarled, so viciously his friend stepped back a little. 'Which ships are ready to go?'

Verak blinked at him in shock, then said, 'Uh – the *Draxan Princess* and *Love's Folly*.'

Kael almost laughed aloud at their names. Almost.

'Get the *Ghost* ready to go. Find a cabin for the boy. We leave on the tide. Go.'

He leapt into a boat about to push off, and didn't look back at the shore.

Ishtaer left on the last ship, more than a week after Kael had walked out on her. Her body healed well, her heart less so. Hanna had promised not to breathe a word to anyone about it, but Ishtaer told Eirenn what had happened.

'Bastard!' he exclaimed, touchingly outraged on her behalf.

'He's entitled to be angry,' she replied.

'Yeah, but to leave the country? He can't take anything happening that he's not in charge of, can he?'

Ishtaer knew it was more than that, but she was so tired of the arguments chasing themselves round inside her head that she shrugged and changed the subject.

Most of the soldiers were put to work clearing out Samara's compound. Ishtaer had thought she couldn't face going back there, but then she told herself not to be so stupid and steeled herself to do it.

'They're just buildings,' she said, standing in the courtyard. 'Just stone and brick and wood. They're not evil.'

Nevertheless, she ordered it all to be burnt down, and stood watching the orange glow from the stern of the ship taking her away from the New Lands for good.

'What will happen to the oil fields?' asked Marcus, standing beside her.

'I imagine they'll belong to the Empire. Or maybe to Lord Krull. He's probably already signed the paperwork.'

'He'll still be under sail,' Marcus pointed out.

'He doesn't leave things to chance,' Ishtaer said.

They were silent a while, watching the bleak shore recede. Eventually Ishtaer said, 'Was there something you wanted, Marcus?'

'Yeah. Um. I wanted to say sorry.'

'Why, what have you done?'

A short pause, then he said, 'Said some pretty nasty things to you, as I recall.'

She looked at him, then back at the glow of the fire visible for miles around.

'I imagine I'll survive,' she said drily.

'It's just, you were right when you said I'd understand once I'd been here. I mean, all those people, the things she'd done ... it was ...'

'I know.'

'Animals in slaughterhouses get treated better than that. When you said "slave" I thought you meant like the ones we had in the Empire, valuable and taken care of.'

'I know.'

'But this was just ... how could a person do that?'

'The same reason you were cruel to me,' Ishtaer said, and she felt him flinch. 'Power. There was nothing to stop Samara. She got drunk on it.'

342

Marcus watched the glow fade with her, then said, 'You must have loathed me.'

Ishtaer turned, and smiled at him. 'I've been bullied by the best,' she said, 'you were a mere amateur. Besides. You've spent the last week helping Samara's victims. I'd call that making amends.'

'You're a forgiving woman,' he said.

'Not really. I'd quite like to have hacked Samara to pieces like I did with her men, but they'd already burned her by the time I came round.'

'Did you really, er, hack those men on the boat to pieces?'

'Kael wasn't joking when he said they had to count limbs.' She shook her head. 'I don't really want to think about it.'

'Don't blame you.' Marcus pulled his cloak tighter around his body. The wind was picking up, blowing the scent of smoke after them.

'What will you do when we get home? Are you going back to Krulland?'

Ishtaer let out a bitter laugh. 'I doubt it.'

'You have family in ... where is it? Draxos?'

'I suppose I could visit them. I don't really know.'

But by the time they rounded the Excelsis Cliffs and the shining city of Ilanium came into sight, Ishtaer did know. She came ashore with Marcus and Eirenn and the three of them walked through the streets to the Turris Imperio. Marcus had brought his dress armour, complete with the sigil of his father, but declined to wear it as he walked beside Ishtaer. He wore street clothes, just as she and Eirenn did.

'Marcus,' said Ishtaer, 'your family is rich, yes?'

'Uh, yes,' he said, clearly taken aback.

'They own lots of property? The – er, what do you call them? The tenements that are rented out?'

'Yes,' said Marcus, his expression guarded. Eirenn had told Ishtaer that a lot of Lord Glorius's money came from squeezing high rents out of impoverished tenants in dreadful accommodation.

'How much might one cost?'

Eirenn gave her a curious look, no doubt thinking of that jar of coins in the workroom in Krulland. Ishtaer didn't expect it would be enough to buy a building, but it might be enough for a deposit, and surely a Thrice-Marked Chosen could get credit?

But when they reached the Emperor's audience chamber the question became moot. 'My lady Ishtaer!' he cried, looking ten years younger than the last time she'd seen him. He murmured something to a servant, who quickly disappeared. Beside him sat his sister, Otho cuddled on her lap, neither of them looking as if they were about to let go of each other. Her heart clenched.

That will never be you.

Ishtaer hadn't dreamed of the huge red cat since she'd woken up in that tent in the New Lands. What she saw instead was infinitely worse.

A little girl, with bright blue eyes and shining dark hair, her smile lighting up the room, laughing with her brothers as she waved a wooden sword and her father looked on in adoration—

Every night. And every morning Ishtaer woke up so eager to see her daughter, before she remembered, and the pain was enormous.

'My dear girl, I can't express my gratitude enough. Ask anything of me. Anything you want.'

Ishtaer thought about the dead-eyed slaves on the ship, and said, 'A tenement building. For the freed slaves.'

The Emperor looked surprised. 'But—His Lordship didn't tell you? The villa on the mainland?'

Ishtaer glanced at her companions, who looked as blank as she felt.

'Lord Krull organised accommodation for them as soon as he returned. A quiet house on the mainland, several of the Healers to help take care of them, and I have clerks trying to trace if any of them have family.'

Ishtaer stared. It was exactly as she'd planned.

'And ... employment opportunities?' she said. 'They'll need counselling ...'

'Already in hand.' The Emperor allowed a frown to penetrate his happiness. 'I thought for sure he'd taken your advice on this. Ah, fine. If you'd like to go out there and see for yourself, you're more than welcome.'

The servant reappeared, holding the lead of a large, wolf-like dog.

'Brutus!'

He yelped happily and rushed over to her, nearly breaking the nose of the servant as he did. Ishtaer dropped to her knees and gave her dog a huge hug. 'I am so glad to see you.'

'He's been pining for you,' the Emperor said as Ishtaer stood back up. 'But we were talking about a reward for you! What would you like?'

Her mind went blank. 'I'm not used to asking for things for myself,' she said, and the Emperor roared with laughter.

'Money? Jewels? Another victory title is, of course, yours.'

'I don't want another title,' Ishtaer said automatically, and realised it was true. 'My name is long enough already.' She chewed her lip, then said, 'When I first came here, Lord Krull called me Ishtaer prior Inservio. I'd like that to be added to my name.'

She was met with astonished stares from everyone in the room. 'Ish, do you know what that means?' Eirenn hissed.

'You want the world to know you used to be a slave?' the Emperor clarified.

She looked at the brand on her arm that she could have

healed a dozen times over, and never had. 'I want the world to know I'm not ashamed of it. That it's my victory.'

He looked surprised, but nodded. 'Very well. It shall be written in the Book of Names.'

'And I'd like a house.'

More surprised looks.

'My own house. I was going to try to buy one, but your Imperial Majesty did say anything …?'

He laughed again. 'A house is certainly within our means. A villa, perhaps?'

'No. A domus. In the city. Within the Merchant's Circle. With commercial space.' She turned to Eirenn. 'Malika wanted to set up her own dress shop, didn't she?'

He nodded, eyes wide.

'I see. I'm sure we can manage that,' said the Emperor, straight-faced.

'And an employment program for all Samara's former slaves. Full-time Healers at the house in the country. Which I want to oversee. And amnesty for other escaped slaves from the colonies of the New Lands. To be made into law.'

This time his straight face was of an entirely different nature.

'My lady Ishtaer,' he said, rising. 'Come with me. We have a lot to discuss.'

There was no diving overboard this time. No joyful swim towards his family. Kael rowed himself to shore and wrapped his arms tight around his sons, letting his tears fall onto their warm skin.

'Papa, why are you crying?'

'Are you hurt?'

'I'm just glad to be home,' he said. He pulled back and looked at them, one dark and one fair, one born to him and one not. 'I love you. I'll never let you be hurt, you hear me?'

They nodded doubtfully, and squirmed away from him to greet Verak and his other men.

Kael stood and met Mags's frown. 'Are you all right?' she mouthed.

'Fine,' he said, picking up his kitbag and slinging it over his shoulder.

'I take it you won?'

'Oh yeah. We won. Got the boy home safe. Freed the slaves. Got a pile of gold from the Emperor for it.'

'Then I'd expect you to look a bit happier.'

His footsteps faltered. No, not happy. Maybe not ever again.

'People died,' he said, staring at the cliffs, willing himself not to cry. 'Important people.'

'Oh gods.' Her hand touched his arm. 'Ishtaer?'

She might as well have.

'No. She's alive.'

'Where is she? Is she still on the boat?'

Kael closed his eyes, and he could see her. Strong, magnificent Ishtaer; trembling, passionate Ishtaer; pale, treacherous Ishtaer.

'She's not coming,' he said, and walked away.

Chapter Twenty-Seven

By spring it felt as if this was the way things had always been.

The domus the Emperor had given Ishtaer was on a smart street near the main shopping thoroughfares, and Malika's dress shop was thriving with customers drawn as much by her excellent work as the thrill of wearing something the Empire's only female Warrior might wear.

Ishtaer divided her days between working at the Lady Ishtaer Hospital, as the villa on the mainland had become known, and the Academy, where she and Eirenn had devised a training regime taught entirely in the dark.

'I learned to fight when I couldn't see,' she explained to Sir Scipius. 'To use my other senses and my intuition. Sometimes,' she added, allowing herself to think of the fight on the trireme, 'there's not enough light to see by. It shouldn't be a handicap.'

The class became so popular Marcus had to help out as an instructor. Sir Scipius confided that while it was unusual to have three Tyros teaching a class, their graduation would be a mere formality in the spring.

When she told Eirenn this, his eyes went huge. 'I'm going to graduate? I never thought I'd graduate! Ishtaer!' He threw his arms around her. 'Do you know what this means to me? Do you know I'd never have got here without you?'

She smiled and hugged him back. 'Likewise.'

They had both taken apartments in the domus, although more than once she'd heard him sneaking out of Malika's rooms late at night, and didn't expect it would be long before she needed to advertise for another tenant. In the evenings, while Malika finished up her day's work, Eirenn helped

Ishtaer to learn her letters. The first missive she wrote to her aunt and uncle in Draxos looked like the work of a child, but she was immensely proud of it.

Even Marcus had taken to dropping round occasionally, usually on the pretext of bringing letters or information from the Academy. Eirenn had gone from ignoring him to teasing Ishtaer that Marcus fancied her, which she was uncomfortably aware might be the truth. Even Madam Julia remarked that he might be a good match for her.

'I'm not marrying Marcus,' Ishtaer said flatly. 'I'm not marrying anyone.'

'Not even Lord Krull?' asked her old mentor innocently.

'Not even Lord Krull,' Ishtaer said, her face schooled to the calm expression she always wore when his name was mentioned.

Because his name was mentioned often. The Lady Ishtaer and Krull the Warlord. Every day an eager student asked her what he was like. Every day, Ishtaer realised as her command of the written word improved, the news sheets made mention of her work at the Lady Ishtaer Hospital, and usually worked in a mention of Lord Krull there too. 'Lady Ishtaer, who trained with Lord Krull.' 'Lady Ishtaer, the protégée of Lord Krull.' And in a few of the gossip sheets, 'Lord Krull, who has been romantically linked to the brave and dashing Lady Ishtaer …'

And every time it hurt. The pike wound in her belly had healed perfectly, but every time she heard Kael's name or saw a tall man with dark hair or spied a banner with a red tiger on it, the scar ached.

It had to be done, she told herself, but that was no consolation when she was alone and lonely in the night.

For the first time since autumn the air wasn't bitingly cold. Kael tilted his face up to the sun and felt his skin warm.

He'd felt the warmth of fireplaces, of warm blankets and of aquavit, but not of the sun.

He still felt cold.

'Kael.' Verak's voice seemed distant. 'Kael! Where are you?'

He blinked and looked at his friend, standing a few feet away. 'What do you mean, where am I?'

'Well, you're not here with me. You haven't been since we left the New Lands.'

Kael scowled at him. 'I don't want to hear it.' He lifted his sword. 'Ready?'

But Verak stood still, sword still sheathed. 'To beat the hell out of you again? No. I'm tired of it, Kael. Nearly dislocated your shoulder yesterday.'

'You just got lucky.'

'For the second time.'

'That was ages ago.'

'It was last week. You're not fighting me any more. It's like when you brought Ishtaer here—'

'Do not say her name.'

Verak's eyes narrowed. 'Ishtaer. Ishtaer Lakaresdottir Vapendam, the name you gave her.'

'Shut up.'

'Ishtaer the Healer, Ishtaer the Warrior, Ishtaer the Seer. Ishtaer your lover.'

Kael's hand shook. He brandished the sword at Verak.

'See that? I know you're sitting up all night drinking. It's why you can't fight worth a damn. That and your heart's not in it.'

'You just shut up about my heart.'

Verak sighed. 'Kael, I'm your friend. Always have been. I was your friend when Hasse died and you slept with his wife. I was your friend when you decided to let people believe Durran was Hasse's son. I was your friend when Ilse died and left you with Garik. But I don't know if I can carry on being the friend of someone who walked out on his lover after she lost her baby.'

'*Her* baby?' Kael said, incredulous. 'And who do you think the swiving father was?'

'You,' Verak said calmly, 'a fact which Ishtaer, probably for the first time in her life, knew for certain. How many other babies do you think she's lost?'

The first potion I ever learned to make …

'What's that got to do with it?' Kael said tightly.

'Everything. I might not have seen what happened to her inside my own head like you did, but I'm not an idiot. I've seen the way she acts and I've seen those slaves in Samara's compound. She probably resolved to herself a long time ago that she would never have a child. A baby should be cherished and loved and wanted, and what do you think the chances of that were in that gods-forsaken place?'

Kael wanted to kill him. Instead he wrapped his arms around himself and turned away. The spring sunshine glinted off the water in the harbour, the flash of bright silver fish in a boat, the shine of a child's hair clasp as she ran and played in the village. He ached unbearably.

'And then she met you, and you were kind to her and you loved her and you asked her to marry you, and for once she had that real chance of a family.'

'Not for long she didn't,' Kael said bitterly.

'No. Because she had to make a terrible choice. And don't you get that mulish look on your face, Kaelnar Vapensigsson, I know it's a choice you've thought about. The gods know I have. Ever since I heard that prophecy. If you had to face your child dying to save you, there'd be no choice, would there?'

'Damn right there wouldn't. I'd die for them,' Kael said violently.

'As I would. For yours and for mine. But what if it was you and me who had to die? And everyone else here? Mags, Klara, all the children, Marte and her new baby, old Smed and Valter and—'

'Shut *up*!'

For a long moment Verak was silent, and Kael turned to stare out over the harbour again, fighting the tears that burned his eyes. Because that was the thing, wasn't it? It was all right to get sanctimonious about sacrifice, but had he ever faced it? Really, truly had to make the choice?

'She knew Samara better than anyone,' Verak said quietly behind him. 'Knew what she was capable of. I heard her telling you. You knew what would happen if Ishtaer didn't give herself like that. Back into the hands of a woman who'd tortured her for years. I can't imagine the bravery that took. Or the pain of the knowledge she had. No wonder she never told you about the baby. You'd have locked her on board and attacked and probably by now Samara would be sitting in your longhouse, peeling strips of flesh off your family and friends and roasting them on a fire, and Ishtaer would be dead anyway, or at any rate wish she was—'

'Enough!' Kael whirled round, sword in hand. He might be tired, he might be hung-over and out of condition and so full of self-loathing that he ached with it, but he was still Krull the Warlord and he could still set a sword at a man's throat before anyone had seen him move.

Verak stood calmly as the cold steel lay against his neck.

'The prophecy has come true, Kael,' he said. 'It can't hurt you any more.'

'It hurts me every swiving day.'

'Then how do you think Ishtaer feels?'

Soft and warm and trembling and trusting, that was how she'd felt. And now she was far away, she was cold and distant and treacherous ...

... and hurting and lonely and brave and miserable.

His sword fell to the ground, clattering on the flagstones.

Verak met his eyes, and there was compassion in them. 'You still love her,' he said, and it wasn't a question.

'Don't reckon it'd hurt like this if I didn't.'

'Then go to her. Apologise. She's probably a wreck. Gods only know what something like this could do to someone as fragile as her ...'

Kael dealt him a look. Verak smiled.

'All right, fragile probably isn't the word for her any more.'

'I've never known anyone braver,' Kael said, his throat tightening. He ran his hand over his face and realised he couldn't even remember the last time he'd shaved. 'Verak, what the hell do I do? I don't know how to get out of this.'

'Be brave,' Verak said simply. 'You're Krull the Swiving Warlord, after all.'

'Cousin Ishtaer!' Poppia shaded her eyes, then ran down the steps of the villa and enveloped Ishtaer in a hug before she'd even got both feet on the ground. The carriage swayed alarmingly as the other girl embraced her.

'It's good to see you too,' she said. Beside her, Brutus wiggled out of the coach and nearly knocked them over, probably more out of a desire for water and shade than for company.

'You still have your dog! He's a good dog, aren't you? Who's a good dog?'

While Poppia fussed over Brutus, who behaved like a puppy given half the chance, Ishtaer turned to Liberius, high up on the seat of the carriage, and took her luggage from him.

'I can't wait for you to meet Paulus, I'm sure you'll just love him,' Poppia babbled, linking her arm with Ishtaer's and leading her towards the house. 'He's so eager to meet you too. No one here has ever even seen a female Warrior!'

'No one anywhere else has, either,' Ishtaer said, gently extracting herself from her cousin's grip. 'Let me just bring my luggage—'

'Oh no, let the servants deal with it, it's their job,' Poppia laughed.

'I can carry my own bags,' Ishtaer said quietly, and picked up the larger trunk.

'Oh,' said Poppia. 'Well, then I'll help you. Why not?'

Ishtaer watched her try to pick up the smaller trunk, and hid a smile. It didn't contain anything particularly heavy, but then Poppia looked as if she hadn't lifted anything that weighed more than a hairbrush in her whole life.

Eventually she looked up, pink with exertion, and smiled sheepishly.

'It's all right, you don't have to,' Ishtaer said. 'Liberius, could you bring it in, please?'

He silently hefted the trunk onto his shoulder, apparently impervious to the heat, and waited to follow them.

Poppia regarded him, tall and muscular and silent, his skin like polished ebony. He wore plain clothes like a servant, and had a slate and a piece of chalk slung around his neck.

'Will you be staying with us, Liberius?' she asked uncertainly.

'He will. If someone could show him to the servants' quarters, we'd be grateful. His own room, if that's possible, and one with a door that locks from the inside.'

'Er, yes,' Poppia said, 'I'm sure we can …'

'Otherwise a guest room. So long as it locks. He has offered to help out in any way you need.' Liberius nodded gravely at this. 'As you can see, he's quite strong, and he's very good with horses.'

Realisation dawned on Poppia's pretty face as she hurried

after Ishtaer. 'Is he one of your, you know, from the villa? Your charity hospital?'

'He was a slave, yes,' Ishtaer said calmly. 'He has no vocal chords, he can't speak. But he's been learning his letters, hence the slate, you see.'

'No—? Oh, you poor man! What happened to him? No, I don't think I want to know.'

Ishtaer, who had witnessed Liberius's degradation as one of Samara's favourite pleasure slaves, agreed silently that her sheltered cousin probably didn't.

Once inside the sunny atrium of her uncle's villa, Ishtaer allowed her trunk to be taken off by two eager footmen, and had a moment to admire the ribbons and flowers decorating everything in advance of tomorrow's celebrations. A harp stood in the corner and servants were filling glasses and laying out trays of food in the shade.

'Find somewhere you like,' Ishtaer told Liberius, 'and if there's a problem come and find me. All right? And make sure you drink plenty of water.'

He grinned, bright white teeth in his handsome face, and the attendant servant girls all went a bit pinker.

Ishtaer felt like someone's mother when she said, 'I mean it about the water. It's far hotter here than you've been used to.'

Liberius bowed, never losing his grip on the trunk, and walked off after an imperious butler.

'This way,' Poppia sang, and Ishtaer followed her cousin through a series of covered walkways and pretty courtyards to a small enclosed area with an orange blossom tree and a small tiled pool. A door stood open, leading to a spacious room with tiled floors and a large bed covered by a net. Her trunk stood at the foot of it.

'I expect you'll want to freshen up after the journey,' Poppia said, gesturing to a tray of soaps and oils. 'Take your time bathing – would you like an attendant? I can send my girl to you—? All right then. Whenever you're ready, come and find us in the main atrium. Just through that door and turn right, and if you get lost, ask the servants.'

Ishtaer nodded. 'I will, thank you. Brutus, away from the water.'

Poppia giggled. 'Bring him with you. I can't wait to see my in-laws' faces when they see him! I mean, my in-laws to-be, that is!'

She hugged Ishtaer again and bounded off like an eager puppy.

Ishtaer smiled automatically at her, but it faded as she moved around the little courtyard, bolting the door without really thinking about it and checking for lines of sight over the high walls before catching herself.

Don't be stupid. No one is going to fly out of nowhere and attack you, in your uncle's house, on the eve of your cousin's wedding.

'And I could defend myself if they did,' she murmured, then snorted at the reaction that would get.

She stripped and bathed in the small pool, rubbed sweet-scented oils into her skin, ate some of the fruit on a platter in her bedroom, put on one of Malika's lovely creations, and regarded herself in the mirror. Like the dress she'd worn for her first presentation to the Emperor, this one had a design that mimicked armour, although this time in silver and white. The silk corset bore her finished coat of arms, picked out in bright colours and metallic threads.

'You'll never be like other women,' Malika had said when she'd presented the dress to Ishtaer. 'Why dress like it?'

This much was true, although Ishtaer supposed Malika meant the bright vivid marks on her skin, the delicate tracery around her eye, the still-visible S brand on her arm, and not what was inside.

She smiled at her reflection, and an attractive, well-groomed woman smiled back at her. She'd got very good at smiling, these last few months. She could even fool herself sometimes.

She worked hard for good rewards. More and more of Samara's former slaves were thriving, finding jobs and homes and independence. The Emperor asked often for her advice on some new laws he was drafting on the rights of women in the Citizenry. She was valued and respected at the Academy, and only two weeks ago had been presented with the red sash of a fully qualified Militis at the Imperial Ball. Beside her, almost bursting with pride, Eirenn had stood and received his own sash. He'd celebrated with her and Marcus, and then sheepishly admitted he was going back to the domus to celebrate with Malika.

'You don't mind, do you?' he said to Ishtaer, who found a smile.

'Of course not. Why would I mind? I'm glad you're happy.'

And she was glad. She made herself be glad. Her friends were happy and fulfilled, and she was … she was independent and respected and strong and—

Lonely.

The chasm was still there, only instead of demons and lava it was dark, cold and empty. And it yawned and sucked at her, while up above the sun shone and people laughed and babies gurgled.

Oh gods, someone here was bound to have a baby. Poppia had gone on excitedly about her friends' confinements, about their lovely little bundles of joy, about how she could hardly wait for one of her own. Ishtaer wasn't sure she could bear it.

—*bright blue eyes, shining dark hair, a smile that lit up the room, laughing with her brothers*—

Then she straightened her shoulders and told herself that she'd borne much worse, and that pining for something she couldn't have and had never, until a few months ago, even wanted, was ridiculous, and possibly the actions of a crazy person.

She adjusted the neckline of her dress, the backs of her fingers brushing the warm crystals at her throat. She'd never taken the necklace off, and couldn't justify to herself why.

More actions of a crazy person.

'Well, let's go and be eccentric,' she said to her wolf, who leapt to his feet and submitted to Ishtaer tying a ribbon from her wrist to his collar. It wouldn't hold him, of course, any more than the silk breastplate of her dress would stop a sword. Brutus behaved like a dog most of the time, but that didn't mean he actually was one. He was a wolf, not a puppy.

We're both of us pretending, Ishtaer thought, but she lifted her chin and left the chamber.

A smiling woman in the pale tunic Ishtaer realised was servants' garb directed her back to the main atrium, from where she could hear a harp playing and people talking and laughing. And – yes, there was the cheerful shout of a child, which sounded so much like Garik it made her heart turn over.

She hadn't allowed herself to think of the two small boys she'd cared so much for. She already hurt so much she didn't think she could take more.

'Ishtaer! There you are, my dear.' It was her aunt Nima, elegant in traditional Draxan dress with a scarf covering her hair. She kissed Ishtaer on both cheeks and said, 'It's so good to see you. How was your journey?'

'Not bad, I came by boat most of the way and hired a carriage.' She scanned the atrium, now full of guests in bright clothes, eating and drinking. The pool in the middle had candles floating in it and the air smelled of orange blossom.

'Ah yes, Poppia told me you brought your own manservant with you.' Nima's eyes twinkled, and Ishtaer realised she thought Liberius was her lover. She nearly laughed at the idea. The tall, silent man had adjusted quite well to his freedom, but two people more loath to be touched she couldn't imagine.

'He came with us from the New Lands,' she explained, and saw the understanding in her aunt's eyes. 'He was originally from the far south, we believe. Hates the cold. I asked him if he'd like to see what a Draxan summer was like.'

'And is he surviving?' Nima moved a few paces to stand under one of the huge ceiling fans being operated by a servant. Ishtaer didn't blame her, the crush was becoming immense. She could hardly see more than three or four people away, and the buzz of conversation was so strong she doubted she'd have been able to pick out more than a few voices even with her eyes closed.

'He says it's like coming home. I wonder if perhaps you might consider taking him on permanently? He's very good with horses. Patient and gentle, I've seen him work miracles with very difficult animals.'

'Ah, everyone has an agenda,' her aunt laughed. 'We'll see. Your uncle bought a very temperamental stallion the other week which ...'

There it was again, a child's shout. Brutus's ears pricked up.

One child sounds much like another, Ishtaer told herself, and forced her attention back to her aunt.

'... poor man still can't use his arm properly, I wonder if perhaps you could take a look at it? We called in the local Healer but I'm not sure if there might be some nerve damage.'

Ishtaer nodded and said she'd be delighted to. *This is how it will be for the rest of your life*, she thought as Nima called over a man about ten years older than Ishtaer, handsome and dark, in a red tunic. Small talk and charity and helping out with tricky medical problems.

'... Karam Sadik, who trades in horses. I'm not sure I've asked, Ishtaer, do you ride?'

'A little, and very badly,' she said with a smile. Brutus stood up abruptly at her side, and she wondered why, since Karam seemed entirely unthreatening.

'Some practice will help,' said Karam. 'I should be glad to help you if you're here for a while? My villa is just a few miles away.'

Ishtaer smiled politely and agreed that some help from an expert would be wonderful, whilst wondering what she could do to get out of it.

The future stretched ahead of her, every social gathering a minefield of men who wanted to marry a wealthy girl from a good family, a Thrice-Marked Chosen, a heroine of the Empire.

Ishtaer wondered if she could throw herself under the cool water of the pool and let the noise of the party fade away. She glanced towards the water, but it was blocked from view by the press of people. Something seemed to be going on there.

Brutus's tail started wagging.

'... my lady?' Karam turned his handsome head to see where she was looking. 'Ah yes, I think a child jumped in for a swim. Can't blame him really, not in this heat. Can I fetch you a cool drink?'

The crystals at her neck seemed to get warmer.

'... know you can swim,' came a voice that made her heart stop, 'but this isn't the place for it. Look, you're getting these nice ladies' clothes wet.'

'It can't be,' she murmured, frozen with shock.

'Lady Ishtaer? Are you all right?'

Brutus yipped, and pulled on his ribbon lead. Ishtaer felt her footsteps follow him, as if in a dream.

'My brother nearly drowned once,' a solemn child's voice

informed someone. Ishtaer pushed faster through the press of people. 'If I hadn't gone for help he might have died.'

'Garik, get out of the bloody water. Good gods, son, I can't take you anywhere.'

'But Papa, it's so hot, how can anyone breathe when it's so hot?'

'There are bathing pools in the guest quarters,' Poppia was saying helpfully as Ishtaer pushed into a sudden void and narrowly avoided falling into the pool herself.

She stared. Across the stretch of cool water, past the splashing, grinning child, stood a man dressed all in black, his hand on the shoulder of another boy.

Everything else seemed to fade away. He was here, Kael was here, with his sons. He stood fifteen feet away, across the water, dark eyes burning into her.

'Ishtaer, look who's here,' burbled Poppia's voice from a distant place.

Ishtaer stood like a statue and gazed at him, utterly unable to speak. Every part of her ached to touch him, to speak to him, and every part of her knew it would hurt too much if she did.

Brutus barked again, breaking the spell, and she turned and walked away as rapidly as she could through the crowd.

'Ishtaer!' His voice followed her. 'Ishtaer, wait, please!'

She picked up her pace, but Kael was faster. She hadn't quite made it to the doorway before he caught her, his hand on her arm. 'Ishtaer!'

She stopped dead, her eyes closed.

'What do you want?' she asked, without turning.

'To talk to you. Is there somewhere—'

'Ishtaer! Ishtaer!'

Durran cannoned into her, throwing his arms around her waist and hugging her fiercely. *Oh gods, I've missed you!*

'Where have you been? Papa said you weren't coming

back and then he said we were going on a trip and we went to the Empire to see you but you weren't there and there's a huge tower and so many people and Papa wrote our names down in a book and they don't have carriages there in the day and Eirenn said—'

'That you'd come to your cousin's wedding,' Kael interjected. Ishtaer kept her eyes on Durran's face, alive with animation, tilted up to hers.

'You've grown,' she said.

'That's what grandmama said,' he said scornfully.

At that her gaze flew to Kael's.

'I took your advice,' he said softly. 'Ish, is there somewhere we could talk? Away from here? Garik is – oh gods, he's dripping wet, Garik, don't drip all over those people!'

'There's a pool by my room,' Ishtaer said as the little boy squelched towards her, clearly enjoying the effect he was having. 'This way.'

Garik hugged Brutus, who didn't seem to mind getting wet in the slightest, and she led them silently through the corridors and courtyards to her room. Garik leapt into the little pool with delight, and his brother and Brutus followed seconds later.

Ishtaer stayed in the shade, standing next to a stone bench, keeping her eyes on the boys because it hurt too much to look at Kael.

No, that wasn't true. Looking at him was wonderful. He wore black, with his own crest emblazoned on his chest. His hair had been cut, he was clean-shaven, and he looked more presentable than she'd ever seen him.

'It's so good to see you,' he said, and the words twisted like a knife inside her. 'You look really well.'

She wanted desperately to touch him. 'The boys have grown,' she said stiltedly.

'Kids do that. They've been desperate to see you. So disappointed when you weren't there in Ilanium.'

'You must have travelled fast,' she said. 'If you left after I did.'

In the pool, Durran was peeling off his sodden shirt and throwing it onto the paving stones, where it steamed gently.

'We came by sea. Eirenn says you went by barge.'

'I did. I wasn't in a hurry.' Silence. 'I wanted to see the countryside.'

'Yes,' Kael said, a little too eagerly. 'You must have. I mean, you didn't see it before. I mean …'

Suddenly he slumped onto the bench, and she looked down, startled. Kael ran a hand through his hair, and she realised how tired he looked.

'I'm making a mess of this too,' he said, 'aren't I?'

Someone tapped on the door to the courtyard, and it swung open to reveal Liberius with a large trunk.

'You're not staying here?' Ishtaer said in alarm.

'No. Poppia found us rooms. This is for you.'

The big man set the trunk down and hesitated, eyeing Kael with distrust.

'It's all right,' she said, understanding. 'He won't hurt me.'

'What? Of course I won't!' Kael said, outraged. 'Who are you, anyway?'

'His name is Liberius,' Ishtaer said before Kael could do something stupid. 'He came with me from the New Lands. I spoke to Aunt Nima about getting you a job here, Liberius, but she's understandably busy at the moment, so I'll talk to her again after the wedding, all right? Give you a chance to see if you like it here. I also met a man who trains horses, so he may have something for you.'

Liberius nodded his thanks, and left.

'He's a quiet one,' Kael said cautiously.

Politeness. That was the way to get through this. Treat him like any one of the strangers in that atrium.

'He can't speak. Samara did something to his throat and his vocal chords are damaged beyond repair.'

Kael winced. 'I heard about the work you're doing with the slaves. It's really good.'

'Thank you.'

'I, uh.' He raked his hands through his hair. Ishtaer's fingers twitched, remembering the silky feel of it against her own fingers.

'I didn't know Poppia had invited you,' she said.

'She didn't. I just turned up. I had to see you.' He tilted his face up to hers, something in his eyes that looked very much like hope, and Ishtaer couldn't stand it any more.

'Why? Why are you here?' Her voice started to break. 'I was doing fine without you. I have a house, and a job, and people who respect me, and I'm doing fine, and now you're here and it's like tearing open a healing wound. It hurts, and I wish you'd just go away and let me be—' She broke off on a sob.

Kael leapt to his feet, appalled, and tried to touch her, but she stepped back.

'Don't. Please.'

His hands fell away instantly.

'What do you want? Because if it's to make me feel worse about the hardest thing I've ever had to do, then don't bother, because I already hate myself enough over it for the both of us.'

'I don't hate you!'

'Could have fooled me.' She wiped her eyes and glared at him. He looked as if he'd been slapped.

'All right, so I was angry. And I was hurt. And I ... I hated you a little bit. I reacted really badly, and I'm sorry. That's why I'm here. To say sorry.'

Ishtaer regarded him suspiciously.

'Verak told me a few home truths. I was just thinking about me, and how hurt I was, and I took it out on you, and I know now it was much harder for you than it was for me, so I'm sorry.'

He said the last bit in a rush, as if it was a speech he'd practised and wanted to get out.

'Did it hurt?' she said. 'Apologising?'

He nodded. 'Yes.'

'Good. Just so you know, getting impaled on a pike also hurts.'

He flinched, and reached out as if to touch her where the pike had hit.

'But not quite as much as it hurts when you have to make a really, really terrible decision and sacrifice the one thing you'd do anything to protect, and the man you love doesn't even wait around to listen to your explanation.'

Ishtaer realised she had her arms wrapped around herself. Kael stood mere inches away, and she'd have given anything to press herself against him, to feel his arms around her. To get back that comfort and strength he'd given her last time he'd held her.

'I'm sorry. Ishtaer, I'm sorry. I don't know what to do or say to make it right.'

He touched her shoulder, drew her to him when she didn't resist, and for a moment he held her and it was wonderful.

What could be the harm in just being held, in resting her head against his shoulder, in breathing his scent and pretending everything was all right?

She made herself straighten away. She couldn't pretend everything was fine between them.

'I see her, you know. Every night I see her.'

He frowned. 'Samara?'

Ishtaer controlled her shudder. 'No.' She glanced at the pool where the boys had stripped off most of their clothes and were throwing sticks for Brutus. 'Their sister.'

'Their—' She watched the comprehension dawn. 'Our daughter.'

She closed her eyes, feeling tears start again. She'd never cried until she fell in love with Kael.

'Oh gods. Ishtaer ...' He reached out for her but she stepped back. If she let herself be comforted by him again she wouldn't be able to stop.

'Show me.' His chin came up. 'Show me what you see. The way you did at the Ball that time.'

'I don't even know how I did that.'

'Please.'

She chewed her lip, then nodded and placed her hand on his face. It felt horribly good to be touching him. And she opened up the memory she'd been trying to run from, and showed him—

—a *little girl, with bright blue eyes and shining dark hair, her smile lighting up the room, laughing with her brothers as she waved a wooden sword and her father looked on in adoration*—

—and when she opened her eyes again Kael's tears were running over her fingers.

He took her hand, and kissed it. And he smiled.

'You think it's funny?' she said, snatching her hand back in disgust.

'No. I think it's wonderful. Ishtaer, what if she's not the baby that—that—I mean, what if she's a different child? One we've yet to have?'

She stared, incredulous. 'Are you mad?'

'No,' he said, still smiling. 'No, I'm happy. I don't think that was a might-have-been vision. I think that's the future. I think you and I could have that beautiful daughter. I think the boys could have that wonderful sister.'

'But,' she began, trying to get her head around the idea. 'I don't even know—What are you suggesting? Is this like when you tried to get me to marry you without actually telling me?'

He winced. 'I really have ballsed this up, haven't I? No. Look. On the ship, that last day, I said I was going to ask you to marry me again and you said you'd say yes.'

'Yes, but that was before—'

'Before something you knew was going to happen, happened. Did you mean it? That if I, uh, hadn't reacted the way I did, that you'd still want to marry me?'

She sat down on the bench with a thump, unable to cope with such an about-face. To her horror, Kael got down on his knees before her.

'Marry me. I love you. I won't ever cage you. Look, I brought the boys here, I took them to see my mother, I wrote their names down in the Book after mine. I won't lock you away. I never could.'

'And this daughter? Will you lock her away in your castle? Make her another possession?'

He closed his eyes for a second, and whatever he saw there made him smile. 'I will give my life to protect her, and you. And I won't cage her either. I told you before, Ishtaer, I could never possess you.'

She couldn't speak, too shocked and too hopeful. Hopeful?

Yes, because wasn't this what she wanted?

Her gaze strayed to Durran and Garik, who'd got bored with the pool and were trying to climb the orange blossom tree. He'd brought them here, away from the safety of his secret stronghold, and he'd told the world they were his.

He wouldn't lock her away. He wouldn't hurt her. He loved her. He actually loved her, and she loved him, and now, all of a sudden, there wasn't any reason to push him away.

I'm not afraid any more.

He stood up, and she opened her mouth to tell him not to go, but he was only walking as far as the trunk Liberius had brought in. He opened it, and withdrew a large package wrapped in cloth.

'I brought this for you. So you always know who you are, and you're always protected.'

Self-consciously, he held it out, and Ishtaer unwrapped it.

The cloth was silk, brightly coloured and embroidered, and it held a breastplate which had been enamelled with a shield of red, blue and silver.

She looked up, astonished.

'I didn't know the Emperor had granted you supporters,' he said, gesturing to the animals flanking the shield on her silk corset, 'until I arrived in Ilanium. So I had these modified to match.'

He withdrew a pair of vambraces, one painted with a silver wolf, the other a red and blue phoenix.

'Good choices,' he added with a smile that didn't quite reach his eyes.

'But—' She looked down at the breastplate again. 'But this isn't painted on, it's engraved. It must have taken months ...'

'Ever since we visited the smith in Utgangen, yes. You couldn't wear just any old armour. You're Ishtaer Vapendam.'

He took the silk cloth from her and shook it out. It bore her full coat of arms, the shield that incorporated her mother and father's designs, her own three Gifts, and the wolf and phoenix she'd chosen to flank it.

He held out the fluttering silk, but her gaze strayed to the ceremonial doublet he wore with its own shield, black and red, flanked by its crowned red tiger and black gryphon, and her lips curved in a smile. *Out from the darkness, a huge red cat loomed.*

Her hand rested on her belly. The sword might have been metaphorical, but the red cat had been there all the time, if she'd only seen it.

'You like it?' he asked hopefully.

'I love it,' she answered, smiling wider. 'Will it be displayed beside yours?'

'What do you mean? When they hang the banners for the Imperial Ball? I assume yours will go ahead of everyone else's, since you're Thrice-Marked—'

'No. I mean on the wall in your bedchamber.'

She watched the implication sink in, watched the smile come over his face like the sun coming out.

'Ask me to marry you,' she said.

He dropped instantly to one knee and took her hand in his. 'Ishtaer, my darling girl, I love you. Will you marry me?'

She smiled back. 'I will.'

He whooped in delight and scooped her up into his arms, the banner tangling around them both. Ishtaer didn't care. He kissed her, that wonderful deep kiss, and she wrapped her arms around him and kissed him right back.

Brutus barked, Garik yelled 'Papa!' and Durran made noises of disgust.

'Get used to it,' Kael informed them, setting Ishtaer on her feet and holding her tightly. 'You'll be seeing a lot of it.'

'Yuck,' said Durran.

'Does this mean you're coming home with us?' Garik asked, eyes wide and hopeful.

'Yes,' Ishtaer said. 'I'm coming home.'

About the Author

Kate's a prolific writer of romantic and paranormal fiction. She is a self-confessed fan of Terry Pratchett, whose fantasy fiction has inspired her to write her own books. Kate worked in an airport and a laboratory before escaping to write fiction full time. She is a member of the Romantic Novelists Association and has previously published short stories in the UK and romantic mysteries in the US. She's a previous winner of the WisRWA's Silver Quill and Passionate Ink's Passionate Plume award.

Impossible Things is Kate's third novel published with Choc Lit. Her second novel *Run Rabbit Run* was published in 2012 and was the first of Kate's *Sophie Green Mysteries* stories to be published in the UK. *The UnTied Kingdom* was Kate's UK debut and was short listed for the 2012 Romantic Contemporary Novel of the year award.

For more information on Kate visit:
http://www.etaknosnhoj.blogspot.co.uk/
https://twitter.com/k8johnsonauthor
https://www.facebook.com/catmarsters

More Choc Lit

From Kate Johnson

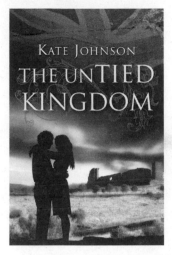

The UnTied Kingdom

Shortlisted for the 2012 RoNA Contemporary Romantic Novel Category Award

The portal to an alternate world was the start of all her troubles – or was it?

When Eve Carpenter lands with a splash in the Thames, it's not the London or England she's used to. No one has a telephone or knows what a computer is. England's a third-world country and Princess Di is still alive. But worst of all, everyone thinks Eve's a spy.

Including Major Harker who has his own problems. His sworn enemy is looking for a promotion. The General wants him to undertake some ridiculous mission to capture a computer, which Harker vaguely envisions running wild somewhere in Yorkshire. Turns out the best person to help him is Eve.

She claims to be a popstar. Harker doesn't know what a popstar is, although he suspects it's a fancy foreign word for 'spy'. Eve knows all about computers, and electricity. Eve is dangerous. There's every possibility she's mad.

And Harker is falling in love with her.

Visit www.choc-lit.com for more details including the first two chapters and reviews, or simply scan barcode using your mobile phone QR reader.

Run Rabbit Run

Sophie's in trouble.
Must be Tuesday.

Sophie Green's an ex-spy, or trying to be. You wouldn't believe the trouble she's in. An MI5 officer has been shot with her gun, her fingerprints all over his office. And no, she didn't kill him.

But she has gone on the run.

Now Sophie's desperately seeking whoever's trying to frame and kill her. She's being forced to work with the least trustworthy man in Europe, MI5 is following her every move, and she's had to leave the tall, blond, god of a man she loves behind.

Luke Sharpe works for MI6. Or did, until his girlfriend became a murder suspect.

Doing nothing wasn't an option, so he started investigating. Who cares if it means jeopardising his career? Sophie's everything he used to say he never wanted. Young, irresponsible, bright and mad. Now she's just everything – and she has to live.

She will live, won't she?

Visit www.choc-lit.com for more details including the first two chapters and reviews, or simply scan barcode using your mobile phone QR reader.

More from Choc Lit

If you enjoyed Kate's story, you'll enjoy the rest of our selection. Here's a sample:

A Stitch in Time
Amanda James

A stitch in time saves nine ... or does it?

Sarah Yates is a thirty-something history teacher, divorced, disillusioned and desperate to have more excitement in her life. Making all her dreams come true seems about as likely as climbing Everest in stilettos.

Then one evening the doorbell rings and the handsome and mysterious John Needler brings more excitement than Sarah could ever have imagined. John wants Sarah to go back in time ...

Sarah is whisked from the Sheffield Blitz to the suffragette movement in London to the Old American West, trying to make sure people find their happy endings. The only question is, will she ever be able to find hers?

Visit www.choc-lit.com for more details including the first two chapters and reviews, or simply scan barcode using your mobile phone QR reader.

No Such Thing as Immortality

Sarah Tranter

I will protect you until the day I die … forever!

A vampire does not have to feel any emotion not of his choosing. And Nathaniel Gray has spent two hundred years choosing not to feel. But when he accidentally runs Rowan Locke off the road, he is inexplicably flooded with everything she's feeling, and that's rage, and lots of it.

He is consumed with the need to protect Rowan at all costs including from himself. To Nate, what is happening is unthinkable and is pretty much as unbelievable as the existence of faeries.

But you see, 'There is no such thing as … immortality.'

This is Nate's story …

Visit www.choc-lit.com for more details including the first two chapters and reviews, or simply scan barcode using your mobile phone QR reader.

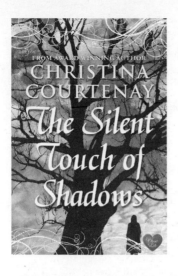

The Silent Touch of Shadows

Christina Courtenay

Festival of Romance

Winner of the 2012 Best Historical Read from the Festival of Romance

What will it take to put the past to rest?

Professional genealogist Melissa Grantham receives an invitation to visit her family's ancestral home, Ashleigh Manor. From the moment she arrives, life-like dreams and visions haunt her. The spiritual connection to a medieval young woman and her forbidden lover have her questioning her sanity, but Melissa is determined to solve the mystery.

Jake Precy, owner of a nearby cottage, has disturbing dreams too, but it's not until he meets Melissa that they begin to make sense. He hires her to research his family's history, unaware their lives are already entwined. Is the mutual attraction real or the result of ghostly interference?

A haunting love story set partly in the present and partly in fifteenth century Kent.

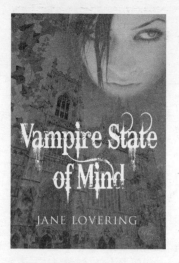

Vampire State of Mind

Jane Lovering

Jessica Grant knows vampires only too well. She runs the York Council tracker programme making sure that Otherworlders are all where they should be, keeps the filing in order and drinks far too much coffee.

To Jess, vampires are annoying and arrogant and far too sexy for their own good, particularly her ex-colleague, Sil, who's now in charge of Otherworld York. When a demon turns up and threatens not just Jess but the whole world order, she and Sil are forced to work together.

But then Jess turns out to be the key to saving the world, which puts a very different slant on their relationship.

The stakes are high. They are also very, very pointy and Jess isn't afraid to use them – even on the vampire she's rather afraid she's falling in love with …

This is the first of a trilogy in Jane's paranormal series.

Visit www.choc-lit.com for more details including the first two chapters and reviews, or simply scan barcode using your mobile phone QR reader.

CLAIM YOUR FREE EBOOK

of

IMPOSSIBLE THINGS

You may wish to have a choice of how you read
Impossible Things. Perhaps you'd like a digital
version for when you're out and about, so that
you can read it on your ereader, iPad or even a
Smartphone. For a limited period, we're including
a **FREE** ebook version along with this paperback.

To claim, simply visit ebooks.choc-lit.com
or scan the QR Code.

You'll need to enter the following code:

Q201311

Introducing Choc Lit

We're an independent publisher creating
a delicious selection of fiction.
Where heroes are like chocolate – irresistible!
Quality stories with a romance at the heart.

Choc Lit novels are selected by genuine readers like yourself.
We only publish stories our Choc Lit Tasting Panel want to
see in print. Our reviews and awards speak for themselves.

We'd love to hear how you enjoyed *Impossible Things*.
Just visit www.choc-lit.com and give your feedback.
Describe Kael in terms of chocolate
and you could win a Choc Lit novel in our
Flavour of the Month competition.

Available in paperback and as ebooks from most stores.

Visit: www.choc-lit.com for more details.

Keep in touch:
Sign up for our monthly newsletter Choc Lit Spread for
all the latest news and offers: www.spread.choc-lit.com.
Follow us on Twitter: @ChocLituk and Facebook: Choc Lit.

Or simply scan barcode using your mobile phone QR reader:

Choc Lit
Spread

Twitter

Facebook